PRETTY WICKED SECRETS

RUTHLESS HEARTS BOOK #2

CALLIE ROSE

For updates on my upcoming releases and promotions, sign up for my reader newsletter! I promise not to bite (or spam you).

CALLIE ROSE NEWSLETTER

1

RILEY

My whole body is buzzing with pleasure, betraying me just as ruthlessly as these fucking Reapers have. That last orgasm was so intense that the afterglow feels almost radioactive—and all from a man I fucking hate.

Something twists inside my chest as Maddoc's cock pulses inside me again, his muscled body pressed against mine in the aftermath of our heated, rough fuck.

Maddoc Gray. Leader of one of Halston's most dangerous gangs. A man I was stupid enough to start to believe in. To count on.

To... care for.

I try to focus on something else besides the anger and hurt crawling through my veins like poison. *Anything* else. The way the edge of the counter he just fucked me on digs into the backs of my thighs. The silence in the kitchen that tells me my distraction worked, that my sister got away.

"*Shit,*" he breathes, the sound dragging out on a slow exhale. "I've imagined this way too many times. But this was better."

He nuzzles my neck, and my skin crawls.

I have to get out of here. I can't fucking be here anymore.

Chloe is long gone by now, I'm sure of it. She's free. But I never gave any thought to how I might get out after she escaped. All I cared about in the moment was covering for her so that she could get out of the house without being seen.

As Maddoc lifts his head and smooths my multi-colored hair back, his eyes warm and his face flushed, my gaze drops to the gun he left on the counter.

Moving in a flash, I wrap my fingers around the cool steel, gripping it tightly. Before I can stop to consider what I'm doing or second guess myself, I lift it to Maddoc's temple.

He stiffens, the warmth in his expression turning to shock. He pulls back, just far enough to look into my eyes... and rolls his hips just enough to remind me that his cock is still buried inside me.

"What the fuck do you think you're doing, butterfly?" he asks, his voice eerily calm as he narrows his eyes.

I grit my teeth and press the gun harder against his skin, grinding it into his temple.

"What I have to," I bite out. "What you *made* me do. You forced my hand when you betrayed me."

My finger curls around the trigger, my pulse racing. Maddoc's nostrils flare as he senses the movement, and tension crackles in the air as he holds my gaze, his gray eyes churning like storm clouds.

Then he moves.

It's so sudden and smooth that it catches me by surprise, one muscled arm shooting up and knocking into my forearm with bruising force.

The gun flies out of my gasp, and he jerks away from me, his cock slipping free as he dives for it.

Fuck. No!

I push off the counter and land on him with a grunt, grappling for control as we both reach for it, my hands sliding on his naked, sweat-slick skin. The gun goes skittering across the floor, and I cling to his back as he lunges for it, then scratch and

2

claw at his face, digging my fingers into his hair and yanking his head back to keep him from reaching it.

He's a better fighter than me, stronger and more well-trained, but I'm running on pure adrenaline and a primal, bone-deep will to survive. I lash out with everything I have, managing to land a lucky blow against the back of his head with my elbow.

He grunts, going down to the floor, and I scramble forward and grab the gun. The second it's in my hands, I roll onto my back, holding it with both hands this time as I aim it at him.

Maddoc freezes, already up on one knee with an arm extended toward me.

"Don't. Fucking. Move," I bite out.

Slowly, he lowers his arm to his side, shaking his head. "Whatever you're thinking about doing, butterfly, I promise you, it would be a mistake."

"Don't call me that. And my only mistake was trusting you," I say. I'm panting as hard as I was while he fucked me, but now it's from adrenaline and fury. "This whole goddamn time, you three assholes have been after Chloe for your own gain. I *heard* you and Dante in your office. You lied to me. You want to use her for something that will benefit you. Rescuing her was never about helping me."

My voice cracks on the last part, and something shifts in his eyes, his expression hardening.

A part of me is still waiting for him to tell me I'm wrong. That there's some other explanation. That I can trust them after all.

That I mean something to him.

But of course, he doesn't.

I don't dare blink as I steady the gun with both hands and keep it pointed at his face, slowly sitting up, then getting to my feet.

"What do you want with my sister?" I demand.

3

"That doesn't concern you," he murmurs, his face completely shuttered now. "And I never lied."

"The *fuck* you didn't," I hiss. My hands shake before I steady them again. "I need to know what this is about. Why do you want her? Tell me!"

"That wasn't part of the deal," Maddoc says flatly. "We did what you asked. We got her away from McKenna. We never discussed what would happen after that."

His words twist in my chest like a knife, the sharp pain making it hard to breathe. I knew he could be cold and calculating, but hearing him speak so callously of the bargain we made breaks something inside me.

Maddoc slowly rises to his feet, his hands at his side as his gaze locks with mine. I know he'll try to get the gun again, that he's probably already looking for an opening or a weakness in my stance. I know he's used to winning, and that he built his gang up into the force that it is because he'll do whatever it takes to survive.

But so will I.

I shove aside the painful, chaotic mess of emotions in my chest and raise the gun. I know by now that the man in front of me doesn't have a heart, but I aim the barrel where one should be.

"You're right," I say calmly, my hands completely steady this time. "None of that was part of the deal. And neither was this."

Then I squeeze the trigger.

The big gun jerks in my hands, the sound of the shot ringing out like deafening thunder. The kickback catches me off guard, making my wrists burn, and the moment of calm, deadly focus I felt a moment ago goes up in smoke as Maddoc's body jerks from the impact, his blood spraying out in a vivid red arc.

It's the middle of the night. Nothing should look that bright in such dim lighting, but it does.

He staggers backward, cursing.

Cursing and *bleeding.*

That sight does something to me, and a flurry of emotions I can't even name well up inside me, hot and fast. My chest is so tight I can barely breathe, and I try to steady the gun again as the shakes set in.

Maddoc's face contorts with pain as he stumbles and crashes into the island in the middle of the kitchen. The bullet struck him, but it went wide, hitting his shoulder instead of his heart. He's hurt, but he's not down.

I'm breathing in harsh, uncontrolled pants as I take aim again. I have to end this.

But my ears are still ringing, and my hands almost feel numb from the force of the first shot. I can't seem to steady them this time, no matter how hard I fucking try.

"Dammit," I pant, raising my arms and locking out my elbows.

Maddoc grunts and slaps a hand over the bullet wound, his knuckles turning white where he clutches his shoulder. Then he looks up, meeting my eyes.

His dark brown hair is sex-mussed and tangled, and a huge black tattoo covers his bare chest. One that looks fucking ominous covered in all the blood splatter, like a sinister omen that I'll never win.

Fuck that.

I glare at him, and in the space between one breath and the next, his pained grimace smooths out, returning to the same calm, unreadable expression he wore when I first walked into Clancy's and asked him to help me get Chloe back.

Like we're strangers.

Like he hasn't been lying to me this whole time.

Like we're not both still naked, with his cum running down my thighs.

I grip the gun even tighter, my body suddenly cold all over and my adrenaline so high I almost feel sick with it.

Blood wells out from between Maddoc's fingers, dripping down his hand. His wrist. Running in winding rivulets down his sculpted pecs, adding chaotic new patterns to the ink there.

A lot of blood.

Too much.

I force away the thought and the twinge of worry that comes with it. It doesn't matter. I need to shoot him again, put him down for good, and go after my sister. I shouldn't be worrying about how badly I've wounded him when that was the entire point.

But my fucked up feelings make me hesitate too long, and when he bursts into motion, I'm not prepared for it.

He bum rushes me, charging toward me like a freight train.

"Fuck," I gasp, firing wildly and missing completely this time.

A chunk of drywall explodes out of the wall behind Maddoc's head, and then he's on me, wrestling for control of the gun. His skin is slick with sweat and blood, and he's so much bigger than me, so fucking strong, that the slipperiness is the only thing that gives me an advantage.

I yell, squirming and fighting, twisting in his grip and jabbing him with my elbows, knees, whatever I can use. I can feel the stitches at my waist pulling again, stinging hard, like they're about to tear through my skin, but it doesn't matter. I slam my forehead into the bloody crater where the bullet entered Maddoc's shoulder, and he spins me around so my back is plastered against his front, letting loose with a string of vicious curses as he wraps one arm around my ribs and strains to reach the gun in my hand with the other one.

I stretch away with all my strength, holding it out of his reach.

Fumbling it.

Trying to turn it back toward him.

"Not happening, Riley," he grits out, the grim tone of his voice telling me all I need to know.

"Fuck you," I hiss.

"You just did," he growls, torquing my arm back until I grunt with pain as he tries to get to the gun.

Whatever connection I fooled myself into believing existed between us before I discovered that the Reapers have just been using me to get to Chloe is gone. I was shooting to kill, and Maddoc will never forgive me for tonight, and neither will his brothers.

But that's fine, because I'll never forgive any of them either.

I strain even harder to keep the gun out of his reach, fighting him with everything in me. Fighting not to let my emotions overwhelm me, and for *damn* sure not to cry.

Right the fuck now is the only chance I'll have to get away, and I know it. I can already hear pounding footsteps heading our way.

Dante and Logan must have heard the gunshots, and once they get here, it will be three pissed off Reapers against one.

I won't stand a chance.

"Give it up," Maddoc grunts, twisting away just as I try to slam my head back into his shoulder again. He tightens his arm around me so hard I can barely breathe.

My neck strains as I turn my head to glare up at him.

Those unique, deceptively beautiful eyes of his burn into mine, igniting a wave of fresh adrenaline that mixes with the post-orgasmic afterglow my body is still buzzing with. I'm all too aware of the intimate feel of his cock, thick and soft now and still wet from my pussy, where it presses into my ass. The evidence of what we just did is smeared across my skin, but the electric tension thrumming through my blood isn't arousal.

It's pure fury.

"Never," I wheeze defiantly, my ribs aching when his arms tighten around me to the point of pain. "I'll *never* give up."

"I know," he says, his jaw tight as he stares down at me.

Then he sighs, almost silently, his arms loosening for nothing more than a split second.

It's all I need.

I twist my body hard and fast, making sure to keep the gun out of his reach and intending to slam my knee up into his unprotected ball sac and make a break for it.

He stops me before I can even turn, but like I just said, I will never give up. Never stop fighting him.

I drop my fist back like a hammer, letting my arm hinge at the elbow to try to bring down the butt of the gun on his head... but the fucker denies me that too, not even flinching as he forces my arm straight again, then pushes it out and back at an unnatural angle so I can't move.

He yanks me back against his body.

"I told you," he says grimly, his heated breath branding the side of my neck, "not happening."

A furious, incoherent sound leaves me as Dante and Logan finally burst into the kitchen, one of them slapping the light switch on.

I flinch under the onslaught of bright light, and they both skid to a stop. Dante stares at us incredulously as Logan's shuttered gaze moves rapidly around the room, as if he's mentally cataloging the blood, the damage, the clothes strewn everywhere.

Dante is the first to find his voice.

"What the fuck?" he demands, crossing the kitchen in two long strides and reaching for my gun hand.

I twist away, despair washing through me as I meet Dante's vibrant green eyes, staring out at me quizzically under his sleep-tousled chocolate brown hair.

He freezes, his brows drawing together in confusion.

How fucking dare he look concerned? I'm sure all three of

them were in on the plan to use my sister, but he was the one I overheard talking to Maddoc about the details.

He was the one I started to trust.

He was the one I let myself open up to the most, develop fucking feelings that felt real for, the one I most thought I was going to *miss*.

"Fuck you," I hiss, narrowing my eyes at him as I fight off the hopelessness that threatens to drown me.

I lunge at him, and Maddoc wrenches me backward.

Dante shakes his head, pressing his lips together in a tight line, then reaches for the gun again.

I curse him out, struggling harder.

I have to. Chloe made it out of the house, she must have, but she's all alone and this fucking gang war of theirs, the one we landed right in the middle of through no fault of our own, means that being alone in Halston right now isn't safe for her.

I *have* to get away.

"Do you want to tell me what the hell is going on here?" Dante asks grimly, dodging backward when my struggle against the force of nature known as Maddoc motherfucking Gray sends the two of us stumbling into him.

"Riley shot me," Maddoc tells him flatly, wrenching me back against him yet a-fucking-gain.

"What? Why?" Dante asks, his eyes locking onto mine.

I pant for air, immobilized but channeling all my rage into the death glare I send back at him.

He pats the air in a calm-down gesture that pisses me off even more. His lips quirk up, proving he can still read me like a book, but then he looks past me, addressing Maddoc over my shoulder. "Why are you two fighting? And why are you both naked?"

Maddoc's entire body goes still, his arms like a steel vise around me. I've got no doubt he's staring Dante down, trying to prove he's the top dog here and doesn't have to answer to anyone no matter how close he and his brothers are.

Dante just raises an eyebrow, waiting him out.

"Why the fuck do you think?" Maddoc finally growls.

From behind me, Logan hisses, a sound that would have scared me if I wasn't so furious at all of them.

Dante just snorts, shaking his head, then smirks knowingly at Maddoc.

Like he almost expected it.

Motherfucker.

I look away. I don't want to see Dante's perpetual good humor or, as he crosses his big arms over his chest, inked-up muscles bulging out enticingly, all the vibrant, beautiful colors that decorate the body I've started to get so familiar with.

I don't want to think about how I've let myself imagine that one day I'd get the chance to trace those images with my fingers, my tongue. Follow the ink to more intimate places and let him tell me about what each tattoo means as we lay tangled together with smooth whiskey on our tongues and all the time in the world.

A stupid fucking fantasy.

And I don't give a shit if both Dante and Logan know that Maddoc just fucked me, either. They *should* know, since it means I'm not the only one he's lied to. After all, he's the one who made it off limits for any of them to touch me while he forced me to live here with them, the fucking hypocrite.

But the last fucking straw is when the silence stretches, the three Reapers engaged in some kind of stare-off, and I feel Maddoc's goddamn cock start to swell, thickening against my ass like he just can't help himself. Like he gets off on winning. On dominating me. On sharing that fact with his brothers.

"You fucking bastard," I pant, coming back to life.

Struggling against him again with renewed fury. "Get the fuck off me!"

I throw my weight to the side, then slam my heel back, aiming for Maddoc's knee this time.

I connect, but bare feet don't do enough damage, and he just grunts without letting me go.

"Get the fucking gun away from her," he says to Logan and Dante.

They both close in, obeying him instantly, and I shout, bucking against Maddoc's suffocating grip in a desperate bid for freedom before they reach me.

This time, I'm not *trying* to fire the gun again, but I'm gripping it so tightly my hand is almost numb. Waving it around as I desperately try to keep the three Reapers from gaining control of it... and my finger is still wedged around the trigger.

When it goes off, the recoil slams my whole arm back, wrenching my elbow and flooding my arm with pain.

It was pointed at Dante this time, and something on the counter behind him shatters, shooting shards of plastic toward all of us like shrapnel.

"Jesus fuck," Dante shouts, his body jerking when some of it hits him. Then he lunges toward me and grabs my forearm in an unbreakable grip, holding my gun arm away from my body as he stares down at me grimly, all traces of his charming humor gone. "Quit it, princess."

Logan silently glides toward the counter behind him, picking up one of the shiny black shards of broken plastic. He stares at it, then lifts his freakishly pale eyes to mine, holding my gaze with an eerily blank stare for a moment. "We'll need a new coffee maker."

"Fuck your fucking coffee maker," I pant, straining against Maddoc's hold and kicking out at Dante's shins.

Dante sidesteps without releasing my arm, and Logan blinks

at me, then turns away and slips out of the kitchen with his precious piece of broken bullshit in hand.

"Drop the gun, Riley," Maddoc says from behind me, steel in his voice.

His hot breath plays over the back of my neck and his fucking cock is even harder now, but I will *never* do what he wants. Never again.

I snarl, tightening my grip on the gun and flexing my wrist, trying with all my might to turn it and get the weapon to point toward either one of them.

I can't.

Dante locks out my elbow and grabs my wrist with his free hand, then squeezes hard on some kind of pressure point that has my hand spasming open without my consent.

"You fucking asshole," I hiss as the gun falls to the floor with a clatter.

Dante gives me a grim smile, kicking it away as Maddoc wrenches both my arms behind my back and locks my wrists together in one of his hands. Dante immediately steps in so that I'm sandwiched between them, trapped with my blood-smeared breasts heaving against Dante's chest while Maddoc's naked body is an immovable wall behind me.

"It didn't have to be this way, princess," Dante says, running his finger down my cheek.

I jerk my head back, glaring up at him with all the hurt-fueled hate in my heart.

"Okay," he says, nodding. Then he looks past me, meeting Maddoc's eyes with his trademark lazy grin back in place and a hint of a challenge in his bright green eyes. "So much for none of us fucking her."

"And this is why," Maddoc growls. "It's a fucking distraction. She kissed me to divert my attention. Got me to fuck her so she could try to kill me."

"Kill you?" Dante asks, looking down at me with a flash of surprise on his face.

I lift my chin in defiance and he quickly covers up his real expression with the laid-back mask he wears so often and so well, dragging his eyes back up to meet Maddoc's. "If she tried to kill you," he drawls, "it sounds like you were doing it wrong, Madd."

A teasing smile hovers around Dante's lips, but it doesn't quite reach his eyes.

"Sex is a weapon. It makes us let our guards down," Maddoc says tightly, clearly not amused. "I've got the bullet wound to prove that fact if you have trouble remembering the rule from here on out."

Dante holds his gaze for a moment, then nods.

And it hurts, a twinge of pain inside me at the idea that what I just did with Maddoc, *why* I did it, betrayed whatever it was that was starting to grow between me and Dante.

But I ignore that pain, because whatever I thought was between us wasn't real, and this little fucking twinge is nothing, not compared to how it felt when I heard him talking to Maddoc about their plans for my sister.

No matter what I did, Dante was the one who betrayed me first.

I harden my heart, and when Maddoc's body subtly shifts behind me as he adjusts his grip on my wrists, I throw my head back again, this time managing to connect with the bloody bullet wound in his shoulder.

"*Fuck*," he shouts, his grip loosening enough that I actually manage to yank loose this time.

I shove Dante away and bolt toward the kitchen door, desperate to get out and go after Chloe. Desperate to get the fuck away from the Reapers.

Instead, I round the doorway and slam straight into another one.

Logan's arms silently snap closed around my body, trapping me against his lean, muscled frame.

"Motherfucker," I hiss, helpless rage consuming me as I try to fight my way free.

He barely reacts, and he sure as fuck doesn't let me go.

But of course he doesn't, because he's in on it too. He has to be. He may not have been part of the conversation I overheard, too busy fooling me into believing there might actually be something more than hate happening between us as he stitched up the bullet wound I got while we rescued Chloe earlier tonight, but these three assholes really are as close as brothers.

Inseparable. Always in sync. A united front.

My enemies. All three of them.

"You—" I start to say, only to have the vicious words I intend to throw at Logan muffled by the cloth he covers my mouth and nose with.

No fanfare. No expression on his face. No chance for me to get away.

I cough, then gag on the pungently sweet odor and try to hold my breath as I struggle against him anyway.

But I can't fight this. Not forever. And when I reflexively inhale, my body growing desperate for air, the sickening chemical sweetness overwhelms me and a wave of dizziness loosens my limbs.

Logan cocks his head to the side, his blond hair glinting in the dim light. He stares down at me like I'm a curious zoo specimen, holding me tightly as I sag against him, everything starting to go fuzzy.

Everything except those ice-colored eyes of his, as empty as his soulless heart.

They're the last thing I see as the world fades to black.

2

DANTE

I SHOULD HAVE EXPECTED Riley to make a break for it once we pinned her, but I'm still a little thrown by how much this whole shit with the gun has surprised me tonight, and it takes me a half second to catch my balance after she shoves me back. By the time I make it out of the kitchen, one step behind Maddoc, Logan's already handled it.

"She's out?" Maddoc asks, his emotions on the kind of total lockdown I usually see from him when we're facing off with pussy-ass shit heads like Austin McKenna's people.

Logan looks up after lowering her to the floor, his face blank, and nods.

He heads back into the kitchen, leaving Riley on the floor at our feet. She's sprawled at an awkward angle, naked and smeared with blood, sweat, and cum.

Maddoc's cum.

Huh.

I can't say I'm all that surprised he gave in and broke his own rule about not fucking her. There are certain things Madd and I are both drawn to, and Riley has them in spades. No reason he should be able to resist when I haven't.

This shit with shooting him is another thing entirely though.

That fucking surprised me. A rare occurrence, since I'm usually hella good at reading people and I legit thought things were going a different way with her.

I wanted them to.

I shake off the pinch of disappointment about being wrong. No time for that shit. Besides, I still don't know what actually went down.

"What happened?" I ask Maddoc, catching myself before I crouch down to check on Riley.

No need. Logan knows what he's doing. She'll be fine.

More importantly, whatever the fuck her justification was for shooting Madd, there shouldn't be any question where my loyalty lies now that she has.

There *isn't* any question. He's my brother.

I turn my back on her sprawled body, raising an eyebrow when Maddoc's slow to answer.

"You okay, Madd?"

He nods, his gray eyes flicking toward Riley and his frustration coming through loud and clear.

It sounds a lot like his teeth grinding.

Or that could be from the pain.

He's got his hand pressed against his shoulder, but the blood flow has slowed, so I'm not too concerned. It probably hurts like a bitch—and there's no exit wound, so that'll be fun for him when Logan digs the bullet out—but it's not gonna kill him.

"Riley knows we've got plans for Chloe," Maddoc finally answers me, the clipped irritation in his voice telling me I was right the first time.

It's not from the pain.

Maddoc fucking *hates* being blindsided.

"Does she know what those plans are?" I ask, resisting the urge to turn back and check on Riley again. Also avoiding thinking too hard about the nature of those plans Madd just mentioned, since I'm all in—'course I am, because it's not just

16

smart, but also fucking brilliant and a hundred percent necessary—but that doesn't mean the idea of one of us getting shackled like that doesn't sit a little funny with me.

"No," Maddoc says, scrubbing a hand over his face and painting it with blood. "It sounds like she heard you and me talking earlier. All she knows is that we had our own reason for getting Chloe away from West Point."

I smirk. "Hell, she knew *that* going in."

He gives me a scathing look, and I rein it in. My default may be to make light of shit and dissipate tension, but yeah. Now's not the time, no matter how much I fucking hate the current complication.

And this most definitely is one.

Riley knew it would fuck with McKenna's gang when we saved her sister from them. It's why we agreed to help in the first place. But whatever plans Maddoc had for easing her into the knowledge that we now need to use Chloe for our own gain are out the window, and that's gonna change things between Riley and the three of us.

Hell, it clearly already has.

I sigh, staring blindly into the kitchen for a second. It's fucking trashed, and in any other circumstances I might be amused at the look of disgust on Logan's face as he takes in the broken appliances, knocked over chairs, and blood splattered everywhere. It's exactly the kind of mess that he can ignore when we're out on a job but can't fucking abide by here at the house, and I've got no doubt at all that whatever else tonight entails, he won't rest until he's put it all to rights.

Gonna take more than some elbow grease to move ahead with Riley and her little sister, though.

"So, does she realize that Chloe is—" I start to ask, turning back to Madd.

"Gone," Logan snaps before I can finish what I was actually trying to ask.

But if I had to guess? No, Riley had no clue. Not with the craptastic apartment the two sisters were living in before West Point took Chloe.

Logan tosses something at Maddoc. His boxers.

Maddoc nods grimly as he slips them on, the muscle in his jaw twitching harder than a stripper when the beat drops. "I figured the girl got away. Seducing me had to be Riley's way of covering for it."

I snort, crossing my arms over my chest. Riley seducing him? That's what he's going with? I'm pretty sure Madd's been wanting to fuck her ever since she first hit us up back at Clancy's, but okay.

He spears me with a sharp glance. "I know you were fucking her too, despite the rule I had in place, so I don't want to hear any shit about this, Dante."

I hold up my hands and shake my head as if I wouldn't dream of it, even though we both know that normally, I absolutely would. The truth is, that's just a knee jerk reaction, though. The longer Maddoc holds my gaze, staring me down, the more I realize I'm not actually in the mood to give him shit about whatever went down tonight.

Besides, nothing feels fucking normal right now.

Madd doesn't let women in his life anymore—at least, not as anything other than an occasional fuck toy—and I'm the king of casual with my hook-ups. I sure as hell don't normally develop... *feelings* when I decide I need to get my dick wet.

Riley's different, though. Even Logan's been a bit off around her recently. So even if no one's gonna come right out and say it, I'm pretty sure this shit tonight has rocked all of us out of whatever the hell normal is supposed to be around here.

Maddoc finally nods at me, and when he turns to stare back down at Riley, I catch the slightest wince.

"You should get that shoulder taken care of, Madd."

He looks back at me with a scowl. "Later. It's not that bad."

I raise an eyebrow. "Yeah, but it's still gonna need stitches... after Logan gets the bullet out."

Logan gives the kitchen one more tight-lipped glare, then nods at Maddoc. "Best to handle it now so it's done, then I'll check the security tapes for the sister." He walks over to us and nudges Riley's body with his toe. "What are we going to do with her?"

Maddoc's jaw starts twitching again. He's fucking pissed, as anyone should be when they get shot.

I'm pretty sure that's not all he is, though.

Something I don't mention, since, no matter how close we are, there's just some shit that you don't remind a guy of, and his history with women who fuck him and then betray him definitely falls in that category around here.

"Take her back up to her room," Maddoc finally says. "We'll keep her there."

I'm about to point out that that's gonna be a fucking challenge, but Madd's already one step ahead of me.

"Cuff her to the bed," he adds. "If we're lucky, we'll have her sister back before she comes around."

Maddoc heads for the stairs, and Logan and I share a look that says it all. We're not gonna be that fucking lucky. Our surveillance doesn't extend beyond the property, and Chloe's already got a head start.

We *will* find her, but she's Riley's little sister. She survived weeks of captivity under West Point's sadistic asshole of a leader. I've got no doubt at all that she's inherited Riley's grit, and she's not gonna make it easy on us.

"It's a good thing we're the best," I murmur, not needing to spell out what I'm talking about since Logan gets it.

He almost smiles. Not that anyone who didn't know him like a fucking brother would have caught it. But then he glances back at the blood-splattered disaster zone our kitchen has become with a pained look, and sighs. "I guess that will have to wait."

I nod. Maddoc will come first, then he'll start the hunt for Chloe before letting himself come back and take care of this shit.

"Want some help cleaning it?" I ask anyway, knowing that with Logan's chronic need for order, he's already jonesing to make it right despite having the self-discipline to stick with priorities. 'Course, I also know he's going to say no, because it's the kind of thing he'll need to make sure is done to his own exacting standards.

But he'll also take the offer as it's meant—a reminder that I've got his back. Fucking always.

"I'll handle it," he says, just like I expect. Almost-smiling again. Then he nods down at Riley, his expression going totally unreadable, even to me. "You handle... her."

"Sure," I say to his back as he turns and follows Madd upstairs.

I look down at Riley's body, then can't fucking help myself and crouch down and straighten out the awkward angle he left her at.

Even passed out and fucking filthy like this, she's gorgeous. Every single thing about her just does it for me, and I'd be lying if I said the streaks of blood smearing her satin-smooth skin—and fuck, even the sight of Madd's cum drying on her thighs—doesn't add to my attraction.

Still, I don't like seeing her so fucking limp and lifeless, and that part *is* hard to acknowledge.

I've watched her sleep, but this is different. Drugged up like this, she's just gone. She's missing that spark, that fiery spirit that makes her so fucking alluring. She looks... smaller like this. More breakable. Vulnerable in a way that brings a whole host of protective bullshit up inside me that I'm not sure I want to feel about her. About anyone.

"Too fucking late," I murmur, sighing as I lift her into my arms, then rise to my feet.

For someone with such a big fucking spirit, she's a little slip of a thing. Her slim, athletic body is almost as strong as her heart, but it sure as shit doesn't weigh much.

"What the fuck were you thinking, princess?" I ask her, pausing on the landing of the stairs to brush some of that vibrant, blue-and-purple-streaked hair back from her face. But those dark eyes of hers don't open, don't even fucking flicker, and I miss the angry glare I'd get if she could actually hear my question right now.

Not that it was anything but rhetorical.

"Protecting your baby sister," I answer for her, resuming my trek to her room. "I know, I know. But shit, you've just made it that much more complicated. You know that, right? I respect how fucking loyal you are to Chloe, but..."

I sigh.

But nothing. I'm just talking to myself here, and it's that damn no-holds-barred loyalty of hers that's the whole problem right now.

I don't just respect it, I understand it down to my DNA, because I'm the same way.

Hell, I'm that way even deeper than DNA, since Maddoc and Logan don't share any with me but are my brothers all the same. And I may know fuck-all about how close siblings-by-blood actually are to each other, never having had any, but what I do know is that blood alone doesn't guarantee a damn thing.

Not everyone is as dedicated to their family as Riley is to her baby sister, and even without blood to bind us, I'd kill or die for my chosen brothers in a heartbeat. I'm loyal to them above all else, and no one has ever tested that bond between us.

Except her.

Riley... puts a strain on it. I still know where my loyalty lies and I always will, but I can't deny that it doesn't feel right to be on opposing sides with her, either.

"Fucking stupid," I mutter, this time talking to myself. Of course our plans for her little sister were always gonna put us at odds. I just didn't want to look too closely at that, because I didn't—I still don't—like it.

I make it up to her room and lay her out on her bed, then go fetch a pair of handcuffs.

Some dirty-ass shit flashes through my brain when I get back with them.

"We could've had some fun with these, princess," I whisper, swinging them around my fingers as I stare down at her still-too-silent form. And it's true, but my cock isn't interested when she's so unresponsive, and instead of cuffing her to the headboard right away, I hesitate for a second, battling with all these insidiously soft feelings that have crept up on me, then toss them aside.

She's definitely gotten under my skin.

"Be right back," I promise her, making quick work of gathering a warm, damp washcloth from the bathroom and then some comfortable sleep clothes from the chest of drawers.

I clean her up, going carefully around the fresh, angry-looking stitches in her side, then get her dressed. And it's a damn good thing I have faith in Logan's knowledge of pretty much everything, because the way she's so fucking out of it from whatever he drugged her with is really starting to bother me.

He wouldn't hurt her, though. Not right now, and not this way.

I run my finger over her neck, then gently grip it, mirroring the way he had his hand wrapped around her throat when I found them alone that night, right after she came to stay with us. He has such control that he barely even left a mark on her.

Part of me thinks it's a shame. It's not that I want her to be hurt—at least, not any more than it takes to get her off—but I have liked seeing our marks on her body.

Maybe some new ones will show up from her scuffle with Maddoc.

I release her throat and shove those thoughts aside, because now isn't the fucking time. I don't know how to fix shit between us now that she's taken it this far. And the fact that I'm even worrying about it just goes to prove what a mistake it is to go soft for her.

I fix the cuffs on her wrists, then attach them to the headboard.

And then, despite having just told myself I know better, I lean down and bury my nose in her hair, breathing in that unique spice-and-smoke scent of hers, overlaid now with the musky tang of sex.

It's fucking addictive.

I press a kiss against her forehead, then wipe it away with my thumbs. "Sorry about the cuffs, princess. It's not personal."

Then I shake my head in disgust and make myself walk away, because that's not really true, and I know it.

I head toward Logan's room, then go on through it to the attached bathroom, where I can hear Maddoc's voice.

The truth is, shit has gotten far *too* personal with this girl, so maybe Madd was right. Fucking her that first time, at the strip club, was sheer goddamn heaven. But once she got mixed up in Reaper business?

Yeah, that might have been a mistake.

It definitely was for Maddoc.

I see the bloody bullet Logan pried out of him lying in the sink, and Logan's just about done stitching up the hole it punched in Maddoc's shoulder when I join them.

"...a grid search," Madd is saying into his phone, nothing in his voice giving away the fact that Logan's currently pushing a needle through his skin. "Call in everyone... no, that's not...

23

yeah. Okay... No. I don't care, Payton," he finally growls, "pull them off and make this a priority, right the fuck *now*."

He stabs a finger at his phone, ending the call, and tosses it down with a curse.

"No luck on the security cameras?" I ask, knowing for a fact that Madd wouldn't have held still for this shit until Logan did at least a preliminary review of the footage.

"Nothing useful," Maddoc says tightly. "The cameras caught her leaving, of course, and we know she went east when she left the property."

"I... shut off a few of our security feeds a while ago," Logan adds, his face even more stone-like than usual. "I should have turned them back on, but I didn't. So we don't have a more clear picture than that."

My brows jerk upward a bit, surprised to hear that. It's not like Logan to leave anything to chance or forget something like that, and I can't help but wonder if it has something to do with Riley. In a way, he's been the least affected by her, out of the three of us. But at the same time, the fact that she's affected him at all means a hell of a lot. My brother is usually completely unflappable.

"There aren't enough nearby surveillance feeds once our cameras lose her trail," Logan adds, and I know he's referring to other home security systems he's able to hack into. "Not until that house on Downing."

I nod. That part isn't news, but it still would've been nice if we were able to get an easy win here. We're in a residential area though, so no traffic cams or convenient ATM machines to tap into if we want to see farther than our own setup, and most of our neighbors don't have decent security. The closest one with a camera system pointed anywhere worth watching is a four-bedroom owned by a bank manager on Downing Street.

Of fucking course Riley's little sister wouldn't have waltzed by right in front of it, though. She's gotta be smarter than that. It's in her blood.

"So Payton's organizing a street-by-street search?" I ask, picking up on the tail end of Maddoc's phone call.

"You heard me," he says. "I've pulled in every able body we have. We need to fucking find her before any of McKenna's people do."

I nod. "We need West Point to keep on thinking Chloe died in that drop at the warehouse."

The drug deal McKenna's gang was trying to initiate with Capside.

The one where we gunned everyone down to get Chloe out, then burned the place to the ground—along with a dead body we tossed in that was as close to Riley's sister's description as we could get on short notice—all to make sure the girl would stay off West Point's radar once we got our hands on her.

"If they find out that shit was staged, if West Point realizes Chloe Sutton is still alive..." Maddoc says grimly.

He doesn't have to finish. We all know that for as big of a bastard as Austin McKenna is, he's not stupid. Chloe meant nothing to him when he accepted her as payment from her father for her father's debts. He treated her like she was disposable. But after all the trouble we went through with this shit, he'll be like a dog with a bone until he uncovers what she's really worth.

He'll wonder why someone went to so much trouble, but he'll also know that whatever the answer is, it means she's valuable.

Logan snaps off the end of the surgical thread and efficiently wipes down the blood dripping from the neat row of stitches in Madd's shoulder, then quickly bandages it.

He steps back to clean up his supplies while Maddoc shrugs into a fresh shirt. "After that scene Riley made in McKenna's club when she saw Chloe dancing there, it won't take long for him to figure out that we're involved," Maddoc says.

"*If* he finds her," I point out, still holding out for things not to go to total shit. "So how about we don't let him?"

Maddoc gives me a tight smile. "That's the plan. This is a fucking war, and we can't afford to lose the advantage Chloe will give us. We need her."

And none of us say it, but we also need to keep her out of the hands of our enemies. We can't afford to let them discover the same thing we did, and turn that same advantage against us.

Destroying West Point isn't just a personal vendetta against Austin McKenna, it's also necessary. His gang is a fucking parasite on the streets of Halston and, more importantly, a threat to every last member who's sworn allegiance to the Reapers, each and every one of whom deserves the protection and security that come with the loyalty they give us.

"Well, fuck," I say, raking my fingers through my hair in frustration as the enormity of just how big of a cluster fuck this might turn into hits me. "This night has really gone to shit, hasn't it?"

Maddoc and Logan both meet my eyes, neither one of them answering and all three of us grim as hell.

I don't need to hear them say they agree. I can see in their faces that they feel it too.

The minute Riley pulled that trigger, shit started to spiral out of control.

And the longer it takes us to find her sister, the higher the body count is likely to be.

3

RILEY

My head is so fuzzy when I wake up that I'm not even sure I *am* awake, but I already know for sure that I don't want to be. Not when I feel this groggy, with my mouth dry enough to seriously make me wonder if someone wiped it down with a cotton ball and no memory at all of coming to bed even though I'm definitely lying on the same stupidly comfortable mattress at the Reaper house that I've been sleeping on for weeks.

I crack my eyes open. The room is dark enough that it must be the middle of the night, and I'm tempted to just close them again and get some more sleep. I clearly need it.

But I can't. Something important is nagging at the back of my mind. It's... *Chloe.*

I smile as soon as I remember, my heart instantly lighter despite how rough my body feels.

We actually did it. We got my sister back.

Is that why I feel so horrible right now?

Were we drinking last night to celebrate finally getting her away from West Point?

For some reason, my memory is somewhere between hazy and non-existent, but that seems the most likely answer. But then I realize I must have celebrated with more than just a few drinks. I'm deliciously sore between my legs, and underneath the cotton mouth, I can taste—

Maddoc.

Jumbled memories of last night start to surface despite how groggy I'm feeling, and warm satisfaction pools inside me. I knew there was something between us, and now I know Maddoc feels it too.

I remember him kissing me like he was starving for it. Eating me out until I screamed for him. And fucking me... fucking me...

While I was crying?

I blink, confusion flooding through me as I try to make sense of the blurry memories. Even when I hated him, I felt this crazy pull to him right from the start, and I definitely remember how fucking good it was once we both finally acted on it last night.

Don't I?

But no. It *wasn't* good. It was—

"Oh god," I rasp, my mind finally clearing enough for me to remember.

And then immediately wish I hadn't.

I shake my head in denial, my throat as dry as sandpaper and my chest tightening painfully as I squeeze my eyes closed. Childishly, a part of me just wants it to go away. To fall back into that fuzzy state I woke up in, where reality didn't fucking suck so hard.

That's not how life works, though.

It always fucking sucks.

And now that my memories are surging back, I don't have time to wallow in hurt feelings or give in to rage over the Reapers' betrayal. I just need to get away. I need to get to Chloe.

I jerk upright, my heart suddenly pounding when I realize I don't actually remember everything from last night, because I don't remember how the fuck I got in *here*.

Pain flares in my wrists and my body slams back down onto

28

the bed before I make it upright, and I twist around to stare up at my outstretched arms in disbelief.

"Fucking *fuck*," I grit out, rage and terror flooding through me in equal measure when I realize I'm handcuffed to the bed.

I shot Maddoc.

Dante took his side.

And then I ran into Logan...

I swallow a sob and yank against the cuffs, desperation fueling me as the cold metal bites into my flesh. Logan, that fucker, must have drugged me.

I ignore the pain and fight against the cuffs even harder. Chloe's out there alone. At least she has my cell phone and the envelope of cash I stole back from Maddoc's office, but that's cold comfort given that there's nowhere in Halston safe for her to go right now. Not when the entire city is crawling with gang members, most of whom are either loyal to lying assholes like Maddoc, or to sadistic fuckers like West Point's sorry excuse for a leader.

My eyes sting with a hot rush of tears, but I blink them away before they can fall. There's no time for that shit. I honestly don't know which would be worse, having one of the Reapers spot Chloe and return her to Maddoc so he can use her for I still don't know what, or Austin McKenna realizing she's still alive... and then wondering why.

Fuck, even *I* don't know why.

I still don't know what the hell the Reapers saved her from West Point for, since it sure as shit wasn't for me.

"Goddammit," I curse through gritted teeth, welcoming the pain as I keep struggling against the handcuffs. Thinking about the shit storm I might have sent my sister out into hurts a hell of a lot worse.

I pull against them hard enough that it feels like my thumbs are about to rip off. Twist and yank with all my might, knowing I'm shredding my skin and not caring at all.

I can't let anything else happen to Chloe. That's all that matters. I've got to find her before anyone else does.

I jerk against the unyielding restraints with another violent curse, and Dante's low drawl rolls out of the darkness, making me freeze like a cornered rabbit.

I thought I was alone.

"Don't bother, princess," he says. "Not the first time I've had to restrain someone with cuffs, and no one's ever managed to slip out yet. Since I don't plan on having that record broken tonight, all you're gonna manage to do is hurt yourself."

"As if you fucking care," I spit out viciously, twisting toward his voice and finding nothing but darkness.

But my eyes start to adjust, and after a second, I can just make out the shape of him, a darker shadow wreathed in black, sprawled out on a chair by the wall with his legs kicked out into a patch of moonlight that's spearing through the window.

I can't see his face, but I don't need to. I already know him well enough to picture him perfectly.

Those intense green eyes of his will be hooded and ever so slightly amused, beefy arms crossed in front of his chest and a lazy smile on his firm lips as he watches me like I'm fucking entertainment.

Which, I realize all at once, must be exactly what I am to him. What I've been this whole time.

Hurt flares in my chest, so bold and bright that I gasp when it hits me, as if it's physical pain.

Then I lock that shit down and glare at him.

He's not fucking worth it.

No man is, not when every last one of them only wants to use me.

It's a lesson I thought I'd already learned, but apparently not. I damn well won't ever let myself forget it again, though.

"Get these handcuffs off me," I hiss, glaring at him. "Let me fucking go, Dante."

He leans forward, resting his elbows on his knees and bringing his face out of the shadows, into the silvery moonlight.

The sight hits me like a punch in the gut. Not just because of how handsome he is, but because he still has the balls to look at me like he fucking cares.

"You know that's not gonna happen," he says gently, the words driving home the truth.

He doesn't care, and he never did. He's just damn good at faking it.

"Thanks for proving that nothing between us was real," I spit out before I can stop myself, immediately hating that I showed him any vulnerability.

Ever, but especially now, about us.

"That's not true," he says, frowning at me.

"Of course it fucking is," I scoff. "If you and I had actually mattered, you'd never have tied me up like this."

Something flares in Dante's eyes when I jerk my wrists against the cuffs again, making them rattle against the headboard.

His lips quirk up in a too fucking familiar smirk. "I mean, I might have," he says, the teasing tone to his voice making my eyes sting again. "If you'd asked me nicely."

"I hate you," I whisper, my throat closing up.

Dante's face turns serious, and he gets to his feet, crossing over to the bed and smoothing my hair away from my face.

I jerk away from his touch, and he sighs.

"I could say the same, you know. About what was and wasn't real between us." He waits a beat, then, "You shot Maddoc. You shot my brother."

Of course that's what he cares about.

Of course it's *who* he cares about.

A shard of hurt spears me all over again, but I grab on to it hard before it can gut me and twist it into the familiar armor of anger.

"I had a reason to," I hiss. "All three of you have been lying to me this whole time. You fuckers made me believe in you. You betrayed me."

Dante doesn't deny it. His eyes shutter, his normally expressive face closing down.

Closing me out.

"What do you want with my sister?" I demand, choking back the other questions burning in my throat before they can come out.

No way am I asking him how long they've been planning whatever it is they want Chloe for. I don't think I can stand to hear about it if it was all lies from the start, or to find out whether any of those moments of connection between us were actually real.

Not the sex, but all the rest. The shit that made it feel like something more.

"Shooting Madd was a mistake," Dante says after a minute, not bothering to tell me what I want to know.

Not about Chloe, at least. But not answering me pretty much is an answer, when it comes to all the things I didn't ask.

"You just made shit a lot harder for yourself," he goes on. "You know that, right?"

I glare up at him. "You fucking Reapers are the ones making shit hard for me."

Dante's lips tighten, then he blows out a harsh breath. "*Jesus*, princess. You wanna know how many people have pulled a gun on Maddoc and survived to tell about it? Because it's not a hell of a lot, and the ones who actually pulled the trigger are all six feet under now."

Dante isn't threatening me, he's just stating facts.

Maddoc's fucking ruthless. I knew that going in.

"Is that why you're here?" I ask, tilting my chin up to hide the fear that washes through me. "Did he send you to do his dirty work and kill me?"

Dante stares down at me with such intensity that it feels like a physical force.

"I'm Maddoc's second," he says, leaning over me and bracing his hands on either side of my body.

I narrow my eyes. I fucking know he is, and I know what it means too.

Of course he handles Maddoc's dirty work.

But even knowing what he's trying to tell me, having his big, imposing body loom over me, having him so close, makes me respond. My breath starts to come faster as I react to him in ways I shouldn't, not now that I know the truth.

But I can't help it... and I can't stop it, either.

Heat spreads through me, my body craving his. Like it knows, remembers, that every time he's ever been this close to me, he's either made me scream with pleasure or...

Or he's made me feel safe.

But I'm not, and it's like a dash of cold water.

I turn my face away, blinking fast as that's ripped away from me too.

It was one thing to know I'd be leaving him, all of them, once we got Chloe back. That was my choice, and I accepted the loss—accepted that I'd miss Dante, Maddoc, and even Logan, no matter how stupid it was to develop feelings for men like them—because I had to. I had to give Chloe a fresh start.

But this is a different kind of loss. This is being smacked in the face with the truth and realizing that nothing here was ever mine to lose. That none of it was *real*.

Dante trails his hand over my cheek, then digs his fingers into my hair and grips my skull, forcing me to turn back and meet his gaze.

"I'm Maddoc's second," he repeats forcefully, holding me tightly enough that I can't look away this time. "I'm loyal to him to the grave. I have killed for him, and I'll do it again. Every time he's asked me to take someone out, I've done it without question. *Every* time, princess. It's my skill set. It's what I do. It's what I'll always do for my brothers."

I know.

I even understand.

Loyalty is Dante's lifeblood, it's what the Reapers stand for and it's what attracted me to him, just as much as the darkness that lives inside him and the light he brings to the surface did. So yes, I get it.

But he didn't say no.

He didn't tell me he *isn't* here to kill me.

And while I might be moments away from death right now, I'm not sure if it's knowing that, or how fucking much it hurts to be reminded that he'll always pick his brothers over me, that has my stomach dipping, my breath coming in short, shallow pants, my eyes squeezing closed in denial again.

He may not let me turn, but I'll be damned if I watch it coming.

Dante's fingers flex, moving through my hair like a caress. Then he brushes them across my closed eyelids... trails them softly over my cheek... traces my lips ever so lightly before dragging his fingers down to my throat and resting them over my fluttering pulse.

"Look at me, Riley," he says, and I instinctively obey him and do it. He stares into my eyes with an intensity that has my breath hitching. "I don't want to kill you. I'll never want that."

I swallow hard. I... believe him. Maybe it's because he used my name instead of calling me "princess," or maybe it's just wishful thinking, but I do.

And I also know that telling me he doesn't want to isn't the same as saying he won't.

I suck in a ragged breath, my shoulders aching from being pulled above my head for so long and a stinging pressure behind my eyes that makes me feel both weak and angry.

Dante opens his mouth like he's got more to say, but I shake my head.

He can kill me if he has to, but he doesn't get to see my tears. He doesn't deserve them.

"Don't," I whisper, turning my face away from him again.

This time, he lets me, and I hate how grateful I am for that. But even if whatever had started to grow between the two of us before all this shit went down actually meant something to him, he's still planning on helping Maddoc and Logan use my sister for the Reapers' benefit.

He still lied to me. Betrayed me. Used me to get to her in the first place.

Because, as he just made a point of reminding me, his loyalty lies with Maddoc, and if Maddoc has decided I need to die for putting a bullet in his shoulder tonight...

Well, like Dante said himself, it's what he does, and there's no way he would ever pick me over his brothers.

Would he?

I know the answer to that one. And yet, when Dante sighs and straightens up without killing me, when he adjusts my cuffed hands so that my shoulders don't ache quite as much and then presses a warm kiss to my forehead before silently returning to the chair by the wall... I can't help but wonder if I'm wrong.

The tears I can't fight anymore start to slowly leak down my cheeks as I stare into the darkness.

Despite everything, I still *want* to be wrong.

And that traitorous feeling is probably the biggest betrayal of all.

4

RILEY

"Shit," I whisper when I open my eyes. My throat is as dry as dust. That's my first thought. My second is that Chloe's been out there on her own all night.

I want to cry. Or scream. But I look around the room, and there's no one to scream at.

Dante was here most of the night, but now I'm alone.

"Of course I am," I mumble, fighting back emotions I really don't want to deal with.

Not right now, and not ever.

It's not like I *want* his company, or any of the Reapers' company, but the part of me that felt... not alone for a while, the part that was starting to believe I actually had people who gave a shit about me for once in my life, people who'd have my back, I guess that part still hasn't gotten the full memo that none of it was real.

Probably just a shitty side effect of the broken sleep I got.

I don't even remember dozing off, but I do remember waking up over and over throughout the night, as my worries about Chloe tore me out of nightmares that were even worse. The low-key headache from those drugs Logan gave me didn't help either, and no matter what the room flooded with daylight is telling me about how long I've been lying in this bed, it feels like I didn't get any actual rest. Not any that counts, at least.

It doesn't matter. I can tell I'm not going to fall back asleep this time. For better or worse, I'm awake now... and I'd kill for some water.

For some *more* water.

I do my best to push away the vague memories of Dante bringing me some during the night. Holding the cup for me while I drank. Brushing stray drops from my lips when he pulled it away.

Keeping his promise to keep me locked in these cuffs the whole time.

"Goddammit," I hiss, yanking on them as desperation and hopelessness well up inside me in an unstoppable wave. It figures that the one thing that asshole didn't lie to me about would be this. That there's no way for me to get free.

But I have to.

Baring my teeth, I twist my body enough to gain some leverage and then jerk my wrists against the warm metal until it bites into my flesh like twin bands of bloody razor blades.

And I've got no doubt they really are bloody. I can't bear to look, but it feels like the only thing I'm accomplishing is scraping my skin raw. Dante's not here to tell me to stop this time though, and it's literally the only way for me to get free, so fuck it.

I pant through the pain, happy to rip my own hands off if that's what it takes. I won't let them win, and no matter how empty this room is, after what they told me about the surveillance system in this place, I know that being alone in here means jack shit. They can still see me.

And I refuse to let them see me give up.

I can't give up. Chloe may have my phone and a little money, but we had no time to make a plan. She knows just enough to know she's in danger, to know that there's nowhere safe for her to go, but the only other thing she's got is my promise that I'll find her.

And the brutal reality that there's no way for her to reach me if I don't.

Not without coming back here.

I squeeze my eyes closed and pull against the cuffs even harder. Pull until I really do feel a warm trickle of blood snaking down my arms.

It doesn't matter. Call it an offering, a blood sacrifice, to anyone listening.

Please, *please* let her be too smart to come back.

Although if I'm going to bother with prayers when there's fuck-all chance of getting them answered, what I should pray for is that Chloe gets herself out of Halston.

But I know better. She won't leave the city without me. And even if I'm somehow wrong about that, it's not like she has enough to make a new start anywhere else. Not on her own.

I don't even try to stop the tears that slip out as I keep struggling in vain against the cuffs. The few thousand dollars in that envelope I gave her will run out all too soon, and she's got no good way to get more, no ID of her own, and no way to use her own name safely even if she did.

Not with Austin McKenna's gang thinking she's dead right now.

"I'm sorry," I whisper, hating that I've failed her.

Then my eyes pop open and I go still, my heart suddenly racing. I've gotten used to thinking of West Point as the enemy over these last few weeks and the Reapers as some kind of fucked-up safe haven for us, but that's only half true. West Point *is* the enemy, and staying out of sight might keep Chloe off their radar, but the Reapers? Well, now I know that they're our enemy too. And they not only know Chloe is still alive, but Maddoc has probably had his people out looking for her all night while I've been lying here doing *nothing*.

What if they've already found her?

What if they brought her back to the house while I was sleeping?

What if they've already forced her to do... whatever the fuck it is they want to use her for?

"*Chloe!*" I scream before I can decide whether or not it's smart, yanking so hard on the cuffs that the pain feels like liquid fire and a distant part of me, buried underneath the panic that claws at my heart at the thought of my sister back in the hands of these *liars*, is surprised I haven't ripped my hands off already. "Chloe!" I can't stop shouting for her. Can't stop the fear that all but chokes me. "*Chloe!*"

Blood runs down my forearms in earnest now, and I don't care if calling out for her is smart. If she's here, I need to know it. If the Reapers found her, if they're holding her, I need her to know that she's not alone. I need her to trust that I'll... I'll...

Fuck. I don't know what, but I'll do *something*.

Protect her.

Save her.

Whatever it takes.

"Chloe!" I yell again, desperation fueling my voice even though it's so hoarse that the word feels like sandpaper scraping my throat raw from the inside out.

But at least this time, I get a response.

Just not one from my sister.

The door bursts open, and Maddoc—flanked by Dante and Logan—strides into the room like he owns it.

I glare at them, panting. Trying to ignore the way seeing them walk in together as a group, a united front, makes my heart stutter with a whole different kind of pain than the fire in my wrists. Each one of them is intimidating on his own, but with all three men together—together and clearly aligned against me—I can't even pretend that I have a chance here.

But I can still fight for one.

And I'll be damned if I let them see how hopeless I feel at the thought of standing against them.

I grit my teeth and use the handcuffs as leverage, pulling myself up into a sitting position. A fresh, hot wave of agony makes me hiss, threatening to steal all my attention for a moment.

But it can't have it... and neither can Dante when his eyes dart toward my wrists and his lips turn down, just for a moment, in a fierce frown. Or Logan, whose icy gaze flickers with something else as he rakes it over me before blanking out his face again.

I ignore both of them and lift my chin, fixing my own gaze on Maddoc. He's in charge. Dante and Logan had made it crystal clear that they're loyal to him, so he's the only one who matters right now.

"Why are you screaming your sister's name?" he asks me, so coldly that only the telltale twitch of his jaw muscles proves how furious he still is.

I lift my chin, refusing to answer.

"Chloe's gone, remember?" he presses on. "You helped her run."

He's goading me, I know he is. But that doesn't stop relief from slamming into me at the words.

Maddoc may be a piece of shit who betrayed me, but he was right about one thing. He never actually lied, and I can't bring myself to believe he's doing it now. There's just something about his dominant nature that makes it impossible to picture, like he's arrogant enough to think lying is beneath him.

And right now, that means he's telling me the truth. They haven't found Chloe yet.

But that still doesn't mean she's safe.

He smiles grimly, like he's reading my mind. "But we will find her."

I swallow hard. "What do you even want with her?"

No one answers me.

Of course they don't.

"You asshole," I hiss, narrowing my eyes at Maddoc. "Just fucking tell me already!"

"The way you're prepared to tell us where it is she's gone?" Maddoc asks in a clipped voice that betrays no emotion at all.

I laugh. It's either that or cry. He's the most stubborn, unbending man I've ever met, and for all that I thought we'd had some *moments*, some kind of connection growing between us, he's put my sister in danger and betrayed my trust.

And he has the nerve to be angry at me.

My throat closes up. No, that's not what guts me. It's that he doesn't even seem sorry about any of it. Not at all.

"You don't know where she is," Maddoc says after a breath, stating it like it's a fact. An accusation that I've failed her.

And he's right.

"But you probably know the parts of the city she's familiar with," he goes on. "Places she'd feel safe. People she might have turned to."

I shake my head, turning away and blinking fast as tears sting the back of my eyelids again.

There's nowhere in Halston Chloe would feel safe. No one in the city for her to turn to for sanctuary.

"I'm not telling you anything," I whisper, hating the way my voice gives me away when it cracks.

Maddoc's jaw tightens. "Then you've done more than just put her in danger by sending her out there on her own. You're the one who's going to be responsible for leaving her out there in harm's way."

The harsh truth in his words hurt worse than when he belted me.

"You asshole!" I scream, lunging at him only to have the handcuffs rip into my abused wrists like molten steel. This time, I don't ignore the pain, I let it fuel me. "*You* did this, not me.

41

Chloe is in danger because of you fucking Reapers! Because all she is to you is someone else to be used! Because you don't fucking care—"

I choke off my words. I've already shown them too much of my heart. They don't get any more.

Maddoc doesn't flinch, but his glare turns murderous. Still, when he finally answers me, his voice is so calm that it cuts into me before I even know he's sliced.

"Wrong, Riley. This one's all on you. And all you have to do to fix it, to save your sister, is tell us where to look. Help us find her before it's too late."

Fear twists my gut.

Fear that he might be right.

But doing what he wants would mean trusting him again, and been there, done that... and instead of a commemorative t-shirt, all I got was fucked over and made to look a fool.

No, all I got was this. Chloe is gone again. I'm still the Reapers' prisoner.

But this time, there's no one to turn to.

No one on my side.

"Never," I whisper, turning my head away when my emotions threaten to betray me again. "I will never tell you anything, ever again."

I close my eyes.

I can still feel the way Maddoc's eyes bore into me, though. The way he waits. Stares. Glares with a frustrated intensity that he probably thinks will break me.

He's wrong.

Eventually, he clues in to that fact and somehow signals to his seconds, because when I finally hear the door click shut behind them, I open my eyes again and find myself all alone.

Again.

Always.

Alone with my thoughts, my worries, my hate.

But mostly, alone with the harsh, inescapable truth Maddoc reminded me of—that Chloe's in danger again.

Even if the Reapers are the ones to blame for that, it's still my fault, because I'm the one who came to them. Led them to her. Fucking *trusted* them. And knowing it's a mistake I won't ever let myself make again is a cold comfort when there's nothing I can do to change any of that.

Nothing I can do to help Chloe.

5

RILEY

I do my best to ignore Dante when he comes in to doctor up my wrists, and I keep right on keeping my thoughts to myself as all three guys rotate through giving me a few bathroom breaks throughout the day. Chloe's out there on her own and I'm stuck here, antsy and agitated, but I've got nothing to say to any of them that isn't a curse word, so I just don't.

At least, not until the door opens late enough in the day that the light is starting to fade, and it turns out to be Logan.

"You need to eat," he says flatly, staring at me with those eerie, pale eyes of his.

My first impulse is to tell him to fuck off, but my stomach growls before I can follow through.

Logan's eyes meet mine at the tell-tale sound, and his face... does something.

I might have called it the barest hint of a smile if it were anyone else, but the expression is already gone before I can decide if I actually saw it or not.

Probably not, since I'm pretty sure he doesn't have that particular skill.

"I could eat," I admit, since my stomach already gave me away anyway.

My voice comes out raspy from disuse, and even though I haven't been thinking about food at all—my stomach twisted into knots since I'm worried like hell about my sister—I'm suddenly ravenous now that he's brought it up.

Logan gives me a curt nod, then comes over and holds some water to my lips, then uncuffs me from the bed once I'm done drinking.

My legs are shaky, and I'm embarrassed by how much I need to rely on him as he helps me to my feet. But then I'm even more embarrassed when he immediately pulls my wrists in front of me and cuffs my hands together again.

Once again, I stupidly thought his support meant something different than it actually does. But Logan isn't touching me out of some desire to help me or because he actually cares whether or not I fall over, he just kept his hands on me so I wouldn't make a break for it before he could restrain me again.

"Asshole," I mutter as he clicks the cuffs closed and slips the key back into his pocket.

That earns me a sharp look, but he doesn't comment. He doesn't even hurt me for saying it. Instead, he silently leads me out of the room and down the stairs, and the split second of fear from the memories that flood through me when we end up in the kitchen eases almost immediately once I actually look around.

The room is spotless now. No broken things. No blood, or cum, or any signs of struggle. There's nothing out of place at all. Nothing left to remind me that I shot Maddoc in here.

And fucked him.

My body clenches, remembering anyway, but I ruthlessly shove those memories aside, sucking in the lemony fresh scent of cleaning supplies instead.

An unwelcome surge of gratitude rises up inside me.

"You did this, didn't you?" I ask, turning to Logan.

Not that he would have cleaned it up for *my* peace of mind.

Hell, if anything, he was probably silently cursing me out for the extra work the whole time. Either that or plotting how to punish me for not falling into line with their plans.

But instead of glaring at me, Logan pans his gaze over the pristine kitchen, finally looking back at me confused. "I did... what?"

"Never mind," I mumble. It was a stupid question anyway. Of course it was him. There's no way Logan's need for order would have let him rest with the state we left the kitchen in. He just doesn't see having taken care of that so thoroughly as anything special, because to him, it wasn't.

Maybe he really is a robot... one who's still staring at me with a quizzical look on his usually expressionless face, like I'm a problem he has to solve.

Or, more likely, a duty he's been assigned.

I thrust my cuffed hands at him, suddenly exhausted in a way that has nothing to do with how bad my sleep was. "Are you going to take these off so I can get something to eat?"

"No," Logan says flatly, cocking his head to the side. "That would be imprudent."

I snort. Imprudent? Who talks like that? But whatever. I'm just here for the food, so I can get my strength back and find a way to help Chloe. If he wants to make it difficult or play some kind of power game by keeping me locked up, I'll deal with it just like I have with all the other bullshit the Reapers have thrown at me.

Logan's still staring at me, his bold, dark eyebrows drawn together in the middle.

For a second, I almost think he's going to say something else, but silence is almost like a religion with him, so of course he doesn't. Instead, he just shakes his head and leads me over to the same tall stool I sat at when he cooked me breakfast that one time, his long fingers wrapped around my wrist in a surprisingly gentle hold that almost has me considering making a run for it.

46

I'm not that stupid, though.... and I *am* that hungry, now that he's brought it up.

Once I'm seated, he clears his throat. "Do you have any requests?"

I blink in surprise, then hold out my wrists again. "I just made one."

"I meant about what you'd like me to cook for you," he says, his voice as flat as ever despite the fact that, this time, I'm almost positive I saw that almost-smile cross his face for a second.

"You're going to cook for me?"

"Of course," he says promptly, even though there's no "of course" about it.

Other than the low-budget meals Chloe would save for me after a shift, he's the only one who's ever gone to that kind of trouble for me, and I still don't know why he even did it the first time, much less why he'd want to now that we all know we're not on the same side.

"Why the fuck would you do that?" I blurt out.

He stares at me in silence for a moment, and this time there's definitely no almost-smile. There's no expression on his face at all.

"We're not trying to starve you to death," he finally says. "Maddoc wants you alive and functional. Food is essential to that."

"Anything you want to make is fine," I mumble, looking away and willing myself to get a grip. Of course that's all it is.

I can feel Logan staring at me in silence for another minute, but then he finally moves away, rummaging through the refrigerator and pulling out a bunch of shit that I don't pay attention to.

As soon as his back is to me, I bring my cuffed hands to my face, scrubbing furiously before my stinging eyes spill over and can give away how stupid I am to keep looking for something that isn't there and never was. I've been on my own forever, not counting Chloe, so I'm not exactly sure why this current bullshit with the Reapers makes me feel even lonelier than I did before I met them.

What I am sure of is that it's time to clamp down on my unruly emotions and get some answers about the one thing that truly matters here.

"How's the search for my sister going?" I ask as Logan lays out some vegetables on a cutting board.

He looks up, giving me another of those eerily blank looks of his.

"Have the stitches been bothering you?" he asks, ignoring my question. "You were very... active earlier. Twisting at the waist may have popped a few loose."

Which means he was watching me thrash around on the bed this morning through the security system.

I lift my chin defiantly. Fucking perv.

"I don't care about my stitches," I grit out, ignoring how the bullet wound he closed up for me aches in response to his question. Maybe I did pop a few. "I care about Chloe. You guys *are* out there looking for her, right?"

His hands fly with practiced precision over the colorful jumble of vegetables he laid out, reducing them to perfect little cubes that he tosses into a prep bowl.

"I'll check them after you eat," he says without looking up.

"You'll check... what? Forget my fucking stitches! Just tell me what's going on with my sister!"

He turns away, pulling a flat pan out of a cupboard and placing it on the stove. "My stitches were very precise, but if you insist on disrupting them, you might end up with a scar."

"I. Don't. Care," I grit out as he gets out another cutting board and quickly slices up a cooked chicken breast. "What is it you guys want Chloe for?"

He doesn't answer, just pulls a carton of eggs out of the

48

fridge, then opens another cupboard and plucks out a bunch of little spice jars.

I look away, trying to hold on to anger in the face of the overwhelming hopelessness that threatens to overtake me.

When I first came to the Reapers, it was a last ditch, desperate effort to save my sister. But that's the problem with "last ditch." Now that I've used up that option, there's nowhere else to turn.

Especially when I'm not even sure what the Reapers want with her.

Whatever Logan's doing at the stove starts to smell amazing. I try to ignore it, but I can't stop my mouth from watering. When he finally brings me a plate of colorful stir fry, my stomach doesn't just growl again, it practically attacks him.

I refuse to look at Logan's face to see if he finds that as amusing as he did the first time. If he's going to ignore my questions about Chloe, I can damn well ignore him right back.

What I can't ignore is the loaded fork he brings toward my face.

I jerk back, almost tumbling off the stool.

"Oh, fuck no," I bite out, glaring up at him.

He raises an eyebrow, maddeningly calm. "You need to eat."

"Then I'll eat, but no way in hell am I going to sit here and have you feed me like a fucking child." I hold out my cuffed wrists to him again. "I can do it myself."

He does that head-cocked-to-the-side thing again that makes me feel like I'm a puzzle he wants to solve.

"I already told you, I'm not taking those off."

I glare at him, but it has no effect whatsoever.

"Fine," I say, awkwardly grabbing the fork out of his hand and sending some of the stir fry flying over the countertop. "I still don't need your help."

He frowns down at the scattered food, then turns and

retrieves a bottle of spray cleaner and a cloth from under the sink.

I ignore him as he cleans up the mess I just made, trying to work out how to actually feed myself without adding to it.

It turns out to be harder than I expected. It's awkward as hell to scoop the unfairly delicious food onto the fork with my hands locked together like this, and even when I do, getting it to my mouth without half the forkful falling off on the way is almost impossible.

"Goddammit," I finally mutter, letting the fork fall from my grip with a clatter. "Fine. Go for it. Fucking humiliate me, Logan."

He stares at me in silence for a moment, then cleans up the newest mess I've made with quick, efficient strokes before plucking the fallen fork from where it's landed and loading it with food.

I stare at him right back.

I tell myself it's to make a point, but the problem is I'm not sure what that point actually is. What I am sure of is that the whole thing suddenly feels oddly... intimate.

Opening my mouth and having him place the delicious food he cooked carefully on my tongue. Holding eye contact while I close my lips around the fork. The way he takes care to pull it out of my mouth slowly, so he doesn't hurt me.

He brings another bite to my mouth.

I take it, but pull my hands as far apart as they'll go, needing to feel the metal cuffs bite into my wrists. Needing the reminder that I'm a prisoner here now.

Logan's careful attention doesn't mean shit. He's just trying to keep me "alive and functional," and even that is only on Maddoc's orders.

"Did you know?" I blurt out between bites, needing to distract myself from the effect all this focused intensity is having on me.

Logan pauses, the fork halfway to my mouth.

"About Chloe," I add, my throat suddenly tight. "Did you know about Maddoc's plan to... use her?"

Logan blinks. "Yes."

He pushes the fork toward me, and I flinch, then square my shoulders and glare at him.

He lays the fork down on the plate.

Yeah? Well, fuck him. I don't need his food, and I'm not even surprised he's in on whatever it is they're planning for my sister. He's probably the one who came up with it in the first place.

Logan is giving me that puzzle-look again, and I swallow and glance away to try to hide how much that hurts from him. Stupid, since of all of them, he's the one least likely to have even thought twice about betraying me.

But when I look back and meet his eyes again, I'm the one who has to blink.

Logan actually has an expression on his face this time, one that looks an awful lot like regret. But then he catches me watching and it's gone so fast I'm sure it's just another thing I imagined.

"Tell me what you want her for," I beg, my voice cracking.

The plate is only half empty, but Logan stands abruptly, his posture stiff and movements jerky, and takes it to the sink. "You need to go back to your room."

I glare at his back, but then notice something glinting on the counter, tucked under the edge of the fruit bowl there. Shiny. Metallic. Probably a piece of something or other that broke during my struggle with Maddoc earlier.

It's hard to believe that an obsessive clean freak like Logan missed something like that, and even harder to convince myself I'll be able to do anything with the tiny little shard, but I need any advantage I can get.

I hold my breath and reach out with my cuffed hands,

snatching it up as quietly as I can. I half expect Logan to whirl around and catch me at any moment, but he doesn't.

It's a piece of wire. I've got no idea what it's from, but I quickly tuck it into my cleavage, ignoring the sharp prick as I shove it out of sight a moment before he turns back to face me.

Logan is scarily observant and always three steps ahead of everyone else, and my heart starts to pound as his light blue eyes meet mine. But maybe he's feeling just as off kilter as I am, because he doesn't call me out. Doesn't shove his hand between my breasts and fish out the tiny piece of broken wire. In fact, he doesn't say a single goddamn word to me. Just wraps my arm in an iron grip and hauls me to my feet, then leads me back upstairs to my room.

I don't resist. That will come later. A broken piece of wire may not be much to work with, but I'll take what I can get and run with it. Run all the fucking way out of here.

And never look back.

6

MADDOC

"...ALL the way down to State and 26th," the kid in front of me says as he finishes his report, flinging a hand out to point toward the part of town he's describing, as laid out on the map pinned to my office wall.

"Watch it, Levi," Payton snaps, dodging back when he almost smacks her in the face.

Levi's face turns a shade of red that tells me he's thinking with his dick, and he mumbles an apology as he drops his hand and scoots out of her way.

Isaac, the third Reaper I called in to report on the search for Chloe, smirks at him, then catches my scowl and straightens up. "No sign of her in the warehouse district either, boss," he says.

"You tapped your contact with Mathis over there?" I ask, frustrated with his answer even though it doesn't surprise me.

Isaac nods. "He promised they'd keep their eye out for us."

Sure they will. Mathis is a small organization with questionable loyalty, and even though I've marked their territory as an ally on the city map, I don't have a hell of a lot of faith that loyalty will hold if they're the first to find what we're looking for. But Halston is a big city, and there's no way to cover all of it on our own.

I turn to look out the window, trying not to let my frustration show, as Isaac, Levi, and Payton go on with their reports. Nothing but more fucking dead ends, but I nod to let them know I'm listening, pinching the bridge of my nose because this shit is giving me a fucking headache.

I've had every Reaper I can spare scouring the streets all night, and even though Riley's... *distraction* last night lost us some time, Chloe shouldn't have been able to get ahead of us like she obviously has. She's just a kid herself, younger than Levi even, and all alone out there with no resources, no one to turn to, and no fucking skills? There's no way she could have gotten very far.

Then again, she's Riley's sister, and Riley's not just a fighter, she's also smart, savvy, and scrappy as hell. A survivor if there ever was one. So of course the girl she basically raised must have learned a thing or two about looking out for herself too.

I grit my teeth, but an irritated sigh escapes me anyway.

"Boss?" Isaac asks, jerking my attention back to the three of them.

I nod at him to go on, and he gives me a few more facts that boil down to no one's seen any sign of the girl. But we *will* find her. We have to. West Point's become a real problem lately, and we need her.

I turn to Payton. "Anything from the 17th Street Gang?"

She shakes her head. "They haven't seen her, but I've passed her picture around."

The picture of Chloe that I got off Riley's phone.

That day she let me flip through her photos, it was easy to see how much love there is between the two sisters. The kind of love and loyalty that makes what Riley did not just understandable, but something a part of me fucking admires.

That doesn't mean I can let it slide, though.

I scrub a hand down my face and shake off the unpleasant

thought. I'm still too fucking pissed to go there. Right now, I need to stay focused on bringing Chloe in.

"Did you tell them her hair is different now?" I ask Payton, gesturing with my hand to show her the length as I picture the trembling, scared teenager we snatched from the middle of a drug deal last night.

Payton nods. "It doesn't matter. We'll still find her."

Of course we will. It's the only outcome I'll settle for. Still, the hair isn't the only difference between the girl we found last night and the smiling, happy little sister Riley had so many snaps of on her phone. I've got no doubt that Chloe has the same thread of strength running through her that makes Riley so fucking appealing, but remembering the way the girl clung to Riley when we brought her back here to the house gives me a twinge of guilt.

I shake it off. The dull, throbbing pain in my shoulder, the shoulder Riley fucking *shot* me in, is all the reminder I need that there's no place for that kind of sentimental shit. My loyalty lies only with those who've sworn allegiance to me, with the Reapers, and my only responsibility is to do what's best for them.

Right now, that means strengthening the organization I built from the ground up. Doing whatever it takes to look out for my people. And if that includes making the hard calls—the ones that may or may not result in collateral damage—fine. That's my job. It's what a leader does.

Even when he doesn't want to.

I refocus on the task at hand, pinning the three gang members in front of me with a hard stare. "What about sightings? Did that lead from Ruiz pan out?"

Levi's the one who shakes his head this time. "It was a false start. Just a teen runaway."

I narrow my eyes, wondering if Chloe could have played that off. But no. My people know what they're looking for, even if she managed to change her appearance. If there'd been any doubt that the teen was her, they would have brought her in.

I look back at the map and mark off the areas we've already cleared, then give Levi, Isaac, and Payton new marching orders.

I know they're tired—fuck, we all are—but they're Reapers, they don't bitch about being sent out to keep searching. They don't question why I'm putting so many resources on this. They trust me.

Which is why I can't let myself get fucking soft about this.

Levi and Isaac head out, but Payton lingers, resting her hand on my bicep. Stroking it a little.

"Did something happen?" she asks, swaying toward me. "It looked like you were wincing a little when you used this arm."

"It's nothing," I say, brushing off her concern and taking a step back so her hand falls away. "A minor injury."

It's not nothing, though. No one outside the four of us who live here know that Riley shot me, and I've got years of fucking practice ignoring pain. If Payton caught on, it means I let it show.

It means I'm letting my people down.

Her eyes narrow, zeroing in on the bulk of the bandage under my shirt. "Was it West Point?"

"No," I bite out, my jaw clenching tight. But I force it to relax when I see Payton gearing up to press me for more details and give her a reassuring smile. "It's nothing for you to worry about. It's been handled."

"So this 'minor injury' needed to be *handled*?" she asks, not letting it go. She reaches for me again. "If there's anything I can do..."

I catch her hand before she touches me, using it to steer her toward the door. I appreciate her loyalty, and she's got the kind of skills the Reapers have really benefited from, but I can't let her think there's an opening for anything more here. There's not, but give Payton an inch and she'll take a mile. It's a quality that makes her a fucking badass when we need one, but not anything I have the time or interest for on a personal level.

I keep my tone brisk. "The best thing you can do for the organization right now is get back out there and keep searching for Chloe."

She stalls as I try to usher her out. "It's not just the organization I'm worried about, Maddoc. If *you* need anything, anything at all, I'd be happy to—"

"Dante," I interrupt, talking over her to greet him as he walks up behind her.

Payton presses her lips together in what might pass for a smile as she turns to him, but the effect is spoiled by the irritated look she gives him. If I was in a better mood, it would almost make me laugh.

I'm not.

"Hey, Payton," Dante says with a smirk before turning to me. "Any news, Madd?"

"Not yet, but Payton's about to go out and get me some. Isn't that right?"

"Of course," she says, accidentally-on-purpose rubbing her tits against me as she moves through the doorway, out into the hallway. "Like I said, anything you need."

"Finding Chloe is important, and I appreciate what you're doing out there. It's good to know I can count on you."

She brightens up a little too much at the praise, but with a nod, she finally leaves.

Dante watches her go. "She's getting less subtle every day."

I brush that off. "It's fine. I've got it handled."

He grins. "If you really had it 'handled,' I'm pretty sure she'd have been a lot less irritated about me interrupting."

I snort. Payton's attractive, but I don't want her and Dante knows it. Besides...

"I learned my lesson with Sienna."

"I know," Dante says with a flash of sympathy on his face

that's thankfully gone as quickly as it appears. Fast enough that I don't have time to get pissed off about it.

I don't need fucking sympathy. Sienna may have screwed me over, but all valuable lessons come at a price, and I've never shied away from paying my dues. That's what it takes to get stronger. Better. To come out on top.

I change the subject, giving Dante a quick rundown on the areas of Halston we've already searched... and letting some of my frustration with the big fat nothing that we've found bleed through into my voice now that it's just the two of us.

"How the fuck has the girl managed to go to ground?"

Dante frowns. "I don't know, Madd, but she won't be able to stay hidden forever."

"I'm not worried about forever. I'm worried about finding her first," I growl.

Dante nods. "You're right, it's time sensitive, but have you slept at all, bro? Showered at any point in the last twenty-four hours? Because she's not gonna get found any faster by you killing yourself here."

I glower at him. "You're right, this shit *is* time sensitive," I say, ignoring the rest... but it's fucking Dante, so of course he doesn't back down.

"It's not gonna do any of us any good if you snap. But hey, if you don't want to take the time to actually get some sleep, I could always call Payton back here so you can relax another way. Take her up on—"

"*Hell* no," I cut him off. Then I scrub a hand over my face with a sigh when he laughs.

He's needling me, trying to get a reaction, and it worked. But he's also fucking right. I'm the leader, and it's one thing to make sure I'm holding it together when our organization has eyes on me—I'll always do that, no matter what it takes—but it's something else entirely to make sure I'm truly good to go when it's time to move.

And for that, I do need to unwind a little.

"Go," Dante says, jerking his chin toward the stairs like he can sense he's won. "Shower at least, yeah? And think about catching some shut eye. Logan and I will hold down the fort."

It's the one thing in life I can always count on. My brothers have my back. Always.

I give in with a nod. "I guess taking a few to decompress isn't a bad idea."

"And Payton *did* offer..." Dante starts in, his eyes twinkling as he drags the joke out too far.

I answer him with my middle finger, heading toward the stairs, but Dante's still not done.

"You want me to get you someone else?" he calls out from behind me, not trying to goad me this time.

He really does know that I've got no interest in Payton despite her blatant come-ons, but he also knows that a good hard fuck is my go-to when I actually need to release some tension. What he doesn't know is that there's only one person on my mind these days, only one woman I want to sink back inside now that I know how fucking perfect it feels to be balls deep in her tight little body.

Riley.

Right up the stairs, but after what went down in the kitchen, completely out of reach.

I shake my head, waving the offer off without turning around. "I just need a quick shower, like you said."

I take the stairs two at a time and silently curse Dante's "helpful" suggestion as I pass Riley's room and head toward mine, because now I'm thinking with my cock... and I really *could* use a good fuck right now.

The problem is, last night I had the hottest one of my life, and now nothing else appeals.

Especially because it wasn't just the hottest, it was also the fucking stupidest.

I let my guard down.

"Goddammit," I grit out as I reach the private bathroom off the master bedroom I claim as my own, pissed off all over again.

I methodically strip my clothes off and slam my hand down on the faucet in the shower, pushing it all the way toward the left. If nothing else, I can get it to burn off some of the fucked up mess happening in my head right now.

I just got done reminding Dante that I learned my lesson when Sienna fucked me over, but did I? Because as the bathroom starts to steam up and I quickly wrap my shoulder in plastic before stepping under the scalding spray, I can admit— only here, only to myself—that I fucking fell for it all over again last night. That over these past few weeks, I've started to... *feel* things for Riley.

Things that were above and beyond what I'd ever felt for Sienna.

Things I started to think might be real.

But just like with that bitch Sienna, it turns out I wasn't just wrong, I let those fucking feelings completely blind me to Riley's actual motives. When she suddenly wanted to fuck out of the blue last night, I wasn't thinking distraction. I wasn't worried about whether or not she might be using my cock to break down my barriers. I didn't even question why she wasn't with her sister, when making sure the girl was safe was all Riley had cared about since we met her.

I just figured something else was happening. Something between us that I'd been resisting, but that felt inevitable too.

And I figured wrong... but I still can't get her out of my head.

I close my eyes and tip my head back against the tile with a vicious string of curses, letting the hot water sluice down my face even though it's doing a shit job of burning out the memories I'd rather bury.

How fucking good it felt to finally take her after holding

back for so long. How goddamn perfect she tasted, like honey and smoke and the kind of sex that could fucking ruin a man for all other pussy. How her body opened up to me, how my name sounded when she came, how fucking hot it was when she begged me, fought me, moaned for me...

"Fuck," I grit out, squeezing my cock—hard and dripping now—out of sheer rage.

At myself.

Because even knowing the truth now, even knowing how fucking wrong I was about it all, I still can't stop, I don't *want* to stop, replaying those memories in my head.

So I give in and do it. Start working over my shaft because if nothing else, I need the fucking release.

I've got no interest in drawing it out. I want it to come hard and fast, and my body obliges, balls pulling up heavy and tight as everything that's pent up inside me prepares to unleash.

I pump my cock harder. Faster. Almost brutally. I hiss from the friction, welcoming it. I want to strip myself raw. Strip away those fucking feelings. Make my dick forget the feel of all that soft, plush, perfect I found inside Riley's sweet little body.

But fuck, I can't. I'm never going to forget it. The feel of her is burned into my fucking soul now.

I curse and let my hand slow, sliding up and down my cock as images from last night flicker behind my closed eyelids. I twist my palm over my cockhead, sending a delicious shudder up my spine, and tighten my grip, trying to chase what it felt like to be inside her.

I've never had any use for religion and don't believe in any power higher than my own, but god*damn*. Riley's pussy? It could almost make me a believer. It's the closest thing to heaven I've ever found, and something I didn't even realize I was craving until I was finally balls-deep inside her.

She's the perfect mix of softness and strength, temptation

and torment, and I still want to break her... but that's not the memory that sends me over the edge.

I grit my teeth and turn toward the wall, pressing one hand flat against the tile as I lean into it and pump myself faster. My skin practically sizzles, the water so fucking hot it's gotta be stripping off the top layer and cooking whatever's left, but it's got nothing on the heat that explodes in my groin when I picture Riley the way she was last night, at the end.

Not when she was gasping out my name.

Not when she was clenching that perfect fucking pussy of hers around my cock as she shattered yet again for me.

"Jesus fuck," I hiss, my hand flying as I picture the moment after that. The moment she should have been soft and spent and pliant, completely fucked into submission.

But instead, she'd had fury flashing in her eyes. She'd scrambled for my gun. Raised it fearlessly, with trembling hands but rock-solid determination. Pointed it right at my head as my cum trickled down her thighs, and then pulled the—

"Fuck, fuck, *fuck*," I shout, spilling over my hand with a tortured groan as my release slams into me without any warning, hitting me just as hard and fast as that bullet had.

I slap the tile, coming hard enough that I need a minute. It's not as good as coming inside her, but it's pretty damn close. Eventually, the aftershocks fade away, and I mutter another quiet curse, resting my forehead against the wet tile. My shoulder well and truly aches now, I've got no doubt I've fucked up Logan's stitches, and every inch of my skin is painfully red from the torturous temperature of the water still beating down on me.

And every bit of that pain serves me right, but I'd still do it again. Fuck, I'd do *her* again, even if it meant taking another bullet.

Or maybe... especially if it meant taking another bullet.

A truly fucked-up thought that I do my best to drown in a glass of whiskey once I get out of the shower.

But just like everything else about Riley, it's too fucking stubborn to let go, and when I finally give in and lie down to catch some shut eye, my last thought is of her.

And so are my goddamn dreams.

7

RILEY

LISTENING to the faint sounds of the men moving around the house as I wait for them to quiet, hopefully for everyone to finally go to sleep, is an awful kind of déjà vu. Of course, last time I did this Chloe was at my back, and I wasn't cuffed to the bed.

Fuck. I can't believe we actually rescued her, and less than twenty-four hours later, she was lost to me again.

Not for long, though. I'm going to get out of this fucking prison, and I won't look back.

I need to find her.

I hear footsteps out in the hall and force my body to relax, feigning sleep. My eyes stay cracked open, though. Just enough to allow me to watch my door in the moonlight.

It doesn't open, and whoever just passed by keeps on going.

I wait another few minutes, but it's truly silent now. I was worried that one of the guys would come in here tonight, that Maddoc would assign someone to watch over me the way Dante did last night, but when I crane my neck to see the clock, it's after two in the morning.

Since I haven't seen any of them since Logan brought me back up here, I think that means I'm safe.

A crazed kind of laughter suddenly bubbles up, feeling like it comes from my very soul and threatening to spill out of my throat and bring the kind of attention I can't afford right now.

I stifle it, and panic swells in its wake.

"Safe" is the last thing I am. I can't even remember what safe feels like.

I take a few deep breaths, forcing myself to relax as I reach for the skills I learned on stage. I never let anything get to me when I was stripping. I couldn't. Emotions weren't useful when I had a job to do, and I've got another one now, so I've got to keep them locked down a little longer because it's time to do it.

I haven't heard any movement, any sound at all, for long enough that I figure the men must have either gone out or finally retired to their rooms. And sure, I thought the same thing last night when I tried to escape with Chloe, so I know damn well I could be wrong, but I've got no other choice. If they're asleep, this is the best chance, maybe the only chance, I'm going to get to escape.

I've got to take it... and pray to higher powers who've never given a single shit about me that my luck will be better than it was last night.

"No more stalling," I whisper to myself. It's the world's worst pep talk, but it's all I've got right now.

I'm not sure how long it takes to work the thin piece of wire I stole from the kitchen out from between my breasts, and once I finally do, it's even more frustrating to move it from where it falls on the mattress to one of my cuffed hands. I use my teeth and twist into positions that make me feel like a fucking pretzel, but I finally manage it.

I couldn't have if I hadn't convinced Logan to lock my hands around a single post in the bed frame instead of keeping them spread apart the way Dante had done last night, but I don't feel guilty for preying on his moment of unexpected kindness. I don't.

"Because I've got no fucking reason to," I whisper in an effort to convince myself as I awkwardly try to work the wire into the locking mechanism for the cuffs.

I've got no idea what I'm doing outside of having watched a few heist movies with Chloe, and the frustration almost brings me to tears. It's my one chance though, and even though the house has stayed quiet, that won't last forever.

"I've got this," I repeat, my eyes darting to the door.

Still closed. Still silent. But that doesn't stop the rush of adrenaline that's got me ready to vibrate right out of my skin.

I take a breath and refocus. It can't be that fucking hard, and when I concentrate, I can just feel the tiny wire catching on something inside the handcuffs.

I push. Twist. Curse up a storm. And finally, *finally,* I feel something give.

The first cuff pops open, and I can't hold back a gasp of relief as my hand comes free. But I've got no time to fall apart, so I get on with it, and even though I'm still not confident I understand how I managed the first one, the second cuff comes off faster.

The minute it clicks open, I hear a sound and freeze.

"Shit, shit, shit," I mutter, staring hard at the door as my heart jumps up into my throat. But the house is as still as a tomb, and after a second, I relax. It must have been a car passing by outside. If they were watching me, if they'd heard me, they'd already be in here.

I toss the cuffs aside and scramble off the bed, my whole body shaking with adrenaline.

I use it as fuel, and move. If they locked me in here—

They didn't.

"Thank fuck," I whisper when the knob turns and I ease the door open to find the hallway silent, dark, and empty.

I close it and quickly put on some warmer clothes and a pair of shoes. I'm almost surprised that Logan didn't come shred my

66

clothes again, or that Maddoc didn't simply take them all away. I'd still leave, even if I had to head out naked, but this will definitely be easier.

I look around for anything else useful I can take, but then realize I'm stalling. The most important thing is to get myself gone. I'll figure out everything else once I'm free.

I turn away from the room that I've made my own these last weeks and slip out into the hall, every sense on high alert. But as I carefully creep down the hallway and then the stairs, no one tries to stop me. The house stays dark. And underneath all the adrenaline, a tiny, bright sliver of hope sparks to life in my chest.

I'm getting out of here. I'm really going to do it.

And then I'm going to find my sister.

I hesitate at the bottom of the stairs, debating which way to go. I instinctively want to head to the back of the house, go out the back door, past Maddoc's office, like Chloe did. That's stupid, though. She's long gone, so it's not like I'm going to pick up her trail that way, and the front door will give me easier access to the street, which will be faster.

Decided, I turn that way and move as silently as I can through the dark. I know I'll have to run as soon as I hit the porch, because once I open the door they'll be alerted, but for now, I can't risk waking up any of the Reapers.

Too late.

With no warning at all, strong arms wrap around me from behind, yanking me back against an unyielding body that I now know all too well. Then the cold, hard prod of a gun presses into my back.

His gun.

The one I shot him with.

"You may have missed with this thing," Maddoc hisses into my ear, "but at this range, there's no way I will."

My heart lurches, a wave of fear flooding through me that

would have taken me to my knees if he hadn't been holding me so tightly.

But I don't have time for fear, and I've sure as shit got nothing left to lose.

I slam my head back, hoping to break his face with it, but Maddoc is faster. He feints to the side, so all I manage is a glancing blow... but he also loosens his grip on me.

I shove myself away and dart for the door, but I'm not fast enough.

Maddoc grabs me before I can open it.

"Let me fucking *go*," I scream, kicking and clawing, fighting him like a feral wildcat.

Fighting, and losing.

Maddoc spins me around and slams my back against the door, then presses the gun under my chin, right in my face. And the look on *his* face...

I swallow hard, fear freezing my veins.

Oh god. I don't want to die.

"Don't make me kill you, butterfly," he growls, as if he read my mind. Like we actually do have that connection I was stupid enough to imagine existed... before.

But we don't. The cold metal digging into the soft skin under my chin, making it hard to breathe, to even think, is all the proof I need. The seething anger in his Siberian Husky eyes —cold and flat as he stares down at me—is almost overkill.

"You're not going anywhere," he bites out as Dante and Logan step out of the shadows too.

I close my eyes, despair washing through me... and worse, leaking out my eyes. It's not even that they caught me. It's that they've snuffed out my hope. I know, deep in my heart, that I'll never give up. Never stop working toward the goal of saving my sister.

But right now, it's hard to see how I'll ever get another chance.

"How?" I ask brokenly, opening my eyes and pretending I don't feel the twin tracks of moisture down my cheeks.

It's dark. Hopefully, the guys won't see them.

"I saw you pick something up in the kitchen," Logan says flatly as Maddoc finally lowers his gun, holding it loosely in one hand as he captures my wrists in a punishing grip with the other one.

It hurts, but I don't give a fuck. Rage is burning away the useless, hopeless feeling I almost gave in to for a second there as I glare at Logan where he stands in the shadows.

He set me up. He knew I'd try to escape, and they were lying in wait for me. But worse, he didn't let on. He saw, and he let me think I got away with it.

He was almost *nice* to me.

For some reason, it feels like a whole new level of betrayal.

I press my lips together tightly. I don't have a death wish and Maddoc still has his gun out. Anything I say right now really is liable to get me killed.

I expect some form of punishment, or at the least, to be marched back up to my room and locked to the bed again. Instead, Maddoc drags me into the living room, the other two following, and tosses me onto the couch.

"What the fuck do you want from me?" I hiss, glaring up at the three of them. Staying pissed off is the only armor I have right now.

The three of them spread out in front of where I landed on the couch, looming over me. They'd be intimidating as hell even without the gun in Maddoc's hand, but when he scowls down at me without putting it away, it's all I can do to not flinch away.

"This isn't going to work," he says, just about making my heart stop.

I swallow hard, half expecting him to raise it and end this thing. Like he said a few minutes ago, there's no way he's going to miss like I did. Not at this range. Not if he really wants to be done with me.

He sighs and tucks the gun back into his waistband, and a watery kind of relief goes through me, making me feel as shaky as a virgin on stage for the first time.

Logan's face predictably gives away nothing, and Dante has a look on his face that I don't even want to try to understand. Maddoc clenches his jaw as he stares down at me, but then finally gives a single, curt nod, as if he's come to a decision.

"We can't keep wasting our fucking time trying to stop you from escaping."

"Then let me go. I need to—" My voice cracks with emotion, but I lift my chin and silently dare them to call me weak as I swallow and go on. "I need to find Chloe. I need to find my sister."

Maddoc's face shutters, his voice grim. "So do we, so we might as well work together."

I narrow my eyes. "Never."

"She's on her own," he says, going on as if I never spoke. "Out there in the city, hiding from West Point. Do you really think she's safe out on the streets, all alone?"

My eyes well up, and I look away, scrubbing at them furiously. "Fuck you. She's on her own because of you. In danger because of *you*."

Maddoc crouches down and turns my face toward him, keeping a tight grip on my chin so I can't look away. "Then let's find her," he says, his gray eyes boring into mine. "Help me, butterfly. Let's call a truce and bring Chloe home."

I laugh in disbelief. I don't know what the fuck he's playing at, because *home*?

Chloe and I don't even have one anymore.

8

RILEY

I IGNORE the pang in my heart from Maddoc's careless, casual reference to "home." A side effect of missing Chloe, and how fucked-up this whole situation is.

"Why the hell would you ever think I'd help you find my sister?" I demand instead, biting my tongue before I can add, *after I shot you to make sure she got away.*

No need to remind him about his gun when he could all too easily pull it out again. I hate how much I'm at their mercy right now. I've got no options left at all, but I'm still stunned at Maddoc's arrogant audacity in asking me for help after the way they've used and betrayed me.

"You'll help me because her safety matters to you," Maddoc says as if it's already a done deal, holding my gaze as he adds, "and she's in a hell of a lot more danger out there on her own than she would be here."

I almost lash out with a denial, but I can't. No matter what it is the Reapers want with Chloe, I don't deny the dangers that exist for her on the street. I just don't know which is worse, because he still hasn't told me anything.

"What do you want with her?" I ask, looking past Maddoc to take in Dante and Logan with the question. "Why are you doing all this? What could you possibly want with my sister? You didn't even know she existed before West Point took her!"

"But you always knew we were going to help you because it would help us strike a blow against McKenna's organization," Dante murmurs.

I send him a death glare. "Of course I knew that. And you told me that fucking up West Point's drug deal with Capside was how getting her back would help you with this gang war of yours."

I was okay with that. This is something different.

Dante looks like he's going to argue the point with me, but Maddoc sends him a look that quiets him. "You're right," he says, turning back to me. "We thought that would be enough. But then we found out that she can be... useful to us."

"The fuck she can." I glare at him. "Up until our father showed his true, spineless colors, I've managed to keep Chloe away from the gang activity in this city all her life. At least out there on her own, I know she's not going to be used by *you*."

That muscle in Maddoc's jaw starts twitching, and he looks murderous for a minute, but then it's like he suddenly comes to a decision, and a wall comes down. He straightens up from his crouch and nods to his seconds, and they all take seats around me.

"Your father did sell her out," Maddoc says, an urgent intensity in his voice. "But it could have been worse."

I blink. "How?"

"Frank Sutton was not a faithful husband. Chloe is your half-sister. The product of an affair."

A rushing sound fills my ears, and I stare at him for a moment as I process his words.

The product of an affair...

Did Mom know? She must have. Maddoc is telling me that she raised another woman's child. She may not have given birth to Chloe, but even if Chloe and I don't share all our blood, don't share *her* blood, that doesn't actually change anything. Blood does matter, but Frank selling us both out is living proof that sometimes it also doesn't.

"You didn't know," Logan says, jerking my attention over to him.

I stare into his pale eyes and for no good reason at all, find myself fighting off tears.

I look away. "She's my sister."

It's not really an answer, but then again, Logan didn't exactly ask a question. Besides, it's the one thing I do know, so I glare at Maddoc and say it again. "Chloe is *my sister.*"

"She is, but she's also more than that, and if Frank had known, then he could have done a lot worse than trade her to McKenna in lieu of his debts," Maddoc says grimly.

I can't think of anything worse, but then again, right now these fuckers have my head twisted around about this so much that I can't think very clearly at all.

"What do you mean?" I demand. "What the hell are you talking about?"

"We think that the woman your father had an affair with was the estranged daughter of William Sutherland. Which makes Chloe William Sutherland's granddaughter. And his heir," Logan says flatly.

My brow furrows as I try to place the name, but it doesn't ring any bells. "Who's William Sutherland?"

"He was born into old family money that he increased by an obscene amount by buying up half the state," Maddoc explains. "His wife died years ago in a boating accident, and he became a bit of a recluse after that. When he died last year at the age of seventy-three, leaving behind an incredibly wealthy estate and no living heirs, the vultures started circling."

I frown. "But you just said—"

"No *known* living heirs," Maddoc interrupts, correcting himself with a faint smile. "Well, no publicly acknowledged ones. But when Logan was doing some research to help us get your sister back, he found out that part of the reason the Sutherland estate still hasn't been settled is that William Sutherland's will did identify an heir. A daughter."

"Okay, so he had a daughter," I say, my heart starting to pound. "What does that have to do with Chloe?"

"We believe that William Sutherland's daughter is Chloe's real mother. She was estranged from her family and went by a different name after the estrangement, so we don't think Frank was ever aware of her true identity. She was just some woman he was fucking. And according to our research, that woman has died as well. Leaving only..."

"Chloe," I whisper, the pieces clicking into place in my head. "You want her money. You fucking asshole. That's what this is about? You want this inheritance of hers!"

Maddoc stares back at me calmly, not denying it.

"If West Point realizes she's alive, they're going to want to know why. And once they figure it out, once they realize she's the key to an estate with a huge amount of money, they're going to want her too." He leans forward, resting his elbows on his knees as those striking gray eyes of his bore into me. "And who do you think will treat her better? Us, or McKenna?"

"Fuck you," I whisper, shaking my head. I can't wrap my mind around what he's saying. It's like he's pulled back the curtain and shown me a world I need to protect Chloe from that's something totally different than I thought.

I keep trying to make sense of it all, running through the timeline in my head. My mom and dad split up a few times when I was younger, although he kept pulling her back into his orbit in the end. But one of their separations was in the time before Chloe was born, and I ended up having to stay at my dad's place, although my mom called all the time to checked in on me.

After Chloe was born, they got back together and stayed

together, which I always assumed was because of us. Mom had two kids to protect by then, and she didn't want him to take both of us away from her, so she stuck around and did her best to shield us from the worst of his qualities.

But now I can't help but wonder if their separation before Chloe's birth was because she found out about his cheating. And even after all of that, even after his betrayal, she still agreed to raise Chloe as her own. She loved my sister like her own daughter.

"You can keep trying to run," Maddoc goes on relentlessly, dragging me from my thoughts. "You can fight us. And at some point, you'll either end up dead or actually manage to escape. But if you do, then what?"

"Then I find my sister," I say angrily.

Maddoc nods. "You find her, and you try to protect her... and you fail, because you're out there on your own."

"I've always been on my own."

"But now there will be too many other players involved," Maddoc says. "Ruthless ones. Men like McKenna, who won't give a shit about collateral damage to the two of you as long as he gets his hands on the money."

"I won't let him."

"You won't have a choice."

He stares me down, and I hate myself a little for it, but I blink first.

I look away, a lump in my throat. "I've never had a choice. That doesn't mean I just give up."

"I know," Maddoc says, grabbing my chin and forcing me to look at him again, his eyes burning with intensity. Then his lips crack in the smallest of smiles. "But you've got a choice now. Help us."

"So you can be the ones to use her instead of Austin McKenna? How would you even..." I let the question trail off,

75

my mind racing until the final piece clicks. "You'll force her to marry you."

Again, Maddoc doesn't deny it.

"Which one of you?" I demand, my glare taking in all three of them as something ugly and hot tries to claw its way out of my chest. "Which one of you is planning on—"

I snap my mouth closed. I almost said *betraying me again*, but that's not right. I don't even know where it came from.

Fine, I do. And it hurts in ways it shouldn't.

Here I thought there was something growing between us. Something real with Dante. A magnetic connection with Maddoc. Even something with Logan that resonates inside the darkest, most fucked-up parts of me in a way that nothing else ever has. And all along, one of them planned on marrying my sister.

I swallow hard, forcing the words out of my tight throat. "Which one of you is planning on forcing yourself on her?"

"If we leave her out there too long, it will end up being McKenna," Dante says, his grim tone so at odds with his usual demeanor that it brings my priorities back into focus.

It doesn't matter what they're planning and which one of them was going to do it. I still don't plan on letting them win. What *does* matter is that they're right about how much danger Chloe is in.

More than I realized, and more than I can protect her from on my own.

"Help us bring her in before it's too late," Maddoc says. "You don't know what McKenna's capable of."

I do. I fucking do. And while he's a fucking monster, so are they.

I've never hated the three men surrounding me more than in this moment. Chloe being in danger is my fault. I'm the one who sent her out there with a target on her back.

But only because they lied to me. I'd have found another way if I'd known the truth.

I lift my chin. "I don't need to help you. She's probably already left Halston, and West Point's reach isn't that far."

If I just give her enough time, refuse to cooperate, Chloe can get far enough away to build a new life for herself. Eventually, I'll find a way to let her know about the inheritance, and then she can use it to keep herself hidden and safe forever.

It's a pipe dream that Maddoc shatters with a single question.

"Do you really think she's left the city?"

"No," I have to admit, swallowing hard but refusing to cry again. "I wish she would. I told her to go. But she'll wait for me."

The truth is, there's almost no way Chloe would leave town without me. I honestly don't know where she would have holed up, but the idea that she'd leave me behind is ridiculous. She'd no more do that than I ever would.

Which means Maddoc is fucking wrong. I still don't have a choice.

But I do have conditions.

"I'll help," I say, the words feeling like razorblades as I force them out, "but only if each of you swears that you won't use her. Won't...force her into a marriage just so you can control her money."

"You don't understand what's happening out in the streets, princess," Dante says, crossing his arms over his chest. "This fucking war..."

"I don't care," I snap. "I'm talking about my sister's whole life!"

"We need the money," Logan says flatly. "But Chloe will be taken care of. All Reapers are."

I see red and I can't even be sure which part of that statement to blame it on. "Taken fucking care of?" I repeat, practically spitting as I surge to my feet.

"Riley," Maddoc says sharply, grabbing my wrists as he stands too. "We're wasting time."

And still, none of them promised they won't use her once we find her.

But that's something I'll have to deal with after we get her back, because he's right, damn him.

I give him a jerky nod. "Fine. I'll quit trying to run and help you guys figure out where she went, but not if you're going to treat me like a fucking prisoner." I jerk my wrists out of his grasp. "You're not tying me up again."

"You don't like the cuffs?" Maddoc says with a cool smile. "That's... surprising."

I narrow my eyes. "You're a fucking asshole."

"And you're our partner now," he replies calmly enough that I'm tempted to grab that gun from his waistband and shoot him all over again just to get a rise out of him. "We've got no reason to restrain you again."

"None?" I ask before I can stop myself, my face flushing with heat as I realize how that might sound... and try to figure out if that's how I meant it.

Something flashes behind Maddoc's eyes. "None," he repeats, giving me a predator's smile as he grips his shoulder. The one I shot.

He doesn't trust me, and he shouldn't. Not while he's still planning on using my sister as a pawn.

"Get some sleep. Dante will take you back to your room."

There's no way in hell I want to wait. I want to find Chloe *now*. But like he's reading my mind again, Maddoc pins me with an alphahole look that doesn't leave any room for argument.

"We need you to be alert tomorrow. I've already got people all over Halston looking for her, but with your knowledge of her habits and connections, hopefully we'll be able to predict her actions and find her."

"But West Point—"

"Hasn't figured it out yet," Dante cuts in, taking my arm and tugging me toward the stairs. "Trust me, princess. We've got ears to the ground. You'll be more useful when you're not crashing from adrenaline."

Useful? Fuck him. Especially because I know he's right. At least I'm reassured by his words about West Point, though.

Which, I realize with a scowl, means a part of me still trusts him.

But I refuse to overthink it. Honestly, I don't have the energy left for that shit right now. Besides, like Maddoc said, we're partners now.

For this, at least.

"No one's seen any sign of her?" I ask as we climb the stairs, suddenly desperate for news of how the search is going.

I'm completely torn about what kind of answer to hope for. Of course I want to find her, but wanting them to find her too is a one-eighty I'm having trouble making.

Dante shakes his head. "Madd's got everyone with a pulse out looking, but your girl's gone to ground. We know you gave her your cell phone and that envelope full of money. But so far, Logan's had no luck tracing the phone. That means she probably either ditched it or is keeping it turned off intentionally so that it can't be tracked by pings to nearby cell towers." He gives me a smile that's a faint echo of his usual grin. "You taught her well, princess."

His words spark a surge of pride... immediately followed by a surge of fear.

"What will happen to her if West Point finds out what she's worth and goes after her?"

His face turns grim. "Their goal would be the same as ours. That kind of money is going to allow whoever has access to it to come out on top. West Point will just be a lot less nice about how they get what they want from her."

I shiver, feeling sick. I can't let that happen, no matter what it takes.

Even if it means seeing her married to one of—

No.

Not that. There *will* be another way.

Dante's steps slow as we reach the door to my room. "You know, Maddoc might be pissed at you right now, but he also respects you. And trust me, princess, he doesn't respect a lot of people."

I make a rude sound. Mostly to cover up the flare of warmth those words bring. "I fucking shot him."

"Yeah, maybe don't do that again," Dante deadpans, startling a laugh out of me.

I immediately narrow my eyes, which has him backing off and putting his hands up to ward me off.

I look away. I don't want Dante to make me laugh right now, and I definitely don't want to feel anything about what Maddoc may or may not think about me. This new partnership idea already has me feeling way too off balance, and with as messed up as everything is between us right now, I don't have it in me to joke around with him.

He's still not on my side. Not my friend. Definitely not my anything else.

And neither is Maddoc.

Dante's looking at me with an expression I don't want to decipher. But just when I'm about to snap at him to break the tension, he smiles. "Good night, princess."

He turns and starts walking away.

"What?" I blurt, thrown off balance all over again. "You're leaving?"

"Gonna miss me?" he asks, turning back to me with a smirk and a raised eyebrow. "Because if you're inviting me to come in..."

My body instantly reacts to that, and I force myself to scowl, crossing my arms over my chest. "Since when do I *invite* any of you into my room? I'm the prisoner here, remember?"

"Not a prisoner," Dante says mildly. "You're our partner now... remember?"

"So you're actually just walking away? You're going to leave me unrestrained in my room all night and trust me not to make another break for it?"

I don't know why the hell I'm pushing him when it would be smarter to keep my mouth closed and be thankful for it, but I can't seem to stop myself.

Dante grins and saunters toward me, only stopping when he's close enough that I have to tip my head back to keep glaring at him.

He trails a finger over my lips, sending sparks skittering over my skin, then wraps his hand around the back of my neck and leans in.

I'm prepared to knee him in the balls if he tries to kiss me, but he doesn't. Instead, he gently pushes my hair out of the way and dips his head down.

"Of course we don't trust you, princess," he whispers, his breath on the sensitive skin under my ear sending more of those aching, wanting sparks through me. "That's why Logan put up cameras in there."

And then he's gone, and I stand in the hallway blinking as I process that.

Fuck.

Of course.

I feel stupid for ever thinking I could have actually escaped. Between them watching me in my room and Logan having seen me swipe that fucking piece of wire, I never had a chance. All that time I was lying silently, waiting until the house was quiet, was useless.

"Fucking assholes," I mutter, stomping into my room and slamming the door closed after me. Not that it matters. They can watch me, come in uninvited, do whatever they want. They may say I'm not their prisoner, but I'm still one hundred percent at their mercy. Even here, in private—

"Shit," I whisper, freezing in place as I realize there is no "in private" here.

Dante didn't say *when* Logan put up the cameras, but I can only assume that everything I've ever done in this room has been watched. Every time I've changed my clothes, talked to myself, or even...

Touched myself.

I flush with embarrassment. The idea of Logan, Maddoc, or Dante having watched me get off without my permission bothers me way fucking more than it should. Especially since I've made my living being an object for men to stare at for years now.

This is nothing like when I've stripped on stage, though. Rubbing my pussy and playing with my tits to get a few more dollars from the shitbags who flock to places like the club I used to work at is just a show, even when it felt good.

But behind closed doors, it's real. Uncensored. Raw.

Private.

I glare around the room, wondering where the hell these cameras are.

"Fuck. You," I say clearly, pushing myself away from the door.

And fuck my embarrassment too. I have no reason to be ashamed of what I do in private. They're the ones who should be ashamed for spying on me and invading that privacy without my consent.

I pull my shirt over my head and run my hands up my sides to cup my breasts, exactly as I'd do on stage, then drag my finger over the small scar between my breasts.

The healed slash from the knife wound Logan put there doesn't hurt anymore, but it definitely makes me feel something to touch the mark he left. Another sign of how fucked up my reactions to these men are, but right now, I'm happy to roll with it.

They want a show? Fucking fine. They'll get one. But it's not for them. It's for me.

My nipples tighten as I rub my fingers over the little nubs, and all the uncertainty and heartache of the last twenty-four hours starts to fade into the background as my body responds.

I need this, and fuck all three of them and their voyeuristic tendencies.

I'm taking it.

9

LOGAN

Riley is... disruptive. I don't like it. Should, in fact, be repelled by it.

The fact that I'm not unsettles me.

Watching her through the security feeds after retreating to my room is easier. It puts some distance between us and allows me to analyze her more clinically than when I'm confronted with her passionate, chaotic nature in person. But as I watch her trail her finger over the scar I put on her chest, I don't feel clinical. I... react.

It takes me a moment to identify the feeling.

My cock is twitching. Filling. Responding to not the sight of her naked flesh, but to a possessive sense of satisfaction at the knowledge that I've marked it.

The feeling is dangerously addictive, so I quickly flick the monitors off, frowning as they go dark.

She's trying to fuck with me, that's clear from the way she deliberately looked around the room, cognizant somehow of the cameras even if she clearly doesn't know where exactly they're placed. But turning off the monitors doesn't stop my body from responding to the knowledge that she and I are connected now. I've touched her. Left permanent proof on her body. And failing to observe her after the volatile way she's reacted to the situation with her sister could put us at risk.

It's the only justification I need to turn the monitors back on.

The moment I do, my eyes zero in on the scar again.

I'm no more used to feeling guilty than I am to the way the sight of her like this affects me, but that doesn't stop both reactions from being true.

The scar bothers me. I hate knowing that I wasn't able to repress the monster inside me when I put it there. That I lost control the night I marked her.

But I also wouldn't change it, because it doesn't *only* bother me.

It also turns me on.

I press my hand against my cock as Riley slips her pants off and stands in the middle of the room defiantly naked. She is... very aesthetically pleasing. But it's the defiant lift of her chin as she deliberately scans the room again, eyes narrowed as if she's still trying to locate the glimmer of the hidden camera lenses, that intrigues me the most.

She hasn't found them and most likely won't. I'm very good at what I do. So it makes no sense that I'm annoyed at the way her gaze is off center. That, not knowing where to look, she isn't facing me directly as I stare back at her through the monitors.

I want to see her eyes.

I want to see what's in them as she shows herself to me this way.

I move without taking the time to consider why that matters, leaving the order and serenity of my room and letting my feet guide me toward hers before I can second guess myself.

I open the door to her room without knocking, and Riley spins to face me.

I smile. Yes, this is better. Having her eyes on me. Watching the rise and fall of her chest as she meets my gaze with a courage and composure that I know for a fact is rare to find.

She's... lovely.

The tumbled waves of her hair do little to hide her satin-smooth skin, but I like the way she doesn't flinch away from my gaze. She's used to displaying herself, of course, but now, anyone who sees her this way will also see that I touched her first. *My* stitches decorate her slim waistline. *My* slash marks her breastbone.

"What are you doing here?" she asks, a slight tremble underneath the hostile challenge in her voice.

I blink. I don't have an answer for her, and I don't like that at all.

Riley lifts her chin. "Did you come to shred my clothes again?"

I stiffen, the question unpleasant. The night I did that is all too clear in my memory, and yet it still feels like it was someone else who did it. Like the monster that lives inside me, my own personal demon, possessed me.

I don't like the reminder, or the way that facing her now has me uncertain what my actual intention was in coming to her room tonight.

I do know one thing, though. "No," I answer her, carefully folding away all the feelings I have no explanation for and tucking them out of sight. "I won't destroy your clothes again, but you should get dressed now. You need to get some sleep so you can be alert tomorrow."

Her eyes blaze. "So I can be *useful* to you guys," she says, venom in her voice. "God, all of you are the same."

We're not, but she turns away to take sleeping clothes out of the dresser, so I don't bother explaining that. Besides, in some ways, as different as Dante and Maddoc and I all are from each other, Riley is actually correct. The three of us share core values. Ones I rarely find in others and that have made it possible for me to trust my brothers the way I don't with most people.

Ones I also see in Riley.

That thought unsettles the stability I require in my world, so I delete it. In fact, now that I've established that I have no logical reason to be here, I should leave.

I don't.

Riley finishes dressing and glances over me as she pads toward the bed. "Why didn't you take that wire away from me if you saw me grab it down in the kitchen?"

"Because I wanted to see what you would do," I answer, her question surprising raw honesty out of me.

"Sadist," she mutters, climbing into bed and settling herself amongst the pillows.

I cock my head to the side. "No. I don't enjoy your pain."

"Don't you?" she taunts, raising her eyebrows.

I think about it. It's true that I've found hurting her to be both arousing and satisfying, and watching Maddoc belt her was the same. But it wasn't the pain I enjoyed, it was her reaction to it.

And the fulfillment I found in control of that reaction.

"Go away, Logan," she says with a huff, closing her eyes before I can decide if I actually want to tell her any of that or not.

I run my eyes over her, noting the sensual way she shifts under the blankets and the way the irritated furrow in her brow draws me in. I really should leave. She needs to sleep. I need to... not be here.

But I don't.

I don't trust women, and I haven't cared to be around them often. Riley is different, though. I'm curious about her. Addicted to trying to figure her out and understand her actions. She doesn't fit into any of the orderly boxes I typically classify people in, but instead of frustrating me, the ongoing effort of trying to make sense of her feels... invigorating.

Oddly enough, I'm not sure I want to understand her. Not if it means the end of the quest to figure her out.

That's illogical in the extreme, and the moment I realize it, rage overtakes me. I don't like feeling out of control, and I can't remember anyone else who's made me feel that way as often as she has.

Well, one person. But my mother was a true monster. Riley is something else.

She opens her eyes with a sigh. "You're still here? Honestly, you could have saved me the trouble of picking the lock on those handcuffs and almost getting shot by Maddoc. Is it some kind of sick game to you?"

"No," I say, all the rage from a moment ago dissipating like smoke now that her eyes are on me again. "You were very... competent." I pause, trying to define what I felt, watching her efforts to get away and help her sister. "And brave."

Her cheeks turn pink. "Whatever," she mutters, looking down.

I start to frown, but before I can get annoyed at the way she's not looking at me anymore—or have to figure out why it bothers me so much—she looks up again. "Are you really okay with having me help you guys look for Chloe? I know you don't trust me."

I smile. I appreciate how intelligent she is. "Correct."

She gives a delicate snort, her lips twitching. "You never have, have you? And Dante said you're the one who put the cameras in here, so probably even less so now that you've watched me try to escape, right?"

I don't bother answering. Obviously, the question is rhetorical. "We've got an agreement now."

Riley rolls her eyes. "Sure we do, but this truce thing between us is shaky at best. None of you trust me, and I sure as fuck don't trust you. You're really just going to sit back and accept it?"

I blink. "Of course I am."

She scowls. "I don't get you."

And normally, that wouldn't bother me. For some reason though, it does. An uncomfortable, untouched part of me wants her to "get me," so I explain.

"Maddoc is one of the two people in this world that I do trust, and I understand why he made the decision to include you in our efforts. It's clear you'll do anything to protect your sister. I may not trust you, but I do understand you." I pause, frowning. That's not true. I don't understand her. I correct myself. "I understand *that*. That kind of loyalty, that love. It supersedes everything else. When my sister—"

I stop abruptly, shocked at the fact that I mentioned Emma. I don't talk about her. Ever.

Riley sits upright, smoothing her hands over the blankets covering her lap as curiosity flares in her eyes. For a split second, I relish her interest, being the object of her focus. I note that the warm brown of her eyes is more than just pleasing. It's as beautiful and nuanced as those bold paintings Dante pours himself into. But then that second passes, and it takes all the self-control I have not to flinch away from her gaze.

Accidentally bringing my sister into the conversation feels like I've just ripped off a patch of skin. Like I've flayed myself open and allowed Riley to see inside me.

It's not a pretty place. Certainly not a safe one. I don't like to look at all the darkness that lives there, and whatever this pull toward her is, whatever this inexplicable attraction is, it's not worth exposing that part of me.

"Logan?" Riley asks, leaning forward.

"Go to sleep," I say, cutting off whatever it is that she's about to ask. Then I turn and leave, shutting the door behind me and keeping my mind carefully blank as I head back to my room.

I've left the monitors on, but I don't let myself look at them. Not even to go near enough to turn them off. I can't. Not while I'm feeling so... raw. Disordered. Out of control.

Luckily, I have a series of exercises that have never failed to settle me when emotions threaten to become distracting.

I go through the series. And then I do it again. Eventually, I lose track of the repetitions, only aware that for the first time I can remember, they don't work. My mind stays in turmoil. I don't find any peace. Even once my body is exhausted, I still feel like something inside me is on the verge of spinning out of my control.

Because of *her*.

Riley is disrupting everything.

10

RILEY

THE WAY LOGAN cuts off our conversation and leaves so abruptly is so... so... *ugh*.

It's just so him. It's fucking maddening, is what it is. Especially because he did that thing again. Almost opening up to me for a second. Showing me that there's more to him than the cold-blooded killer facade he wears every day. He's not like anyone else I've ever met, and every time I start to feel like I know what to expect from him, he proves me wrong. He's a total mystery to me, and talking to him feels like playing Russian roulette. I never know which chamber will hold the bullet.

And still, I can't deny that I'm drawn to him. Everything I learn about him is hard won, but each new facet just makes me more curious to find out more.

That's not going to happen tonight, though. Or ever, I guess, since this partnership between me and the Reapers ends the moment we find my sister.

Both parts of that thought leave a sour taste in my mouth for different reasons, so I do my best to shove the whole thing out of my mind and settle down to actually do what they all seem to want me to: get some fucking sleep.

It's not easy. I close my eyes and slow my breathing, but my brain doesn't get the memo, my thoughts racing almost out of control. Now that I don't have the distraction Dante and then Logan provided, I'm left reeling from everything I learned tonight. I need to sift through it all, make sense of it, come up with a plan. But I also really, really want to just sink into oblivion and not have to deal with all these changes to the world I thought I was living in. The one where Chloe was my one constant, and I thought I had the Reapers figured out too.

They never did answer me about which one of them planned on marrying her to take control of her inheritance, but honestly, I don't know why I even bothered to ask. It won't be Logan. I can't even fathom it. And Dante... okay, I *can* picture that, and the image bothers me more than it should.

But it wouldn't be Dante. I smother a silent laugh, rolling over and punching the pillow into a more comfortable shape. All three men clearly have control issues—and I'm just fucked-up enough that contemplating that fact has my body responding in ways that remind me of the relief I didn't give myself after Logan barged in and interrupted me—but the truth is, if someone's going to control the wealth that the Reapers need to come out on top in this stupid gang war of theirs, there's no way in hell Maddoc would ever let it be anyone but him.

So, fine. Maddoc then. He wants to marry my sister.

Something ugly and dark rushes through me. It's anger on Chloe's behalf, helpless rage at Maddoc's high-handed plans to use her for his own ends, and... something else too. Something that spreads like spilled ink in my chest, blotting out all those moments that I'm still trying to tell myself didn't mean anything between us.

Fuck being hurt, though. And fuck any jealousy too. Neither of those feelings is going to do either me or Chloe a damn bit of good, and Maddoc—none of the Reapers—fucking deserve them.

Besides, it won't even be an issue. I won't let Maddoc,

92

Austin McKenna, or any other man use my sister. I may agree with Maddoc that the best way to find her is to work together, and I'm a hell of a lot more comfortable now that I'm not cuffed to the bed, but the moment we find Chloe, the deal is over.

If anyone should understand that, it's Maddoc.

I'm exhausted by the way my thoughts keep circling back to him. Thankfully, my exhaustion eventually pulls me into a deep sleep... but that does fuck all for me when I immediately start dreaming about him.

"I hate you," I murmur, letting my head fall back as Maddoc drives his cock into me. I'm not sure where we are. Not sure it even matters. But then I realize of course it does, and everything snaps into place.

We're in the kitchen again, but this time it's as pristine and orderly as it was after Logan set it to rights. There's no sign of the struggle we got into the night I shot him. Nothing is broken yet. There's no blood, no bullet wounds, nothing but swiftly rising pleasure that threatens to overwhelm me.

I can't let it.

"I fucking hate you," I pant, not sure if I'm reminding him or myself.

Maddoc doesn't react. If anything, he fucks me even harder. And goddammit, just like when it happened for real, I like it too much.

I have to end it.

I reach for the gun he left on the counter, knowing exactly how to make that happen, except this time, it's not there.

Maddoc grips my throat, his hips grinding against me as he smiles down at me with heat in his eyes. "What do you want, Riley?"

I try to ignore how good he feels inside me. "Your gun."

He laughs, the sound slow and sensual. "Why? I know you won't kill me."

"I can't. Not without that fucking gun."

He drags his hand from my throat down the center of my chest. Passing over the scar. Trailing down over my stomach.

He rubs my clit, his thrusts slowing as need, white-hot and urgent, slowly builds inside me. "That's not why."

I want to look away, deny that I know what he means, but the dream doesn't allow for it. My eyes stay locked onto his as I shake my head, then arch against him with a gasp when he drives in to the hilt.

"That's it," he says, his hands taking possession of every part of me as he fucks me even deeper. "You can't deny me. You can't deny this."

I want to.

I try.

But he feels so fucking good, his cock giving me exactly what I've needed so badly all night, and since a part of me knows it's not real, it's all too easy to give in. To lose myself in the rhythm and heat of his thrusts, in the seductively dirty promises he makes as he pushes me higher and higher.

"You feel so fucking good. Like you were made for my cock. The only one—"

"Fuck you," I rasp, a sharp pain lancing through the rising pleasure.

Because that's a lie. I'm not the only one.

He wants to marry my fucking sister.

Maddoc's eyes blaze, and before I know what hits me, he pulls out and flips me over so I'm facing away from him. Facing the same counter he fucked me on for real.

"Fuck you," I repeat, bracing my hands against it and pushing backward as all the feelings I tried to suppress while falling asleep rise up inside me again.

It's an unstoppable tide that I can't escape, not even here. Not even now.

It pisses me off. I just want to come. I want to enjoy this.

And I want to hate him and end it too.

But Maddoc is fucking Maddoc, so of course he doesn't give me a choice. He crowds up against me, the heat of his body melting everything else away, and for one sweet-as-sin, shamefully perfect moment, nothing else matters.

"Yes," I whisper, letting it happen. "Fuck, yes."

His hard, wet cock digs into me from behind and he tangles his hand in my hair, then yanks my head back, taking my mouth in a vicious kiss.

"It's you, butterfly," he growls once he releases me. "It's only you."

I don't know what that means, but it's exactly what I needed to hear.

"Please," I gasp. Then, "fuck," when he slams me down on the counter, bending me over it and holding me there as he shoves back into me.

It's rough and dirty and fucking perfect.

"That's right. Gonna fuck you until you stop fighting it. Take it just like that, baby. Let me give you what you need."

Yes, god. Fuck. More.

I'm so close, but I can't seem to get there. He promised to give me what I need, but I don't even know what the fuck that is. Then he slaps my ass hard enough to sting, and I scream, pleasure mixing with pain and blotting everything else out of my mind.

I sag against the counter, surrendering. It doesn't matter if I know or not. Maddoc's in charge, just like he fucking likes it... and maybe that is what I need.

The moment I have that thought, I realize we're not alone... and I also realize I was wrong. Because this is what I need more than anything. I need his two best friends here too. A part of this, like they've always been.

Dante and Logan are watching, and suddenly I'm right there, teetering on the edge of an orgasm.

When Maddoc slams that thick cock of his into me again, I scream, coming so hard I—

I wake myself up.

"God, fuck, *shit*," I whisper, panting in the dark as my body throbs in the aftermath of pleasure. I'm wet between my legs and the sheets are tangled around me, and the afterimage burned into my brain from that dream almost has me coming all over again.

I fist my hands in the sheets, trying to get control of my breathing and deny the intensity of what just happened, but before I manage either of those things, the door to my room slams open.

Maddoc bursts in, throwing on the overhead light and sending my heart right up into my throat.

"What the fuck?" I gasp, scrambling upright as reality careens into the aftermath of that dream, throwing me into a surreal moment of confusion. "What are you *doing*?"

His steps slow, his gaze finally settling on me after searching the room. "You're alone."

My heart starts to pound. "Of course I'm fucking alone."

"I heard you scream," Maddoc says, scowling as his eyes rove through the corners of my room again. "I thought..."

He doesn't finish, just stares at me with an intensity that has my pussy flooding with heat again.

He thought I was in danger.

He came for me.

I look away, too confused to even start to know how to react to that.

Anger. Anger would be good. Safest, at least. But all I can hear is his voice in my dream, laughing seductively when I told him I wanted to kill him. Knowing I didn't mean it.

"Riley?"

I glare at him.

It has no effect.

"Why did you scream?"

My cheeks flush with heat, and I hate him harder than I ever have before. He stares back at me like he fucking gets off on it, the intensity of his gaze slowly going from concern to something... hotter.

"Fuck you," I mutter. "It was just a nightmare."

The asshole smirks. "Was it?"

"Yes," I snap, my whole body thrumming with tension as something builds between us.

Then he sighs and the tension breaks. "Since you're up, we need you downstairs," he says, jerking his chin toward the door. "Come on. We're working on a search plan for the day."

"I'll be right down," I say stiffly, clutching the covers to my chest as I realize they're pooled at my waist, exposing me to him.

"Hurry," he says with a curt nod, his face shuttered and cold again.

He turns and leaves, and I shower quickly, keeping the water as cold as I can stand. I have to. I refuse to think about the fact that I just had a sex dream about not just Maddoc, but Logan and Dante being there too.

It only happened because I'm so stressed out. Obviously, I needed the fucking release, and they were just what my brain conveniently pulled up to get me there.

It's the story I stick with as I quickly wash up and dress, and by the time I head downstairs, I've pushed it out of my head completely. In fact, I feel almost... *good*.

The guys are all in the kitchen, and I don't let myself think about what happened here—not in real life, and not last night in my dream—when I sit down where Logan directs me and let him feed me another one of his home-cooked breakfasts.

Just like every other time he's fed me, it's fucking amazing, and I have to bite my tongue not to say so. I'm definitely hungry, though... and dammit, even though I don't admit how good it is,

I can't help noticing the ghost of a smile he gets as he watches me enjoy it.

Thankfully, Maddoc gets down to business, and my priorities click back into place.

"You guys really haven't found any sign of her?" I ask, worried more than I care to admit if that's true. Now that I've agreed to help them and know what's at stake, Chloe staying under the radar has gone from reassuring to frightening the fuck out of me.

Chloe doesn't know what's at stake, and she's been gone for a few days now. I honestly have no idea where she might have gone. Worse, it's all too easy to imagine her accidentally reaching out to the wrong person and walking right back into a trap.

Dante drums his fingers over the map they've laid out on the counter. "Who would she turn to for help, princess?"

"I don't know. Frank fucked her over, and we don't have any family."

"Friends?" Maddoc asks.

I shake my head. "She has them, but..." I shrug helplessly.

Can I list off some names for them? Sure, a few. But Chloe is too much like me. She doesn't trust easily, and even the few people she was closer with wouldn't be anyone she'd trust while she's on the run like this.

"She'll try to make it on her own," Logan states, staring at me in that eerie way he has. "She won't want to rely on anyone else. Not until she can reconnect with you."

"That's right," I whisper, my throat tightening up. I don't have time for that shit though, so I clear it and straighten up on the stool, leaning forward. I push my plate aside and look at the map. "She won't risk coming back here, but she knows I'll... that I would have... that I'd do whatever it takes to get away from you and find her."

"Of course," Dante murmurs, something too warm for comfort glowing in his green eyes when I glance up at him.

I look back at the map, tapping a spot a few miles away from the Reapers house. "This plaza, the one with the fountain? We used to go there sometimes. She wouldn't hang around there for long. It's too public. But she'll probably check in there periodically to see if I show up."

"That's on the edge of West Point's territory," Maddoc says, frowning. "We've got eyes there, but I'll make sure they're around the clock. Where else?"

I point out a few more places that she might expect to meet up with me, then a couple of others where I could see her trying to hole up and stay out of sight. And every fucking one of them ends up being somewhere that Maddoc's already had someone check.

"Maybe they need to check again," I snap, my worry and frustration spilling over.

"And maybe you won't be as much help as we thought," he cracks back, his eyes boring into me.

I bristle, about to bite his head off, when Dante shifts closer to me. He rests his hand on my thigh below the counter in a silent show of support, and I...

Fuck. I hate him for it. It soothes something in me, helps settle my frayed emotions, and that's obviously what he wants. We've already established that neither of us can trust each other, so all he's trying to do is manipulate me into giving them what they want.

I shift away and Dante lets his hand drop, and I finally give in and voice the thought that I've been avoiding. "Maybe we should check in with Frank. He's a piece of shit, but Chloe's always been quicker to forgive than she should be."

"She shouldn't forgive him for selling her to McKenna," Logan states in that flat, emotionless way he has. "Not ever."

"You really think Chloe would reach out to your father?" Maddoc asks, frowning thoughtfully.

I grimace, but I can't deny that it's possible. "He's the only family we have, and he may not be worthy of the title, but Chloe never stopped hoping it meant something. She won't be stupid enough to actually trust him again—"

"Good," Dante says sharply.

I glare at him. I agree, but I don't need his show of support. "—but *if* she's desperate, she might," I finish.

"That really would be fucking stupid," Maddoc says dryly. "Especially with Sutton's ties to McKenna."

I turn my glare on him. "Fuck off. It's not like Chloe has a lot of options. Besides, don't we all do stupid shit when we're desperate?"

Case in point, the last time I got truly desperate, I turned to the motherfucking *Reapers* for help.

Maddoc smirks. Oh, he understands my glare perfectly. Message sent and received.

"Let's pay a visit to Frank Sutton," he says, getting to his feet.

It's the last thing I want to do, but on the bright side, at least it kills off the last, lingering trace of that dream.

And on the brighter side, maybe—just maybe—it will get us one step closer to finding Chloe.

11

RILEY

"Okay, so do I borrow one of your cars, or what?" I ask, belatedly noting that I've given exactly zero thought to what happened to my own car after these guys forced me to come live with them. Is it still parked in the back lot of Clancy's?

It's a piece of shit, so it's not like I care that much, except that when we do finally find Chloe, it might be nice to have it on hand so I can get the two of us out of Halston.

I put a pin in that to figure out later, already suspecting I'm not going to like Maddoc's answer about how I'm supposed to get over to Frank's place, based on his smirk.

"Logan will drive you," he says, wrapping a hand around my arm and hauling me to my feet.

"Fine," I say, shaking his hold off and stalking toward the garage.

It's not just Logan who follows me, though. Dante and Maddoc are right behind him.

I'm not sure why they all plan on coming along. Frank's a piece of shit, but he's a weak one, so it can't be for muscle. I can only assume it's a sign of how little they trust me.

Which is fine, because I trust them even less.

I head toward the big, black Escalade we used when we went to rescue Chloe from the Capside deal, but Logan shakes his head. "I'm driving," he says, nodding toward another car. One that sits low to the ground and looks like sex on wheels.

"In that?"

I definitely don't mind.

"Yes," Logan says in his usual clipped style, but a rare, fleeting smile crosses his lips, and I almost stumble over my feet as I stare in surprise.

He strokes the top of the shiny red car in a way that's almost sensual. It's the first time I can remember seeing him actually *like* something.

Dante catches the look on my face and laughs. "I know, right?" he says, ushering me toward the back and crowding in next to me once I slip into the leather seat. "Logan's picky about what he likes to drive. The Audi is his baby."

It's pretty much what I was just thinking, but I definitely don't need a bonding moment between us, so I ignore him.

I give Logan Frank's address, and he pulls out of the garage with Maddoc in the front seat next to him, already murmuring quietly into his phone.

It sounds like he's checking in with various people who've been out looking for Chloe, but I can tell by the tone of his voice that all the news is negative.

"Any idea how deep your dad is in with McKenna?" Dante asks as Logan navigates through traffic.

I glare at him, but before I can snap about his use of the "dad" title that Frank has never deserved, Dante's already correcting himself. Proving he paid attention to what I told him before, and that it's not my imagination—he really can read me like a book.

"Sorry. I meant Frank. I get that he wasn't a real dad to you."

"Yeah, not even close. And I've got no clue about his involvement with West Point. I worked hard to keep him out of our lives, and didn't even know he did business with them."

"Understandable," Dante says, squeezing my knee in, what? Some kind of support?

I don't need it.

I knock his hand off my leg and pointedly look out the window, giving him my back. I don't need his understanding or support. He's already chosen his gang over me, and it's a betrayal I'm not going to forget and have no intention of forgiving.

I pop out of the car the minute Logan pulls up in front of Frank's place, leading the way up the walk. Frank's been dead to me ever since he sold Chloe out, and if it weren't for her, there's no way I'd ever step foot in his house again.

That's not the way life works though, so despite the knot in my stomach, I don't waste time dithering. I give a brisk knock as soon as I reach his door.

"Who's there?" comes Frank's muffled response.

I roll my eyes and knock again, louder. And then again. He finally pulls the door open, letting out a waft of stale air, cheap liquor, and rank body odor.

"Jesus, Frank," I say, disgusted even if I'm not surprised. Clearly, he's been hard at work doing his usual freeloading bunch of nothing, not torn up at all about what my sister was going through after he sold her off to Austin McKenna.

Frank gives me a sloppy smile, blinking blearily as he shoves his loose shirttail under his beer belly, trying and failing to tuck it back into his pants.

"Riley! Hey, honey girl. Wasn't expecting you. Come in, come in. You're looking good."

I can't believe he's pulling his usual bullshit, acting like everything's okay. Like I didn't punch him in the fucking face the last time I saw him. I'm too worried about Chloe to waste time being annoyed by what a shithead he is, so I shove my way past him, taking him up on that offer to come inside.

The guys are right behind me, and I'd be lying if I said I didn't get a moment of gratification out of the way Frank blanches when he sees them.

"Who, uh, who did you bring with you, Riley?" he asks, his voice cracking as his bleary eyes dart between me and the solid wall of muscle that Maddoc, Dante, and Logan make on his doorstep.

He's scared. It's a beautiful sight.

"Friends," I say. "Of Chloe's." A hundred percent not true, but still fun to say for the way it makes Frank's face go green. "I suggest you invite them in too."

"No need," Maddoc says with a dangerous smile, grabbing Frank's shoulder in a punishing grip and steering him into the house.

Logan and Dante follow, moving around the room until all exits are blocked.

Maddoc lets Frank go, and he swallows with an audible gulp. "You, uh, you guys West Point?"

A faint look of disgust flashes across Logan's face, and Dante makes a rude sound.

"No," Maddoc says simply, crossing his arms over his chest.

"*Hell* no," I spit out, suddenly furious. "Do you honestly think I'd have anything to do with those West Point motherfuckers after *they took my fucking sister*? These are Reapers, Frank. The people I went to for help after you sold her."

I can't tell if the expression on Frank's face is guilt or if he's about to shit himself, and I honestly don't care. Especially not when his go-to response is to deny any responsibility. "More of a business arrangement than an actual sale," he says, holding his hands up as a bead of sweat rolls down the side of his face. "And come on now, no harm, no foul, right? It's just a temporary thing. You gotta know I always planned on getting her back. She's my little girl."

"Fuck you," I spit out, then bite my tongue. I'm not here just to ream him out, as satisfying as that would be. "Have you heard from her?"

Frank's eyes dart around the room again, skittering away from the glowering stares from each Reaper. "You mean, uh, like recently?"

"Yeah, I mean fucking recently. Has she made contact with you at all? Called? Come by?"

His face brightens. "She's not with West Point anymore?"

I ball my hands into fists to keep from punching him. "Answer me!"

"Okay, okay," he says, the smile dropping from his face as he makes a settle down gesture and backs away a little. Then he realizes that puts him closer to Logan, and stops in his tracks. "Not sure why you're so worked up, honey girl. You just said she's not with them anymore, so—"

I don't know what he sees on my face, but whatever it is, he shuts the fuck up and swallows hard.

"Have you heard from her, or not?"

Another bead of sweat drips down the side of his face, and he shakes his head. "Uh, no. I don't think so. No. Definitely not. Not since, you know, before."

"You mean, before you fucking sold her."

"But you said she got away! See? It all worked out, just like I said. I knew they wouldn't hold on to her, right? Didn't I say that? And they didn't."

I stalk toward him. "They did fucking hold on to her. They used her. Degraded her. They hurt her, Frank! *We* got her out. But now she's on the streets of Halston somewhere, all on her own, and I... I need to... I don't know where..."

I'm so angry my voice starts to shake, my thoughts in just as much of a mess as my emotions. His cavalier attitude about the complete shit-fest he got Chloe into and all his self-serving lies have ripped something open inside me, and I'm not sure how to hold myself together. I'm not even sure if I want to try.

"I can't fucking believe you!"

"Now, just calm down, Riley," he starts, backing away from me again. "If you need help finding your sister, I can help with that, but I can't, uh, if you do something silly here, I'm not gonna be able to—*mpgggff*."

The empty bullshit he's spouting turns into a pained gurgle when Logan suddenly grabs him by the throat and slams him against the wall. "Shut the fuck up."

I'm so used to Logan's stillness, his control, that it's a shock to see how quickly he moves. And an even bigger shock to realize he's doing more than just acting like muscle. His whole body vibrates with anger as he glares into Frank's eyes, fury radiating off him in a palpable cloud.

"Your job was to protect your daughters," he says, his voice dripping with venom, "not sell them. You're a pathetic piece of shit. You had something precious. Something to care for. And you *failed*."

Frank's hands scrabble at Logan's wrist, his toes barely touching the floor. His face is starting to turn blue, and I can't find it in myself to care, because Logan's right.

"You don't deserve to live," he says, slamming Frank into the wall again.

Frank's head makes a sickening crack, and his eyes roll up, his nails digging bloody scores into Logan's arm.

Logan doesn't even flinch. He just leans closer, his grip noticeably tightening, and whispers something in Frank's ear. Whatever it is puts a look of utter terror on Frank's face, taking his efforts to get loose from panicked to completely frantic.

It makes no difference. Logan is relentless. And based on

Frank's wildly rolling eyes and the choked, gurgling whine he manages to make, he's finally realized the truth too.

He's not getting out of this.

Logan is actually going to kill him.

12

RILEY

Maddoc crosses the room, coming to a stop at Logan's shoulder.

"We need information," he says calmly. It's just a reminder. He makes no move to stop Logan from choking the life out of the piece of shit who failed to raise me and Chloe, and Logan doesn't act like he heard anyway, so I figure it's a done deal.

And I'm not fucking sorry, either.

Frank gurgles again, his face turning a color that shouldn't exist in nature, and I can't look away. He deserves everything he gets. But that doesn't mean I don't have a reaction to seeing him get it.

My adrenaline is so high it takes me a minute to realize I'm gasping for breath, panting, filled with an echo of residual terror that freezes my blood as Logan's unexpected rage wakes up memories of being held just like that, his fingers digging into *my* throat, choking me, bruising me...

But it's not just terror that has me panting.

In my entire life, no one has ever come to my rescue when I needed it. No one gave a single solitary shit that Frank was a pathetic excuse for a parent to Chloe and me. Not until now.

I don't really know what triggered it, because Logan's

reaction is clearly not part of the Reapers' plan, but watching him unleash all that deadly fury on Frank settles something that's been broken inside me for a long time.

Maddoc's right. We need to know if Frank can help us find my sister. But if that doesn't happen? If Logan finishes this?

I can't say I'll be sorry. In fact, watching it happen has a soul-deep satisfaction that almost feels as good as sex welling up inside me.

"Logan," Maddoc says softly.

Logan blinks as if he's coming back to himself, then opens his hand, releasing Frank. His face is completely shuttered again, but there's a slight tremor in his hands as he tucks them behind his back and steps away, letting Maddoc take over.

Frank falls to the floor, hacking and coughing as he clutches his throat. He's fucking pathetic. Face covered in tears, sweat, and snot, and body reeking of other fluids.

Maddoc crouches down next to him, ignoring all of that, and fists his hand in Frank's hair, yanking his head up. "What do you know about Chloe?"

"N-N-Nothing," Frank wheezes, cringing away from him.

Dante saunters over, tsking as he shakes his head. "Come on now, Sutton. That can't be right. Not after you cozied up with McKenna and his fucking weasels, promising them they'd get good value out of her."

"I didn't—*aghhhhh*."

Logan's face doesn't change expression as he delivers the vicious kick to Frank's ribs, but his hands steady again, and when he flicks his gaze toward me, I give him a small nod, that weird sense of satisfaction inside me turning into a bright glow.

Both Maddoc and Dante act like nothing happened.

"What was that?" Dante asks Frank, cocking his head as he stares down at him like he's been a naughty puppy. "Couldn't hear you very well. Wanna try again?"

"I don't... I didn't... wait!" Frank gasps, flinching as Maddoc suddenly straightens up, hand still gripping Frank's hair as he drags him to his feet at the same time. "Okay, okay, okay. I, uh, I haven't heard from Chloe in a long time! Not since before the, uh, the arrangement. You know, with West Point. Austin never said! Never said she'd got away from them. I swear I didn't know! I'm not even doing business with them anymore, and I haven't heard from either of my girls since that call from Riley the other day." He turns watery, bloodshot eyes on me. "I didn't know it was about this!"

"What?" I say as all three of the Reapers swing around to look at me too.

"You called him?" Maddoc asks, his eyes going cold.

"Fuck no, I didn't call him," I say. "How would I have even done that? He's a fucking liar."

"No! No, I'm not, I swear," Frank babbles, hands scrabbling in his pockets.

Maddoc immediately twists him around, slamming him face-first into the wall and immobilizing his arms. "Watch it."

"It's... it's just my phone. I was just getting my phone out for you," Frank whines, his body going slack. "Let me show you! Riley called me. She did."

Maddoc frowns, then jerks his chin at Dante.

Dante pats Frank down, grimacing because yeah, he's fucking disgusting. "No weapon, Madd," he finally says, gingerly pulling out Frank's phone. "You wanna look at this?"

"Chloe has my phone," I whisper, my heart suddenly racing as I put it together.

"Unlock it," Maddoc says, releasing Frank and shoving it into his hand.

Frank nods eagerly, quickly tapping the screen and then shoving it back into Maddoc's hands. "Yeah, see? Right there! I told you. That's Riley."

Maddoc shows me the screen. "That's your cell number?"

I nod.

His lip quirks up. Just a hair. Just for a second. "Last I saw that, it was in my office drawer."

I lift my chin. "Guess you should learn to lock up shit that matters to you."

"I'll keep that in mind," Maddoc says, holding my gaze before slowly letting his eyes drop down to my wrists.

When he turns his attention back to Frank, I can't stop myself from rubbing them. The cuffs are long gone, but I swear to fuck I can suddenly feel them again.

I can't deal with Maddoc fucking with me like that, though. And it's not what we're here for.

"You know it wasn't me that called," I say to Frank. "Quit fucking lying. What did Chloe say?"

"I don't know! Nothing! Thought it was you, honey gir—uh, Riley. I did! Maybe a butt dial or whatnot. You, uh, she.. there was no message. Just sounds."

I frown. "There was a voicemail?"

He nods eagerly.

"Play it," Maddoc says, shoving the phone back into Frank's hands.

He does, and it's just random noises. Not a butt dial, though. Chloe would have been more careful than that. But even though there's nothing, my eyes suddenly sting as I realize what this means. The timestamp is yesterday. She was alive then, at least, and that's more than I knew before.

I turn away as the guys make Frank replay it a couple of times, scrubbing at my face as I try to get myself back under control. We can do this. We can find her.

And when we do, I'm never letting her go again.

Logan records the voicemail on some fancy little electronic device, both Dante and Maddoc seeming to believe that he'll be able to pull something useful out of the noise.

He probably will. I'm starting to think Logan can work fucking miracles.

"All good, princess?" Dante asks quietly, making me jump. I didn't even hear him walk over.

"Fine," I say, straightening my shoulders. "We done here?"

He glances back over at Frank. Maddoc is still pushing him. Questioning him on some shit about West Point and circling back around to questions about Chloe, but it's pretty clear Frank doesn't know anything. As always, he's fucking useless.

"You want to leave him breathing?" Logan asks when it's clear there's nothing else to get from him.

Maddoc looks at me, but I keep my face blank. I don't need them to kill him.

But I also won't cry if they do.

Maddoc turns back to Frank. "We'll be getting Riley a new phone to replace the one she gave Chloe." He grabs a piece of paper, writes a number on it, and slaps it against Frank's chest, where my father scrabbles to grab it. "If Chloe calls again, or if you remember or notice anything that you think might help us find her, you call that number."

"Right." Frank swallows, glancing down at the paper.

"Oh, and if you're thinking of talking to anyone about this visit?" Maddoc adds, his voice hard. "Don't."

Frank shakes his head. "No, no, of course not! Not a word. Not a peep."

The three Reapers share a look. Logan's the one who steps forward, and Frank just about pisses himself.

"If West Point finds out we were here, I'll find out that they know," Logan says in a deadly monotone.

"I won't tell them! I won't talk to them! I swear," Frank babbles, backing away until he hits the wall again.

"I'm sure your word is as pathetic as you are, Sutton. But just to be clear, if you break it, I'll come back and pay you another visit," Logan promises. "On my own."

Frank is selfish, slovenly, and stupid... but not that stupid. He understands what Logan's saying.

If Logan comes back on his own, neither Maddoc nor Dante will be there to step in and stop him from finishing what he started today.

I don't know why Logan seems to care so much. Hell, maybe his threats are just some kind of strategy that the guys haven't shared with me yet. But still, even though this partnership between us is temporary and I know damn well that the Reapers aren't really on my side—even though Chloe's still missing and we didn't find out anything useful here—when we finally walk out of Frank's house, I don't feel quite as alone.

And I really, really wish that feeling could last.

13

RILEY

Nobody speaks during the drive back to the Reapers' house. As soon as we left, Maddoc had a contact of his put a trace on the phone, trying to find out a general location of where she might've called based on the cell tower pings, but nothing has come back yet. I keep my eyes on the passing scenery, unrealistically hoping that if I scan every street, I might somehow see my sister.

I don't of course, and the tension in the car feels thick enough to choke as Logan navigates through some of the seedier parts of Halston. Or maybe that choking feeling is thanks to all the worries that flood my mind as I go over the phone call Chloe made to Frank.

Even though she didn't speak, I know it wasn't an accident. She decided to reach out to him, which means she's just as desperate and alone out there as I've suspected. But she's also smart enough that she didn't actually trust him enough to make real contact. Thank god. No matter how dire her circumstances are, I trust Frank about as far as I can throw him. He already sold her out once. If he got his hands on her again, I've got no doubt at all that he'd find another way to use her for his own selfish ends.

Still, knowing that Chloe has my phone and hopefully still has the money I gave her reassures me a bit. It means that she might be okay until we find her. As long as she keeps her head down, at least. It doesn't make it any easier to find her, since I really am out of ideas that Maddoc hasn't already had his people check, but I'm still proud of her for staying safe.

And maybe Logan really will be able to figure something out from the voicemail she left—either from the cell tower pings or from the ambient sounds. I can't imagine how, since it just sounded like a recording of random traffic noise for a minute or so, but if anyone can pull something out of that, it will be him.

When did I start feeling like I could count on him?

I know exactly when.

I glance over at him, trying to sort out how I feel about his rage at Frank and the violence he unleashed like a fucking tsunami back there.

Good. I feel good about it. And if that makes me a shitty person, I honestly don't give a fuck.

We make it all the way back to the house without anyone saying a word, and the whole time, Logan looks tense as hell. Shoulders stiff and grip tight on the steering wheel as he stares straight ahead with that laser-like focus he seems to bring to everything, a storm brewing in his normally emotionless pale eyes.

I can't shake the sight of it as we all file into the house. Logan immediately heads up the stairs, and Maddoc takes a call that has him scowling and stomping off to his office as he rips into whoever's on the other end of it.

"You doing okay, princess?" Dante asks, hovering near me in the entryway.

I pull my gaze off the stairs Logan just disappeared up and give Dante a cynical look. "Okay? Not even close. All of our leads are shaky at best, and Chloe's not safe."

He huffs out a quiet laugh, shaking his head. "Fair enough.

It was a bad question. You know we're gonna find her though, right?"

"Of course we are."

He grins. "Good. Just making sure you don't forget that. I've got some work I've gotta go take care of—"

"Then go," I cut in, my voice harsher than he probably deserves. But dammit, his obvious concern shouldn't be so appealing, not after everything that's gone down between us.

There's no denying that it feels good though, and that almost makes me feel like *I'm* the one betraying Chloe.

Dante, of course, isn't fazed by the way I snap at him. "You sure you don't need anything before I head back out?"

"Yeah," I say, trying not to smile as I make a little shooing motion. "I don't need a damn babysitter, so unless you're planning on locking me back up, I'm sure I can manage to keep myself busy until Maddoc comes up with some other way I can be useful."

His eyes flare for a moment, and it's far too easy to imagine all the dirty comebacks he could make to the way I phrased that. Maybe I even want him to. But in the end, he just nods and heads back out the door without going there, and I give in to the impulse I had when we walked in, and follow Logan up the stairs, trying to convince myself I'm not taking my life in my hands when I knock lightly on his bedroom door.

To my surprise, it's not fully shut, and when I rap on it with my knuckles it swings open.

Logan's head jerks up, his eyes narrowing as he shifts to block off whatever he was looking at in the small box I can see open on the dresser behind him.

"Sorry," I rush to say. "I'm not trying to intrude, but I just..."

I shrug, intensely uncomfortable and a little confused over how I'm supposed to end that sentence when I'm not even sure what I'm doing here. And of course Logan doesn't help. He just stares at me until I finally untangle my emotions a little.

"I wanted to thank you. For, you know, what you did with Frank."

His face shutters. "You shouldn't."

"Why not?"

"I did the same thing to you once," he says, his gaze flitting down to my throat for a moment.

I instinctively touch it.

"You did," I acknowledge, running my fingers over the skin there. "But it was different."

It truly was. He has so much control, so much precision, that he gripped my throat tightly but never with enough pressure to cut off my air or even leave bruises. That's completely different from the way he slammed my father against the wall, squeezing so tightly that Frank's face turned purple.

He *meant* to hurt Frank, which only drives home the fact that he chose not to hurt me that night, in spite of his anger.

Because if he'd wanted to, he could have. Easily.

A shiver runs through me at the reminder of how much raw power Logan has at his fingertips, but it's not exactly a shiver of fear. I drop my hand from my throat and lift my chin.

"Maybe it makes me a monster for being glad you did that to my father," I say. "But I am."

Logan stares at me, and the moment stretches out with the same unbearable tension I felt on the car ride home. Just before it snaps, he looks away, his fingers brushing the contents of the small box behind him. "*You're* not a monster."

My breath hitches. This man is so damn hard to read, like he operates on a different level than the rest of us, so it's probably insane to feel like I'm starting to understand him.

But I do.

He put the faintest emphasis on "you're," and I'd bet my life on the fact that he thinks he's the one who's the monster here.

I clench my hands to keep from touching my throat again. A

few weeks ago, I would have agreed in a heartbeat, but now I have to bite my tongue to keep from telling him that he's not.

My reaction is pure instinct. For some reason, I want to comfort him the way I felt comforted and supported by his rage back at Frank's house. But I also don't want to lie, and if I'm honest with myself, I'm not entirely sure whether I do still think he's a monster or not.

I'm also not sure whether I care.

"Can you tell me why you did it?" I ask instead of going there. "Why did you get so mad?"

He jerks his head up, looking away from whatever he's fucking with in his box to stare at me with eyes that blaze with cold fire. "That man doesn't fucking deserve you."

My eyes go wide, and his immediately shutter again.

He looks away. "I have things to do."

It's obvious he wants me to leave, but even though my heart races and the surge of adrenaline that hits me practically screams it's a bad idea, I step into his room instead. "I appreciate that you..."

I almost say "care," but that feels too raw. Or maybe I just don't want to hear him deny it.

So instead, I clear my throat and go with, "I appreciate what you did. That's all I wanted to say."

I fully expect him to rage at me or coldly kick me out, but instead, he turns away. Closing up the little box he's been fucking with, with stiff, precise movements as he haltingly says, "I didn't like seeing your father dismiss you like that. He hurt you. Hurt your sister. And he doesn't care. It's not okay."

I swallow past the lump in my throat. "No, it's not."

"Parents who don't love and protect their children are lower than shit," Logan says in a violent whisper, still not meeting my eyes. "They don't deserve to live."

I nod, even though he's not looking at me. The ragged emotion in his voice speaks to a hurt that's lived inside me, buried deep, for as long as I can remember. One he clearly understands too.

I want to... I'm not sure what.

Ask him about it? Find out more about his past? Share something with him, reach out to him? Connect, maybe?

I have no idea if Logan would attack me for trying or keep opening up to me, and I don't get the chance to find out. Rapid footsteps sound on the stairs, then Dante bursts into the room.

"West Point knows we set up the shootout at the Capside drop," he says without preamble.

Logan goes still, whatever vulnerability he had on display gone in a heartbeat. "Who reported it?"

Dante's lips tighten. "Ruiz from the 17th."

"Fuck," Logan says sharply.

I frantically look back and forth between the two of them. "What does that mean?"

"It means the intel is good," Logan says after exchanging a long look with Dante. "McKenna knows Chloe is alive, and it won't be long until he finds out why."

Dante nods grimly. "And tears the fucking city apart to get her back once he does."

My heart stops. Logan is right.

Fuck.

14

DANTE

I'VE NEVER BELIEVED in sugarcoating shit. Life often sucks, and pretending it's otherwise doesn't do anyone a damn bit of good. But I still hate being the one to deliver this news when it makes Riley go pale.

"It's not anything to panic about yet," I tell her, shoving my hands in my pockets to keep from reaching for her. "We knew it was just a matter of time. This just means we've gotta step up our efforts and move a little faster."

She nods, but I can tell she's not taking my don't-panic advice. And fuck, I hate that. Whatever was happening between the two of us definitely went off the rails with the inheritance thing, but even if shit is fucked up between us right now, I'd be lying if I said seeing her scared like this, seeing her hurt at all, doesn't affect me.

I've still gotta stay focused, though.

"Maddoc wants us downstairs to work on that recording," I tell Logan.

He gives me a tight-lipped nod and starts grabbing up some of his electronic equipment, his movements methodical and precise as always, but something about the way he steals glances at Riley out of the corner of his eye as he does it gives me the oddest sense that he's worried about her too.

That would be a first.

Not one I can find any fault in, though. She's something else.

"Come on, princess," I say, giving in to my instincts and wrapping an arm around her shoulders to usher her out the door. "We'll sort this out. We're not gonna let McKenna win this one. You gotta remember that we've already got our feelers out and have since she took off. Maddoc's made sure we've got eyes fucking everywhere."

She's nodding along, but her breath is still coming short and tight.

I give her a squeeze. "We've already got a leg up on any search efforts McKenna starts, and we'll stay two steps ahead of West Point until we find her."

"Okay," she says like she's trying to convince herself to believe me. "Okay, yeah. We will, won't we?"

She looks up at me, then looks at Logan.

We both nod.

"Your sister is obviously good at hiding," Logan says a little stiffly, following us out into the hall with a bunch of his gadgets and shit in hand.

I let Riley go, not wanting to push my luck, and have to bite back a smile when I notice the way Logan flanks her on her other side, just the way I am over here, as we all head down the stairs.

It definitely wasn't my imagination then. She's gone and gotten herself under his skin too. I'm pretty sure no other woman in existence has ever managed that feat, and I'm a hundred percent sure Logan will deny it if I bring it up, but he's clearly come to care about her too.

Not that that wasn't obvious back at Sutton's place.

Maddoc's back in his office, his face looking like a

thundercloud moved in and took over. McKenna's been a thorn in all our sides for way too fucking long now, but Madd's got a whole other layer of hate for the guy, and I can't say I blame him. It's just another reason, as if we didn't already have enough of them, to make sure this shit with Chloe turns into a win.

"We got a general location from the cell phone ping, but it's not dialed in enough. Which means we need to try to use that voicemail we got from Sutton to narrow it down," Maddoc grits out, stepping back so Logan can do some kind of magic at his desk, plugging shit in and connecting a bunch of stuff.

"It's just noise, though," Riley says, still looking pale and tense.

"Not to Logan," I say, pushing one of those long, gorgeous, indigo waves of hair away from her face.

She jerks away, a spark of fire in her eyes as she glares up at me.

It makes me grin. That's my girl. I honestly don't know if things will ever get back to being easy between us, but fuck easy. That fire in her pulls me like a moth to flame.

And it's a fuckton better than seeing her panic.

Logan finishes getting his shit set up and we all quiet down as he starts playing Chloe's voicemail over the speakers in a continuous loop.

Riley's right. It sounds like nothing but noise. The familiar sounds of Halston's streets, but nothing on first listen that tells us a damn bit of anything.

I'm right too, though. Logan's a fucking genius is what he is, and he's got more tricks up his sleeve than there are shithead losers in the West Point gang. He pulls a few of those tricks out now, fucking around with the settings on his computer to isolate different sounds and change up the volume, until it starts to sound like we're listening to more than just noise after all.

"What is that?" Riley asks, leaning forward, her breath quickening.

No, wait. Not hers.

"Your sister," Logan says, tapping a few keys until the other sounds fade away and the rapid, frantic-sounding breaths come through loud and clear. "Her mouth was right near the phone's microphone, and she was—"

"Scared," Riley blurts, wrapping her arms around her middle like she's trying to self-soothe. "Listen to how fast she's breathing."

Logan nods, but then isolates what at first sounds like just a few seconds that are the same as the rest. "There," he says.

"What?" Maddoc asks sharply, frowning as he leans closer.

Logan replays the loop, and I don't—

Oh.

"Her breath is stuttering there. Hitching. What's up with that?" I ask.

"Something must have startled her," Logan says. "Let's find out what she heard," he mutters, his fingers moving rapidly over the keyboard. All the other traffic noise and shit rushes back in, then parts of it fade away again. What's left is a faint, garbled voice and a distinctive sound I recognize right away.

Logan restarts the loop, and there's no doubt.

"Saint Andrews," I say, nodding toward the speaker.

All three of them look at me.

"Over on 44th?" Maddoc asks, his brows drawing together as Logan loops it again. "That's near the bus depot. And it's within the area where her phone pinged."

Logan's fingers click in a blur, and the church bells all but fade away, the volume increasing for that garbled voice we all heard.

"That could be a boarding announcement for the buses," Riley says, frowning. "Can you make that part clearer, Logan?"

"Not much," he says, sounding as irritated about that as if someone had keyed his precious Audi. "The tone of his voice is too close to the pitch of the traffic noise to properly separate it, but maybe if I use a Fourier Analysis..."

He starts mumbling about shit that I don't understand, but after a minute, he actually does manage to clean it up a bit. Enough for us to confirm that it's definitely coming from the bus station. We even get a route number that allows us to match it with the time stamp from Sutton's voicemail.

Not sure how much good it's gonna do us since the lead is still more than twenty-four hours old, but it's the first solid location we've had since Chloe bolted... and the way Riley's face lights up when Logan confirms it is fucking beautiful to see.

"Oh my god," she says, throwing her arms around me and squeezing tight. "Oh my *god*."

I hug her back, breathing deep to get a hit of that unforgettable spice-and-smoke scent of hers, but all too quick, she realizes what she's doing and stiffens up, pulling away.

"Can we go?" she asks, looking between the three of us and then settling her gaze on Maddoc. "Can we go see if she's still there?"

I bite my tongue to keep from pointing out she won't be. And who the fuck knows, I might be wrong... probably not, but stranger shit has happened. And even though Chloe will most likely have long since cleared out, we still might pick up another lead. Something to point us in the right direction before McKenna's goons sniff out the trail.

Madd obviously agrees. He tells Logan to stay back and keep working the digital file, then grabs the keys to the Escalade, calling in a few more warm bodies so that by the time we get to the area, there are at least half a dozen Reapers with feet on the ground.

"Church or bus station, princess?" I ask. "What was the draw here?"

Riley bites her lip, looking between the two. Bus station is the obvious answer, but Riley—and presumably her little sister, since the girl clearly takes after her—don't always go for the obvious.

Riley agrees.

"I don't think she would have been trying to leave town. Not yet. Not without me," she says, turning away from the bus depot. "But when we were little, there was this other church over by Frank's place that she'd sometimes hit up for after school snacks when I wasn't around."

"After school snacks?" I ask, smirking. "That a thing churches do now?"

"Wafers. Wine. Whatever," she says, flashing a cheeky grin before her worry sets back in. She sighs. "The point is, she'd sometimes hang out there when Frank's business associates were being more dickish than usual, so I could see her maybe ducking into this one to stay out of sight for a while."

"You two go check it out," Maddoc says. "I'm still gonna check the bus station out, and I'll have Isaac, Shae, and Kieran sweep the surrounding streets."

We split up like he said, trying to scope out any likely hiding places where Chloe might still be holed up, but after an hour or so, it's clear that it's a bust.

"Fuck," Riley says when he calls it, her voice cracking as she turns away from us to wipe at her eyes.

It fucking kills me to see, but I leave her be. Bad shit happens every fucking day, and getting a little emotional about it is normal. It's not like me tucking her back against my side is gonna change the fact that Chloe isn't here, so I don't.

Besides, this weird craving I keep having lately, wanting to reach out to her and make shit right, is starting to make me feel a little off-center. Best to leave it alone.

"Let's head back to the house," Maddoc says.

"So, what? You're just going to give up?" Riley snaps, lashing out at him in a way he wouldn't put up with from most people. But he obviously sees through her anger just like I do, because he lets it roll right off him.

"Giving up isn't something I do," he says, grabbing her arm and steering her into the Escalade.

The fact that she doesn't resist speaks volumes.

"Then what do we do next?" she asks, her shoulders slumping in defeat.

I slip in the back seat as Maddoc starts up the Escalade and pulls away from the curb. "I'm leaving a few people here in case she shows up again," he tells Riley. "I also told Isaac to question some players who we know typically work this area."

"She was *right here*," Riley says, pressing her fingers against her window as we drive away. "Goddammit, why couldn't Frank have..."

She shakes her head with a huff of frustration, as if realizing that there's nothing that shithead could have done. Or at least, nothing that would've done Chloe any good.

"It's still a good lead, butterfly," Maddoc says, glancing over at her before returning his gaze to the road. "And if she left any trace at all, my people will find it."

Riley nods, but stays quiet and subdued for the rest of the ride home.

It fucking bothers me.

I guess it bothers Madd too, because as soon as we get back to the house and Logan hits him with some bullshit he's got to step in and handle, he jerks his chin at me, directing me to follow Riley when she heads up the stairs.

I'm already headed that way though, Maddoc and I both on the same page as always.

Riley disappears into the bathroom, and I follow a few steps behind her, not really stopping to question why.

Or whether it's smart to give in to this new craving I've got to constantly be around her lately. To go out of my way to make sure she's okay.

The door isn't locked, and she looks up, startled, when I walk in. She's sitting on the closed toilet, looking fucking devastated, but the minute I enter she straightens up, schooling her features. Shutting them down.

"I'm pretty sure I was here first," she says, an edge to her voice that has me grinning.

"That's right." I take a seat on the edge of the tub, my knees crowding her in so she can't leave without crawling right over the top of me. "And here I am, last to arrive. One of us gonna get a trophy for that?"

She rolls her eyes, but I can see her lips twitching a little. It's a hell of a better look on her than wrung out and devastated, so I've already won.

She crosses her arms over her chest. "What do you want, Dante?"

Man, isn't that the question of the hour? The truth is, I don't really know when it comes to her anymore, and I'd prefer not to think too fucking hard about it, thank you very much. Although at least in the right-the-fuck now sense, the answer is easy. I want to get that look off her face. Even though there aren't any guarantees in this world so hope is something I generally have no use for, I don't like the idea of her not having any. So I go with the facts.

"Maddoc's fucking relentless. You know that, right, princess?"

She raises an eyebrow. "Yeah, I think I've picked up on that personality trait. You're telling me this, why?"

"Because you gotta understand that the news about McKenna today, that changes nothing."

"I'm pretty sure it changes everything," she says, glaring at me. "It means he knows Chloe's out there. That he'll want her. That he's looking for her. That he—*mmph.*"

I cover her mouth with my hand before she can work herself up any further, grinning at the death glare I get for it. I half

127

expect her to bite me. Hell, I'm pretty sure I'd enjoy it. The fact that she doesn't, the way she settles down and lets me get away with that shit without a fight, says a lot.

She might be acting prickly and playing it off like she wants to push me away, but she's craving some kind of reassurance just as much as I'm driven to give it.

So I do.

"What I mean is that when Madd sets his mind on something, he gets it. McKenna being in the game now ain't gonna change that. Or, if it does, it only means it's gonna spur Maddoc to pull out all the stops."

She finally pulls my hand away from her mouth, and neither of us comment on the fact that she lets it fall into her lap... and keeps a hold of it.

"So what you're saying is, he can't stand competition," she says with a tiny wisp of a smile.

I laugh. "Nah, that's not it. McKenna isn't competition. He's fuel. Motivation to get where we're already going, just a little bit faster. What you gotta understand is that Maddoc doesn't just *want* to find Chloe, he's decided—"

I almost say *he's decided we need her*, but I don't want to start that fight right now, so I pivot and go with, "—he's decided we'll get her back, so we will. No other option is on the table."

Riley stares at me for a long time, like she's trying to read the truth of what I'm saying in my eyes.

Then she sighs, looking away. "Okay."

"Okay?" I repeat, grabbing her chin and tilting it back my way so I can figure out what the fuck she means by that. And I do. She's this gorgeous mix of closed-the-fuck-off and vulnerable as hell, and in the few weeks she's been in our lives, I've started to get a handle on her tells.

Right now, "okay" means she's taken some comfort from my words, just like I meant her to.

But not enough comfort.

I don't know why I'm so fucking driven to fix this moment for her, but I need to. Guess that's why, despite a lifetime of knowing some cards should always be played close to the vest and the cardinal rule of the relationship I've got with my brothers is that Reaper business *stays* Reaper business, the last thing I ever thought I'd share with her pops out of my mouth next.

"A few years ago, when the Reapers didn't hold as much territory yet but were definitely starting to make some waves in Halston, some of the other gangs didn't take it so well. The ones who stood against him didn't stay standing for long, because like I said, relentless, right?"

She nods, and something swells in my chest. That defeated look is fading, her interest piqued by my story. So I keep going.

"Anyway, some of the bigger players, like McKenna, didn't feel as threatened as they should have at the time. Madd wasn't big enough yet to go head to head with them, so he gave them their space and focused on making headway where he could. The smaller, scrappier gangs knew he was shaking things up, and some were glad about it, to be honest. But not all of them. So one gang sent in a mole."

"A rival gang member actually managed to infiltrate the Reapers?" Riley asks, her eyebrows shooting up to her hairline.

I nod, my finger instinctively rubbing over the back of my right thumb. A habit that should have died off when the Crimson Crows did. "It didn't take long for Madd to figure out there was a problem, but that didn't mean he moved on it right away. Because you know what he is besides relentless?"

"A lot of things," Riley says drily, making me laugh.

"He is that, but I'm talking about the way he's fucking strategic. Always two steps ahead. He's already planning for the long-term win before the other guy even realizes he's playing the game. It's why, even though McKenna's in it now, he doesn't count as true competition. Madd's already too far ahead, and he *will* come out on top. I need you to understand that, princess. We're gonna get your sister back, because Madd always wins."

She stares at me hard, and in this moment, I can read her like a motherfucking book.

I'm certain she knows that our version of a win and hers don't fully line up, but she also gets that right now, the biggest win is getting Chloe off the streets. And I see the moment it happens. The moment when she finally believes me. Trusts that she can count on us for this. Accepts that it's gonna happen not just because the full resources of our organization are behind it, but because none of us in this house—not Madd, not Logan, and not me—are willing to accept anything else.

"Okay," she says, her shoulders finally relaxing as she gives me a real smile.

A small one, but still. I'll take it.

"But what happened to the mole?" she blurts after a minute, obviously sucked into the story despite herself. "Did Maddoc ever figure out who it was?"

"He did," I say, twining my fingers through hers and lifting our joined hands up so I can admire the way my colorful ink contrasts with all her pale, silken skin.

"Well?" she asks impatiently, the fiery spark I love to see finally back in her eyes as she tugs against my hold. "What did Maddoc do? What happened to the guy?"

I don't let her go. Can't, really. Instead, I lift her hand to my mouth and press a kiss over her wrist where a faint red line still lingers from those cuffs we had her in.

Then I grin at her.

"You're looking at him, princess. It was me."

15

RILEY

I'm so startled it takes me a minute to pick my jaw up off the floor. And then another moment—okay, maybe two—to decide Dante's not just pranking me.

"*You* were a mole?" I shake my head in disbelief even as the words come out of my mouth. I wouldn't have thought anything could truly distract me from my fears for Chloe right now, but Dante's managed it.

He always calls Maddoc his brother, and for all the faults these men have, the depth of loyalty and trust I've seen between the two of them—between all three of them, really—gives truth to that title, regardless of blood. So his bombshell just doesn't make sense. I can't see Dante ever betraying either of his brothers, and yet even though he's still smiling, those gorgeous green eyes of his turn serious as he confirms it.

"I was." He idly rubs his fingers over the red dagger inked onto the back of his right thumb, a habit I've noticed before and wonder if he's even aware of. "After my dad was killed, I was aimless for a bit. Aimless and fucking angry. And then I was recruited by the Crimson Crows."

I flinch without meaning to, and his mouth quirks up in a knowing smirk. "So you've heard of them?"

"Only enough to know Chloe and I were safer staying away from them."

Smarter to stay away from *all* gang activity, of course, but from all accounts, the Crimson Crows were...

"They were brutal," Dante says, like he's reading my mind again.

I shudder. "Yeah. That's what I always heard."

Dante's nodding again. "You heard right. Worse, the Crows treated their people like they were disposable. They had my loyalty at the time because I didn't know there was another way. Not back then. But still, seeing the leadership of that organization rise to power by stepping on the backs of the ones who got them there started to rub me the wrong way even before Shank, that was the name of the dickhead in charge, decided Madd needed to be taken out."

"Taken out?" I repeat, my stomach clenching. "He wanted you to kill Maddoc?"

Dante's expressive mouth tightens. "He wanted me to do a lot of things. First and foremost, he sent me in to find out how the fuck someone with no allegiance and no rep had managed to do what Maddoc had in such a short period of time. He wasn't really a player before the Reapers. Then all of a sudden, out of nowhere, he claims and holds some significant territory, and then goes on to grow it and strengthen his ties every fucking time we turned around."

"And did you find out how he managed to do all that?" I ask, sucked into the story despite myself.

Dante grins. "Fuck yeah, I did. I found out there was a better way to run an organization after all. I found out what loyalty was actually supposed to mean."

"But Maddoc must have found you out too. And he actually let you live after he discovered you were a mole?" I shake my head before Dante can answer. "I mean, obviously he did, but damn. How the hell did you manage to save yourself?"

Maddoc is the last person I can imagine showing mercy after someone betrays him. Which, yeah, is ironic given how easily he decided to do it to me. Or maybe it's not. After all, I guess it doesn't count as a betrayal when he screws over someone he was never loyal to in the first place.

That thought hurts, so I'm glad Dante gives me something else to focus on.

"Find *me* out?" he says with just enough cockiness to make me laugh. "Nah, never happened, princess. But what did happen is he won me over. Not like he was trying to, 'cause he didn't realize I was a threat, but he managed it anyway by being himself. By showing me what it actually meant to lead an organization the right way. He was building it *for* the people who pledged their allegiance to him, instead of on their backs."

I'm not really in the mood to hear how great Maddoc Gray is right now, so I can't resist getting a dig in. "So you're saying he was clueless. That the big, bad Reaper leader had an enemy right under his nose and didn't even know it."

Dante smirks. "What can I say? I guess I'm just that good."

Something in my core starts to heat up. Cocky is a damn good look on him. I'm never going to admit it though, so I punch his arm—which, for the record, feels like punching fucking steel —and he laughs.

"You're wrong though," he says, going on with the story "Madd caught on pretty quick to something being off after I came on board, and he was definitely suspicious. Not of me, 'cause I really am that good, but he knew there had to be a mole in the gang based on the way I managed to start fucking up his operations before I came around to a different way of thinking. And not gonna lie, princess, it would have been easy as hell to frame a member of the Reapers and slip back to the Crows once the damage was done, but I..."

He shakes his head, his usual care-free smirk replaced by a faraway look, like he's remembering.

"You what?" I prompt him, wanting to know.

Dante blinks, coming back to himself. Then he shrugs. "I didn't want to, so I came clean. Told him everything. Who I was, why I was there, what the Crows were planning."

"But... *why?*" I ask, my stomach tightening as I imagine how terrifying that would be. "He might have killed you."

Obviously it all turned out well in the end, but Dante couldn't have known it would go down the way it did at the time. He was either really brave or really stupid... or else he really believed he'd found himself a forever home.

And he was right.

My throat tightens up at that, thinking how up in the air having a home is for me and Chloe now. Will we ever have one again? A place we actually feel safe and don't have to be looking over our shoulders all the time?

I guess it's possible with that money she's going to inherit, but she doesn't even have it yet and it's already causing problems, so it sure as shit doesn't feel like any kind of guarantee. It's all too easy to imagine the two of us actually getting away from the Reapers, but then having to live the rest of our lives wary of who might try for us next, with no one to guard our backs.

Fuck. I've been short on money and scrambling to get just enough all my life. Now, on the cusp of actually having some, it feels a lot like it won't solve any problems at all.

I swallow hard, and whatever Dante sees in my face has his eyes going soft.

He squeezes my knee. "Madd might have killed me, yeah," he admits, thankfully not commenting on my all-too-obvious emotions. Then his lips quirk up and he adds, "Or, you know, he might have tried."

I scowl at him, shoving his hand off my knee. "Cocky, much?"

Dante laughs. "Just calling it how it is. But the thing is, I wasn't worried about it, because Madd had already shown me who he was. He's fucking ruthless against his enemies, but he's just as ruthlessly devoted to those who've given him their loyalty. I decided I wanted to be one of those people. I wanted to be a Reaper. I wanted... something different."

I snort. "Are the Reapers really so different from the rest of the gangs here in Halston?"

It comes out sounding a little bitchy, but of course Dante just grins at me like he knows I'm being petty and he thinks it's cute. He grins like he expects I already know the answer.

I huff out a breath, refusing to admit that I do, and he laughs again, smoothing the hair back from my face and then cupping my cheek.

"Yeah, princess, we are different," he says softly. "Better."

I want to argue it just for the sake of being contrary, but as pissed off as I still am at the three of them, I really can't. The Reapers may be brutal and ruthless, but there's a code behind the way they operate. One that's nothing at all like what I've seen from that sadistic fucker, Austin McKenna, and his West Point goons, or like any of the horror stories I used to hear back in the day about the Crimson Crows.

And then of course there's that gang whose members we took out when we rescued Chloe. Capside. They sounded... bad. Really bad. I shudder, hating the thought that my sister was ever anywhere near them.

But still, Dante talks like Maddoc is the second coming or some shit, and I'm still too raw from everything that's gone down between us to just accept that at face value.

"I saw that map in Maddoc's office, and it looks like everyone's just fighting to be top dog without ever giving a shit who gets caught in the crossfire. I don't really see how you guys are all that different."

I suddenly remember that the Reapers were part of that gang shoot-out at the little bodega Chloe and I used to go to, near our old apartment. It was pure chance that neither of us were there at the time, so Dante can preach about how "different" they are until he's blue in the face, but I've lived in Halston all my life and the truth is it just isn't a safe place to live. Not in the parts Chloe and I can afford, at least. It's honestly a bit of a miracle that this is the first time we've really been caught up in the violence the city seems to thrive on.

Dante gives me an assessing look. "There are dozens of street gangs, large and small, here in the city. More even than Madd bothers to show on that map. And there's always gonna be some fucker trying to make a name for himself, to create an organization that will rise to power. But trust me, princess. The way Maddoc runs shit really is different."

"Trust you?" I snipe in self-protection... because god help me, I realize that that's exactly what my instincts want me to do.

Dante's eyes go soft again, and I want to fucking smack him for confusing me.

Or else crawl onto his lap, straddle him, and thank him properly for it.

"After the Crows sent me in," he goes on before I can embarrass myself by doing any of the above, "it didn't take me long to realize that helping them take the Reapers down would just turn into yet another bloody battle in a never-ending war, ripping this city apart a little more every day. But if I helped the Reapers rise to power instead? That's actually gonna end up keeping the city safer, because unlike fucktards like McKenna who don't give a shit about collateral damage, Maddoc does. He's not ever gonna hesitate to do what he has to, but at the end of the day what matters most to him is his people. And he'll do fucking anything for the people he cares about. It's why I'm ride or die."

A sharp pain spikes through my heart, and I snort, looking away. "Yeah, well, that's all well and good unless you're someone like me. Someone he's willing to destroy to help the people he cares about."

Dante grabs my chin and turns me back to face him. "I get why you may not see it right now, but you're in that second category, princess. Not the first. Maddoc cares."

I shake my head, brushing him off. I don't want to hear it. Sure as shit don't want to think about it or get fooled into believing it again. So I change the subject back to him. "What did the Crimson Crows do when you betrayed them?"

Dante's eyes gleam, his normally laid-back smile turning sharp. "What do you think, princess? They went down."

"You mean, you took them down."

"*We* took them down. The Reapers did. The shit I knew about their organization helped Madd turn the tables on them. He destroyed their entire organization, claimed their territory, and accepted allegiance from every one of their former members who were smart enough to realize that shit was all for the best." He holds up his right hand, tapping his thumb. "You know those gaudy rings West Point wears?"

I nod. I've seen them. The initials WPG in chunky gold that looks more like brass knuckles than jewelry. The goons who our father brought to our apartment when he sold Chloe out all had them on.

"Well, the Crows marked their members with something similar," Dante says. "Tattoos instead of rings. Two black interlocking Cs on the thumb. The day I got rid of those, something inside me finally felt *right*."

I want to tell Dante to shut the fuck up. To stop opening up and sharing real feelings with me. It's just one more way he's adding to the confusing mix of emotions I can't make sense of around him anymore.

But I also want to know more. I want to know everything.

I reach out and stroke my finger over the gorgeous red dagger on his thumb. It's centered over an ice-blue infinity symbol that, now that I know what used to be there, I can tell must perfectly mask the original interlocking Cs. "Why this?"

Dante's quiet for long enough that I almost think he's not going to answer. That maybe he's regretting opening up to me too. But then he speaks again.

"I wanted fucking color in my life," he says, his voice full of an intensity I don't often hear from him. "The dagger is for my father. My past. Everything I came from. And this..." He traces the figure-eight of the infinity symbol, his fingers brushing against mine. "...is how I felt once Madd taught me what loyalty is truly about. It's without beginning and end. Calm and sure. I've got a future now. A sense of purpose."

I swallow hard, something aching inside me. Longing.

"With the Crows, I was part of something," Dante goes on, "but it wasn't a family. I hadn't had that since my dad died, and I didn't find it again until I finally got here. This is my place in the world, where I'm meant to be, and Logan and Maddoc, those two just get me. They see my darkness, they see all the messy colors, and they understand all of it. They accept it, and we just fit, you know? They're..."

"Your brothers," I whisper as his voice trails off, my heart aching a little.

Dante gives me a crooked smile that's more real than any I've seen on his face before. "Yeah, they are. But they're even more than brothers too. Like I said, we're ride or die."

The ache inside me builds and builds. I want that too. I want it so bad it hurts. It's part of the reason I miss Chloe so hard, but even though she *is* my ride or die, Dante's talking about something more than what I've had with her in my life, when it's always been just the two of us against the world. He's talking about something bigger. Being part of something that's more than any of its parts. A family group dynamic stronger than blood.

The kind of family that's forever.

I do my best to keep the longing inside me off my face, but I know I fail when Dante tips my chin up.

"Princess?" he asks, his gaze burrowing deep.

I force a smile. "You're lucky to have Maddoc and Logan in your life."

He nods, serious. "I am. I've almost never met anyone else who gets me the way they do."

"*Almost* never?" I tease, pretty sure he's misspoken since I've seen the three of them together.

They don't just have each other's backs, they're always actively looking out for each other and letting their different strengths support one another without any in-fighting or jealousy getting in the way. They're so tight knit that there's simply no room for anything to ever come between them. And I'm not jealous. Not exactly. But no matter how mad I am for all the shit with Chloe, I can't deny that part of me wishes I could find something like that. That I could have that kind of connection, trust, and security beyond just me and Chloe.

"Yeah, almost," Dante says, still holding my gaze. "Only one other person sees me down to my soul like that."

Now I *am* jealous, even though I shouldn't give a shit.

"Who?" I ask, my voice tight.

Dante grins, my reaction making something flare to life in his eyes that's so hot and bright it burns right through my pissy attitude and leaves me feeling vulnerable and shaken even though I don't know why. At least, I don't until he answers me.

"It's you, Riley."

I shake my head, because it hurts to hear. Hurts to want, to believe.

Especially since he's already betrayed me.

Dante doesn't break, though. Doesn't crack a smile or say he's joking. Instead, he reaches out and strokes the backs of his fingers down my cheek, then wraps his hand around the back of my neck, leaning in to rest his forehead against mine.

"It's *you*," he repeats softly, the vibrant green of his eyes pulling at me like a magnetic force. "Just you."

I suck in a sharp breath, my heart starting to pound, and then, before I can figure out what the hell to say to something like that, his lips are on mine and an embarrassing sound escapes me as I fist my hands in the material of his shirt and hold on like he's the lifeline I'll never admit to needing.

Dante hums, and I can feel his mouth curling up in satisfaction. "I ain't going anywhere, princess," he murmurs against my lips.

"Shut up," I whisper, letting my eyes flutter closed. Shutting out all the bullshit of today and everything that's still fucked-up between us so I can just feel for a little while.

Not feel all my messed-up, chaotic emotions, but just feel this. Him. What he does to me.

He's still smiling against my mouth, the kiss soft, like a gentle promise that twists something up inside my chest. Something that's already too bruised to bear it.

"Kiss me for real," I demand, yanking him closer.

Our knees bash together and it makes it awkward given the angles we're sitting at, but Dante just chuckles, a vibration in his chest that I feel through the tips of my fingers, and does it. He takes over and turns the kiss into everything I need right now. Hot and filthy, just like I'm asking for, but also tender, which I never would but suddenly want like air.

It's like he's telling me without words how bad he wants me, but also that whatever's happening right now, it's about more than just getting off. It's everything that's been simmering under the surface between us all these weeks, suddenly boiling over.

I moan without meaning to, and he thrusts his tongue into my mouth hard and fast, so much like fucking that I shamelessly whine and scoot closer, already wet for him. Wanting him. Wanting *more*.

"That's right," Dante mutters, his hand tangling in the back of my hair. He tugs, forcing my head back, then trails hot, open-mouthed kisses over my jaw and down my throat. "Let me hear you, princess. Let me fucking taste you."

He surges to his feet without giving me a chance to reply, lifting me with him and setting my ass on the edge of the sink before shoving my tight shirt up, bunching it just above my breasts.

"Damn," he says appreciatively as they bounce free.

I'm just not large enough to worry about a bra half the time, so I don't.

Then his mouth latches onto my left nipple, his palm completely covering my right one, and pure fire shoots down to my core.

"Dante." I grab the back of his head to hold him there, arching up against him. "Oh fuck, yes, please."

He makes the most delicious sound, as if I'm the one pleasuring *him*, then starts to take me apart. Licking me like I'm candy. Sucking each nipple until I scream. Biting, just hard enough to sting, like he fucking knows what it does to me, until I'm a squirming, panting, begging mess.

No, not *like* he knows what it does to me. He does know. He said it himself. I see him... but he sees me too.

All the way down to my soul.

The thought rocks through me so hard I freeze, not wanting to look at it. And Dante, thank fuck, doesn't let me. His mouth pops off me the moment I tense up, and his hands are suddenly everywhere, stealing my attention back. Lifting my ass. Opening my pants. Tugging my shirt the rest of the way off and sliding everything off me down below too.

"Fucking gorgeous," he murmurs once he has me naked, running his hands all over me before settling me against the sink again and crowding between my legs.

I brace my arms behind me as the rough denim of his jeans rubs against my inner thighs, and Dante tips my chin up and smiles down at me, then cups my pussy with his other hand and pushes two fingers inside. "You promised me a taste of this."

"I never... promised you that." I start to pant, tremors of pleasure rippling through me. "You just... *you're* the one who said you wanted..."

I give up talking and he grins down at me, a look both wolfish and tender that does really fucking confusing things to my heart.

"Fuck yeah, I did. I still do, princess," he says, distracting me perfectly from my confusion with the wicked things he's doing with those fingers of his.

I give up on trying to talk and give in to what I wanted in the first place, just letting myself feel.

My head falls back as I writhe on his fingers and let my eyes drift closed, and Dante swoops right in with a groan, sucking the side of my throat hard enough to leave a mark.

It stings, and I love it. Almost as much as I love the way he keeps grinding the heel of his hand against my clit, slowly moving his fingers inside me like he's on a single-minded mission to drive me crazy.

It's working. Before I can stop myself, I'm begging again. Promising him anything he wants. The fucker still doesn't go any harder, though. Doesn't speed up the pace or fuck me with his thick digits the way I crave. Instead, he just keeps repeating a slow, sensual beckoning motion, over and over and fucking *over*, deep inside me. Stroking my G-spot so damn well that my knees start to shake and my bones all but liquify, until I know—I just fucking *know*—that if I let him make me come this way, it's going to completely wreck me.

It's too much. It makes things too unequal. With him only giving, totally focused on me, watching as I fall apart... I can't. I just can't.

I force my eyes open and clutch his shirt. "Just fuck me already. Give me your cock."

Any tenderness I thought I saw on his face burns away in a flash of heat so intense I almost do come, right then and there. Then he smiles at me.

"Can't fucking deny you, princess," he growls, sliding his fingers out and straightening up, keeping his eyes on me the whole time as he licks them clean and uses his free hand to pop the button on his jeans. He slides his zipper down and frees his cock. "This what you're asking for?"

Hell yeah, it is.

I knock his hand away and wrap my own around his thick length. "Less talking, more fucking."

That wolfish smile is back. "I do like it when you sweet talk me."

Then, taking me at my word, he slams his mouth over mine and hitches my leg up over his hip, lining himself up and driving straight into me. He goes balls deep in one thrust, filling me so completely that it blocks out everything but this moment.

I lose myself in it, overwhelmed by the dirty things he promises as he finally starts fucking me hard. His fingers dig into my hips to hold me steady, making it clear that he's just as needy and hungry for this as I am. That he doesn't just want the release of sex, but that he *feels* things between us too.

All the things that made the Reapers' betrayal over Chloe hurt me so badly in the first place.

The thought is like fucking ice water on my brain. It doesn't do a damn thing to cool off the inferno inside me—because Dante's cock is like magic, and he's got me so close that I really do want to scream—but at least it brings me to my senses.

Gritting my teeth, I force myself to put my hands on his chest and shove him away. *Hard.*

Dante's cock slides out of me as he stumbles backward, just a step before he catches his balance.

"Princess?" His thick brows draw together as he gives me a

confused look. His hand wraps around his length, which is shiny with the evidence of my arousal. "What's wrong?"

"Fuck you," I grit out as he watches me with hooded eyes.

"Pretty sure I was just doing that," he says, his lips quirking up in a smirk.

I scramble off the counter, pressing my back against the wall opposite the sink to help fight the addiction. I just need a little space between us to get myself under control, but dammit, there isn't any. Not when I'm suddenly bereft of his closeness and still reeling from what I just did. Not when the bathroom is too small and Dante is too large.

Even though he doesn't make a move toward me, I still feel crowded by the sheer overwhelming presence of him. All too aware that he's still *right fucking there*, close enough that I can still feel the heat of his body as the slick-sounding thwap of his hand echoes around us.

I can't escape the awareness of just how close he's standing, how fucking hot he looks as he jerks himself off, how much my body still craves everything I just shoved away.

I squeeze my eyes closed, fisting my hands at my sides. "I hate you."

He leans in, and I feel his breath ghost across my cheek. Sense the motion of his hand, speeding up just like his breath does.

"Nah, that's not what this is," he whispers. "Don't hide from it, wild thing."

That pisses me off enough that I snap my eyes back open and glare at him.

Dante smiles back, bracing one hand against the wall next to my head. Still stroking himself in front of me, *right* in front of me, as if he's not at all bothered by me pushing him away mid-fuck.

"That's it," he says as I narrow my eyes, my whole body still throbbing from his nearness. "Fuck yeah. I love seeing that fire inside you. It's like living, breathing color."

"That's not color you see," I bite out, my chest heaving. "It's rage."

He grins even wider, his hand moving over his cock even faster as his eyes settle on my lips. "It's fucking gorgeous is what it is, but being pissed at me... ain't gonna make this connection between us... go away. It's real. No point hiding from it."

"I'm not fucking *hiding*."

No, what I'm doing is shaking. Wanting. *Craving*, damn him.

"Good," Dante grunts. "'Cause I'm close, and I wanna fucking see you come too. It's so much better together."

"We're not together," I rasp, my body betraying the lie. He may not be inside me anymore, but my core still pulses with the heat he kindled there. My pussy tightens with every ragged breath he sucks in. Every forceful thrust through his closed fist pushes me closer and closer to the edge.

Dante's eyes burn into mine like green fire, his lips hovering close enough that I can taste each exhale. It's all I can do not to grab him and take a real taste. Climb him like a fucking tree to get what I still so desperately need.

What I was so fucking close to having before my head got in the way.

"Dante..."

I don't even mean to say it, but whatever I may or may not have followed it up with is cut off by the sexy-as-fuck groan that rips out of him when he hears me say his name.

And then he's coming. Painting my bare stomach with hot jets of his cum. Stroking his cock as his face tightens in a grimace of pure pleasure, and then cracking his eyes back open and locking them onto mine, just the way he said he wanted to.

I can't look away, and I don't want to. We *are* together. The moment is hot and intimate and obscenely sensual, just like Dante's cum, sliding down my body.

It drips over my swollen, throbbing clit like liquid fire, sending a white-hot shock of pure pleasure through me. I'm so worked up from watching him jerk off that it's more than I can take. It tips me right over the edge, making me come so hard that my knees quake, my bones instantly turning to mush with no chance in hell of actually holding me up anymore.

Dante groans, finally touching me again. He pins me to the wall, keeping me upright with the weight of his body. His breath is ragged, and he strokes my face like I'm something precious as his spent cock gives one final jerk against the heat of my skin.

"Fucking hell, that was gorgeous," he whispers, tangling his cum-drenched hand in the back of my hair and tipping my head back. "It's always so good with you. *Because* it's you."

My breath hitches. God damn him. He can't say shit like that.

Before I can tell him so, he leans down, his nose gently bumping against mine and his breath ghosting across my lips. "Can I kiss you now?"

"No."

The word comes out breathless and needy in the wake of my orgasm, and my fists curl into his shirt without my permission, pulling him even closer.

Dante's lips curl up in a slow smile that turns the warm afterglow curling inside me into something terrifyingly tender, almost too fragile to bear. "Okay." His lips brush lightly against mine as he says the word. "Then I won't."

"Asshole," I whisper, smiling against his mouth despite my best intentions as I go up on my toes and—

And then jump back when a loud, forceful knocking shakes the bathroom door.

16

RILEY

DANTE SAVES my head from slamming into the wall behind me by cradling the back of it, but that doesn't stop my heart from lurching when Maddoc calls out, his voice as sharp and forceful as the sound of his knocking.

"*Dante.*"

Despite the obvious urgency in Maddoc's voice, Dante doesn't show any sign of being fazed by the interruption, his fingers gently massaging my scalp for a moment before he slips them out of my hair, smoothing the waves down as he answers.

"Present and accounted for," he calls back without taking his eyes off mine, a lazy smile hovering around his mouth.

"Well, I need you present and accounted for out fucking here," Maddoc snaps through the door. "There's been a development."

"About Chloe?" I blurt, shoving Dante away and scrambling toward the sink to clean the mess off my body.

The beat of silence that follows my question has my eyes snapping up to meet Dante's as I belatedly remember what he told me. Maddoc, the fucking hypocrite, has a rule. None of them are supposed to touch me.

My face flushes with heat, but Dante just smirks, once again reading me like a book, and gives me a tiny shrug.

"We'll be right out," he tells Maddoc, plucking my shirt off the towel rack it landed on and holding it out to me.

"Fuck," I whisper, snatching it from him and tugging it over my head.

"Nah, it's fine," Dante says, fixing his own clothes before helping me straighten the last of mine. "Come on, princess."

He opens the door, and Maddoc immediately narrows his eyes at us. His irises are a startling mix of grays, lighter near the pupils and darkening near the edges, and right now, they make me think of storm clouds.

Even if I hadn't already seen how well-fucked my mussed hair makes me look in the mirror, the expression on his face tells me loud and clear that he knows exactly what just happened. Or at least, close enough.

He turns a look on Dante, and they have a quick but intense non-verbal conversation that includes Maddoc clenching his jaw and Dante shrugging again. I can tell Maddoc wants to say something, but fuck that. I need to know if they've got a new lead on Chloe.

"What happened?"

Maddoc's attention immediately shifts back to the matter at hand, his jaw clenching even tighter.

"We need to go," he says. "Now."

Nerves shoot through me, killing off the last traces of my afterglow, and Dante's laid-back expression morphs into something deadly serious. Maddoc turns on his heel without giving any further explanation, and even though I've got no clue whether or not I was supposed to be included in that "we," I follow when Dante takes off after him.

Neither of them stop me, and when we get downstairs, neither does Logan. All four of us head out to the car, Maddoc getting behind the wheel and peeling out of the driveway before his seconds even get the doors closed.

The silence is a crushing, almost suffocating weight in the car. Dante methodically checks several weapons he's carrying and Logan's fingers fly over the small screen of his phone in the front seat while Maddoc navigates the Escalade toward a sketchier part of town. It's an area I'm pretty sure Maddoc's map showed as lying right on the edge of the Reapers' territory, and despite the fact that they betrayed me, lied to me, the idea of her stumbling into *another* gang's territory is even worse.

It's enough for my fear to overcome me. Even though I'm not sure I actually *want* the answer—not with the three of them looking grim enough to put shards of ice in my veins—I need Maddoc to tell me.

"Is this... is it about Chloe?" I whisper, the words like sandpaper as they leave my throat.

I swear to fuck, if he tells me she's dead or was taken or something, I'm going to lose it no matter how determined I am not to look weak in front of these men. But Maddoc doesn't draw it out or torture me. His eyes flick up to meet mine in the rearview mirror, and for just a fraction of a second, his gaze softens.

I swallow a sob of relief before it can escape, jerking my hand up to cover my mouth.

Maddoc's eyes return to the road in front of him, his grip on the steering wheel noticeably tightening. "No. It's not Chloe."

"Then what's up, Madd?" Dante asks.

"A West Point attack," Maddoc bites out, causing Dante to punch the seat next to him and let loose with a stream of curses, while Logan goes dangerously still.

Maddoc rattles off a few more details that obviously mean more to his seconds than they do to me, and before I have time to settle my emotions, we arrive at a run-down building that looks abandoned.

A small group of men are stationed around it, looking cagey, but I can tell by the tense way they all go on alert when Maddoc gets out of the Escalade that they're Reapers.

"Report," Maddoc snaps, striding toward the entrance with Logan at his side. Dante takes my elbow and pulls me in next to him, following behind.

One of the Reapers starts spitting out details of the attack, but goes quiet when a woman walks out of the building. A woman with blood on her.

My heart drops. The sight is too close to my worst fears about finding Chloe. But then her eyes flick toward me and I recognize her from having met her at the Reapers' house a few weeks ago, and I realize it's not *her* blood. And she's not my sister.

I repeat that part to myself, trying to slow my heart rate. *It's not Chloe.*

Maddoc didn't lie. Not about that.

"Payton," Maddoc greets the woman, his face as cold as stone, as if he's locked all his emotions behind a fortress. "How bad is it?"

Her eyes glitter, and she shakes her head.

"*Fuck,*" he snarls, the fortress cracking for a moment. "Troy's dead?"

"Yeah," Payton rasps. She clears her throat, then adds, "He wasn't when we got here. We just lost him."

If I thought Maddoc, Logan, and Dante looked grim on the drive over, it's nothing compared to the ice-cold expressions on their faces as we follow Payton into the building.

A couple more Reapers are waiting inside, along with a guy tied to a chair.

No, not a guy. A... body. Or at least, what's left of one.

He was clearly tortured.

"Oh god," I gasp, my stomach heaving and the sour taste of bile flooding my mouth.

Maddoc curses again, low and vicious, and I wrench my arm out of Dante's hold and turn away, squeezing my eyes closed from the grisly sight.

Dante glances at me for a moment, then turns back toward the others, letting me be. The Reapers who were already here start giving Maddoc a situation report, and everyone in the room ignores me while I do my best to pretend the air isn't saturated with the sickening scent of copper and try to get my shit together.

It's not that I don't know what a brutal, horrible place the world can be, it's just that I don't usually have to face that fact in quite such gory detail.

"You said he was alive when you found him?" Maddoc asks, pinning each of his people with a hard gaze.

They all nod, and Payton grimaces. "Barely, and only because they made sure we got here in time."

"They?" Logan repeats.

She nods once, jerkily. "One of those fucking weasels made sure we knew about the attack before they cleared out. Troy was barely conscious when we got here. They *wanted* us to find him like this."

"They wanted to send a fucking message," one of the other Reapers adds furiously.

Maddoc's lips flatten. "Message received."

"He was interrogated," Logan states, looking over Troy's body carefully.

I don't know how he can do that. How he can get up close and personal and stay so unaffected. Or at least *look* so unaffected. But even though bile rises in my throat again, I stiffen my spine and force myself to look too.

This was done by the fuckheads who bought my sister from Frank. The same West Point fucks who treated Chloe like she was just a body to be used, and who will sadistically exploit her, or worse, if they find her on the streets before we do.

I borrow a page from Maddoc's book, and start building a fortress around my emotions.

It doesn't matter that the Reapers betrayed me, or that I still feel a fucking connection to each of them that confuses the hell out of me. None of that matters until we find my sister. It only matters that they're not the ones who did something like *this*.

"We don't know if Troy told them anything," Payton is saying stiffly, "but yeah, they were definitely trying to get something out of him. He was able to say that much before we lost him."

I keep my eyes on Troy's body as she talks, using the gruesome sight to strengthen my new fortress, stone by stone.

I need it, because I'm useless here... and dammit, I wish I wasn't. But I've got nothing to offer as Logan pulls out his phone and starts taking a bunch of pictures while Dante silently moves around the edges of the room, looking for I've got no idea what.

Maddoc snaps off orders to his people, his rage all but boiling under the calm, still surface he presents to them. He tells them to tighten up security around a few key points in the territory and delegates dealing with Troy's body, but stops his people before they disperse to carry out his orders.

"Stick together." He pauses to pin each of them with his eyes. "Have each other's backs. That's your first priority. We're not fucking losing anyone else, got it?"

I turn away as they all murmur their agreement, needing my fortress more than ever. I'm reminded of Dante telling me why he decided to follow Maddoc in the first place, of the way he insisted Maddoc cares about me. And the way Dante acted like he does too.

My heart can't afford to fall for that shit, so I head toward the exit, figuring it's safe enough now that the place is surrounded by Reapers. One of them stops me though, telling me I've got to wait for Maddoc or his seconds.

I sigh, suddenly exhausted by the entire fucked-up roller

coaster of a day. I lean against the door jam, trying to carefully blank my mind of everything I've just seen.

I shudder, then suck in a long, slow breath, desperately needing a distraction. Payton's voice gives me one. The two guys who'd been with Troy's body have already left, but I can still hear her back there, keeping her voice low—almost intimate-sounding—as she talks to Maddoc.

About me. And what the actual fuck? It sounds an awful lot like she's trying to convince him that this whole twisted thing is somehow *my* fault.

I clench my fists, reminding myself that it's none of my fucking business. I'm not a Reaper. I'm not part of their organization, their *family*. And this "partnership" Maddoc insisted on has an expiration date, so it doesn't matter what he believes about me as long as he follows through on helping me find Chloe.

"I just don't think it's smart to trust her," Payton is saying. "Not with her ties to McKenna. She could be working for West Point."

My nails bite into my palms. There's no way I'd ever work with those bastards.

"Riley doesn't have ties to McKenna."

I blink, startled by the sound of Logan's voice. He states it in a dry, cold voice that's nothing but factual. Not like he's on my side, just like he's setting her straight.

It still sends a bittersweet warmth through my chest, and I unfurl my fists and rub at the ache there.

"The fuck she doesn't," Payton snaps. "She stinks of it. Has from the minute you took her in. You should cut her loose before we all suffer for it."

I didn't ask for any of this. My only involvement with West Point is thanks to my father using Chloe to pay his debts to them. There's no way that whatever they were trying to get out of Troy, whatever message they were trying to send to the

Reapers, has anything to do with me. The Reapers were already *in* a gang war with them. Maddoc knows that. He has to.

But he sure as shit doesn't say so. All he says to Payton is that he'll take what she said under advisement, but whatever. It doesn't hurt. It's just another stone to stack in the wall.

I tune the rest of their conversation out, and eventually Payton leaves, the guys finish up, and we all head home. But the problem with ignoring them is that it leaves me with nothing else to distract me from replaying the sight of Troy's tortured, dead body in my mind. Especially once we make it back to the house and they all scatter, each man having plenty of shit to do to deal with the fallout of what went down today.

It leaves me feeling a little lost, which makes me feel weak, which I fucking hate.

"Get it together, Riley," I whisper under my breath

It doesn't work. I'm still unsettled, and it's not just due to the horrific images I can't get out of my head. Troy's death has driven home how dangerous all this shit is. Any one of us could die at any moment. Nothing is guaranteed. It seriously makes me wonder why anyone would even think about coming out from the safety of an emotional fortress.

I mentally retreat to mine, completely overloaded by this day, and head toward the stairs, but my steps slow without my permission when I hear Maddoc and Dante talking in low tones from down the hall.

I would have thought that dealing with the West Point attack would be their only priority right now, but instead, it sounds a hell of a lot like Maddoc is chewing Dante out about what happened between us in the bathroom earlier.

"You fucked her again." Maddoc's voice is low and angry. "After she fucking *shot* me."

I can't make out Dante's low reply, but Maddoc sounds even more pissed—maybe even a little hurt?—when he replies, "Yeah, well, I'm supposed to be your brother."

"You *are* my brother. That's how I know exactly why you didn't end her after she pulled the trigger," Dante replies, loud enough for me to hear this time and with some steel under the laid-back tone I'm used to hearing from him. "Quit pretending that you don't like and respect her even more for having the balls to do it, because we both know that's a lie."

Maddoc makes a rude sound. "You think I like being shot?"

"I think you like the reason she shot you. I know how much loyalty means to you, and how rare it is to find the kind that refuses to break. Riley's got that, and she's one of the strongest, bravest people I've ever met. That's the part you like, Madd. I know you see it in her too."

"All I see is someone who can't be trusted."

Dante snorts. "Oh, you can trust our princess all right. Trust her to do exactly what she told us she would from day one—whatever it takes to look out for the people she loves."

"*Person* she loves," Maddoc corrects him as my heart starts to pound in my chest. "For her sister. It's why she's here."

There's a long pause, and I have to lock my knees to keep from sneaking closer and peering around the corner to get a look at their faces. I'd bet anything that they're having another one of those silent conversations with their eyes that only happens when, like Dante said earlier, two people know each other down to their souls.

After a minute, Dante speaks again. "Things can change. People come into our lives for one reason, but sometimes stay for another. Like the ones who start as enemies and end up brothers."

He's talking about the way he originally infiltrated the Reapers to betray them, but he's also talking about more than that. It makes my chest tighten with emotions that threaten to break down that stone fortress I've been building up all day.

Their voices drop too low for me to keep following the conversation, but I know Dante's right about how Maddoc feels about loyalty, and I'm not sure I want to hear how he reacts to Dante standing up for me like that. Not when my own reaction is confusing enough.

My hands are shaking and my mind is a fucking mess, so I slip up the stairs and head to my room.

Being alone with my thoughts probably isn't going to help sort any of them out, but at least a little space will give me a chance to lay some more stones around my heart. Build up a good, solid wall between my fucked-up feelings and the three men in this house who twist them into such tangled knots, because nothing's changed.

Our partnership is still temporary. They still want to use my sister once we find her.

And if there's one thing that shit Dante said to Maddoc just now makes crystal clear, it's that it's not just the danger out on the streets I have to protect myself from right now.

I close the door to my bedroom and lean back against it, rubbing the ache in my chest.

Fucking Reapers.

17

LOGAN

Maddoc raps his knuckles on the door jamb and walks into my room, a courtesy that I know is meant to avoid startling me, even though it's unnecessary. I saw him coming on one of the monitors.

I swivel my chair around to face him and look up from the surveillance logs I was reviewing, my heart rate steady and my mind deliberately empty of everything but the facts on hand. The trail of digital breadcrumbs I've been following to try and determine how McKenna's people got past ours today. How they got to Troy. To one of *ours*.

Rage surges inside me again, threatening that emptiness, but I automatically tamp it down and tuck it away where it won't interfere with my focus before it gets out of hand. Emotional reactions can't be avoided, but instead of letting this one out to create chaos and destruction, I do what I've become so adept at over the years and compartmentalize it. Store it away like fuel, ready to be lit on fire when it can actually be useful.

"Anything?" Maddoc asks, nodding toward the data on the monitor in front of me.

His rage is also admirably contained. Not being ruled by it is part of the reason he's such a great leader. But it's still there, visible to someone who knows him as well as I do by the tight set of his jaw and the pulsing veins at his temples.

"Nothing we can move on yet, but McKenna's organization is sloppy. I *will* find out how they got to him."

But not necessarily what they learned from him. Troy took the knowledge of whatever they managed to torture out of him to his grave.

Maddoc's lips tighten into a grim line, and he gives me a short, sharp nod. "I know you will, but it will have to wait."

I school myself before I can show any surprise. Maddoc would never let anything get in the way of avenging his people, not unless it was the need to take care of the ones still living. He obviously has a reason to tell me to put my investigation into the West Point attack on hold, so I wait for it.

"I've got to go deal with some shit at our borders in the aftermath of Troy's death," he starts.

My mind takes that statement and immediately races ahead, making a series of connections between the facts I've already uncovered about this attack and the status of our relations with the city's other gangs. I mentally sift through what kind of message McKenna's bold recklessness will send to both our allies and enemies, and after a moment, I've got a pretty good idea of what Maddoc intends to head out and take care of.

I nod, approving. He's not just our leader because of his ruthless drive—although he definitely has that in spades—but also because of his talent for seeing the big picture and strategically looking ten moves ahead of everyone else.

Maddoc nods back, acknowledging that I've brought myself up to speed and don't need him to elaborate with further details.

"While I'm gone," he goes on, "I need you to figure out Chloe's trail, especially where she's been recently in relation to that bus depot she made that call from."

"We need to track her down," I say, weighing and rejecting

158

different ideas on how to manage that when we haven't been able to so far. But failure isn't an option anymore. Gaining access to her inheritance will change everything, and if McKenna found out about it, if his people got that information from Troy before Troy died...

"Finding her just got more urgent," Maddoc says grimly, following the same train of thought. "We don't know what West Point knows now, but we sure as shit know what lengths they'll go to. We need to find her *now*, Logan."

I nod. "I can—"

"Work with Riley," he cuts in. "Get her in here and find out what insights she's got about where her sister might be hiding." He gestures toward the monitors on my desk. "You're going to need her eyes on that to figure out where to focus your attention. What kinds of things Chloe might do when she's scared. Where she'd feel safe."

I stiffen, the idea of inviting Riley into my room without the buffer of my brothers here with us too makes me decidedly uncomfortable. It was different when I had her in here solely to stitch her up. That was a finite task with the added safeguard of her pain to hold her attention. But this space is *mine*. It's where I come as close to relaxing and dropping my guard as I've ever been able to, and I'm not at all sure I'm ready to welcome her into my sanctuary.

Maddoc frowns, and just like I can see through his tells, I know he's seen through mine.

"That's fine," I say quickly, realizing how foolish my hesitation is. "I'll go get her now."

Maddoc is right about everything, and me being uncomfortable is just one more unpleasant emotion I can and will ignore if it gets in the way.

We need to find Chloe.

I stand, intending to follow through and go find Riley, but Maddoc, of course, doesn't let it go that easily. He grips my shoulder, staring into my eyes. "You okay? Got your shit under control, even if she pushes your buttons?"

I nod, but he keeps staring hard, like he's trying to determine whether or not I really mean it.

I'm not offended. Both Maddoc and Dante are better at people than I am, and sometimes they see me better than I see myself.

"I was gonna take Dante with me," Maddoc goes on, "but if you're not sure about working with Riley on your own, I can have him stay and—"

"No." It's my turn to cut him off. "There's no need."

Even though, if I'm honest, it's tempting. But after what West Point just pulled, Maddoc will need Dante to have his back. And also... not *all* my uneasiness at the idea of being alone with Riley is about not wanting her in my space. A part of me is drawn to the idea.

A part I'm not sure what to do with, so I ignore it.

Maddoc takes me at my word, and when we both leave my room, he heads out with Dante while I go to find Riley. She's in her room. I already know it from the monitors, but I hesitate a moment before barging in and, instead, knock.

After a moment, she cracks open the door.

And stares at me.

"I need you," I tell her after a beat of awkward silence, unaccountably put out by her standoffishness. She usually has more spirit, even when she's upset—*especially* when she's upset—but now, it's dimmed, as if she's retreated behind a wall.

I don't like it.

She raises an eyebrow and crosses her arms over her chest, annoying me even further as she waits me out with her face carefully kept blank, clearly expecting more of an explanation than I've given her.

Fine.

"Maddoc pointed out that you can assist me. We need to find Chloe."

"Of course we do," she says, the stiff set of her shoulders softening as she drops her arms. "But do you have something new? Because so far we've had shit luck with that."

"No," I say with a grimace I fail to control. "*We* don't have anything new, but McKenna might."

Riley's eyes go wide. "You think West Point did that to your... to that man, because of *Chloe*?"

"I think they know we've mobilized our people to search for something, and I think McKenna wanted to find out why."

And to let us know in the most brutal way possible that he's getting bolder about interfering in Reaper business, but I don't say that part.

I don't have to. Riley is clearly thinking along the same lines.

"He's a fucking sadist," she snaps.

I nod. Austin McKenna most definitely has a monster inside him, and I've seen what that can do when the host has no desire to control it.

I grew up in the shadow of that kind of monster.

"It's one of the reasons we can't afford to let him take over more of the city. We need..."

Riley's eyes narrow when I don't finish, but of course she understands what I'm alluding to.

"My sister's money," she says flatly.

I don't deny it, and she looks away for a moment, swallowing hard. When she looks back, her eyes are determined. Instead of ripping into me about how cold and calculating she finds our plan for Chloe's inheritance, she lifts her chin.

"What can I do?"

I know she's not agreeing, she's simply being pragmatic. Watching her actively choose not to let her emotions take over

161

gives me an inexplicable sensation in my chest, almost as if it's pulling me toward her.

I've never felt anything like it before, and it's unsettling.

I turn away. "Come to my room."

An odd thrill goes through me when she immediately complies, and when she steps through the door to my room, invades my private space at my own invitation, another strange feeling washes over me.

I'm too aware of her. She's too *present*. Too vibrant. She changes everything, as if she disturbs the very air just by breathing it.

I do my best to compartmentalize the odd sensation and excuse myself to collect a second chair from the library down the hall. When I come back, she's seated in *my* chair, and I freeze.

"Logan?" she asks, swiveling it around to face me.

I mean to tell her to get the fuck out, but no words come out. And when I place the second chair down next to her and slip into it, I don't pull away when our knees touch. When our thighs press together. When she leans into me, smelling of something smoky and intriguing, to see the digitized maps of Halston that I've overlaid with all the information we've already gathered about Chloe's trail as I quickly click through them, explaining what I've inferred so far.

"Stop," she says, an oddly breathless note in her voice as she points to the screen. "Can you switch to a satellite view?"

I do it, an unfamiliar tension thrumming in my body. Light from the monitor glints off the blue jewel in her nose, and the quick smile she throws my way feels like an electrical arc snapping between us.

"We should check there," she says, pointing to a building on the screen. "I know she's caught a few punk shows there with her friends."

I drag my eyes off her face and mark the building with a pin as she rambles on about her sister's taste in music.

"And there," she says, pointing out another. And then another.

I zoom in on the grid-like streets surrounding the bus depot. "Let's concentrate here, then move outward in concentric circles."

She nods, and we spend another twenty minutes discussing her sister's habits and picking out possible areas she may have sought refuge.

Despite my best efforts to stay focused, Riley's subtly enticing scent and the heat of her body so close to mine are distracting... although not quite as distracting as the picture she weaves with her stories about Chloe.

My gaze drifts toward the keepsake box on my dresser, and for a split second, I let myself wonder how different it would have been to have had a little sister to look out for. Then I yank my eyes away and stop wondering, because I know from experience that I won't be able to contain the rage, or the monster inside me, if I let my thoughts stray toward what life would have been like if Emma had lived.

Riley is staring at me.

"What?" I grunt.

She shakes her head, her lips quirking up at the corners. "Nothing."

I narrow my eyes. "If you lie to me, we won't find your sister."

Riley raises a single eyebrow, not looking even a little bit intimidated, and I'm torn between admiration and reminding her that I held her life in my hands—literally—just a few weeks ago.

"Really? You're going to go there? This isn't about Chloe. I was just curious about your... space."

"My space," I repeat flatly, my pulse speeding up without my permission.

She waves a hand in the air, presumably taking in my room decor. "You know, your things."

"What things?" I ask, a dangerous edge creeping into my voice when I realize that instead of putting a hard stop to this conversation, a part of me wants to lean in to her curiosity.

She starts to answer me, but then stops.

Instead of being grateful that she's dropped it, I find myself pushing. "Just say it."

Riley still hesitates, and I can't help noticing how close we are now. Close enough that I can easily read the wariness in her eyes.

"It's just... your room is so neat and tidy," she finally says, "and that first day—"

"When you snuck in," I interrupt.

"When you tried to kill me," she snaps right back.

I nod, a faint flush of shame moving through me, and Riley answers with an equally faint smile before she continues.

"But since I didn't touch anything—"

"Yes, you did."

"Okay, fine! I did, but that's the thing. It's so tidy in here that I made extra sure that anything I did touch got put right back in its spot! So how did you know I was even in here?"

For a moment, I tense. Is she mocking me? I have no reason to care if she is, and yet I still don't like it. But then I realize she's not, so I tell her.

"The rug."

At least, that was my first clue.

She swivels the chair to stare at it. "You, what, saw my footprint on it or something?"

She almost sounds awed, and I laugh, a short, scratchy bark that feels entirely unfamiliar as it leaves my throat.

"No," I say quickly to cover up my own shock at my

reaction. I stand and go to the rug, then crouch down to show her. "The corner of this pattern was out of alignment with the floorboards. This edge... here, should be parallel to the seam... here."

Riley blinks, then cocks her head to the side, staring not at the rug, but at me. "And you actually noticed that?"

I stand. "Among other things."

Like the slight gap where she'd failed to fully shut my dresser drawer. The faint smudge her fingers had left on the metal base of my lamp. The curve in the cord connecting the eReader I'd been charging to the wall, when of course I'd made sure to leave it lying perfectly straight and perpendicular to the wall.

"Did you just notice, or did it... bother you?" Riley asks after a slight hesitation.

I frown. Is she joking? Of course it bothered me. My fingers flex spasmodically by my sides, remembering the soft feel of her skin as I gripped her throat, the rapid flutter of her pulse under my hands, the unsettling tension that built between us before Dante came in and brought me back to myself.

I clasp my hands together behind my back, forcing my fingers to be still. "You came in uninvited. You were in my space. You touched my things."

Riley nods, looking thoughtful.

"What?" I ask, narrowing my eyes.

She answers my question with another question. "Have you always been so particular about things like that?"

No one asks me these things. My brothers understand me on a level deeper than words, and they accept my traits and exacting requirements without question. But we don't *talk* about things like this. We just exist.

And it's much, much more comfortable than Riley's gentle, insidious questions.

I want to lash out at her, but I also have the most absurd

impulse to tell her the truth. To explain that I have a good reason for needing to be particular. That it's a learned skill, a survival mechanism, not a weakness.

Keeping my things in order gave me a small measure of control while growing up in a household where Emma and I had none, and noticing when they were *out* of order was sometimes all the warning I'd get when the monster inside our mother took over. And after she...

Afterward, when it was just me, living on the streets with no space to call my own and no one to watch out for, then yes. I'm not stupid. I know my habit of being "particular" about my things slowly evolved from survival to an actual compulsion.

But it still kept me alive.

And if, now, it feels like a prison sometimes? Well, at least it's one without unpleasant surprises lurking around every corner. Without... dangerous ones.

"Logan?"

I don't even realize Riley left the chair and joined me on the rug until her fingertips brush my arm, so lightly that the touch is barely there. A butterfly kiss.

My eyes snap up to meet hers, and I'm perfectly aware how my gaze typically affects people, but she doesn't jump back.

If my pale eyes are as colorless as chips of ice, her warm brown ones are the opposite.

"No. I haven't always been like this," I find myself answering without meaning to.

She nods like I said more than that, and for a moment I'm overcome with the oddest feeling that I did. That I told her more than I meant to, or else that she simply understood what I didn't have to say, the way Maddoc and Dante—*only* Maddoc and Dante—often do.

"I'm sorry I came in here uninvited," she says after a moment, her fingers still hovering just above my arm. "I didn't know it would matter so much to you."

I blink. I'm not used to apologies. Neither to giving them nor to receiving them.

"I'm also sorry," I say stiffly. "For what I did about it. After. I don't... always have control."

How could I? I'm the child of a monster, and my mother passed that heritage on to me. Order helps. Routine helps. I may have ways to keep it on a leash and—usually—stop it from doing anything awful, but the monster is still there and always will be.

It's a part of me, all the same.

A part that, just by thinking about it like this, has it trying to rise up and break free.

But then Riley pulls her fingers away from my arm and rubs one over her chest, directly between the slight swell of her breasts, and the monster loses its hold on me, my attention suddenly riveted to the spot.

It's where I marked her.

My breath quickens, and I don't even realize I've moved too, until I find my fingers lying over hers.

They tremble. Hers, I think, or maybe mine. Maybe both.

"You cut me," she whispers, not pushing me away.

Heat races through me, swift and overwhelming, and I drag my fingers over the spot. I can't look away. I want her shirt gone so I can *see*. "Did it leave a scar?"

"Yes," she says, a shudder going through her body when I stroke the spot again. Her nipples pebble under her shirt. Then her chin lifts. "And you seemed to have perfect control the night you gave it to me. That wasn't an accident."

She's not wrong about that, but she is wrong about me having *perfect* control. If I'd had that, I never would have gone to her room that night.

But I did have some control. Enough to keep the monster in check. Not enough to keep it from taking over, but enough that I was able to refocus my rage and confusion over the way she affected me—the way she still affects me—into the clean, precise, methodical action of cutting up her clothes.

I systematically shredded each item she brought into our home, and then, when that wasn't enough, I climbed on top of her and cut the ones she was wearing off her while she slept. All without marking her skin.

And that still wasn't enough.

"You *wanted* to cut me," Riley whispers, her voice trembling as she captures my fingers and holds them still.

I can feel her heart beating under my fingertips, and the heat of her body sends a sizzling awareness all the way down to my cock. It starts to thicken and fill, but shame fills me too.

She's right. I cut her on purpose that night. I did have enough control.

I did it because I wanted to.

"I'm... sorry," I repeat, blood rushing in my ears as my body sways toward her, the memory both repelling me and drawing me closer with a magnetic pull.

Riley's breath hitches, her pupils blowing wide, and heat spills down my spine at the way she subtly tips her head back and looks up at me.

Not glaring. Not accusing. It looks like an invitation, and I freeze. I've never done this before. I've never let myself get close to a woman like this. Not physically, and not any other way, either.

I've never admitted the kinds of truths I've just shared with her to anyone.

I've never even wanted to... until now.

The monster starts to rise up inside me, either sensing my weakness or recognizing the danger, but I beat it back down.

It can't have her.

A chime sounds, and Riley jumps back, her cheeks flooding with color as she drops my hand and looks back toward the monitors. "Is that, um, something important?"

Both grateful and resentful for the interruption, I tell her, "It's an alert I set up."

I sidestep around her, careful not to touch her again, and focus all of my attention on the commands I need to type into the keyboard, chasing the information my spyware just coughed up.

Riley slips into the chair next to me, and I don't notice that compelling, enticing scent she has or the soft feel of her long, wavy hair as the bold colors brush my arm. Instead, I fall back on what's familiar. I block out the disruptive... *feelings* and point out what I'm looking for on the monitors in front of us, quickly zooming through the city maps as Riley gives her input.

She leans in close, focusing on the task at hand, and we get back to work.

18

RILEY

My mind is spinning when I finally leave Logan's room. The man takes scary-smart to a whole new level, and I'm beyond grateful to have his help finding my sister.

We spent hours together pouring over the data he'd dug up about the city, and even though nothing's panned out yet, I've got real hope that we've narrowed down some ideas of where Chloe might be hiding.

But unfortunately, he made it very clear that we have to wait for daylight before we follow up on any of the ideas we've cobbled together. Maddoc's orders.

"Dammit," I huff, punching my pillow into a fluffier position before flopping back onto it again. I'm wired and restless and exhausted, all at the same time. And it's not just the progress we made searching for Chloe that has me feeling this way. Being so close to Logan for so long, having the tantalizing scent in my nostrils and the constant, subtle brush of his body against mine all day, has left me with a whole bunch of frustrated energy that I've got no way to handle.

Well, not *no* way, but no satisfying way.

I'm not planning on going there though, so I keep my hands folded under my head and ignore the hum of awareness, of *want*, in my body, determined to shove it aside and get some sleep.

It takes nearly an hour of tossing and turning, but eventually, my eyelids droop and then stay closed.

WHEN I WAKE UP, I'm not alone.

I roll over and rub at my eyes, that distinct scent of Logan's—some heady combination of his crisp body wash and his own enticing, masculine scent—telling me even before my eyes find him that he was thinking of me too.

I look toward the door and see him, our gazes locking in the darkness. Something is brewing between us. It has been all day. And as Logan strides toward me across the room, I stay still, frozen in place as I wait for him.

But not from fear this time.

He drags the covers off my body the moment he reaches me, letting them slide off the bed and pool at his feet as those pale eyes burn into me with the intensity of the white-hot center of a flame. I can't look away as he bares me to his gaze, and it's only once I'm fully exposed to him that I notice the moonlight glinting off the knife in his hand.

I should be scared.

We've been here before, and it was terrifying.

But this time, it's not.

He doesn't say a word, he doesn't even blink, and my pulse starts to race as he climbs up onto the bed, prowling toward me like a jungle cat. He straddles my hips, and heat floods through me. Heat and want.

Logan has his own agenda, though. He doesn't lower his weight onto me. Doesn't pin me down or grind against me. He holds himself aloof even though I can see damn well that I'm not the only one affected here, hovering over me as his fingers drag down the center of my chest, like déjà vu of the intense moment of connection I felt with him in his room earlier.

That's not the thing he seems intent on repeating.

I fell asleep in a thin white camisole and silky matching sleep shorts. Logan slips the cold blade of his knife under one of the thin straps of my top and slices it away, then repeats the motion on the other side.

This time, it's not terrifying. This time is something different completely.

He peels down the top of the cami, baring the scar he marked me with to his view, and heat races through me. I'm used to being looked at, but I'm not used to this. All the single-minded focus and intensity that Logan brings to every single thing he does is on me and me alone. His look is possessive, almost feral, and being the focus of it is an arousing, addictive rush.

He drags the tip of his knife over the scar, not breaking skin, but I swear I feel it slicing straight down to my core. Then he bunches up my shirt in his other fist and pulls it away from my body before jerking the knife through the thin material and cutting it off me.

"Logan," I gasp, my back arching and my hands fisting in the sheets on either side of me.

His eyes snap up to meet mine, but only for a moment. Then they drop right back down to my body, and when he runs the knife under the waistband of my sleep shorts, sliding it deep enough that I can feel the flat part of the blade against my clit, I bite back a whimper.

Before I can decide if he's punishing me or teasing me, he slices the shorts off me too.

I bite back a whimper but can't stop my breath from coming in short, needy pants. I'm so wet there's no way he doesn't see it, even with nothing but moonlight to show him how soaked my panties are. But Logan still doesn't say anything, because of course he doesn't. With him, silence is like another form of foreplay.

He drags the blade back up my body, teasing my nipples with it until they're two pebbled points. Little shocks of lust explode inside me with each touch of the knife, but I'm going to go crazy if he doesn't touch me. I want skin. Heat. Flesh on flesh.

He doesn't give it to me.

He slides the knife over every inch of me, making me aware of every atom of my body in a way I've never felt before. Making me whimper and whine for him and bite my own damn tongue to keep from outright begging. Because this is Logan. He either bolts or shuts down every time things start to feel intense between us, and if he leaves me right now I'll scream.

Finally, he brings the knife between my legs again, slicing through my panties. His thumb drags over my swollen, wet folds as he pushes the silky material aside, and my entire body clenches tight, a shudder of desire rippling through me.

"Logan." It comes out laced with desperation, and Logan goes utterly still in that eerie way only he can pull off.

His head cocks to the side, his eyes drilling into me. "What do you want?"

The truth bursts out of me, a truth I haven't even admitted to myself before now. "Fuck me. Oh god, please."

I try to spread my legs for him, but they're trapped between his thighs. I try to buck up against his hand, but the knife is suddenly at my throat and he's leaning over me, pinning me down, grinding his hard length against my clit until I want to scream.

"You want me."

"Yes." I tilt my head back without any fear, not sure if I'm daring him or offering.

His eyes burn into me like white fire. "You want me inside you."

"Fuck, yes, Logan, do it!"

173

He holds my gaze for an eternity, both of us panting, immobile. Then, with a low curse, he tosses the knife aside and rears back, shoving his pants down to his thighs and immediately driving into me.

"Oh god," I gasp, that white fire ripping all the way through me. And he doesn't stop. He fucks just like he does everything, with total control and barely leashed brutality.

It feels incredible... but I want even more.

He looks down at me with that silent, deadly intensity that makes it feel like he's taking me apart from the inside out as he fucks me, and I feel it everywhere. Inside me with every thrust, on every inch of my skin that he claimed with his knife, and deeper. In that dark, dark place at the center of my soul that resonates each time I'm around him.

"Logan," I whisper, reaching for him. Not sure what I'm asking for.

He gives it to me anyway, hitching one of my legs over his hip and bending over me, crushing me with his weight, bringing his lips toward mine as I breathe in that gorgeous, addictive scent of his. Letting me taste... taste...

I can't taste him.

A frustrated noise spills from my lips, but he's gone.

My eyes snap open. I'm gasping for breath, still aroused to the point of screaming, but alone.

I scramble upright in the bed, kicking off the sweat-soaked blankets tangled around my body and staring toward the door. The closed door. And I'm still wearing the pajamas I fell asleep in.

Logan was never here.

"Fuck," I whisper, pushing my hair back from my face and then clenching my hands into fists as I take a few deep breaths, trying to calm down.

My sex throbs between my legs, my panties so slick inside that there's no way to deny what I was just dreaming, but I'll be damned if I shove my hand down there to finish myself off. It was terrifying enough when Logan actually came to my room with a knife, and while I won't lie to myself and say I'm not attracted, I'm still equally afraid of him.

The only explanation I have for letting myself go like that in a dream is Dante. He got me too worked up in the bathroom, but even if he doesn't scare me the same way Logan's inner darkness does, dwelling too much on what he does make me feel is just as terrifying in an entirely different way.

There's no way I'm risking going back to sleep, not with my core still pulsing with an unfulfilled ache that I can far too easily imagine any of the three Reapers under this roof satisfying for me, so I decide to go down and find some breakfast. It's early enough that I'm not actually hungry, but staying in the bed I now have such vivid images of getting fucked in isn't going to do me any favors, so I throw on a robe and head downstairs.

To my surprise, I'm not the only one up this early.

My steps stutter when I reach the kitchen. Maddoc is sitting at the counter with a plate of eggs and a tablet in front of him, and when he looks up and sees me, we both freeze. I haven't been alone, in *here* with him, since he fucked me and I shot him... and with my body still primed for the kind of relief I'm just not going to get this morning, the memory of both those things slams into me like a freight train.

Maddoc's expression shutters as he gestures to a cell phone sitting on the counter. "That's for you. It's got the number I gave Frank, so if he needs to reach you, he can."

With that, he looks back down at his tablet, calmly taking a bite of his eggs like he's not affected by those memories at all. For a second, I'm so goddamn angry that he's ignoring me that I want to shoot him all over again.

Then I get my shit together and realize it's for the best, so I just snatch up the new phone and then walk past him to get my own breakfast.

I pour some juice into a glass, not quite ready for coffee yet, and pluck an apple out of the fruit bowl, stealing another glance at Maddoc while I do. He looks rough. Stressed the fuck out, and like he didn't get enough sleep.

Or maybe not any.

I crunch a bite of the apple, the hot blast of anger settling into something a lot more dangerous as I watch him.

I should not care about this man, so I tell myself I don't, but I can see how much everything is weighing on him. I can't pretend I don't know by now what kind of leader he is, and how hard Troy's death has hit him. Not just *what* happened to Troy, but that it happened on Maddoc's watch. That he wasn't able to stop it and still hasn't avenged it.

He glances up at me.

"How's your shoulder?" I blurt.

"Why?" he asks dryly, looking back down at whatever it is on his tablet that he's so engrossed in. "Regretting that your shot went wide?"

I bite back a sharp reply but I narrow my eyes at him. Asshole. Was I seriously just emoting for the man?

When he looks up at me again, I hold his gaze and take another bite of the apple, imagining it's his ball sac.

Maddoc laughs, then widens his eyes like the sound startled him. He looks back down at his tablet. "It's healing."

He eats some more of his eggs and I finish the apple, then before I can second guess myself I pour a second glass of juice and take both over to the counter Maddoc's sitting at.

I slide one in front of him and take a seat on the stool to his left.

"Did Logan send you what we came up with?" I ask, nodding toward his tablet.

Maddoc looks at me like he's trying to suss out my angle, but I'm not even sure I have one right now, and after a moment he obviously comes to the same conclusion.

He sighs and finally puts the tablet down. "Yeah, he did."

"But that's not what kept you up all night," I guess, resisting the urge to reach over and rub some of the tension out of his shoulders.

Maddoc shakes his head. "That shit with Troy..."

He lets the thought trail off, reaching for his juice.

"Do you really think it was about Chloe?"

He hesitates, but then nods. "Yeah, but not just about Chloe. We've got a lot of history with them, and they're getting more aggressive all around."

"But... why?"

He grimaces. "Because McKenna is a greedy fuck who wants our territory."

I picture the map in his office. "Don't you want his too?"

Maddoc cuts his eyes over to me, then laughs. "Yeah, I do. But it's not the same. He targeted us specifically a few years ago, deciding we were the gang to take out in order for him to gain some notoriety along with an expansion. We weren't a threat to his organization at the time. At least, not one that he was smart enough to recognize. But he didn't like what we were building here."

He doesn't elaborate, but I'm pretty sure I know what he means anyway. I'm not so naive that I don't realize what the Reapers are. Whatever it is they do to support themselves is part of Halston's criminal underground. I'm not under any illusions about the gang being full of white knights.

But still, there's no denying that Maddoc has built something solid. He's got principles and he sticks to them, a gangster code of ethics that's night and day from the sadistic, self-serving way Austin McKenna seems to run things.

So of course he's threatened by the Reapers. I've known enough small-dicked, power hungry assholes like him to understand that they always feel the need to prove themselves by taking out anyone who does it better.

Someone like Maddoc, who actually inspires loyalty.

"It's personal between you two, isn't it?"

Maddoc stares at me hard, but finally nods. "McKenna made it that way. He got aggressive with our business in ways that were fucking stupid. He hurt both organizations, and now it's escalating. And yeah, he wants more than our territory. He gets off on trying to get one over on me too. He's made it his personal vendetta. That's why Sienna—"

He grimaces, then downs the rest of his juice instead of finishing whatever he was about to say.

Well, too bad for him. I want to know.

"Sienna?" I press.

Dante walks in.

"What about her?" he asks, looking between the two of us. "Is she trying to stir shit up again, Madd?"

Maddoc just grunts.

What the hell is that supposed to mean?

Dante heads for the coffee pot, and he and Maddoc have one of those conversations with their eyes that I'm getting really fucking sick of not being a part of.

I set my glass down on the counter. Loudly.

They both look at me.

"Who's Sienna?"

"A bitch who should die," Dante says cheerfully, at the same time that Maddoc mutters grimly, "My ex."

I'm hit with an irrational surge of jealousy, because of course I am. As if the last few days haven't already been enough of an emotional rollercoaster. There's no place for that shit though, not about some bitch ex of his, and not when it comes to the idea that he's planning on marrying my sister. Not that I'm going to let that happen.. but not because I'm jealous.

A vague memory teases at the back of my mind, and I chase it because anything is better than going down that rabbit hole right now.

I drum my fingers on the counter. Then it comes to me.

"Wait, Sienna? Isn't that the girl who was with Austin McKenna the night we found Chloe dancing at West Point's club?"

They both nod.

"So you two were together, and now she's with *him*?" I press Maddoc.

"That's right," he says, his tone making it clear he's done sharing.

Dante isn't though.

"She cheated on him," he volunteers, earning a black look from Maddoc that he apologizes for by handing him the first cup of coffee, but otherwise ignores. "But worse, she fucking sold him out," he goes on. "It wasn't enough that she went and hopped on McKenna's dick. She also gave up everything she knew about how we operate."

"She what?" A surge of anger hits me. I shouldn't care. This isn't my fight. But I do. "Bitch," I mutter viciously.

Dante grins and hands me a cup of coffee, doctored exactly the way I like it, then pours himself one and clinks his mug against mine. "Damn right."

Maddoc snorts, looking back down at his tablet, but not before I notice the corners of his lips twitching.

I almost smile myself, but then Logan walks in and my body immediately flushes with heat as I'm swamped with vivid flashbacks of exactly how good it felt to have him stare at me so intensely while he fucked me through the mattress—

"Good morning," Logan says calmly, because of course that didn't actually happen.

I mumble something back and gulp my coffee, grimacing when it burns my throat and then yelping with pain when I jerk it away and the hot liquid sloshes over onto my hand. "*Dammit.*"

I shake the coffee off my hand, then look up to find all three of them staring at me.

"You okay, princess?" Dante asks, his eyebrows drawn together.

Maddoc is frowning too, half off his stool and reaching for me, but Logan must have moved faster because he's already by my side, handing me a cool, damp dish towel as he takes my coffee and sets it on the counter.

"Wrap it in this."

"Bossy," I mutter.

"You're just now noticing that?" Dante teases as he quickly cleans up the mess and wipes down my cup, then adds a little more cream to cool it down before handing it back to me. "We wouldn't have passed Madd's vetting process if we weren't."

"It's a Reaper requirement," Maddoc agrees dryly, playing along as he settles back onto his stool.

Even Logan's lips twitch for a moment, and then my cheeks heat up even more as he takes matters into his own hands and wraps the towel around my burn with quick, efficient movements that, thanks to my dream-addled brain, feel oddly erotic in their clinical precision.

It does help soothe the burn, but it doesn't do a damn thing to quench the warm glow growing in my chest as the three of them banter like actual brothers, Dante keeping all of our coffees topped up while Logan starts methodically putting together the kind of breakfast that convinces me an apple isn't going to cut it after all.

They move around each other in the kitchen with a casual ease that speaks of true family, the kind I can completely understand Dante defecting from his former gang for, and with nobody mentioning all the shit we're dealing with—Chloe still missing, the war with West Point, Troy's torture and murder—it feels surreal to have all of us co-existing so peacefully in a room I tried to kill one of them in.

Surreal, but nice.

At least, it's nice until Maddoc's phone rings.

He glances down, the number on the screen making his brow furrow, and the laid-back energy in the room instantly changes as all of us go on high alert.

The call *could* be about anything, but I don't think any one of us expects that "anything" to be good at this point.

And we're right.

The moment Maddoc answers, the sound of shouting comes across the line. Shouting, traffic, and gunshots.

"Report," Maddoc snaps, already on his feet.

And then, I think it's Payton's voice, loud enough that I can hear every word clearly—

"Maddoc? Maddoc! I need backup!"

19

MADDOC

"Where?" I demand, my whole body tense with the need to act as I wait for Payton to spit out the intel.

"We're... near Cliffton." Her harsh, panting breath is punctuated by the rapid-fire sound of footsteps. "Heading north on... on Masters."

I make eye contact with my seconds and they both nod. They heard her too, and Dante is already calling for backup while Logan's fingers fly over the screen of the tablet I was using earlier, no doubt pulling up details that I'm not even thinking to ask.

Because I still don't know what the *fuck* is going on.

"We?" I bark into the phone, my forehead creasing. Pretty sure I'd asked Payton to track down some specific information about a few suppliers last night. Not ones she'd find over in Cliffton, or anyone Luis—a newly vetted Reaper who'd been with us less than a year—would have been involved with.

"Luis is with me," she answers, her voice fading for a moment before I hear a muffled "*shit*" followed by a fuck-ton of yelling.

"Payton?"

"Here," she gasps. "Jesus, tell me you're close."

I grimace, hating the fuck out of the lack of intel I have right now but my mind already firing on all cylinders.

I glance up at Dante and he nods.

"Isaac's taking some muscle and heading there now," he tells me in a low voice, slipping his phone into a pocket and then sliding open a particular drawer under the counter and tossing Logan one of the weapons we keep there. They both arm themselves as I reassure Payton that help is on the way, then demand more answers.

"Why the fuck is Luis with you?"

"I... I got word that someone from West Point was spotted outside... outside their territory this morning," she pants. "I convinced Luis to come with me so we could... take him for you. Find out what he knows. Tit for... tat."

She means for Troy. She wanted to, what, grab one of McKenna's people and interrogate him the way they took out our boy? It's fucking stupid without the kind of planning I know damn well she didn't do and I didn't authorize. Not to mention, like I said when we found Troy, shit like that sends a message. A message which *should* have come from me.

I clench my jaw so hard it spasms, but getting pissed off has to wait.

"Did you get him?" I ask, pretty fucking sure I know the answer to that since shit obviously went south with this little unauthorized vigilante plan of hers. But I'm wrong.

"Fuck yeah, we did," Payton gasps out, surprising the hell out of me.

Dante jerks his head toward the door, indicating we're ready to roll, and I shove the stool I was sitting on out of the way and follow him to the garage with Logan and Riley on my heels.

"Did he know anything?"

"Yeah," Payton says, followed by a clatter that sounds like

she dropped the phone. Then I hear a whole stream of curses as we pile into the Escalade, Dante behind the wheel, followed by the sound of down and dirty street fighting.

Something cracks.

My phone case.

"Hey," Riley whispers quietly, her fingers prying mine off the phone and squeezing them once my grip finally loosens.

I didn't even realize she'd slid into the back seat with me.

She gives me a tiny smile, then pats my hand before dropping hers back to her lap. "Maybe don't break it? We need to keep them on the line to find them, right?"

I give her a jerky nod, then refocus, because Luis is talking. Yelling at Payton to get the fuck up, followed by a grating sound before he obviously snatches up her phone from wherever it fell.

"Boss? Maddoc? *Fuck*. That you?"

"Get those fuckers off your tail and find some cover," I bite out as Dante takes a corner fast enough that my shoulder slams into the door and Riley slams into me. "We're almost there."

"There is no fucking cover," Luis wheezes. "This shit went all to hell. Every time we turn another corner there's another fucking weasel."

"How many?"

"Payton said just the one, but... shit, fine, take it."

The last part is obviously to Payton because she comes back on the line, breathing hard. "If we stop running, we're going down. They're... they're boxing us in."

The girl is normally tough as shit, but I can hear the fear in her voice. Obviously, whoever tipped her off about there being "just the one" was fucking wrong.

And I hate going in blind... but not as much as I'd hate losing two more of mine to Austin motherfucking McKenna.

"We're coming," I grit out. "Isaac's on his way too." I make eye contact with Logan and he holds up four fingers, so I tell her, "Four minutes out."

"Okay," Payton gulps before repeating it like she's trying to make herself believe it, "okay. We can... we can... hold them off. There's at least... six."

Shit.

Payton sounds either winded or hurt, and another quick pop of gunfire in the background has my gut clenching, worry filling me up faster than the busted pipe that flooded our basement two years ago.

I shove it aside and refocus.

"Do that," I tell Payton grimly, knowing damn well it's not the kind of order she can promise to follow even though two Reapers are worth more than six weasels any day. "We're coming."

It feels like both an eternity and way fucking faster than the four minutes Logan gave me until that's true, but when we roll up to the last location Payton gave us—an intersection with a liquor store on one corner and an empty lot surrounded by chain link on the other—it's empty.

"Fuck," I bite out, not surprised since my people are clearly running for their damn lives, but still pissed at the whole fucking situation. "Update?"

I'm asking my seconds, because somewhere along the way the call with Payton dropped

"Isaac's three blocks west," Logan tells me. "He says there's no sign of them."

"Company coming yet?" I ask as we throw open the Escalade's doors and all three of us pile out.

No, all four of us.

"Get the fuck back in the car," I snap at Riley, which gets her back up for all of two seconds. Then, shocking the shit out of me, she gives me a small nod and actually fucking does it. Without even arguing.

It's the first thing that's gone right so far.

Logan telling me no on any incoming police presence is the

second, but that's not gonna last forever. Not with as much gunfire as I heard in the background before I lost touch with Payton. We're right on the edge of West Point territory here, so it's not like that shit is uncommon, but Cliffton is close enough to areas that the cops actually *do* pay attention to that it will still draw attention.

We just need to find our people before that attention comes with sirens and lights.

Another spate of gunfire sounds, and Dante uses the fob to lock down the Escalade as the three of us take off in a dead run, heading toward the problem.

Logan is still on his phone and confirms that Isaac heard the shots fired too. Then he tosses me the phone, the call still connected.

"Head up Jefferson," I bark into the phone, naming a street Isaac and his crew should be close to. If I'm right and he hauls ass, we might be lucky enough to cut off the six West Point fuckers Payton noted and get her and Luis out.

We're not that lucky.

I hear Luis shout something from up ahead and shove the phone into my pocket as the street in front of us turns into a motherfucking shooting range. Looks like the fucking weasels are working together to box Payton and Luis in.

"Shit," Dante shouts, pulling his weapon as he ducks for cover and opens fire.

The West Point shitheads scatter, diving for cover of their own as they realize we've flanked them and that our people aren't quite the easy pickings they'd assumed.

Payton shouts that she's out of ammo, and Luis lays down some cover fire when I direct them toward an alley off to the side. It would be a deadly place to get trapped if we let McKenna's people get to them, but we won't. Isaac has finally shown up from the west with two more Reapers in tow, and a

186

couple carloads of extra bodies I called in for additional backup made it here, parking down by the Escalade and pounding up the street toward us.

The odds are now in our favor. Odds aren't enough, though. Not during a shootout with lead flying in all directions like this.

"Isaac," I shout, giving him some hand signals to coordinate going on the offensive.

He nods, turning to call out my instructions to the men behind him, and we all advance on the alley Payton and Luis ducked into.

The narrow street fills with the deafening echo of gunfire, filling with enough smoke to make visibility a fucking problem for a moment. It gives a few of the West Point fuckers the chance to make a break for it.

I wouldn't mind taking them out, but it's enough to drive them away. All I care about today is getting my people out of this alive, and for that, we need to get them away from that fucking alley so we can extract Payton and Luis.

It's a deadly dance as we all work together to rout the pieces of shit who dared to threaten my people, but they're starting to turn tail and run when I finally make it to the head of the alley.

I round the corner, staying low. It's boxed in at the other end, trapping Payton and Luis in the narrow passage with nothing for cover but a metal dumpster and a stack of wooden pallets. It means the only way to get them out is the way they got in.

"Logan, Dante," I call out, jerking my chin to indicate what we need to do.

They move into position, and I beckon Payton and Luis forward while my seconds lay down cover fire. Payton's got a length of broken pipe in her hand—smart girl, since she's out of firepower—and Luis advances with his weapon at the ready, knowing damn well that it's not over until we're out of here.

One of the last West Point holdouts opens fire from across the street, shooting the gun out of his hand.

"Motherfucker," Luis screeches, stumbling into the pile of pallets behind him.

"Get up," I shout as bullets start tearing chunks out of the concrete next to my head, driving me away from the alley and cutting off their exit. "Come on!"

Payton drops her pipe and scrambles across the alley, snatching up Luis's gun from where it's fallen. She hisses, no doubt from the hot metal, but doesn't hesitate as she moves in front of him and takes up a protective stance, weapon raised, as he extracts himself from the broken pallets.

"Madd, incoming!"

The warning comes a split second before a fresh wave of gunshots ring out, and I spin to the side as Luis and Payton both dive behind the dumpster with a string of curses.

"Get those fucking weasels out of here," I shout to my people, turning back to face the street and help make that happen. My men step up, finally driving the last few stragglers back, and I duck back into the alley. "*Now*, Payton. We've got to go. You good, Luis? Let's move."

Payton stands up, taking me at my word, and starts toward me. "Maddoc, are we—"

Whatever she was gonna ask cuts off as she suddenly flies backward, her body slamming into the brick wall behind her and her chest blooming with red.

"Payton!"

Luis is closer, but I'm already moving and I get there first, vaguely aware of the last West Point shithead—the one who just took her down—racing away up Jefferson. I press down on the wound, shouting for my brothers, vaguely aware that Logan's opened fire on the shooter but that both of them are staying close. Covering me instead of chasing him down.

"She's breathing. She's still breathing," Luis repeats, stabilizing her head and keeping her airway clear.

But it's the kind of wound that's gonna take more than the two of us to keep it that way. My hands are instantly soaked in hot blood, my nose assaulted by the metallic tang of copper, and the only thing keeping me from losing my shit is that we haven't lost her.

"Logan," I yell, refusing to take my eyes off Payton but trusting that they'll do what it takes to help me get her back to the house. "Get the car! Call Shane! Get him to the house!"

Shane's not a doctor, but he's a Reaper, and hands-down I'll trust that over credentials any day. And he definitely knows his way around a bullet wound.

Payton's breath is nothing more than a shallow, painful-sounding wheeze, but her eyes are open, slowly blinking up at me, and her fingers scrabble loosely at my wrist.

"Hold on," I order her, silently cursing when I hear sirens in the distance. The kind that would make our lives a whole lot more difficult.

Then my brothers are there, Logan and Dante lifting Payton while I keep pressure on the wound. And somehow, we get her into the back of the Escalade, Riley scooting all the way over with eyes as wide as saucers before she whips off her shirt and stuffs it under my hands, helping to slow the bleeding.

Logan's behind the wheel this time and he peels out, followed by a few other cars from the Reaper members who showed up to help us end this shit. They follow us, knowing that if either the cops or West Point gets on our tail, it will be their job to get them back off.

"Come on, stay with me," I tell Payton, focusing a hundred percent of my attention on her since I fully trust my people to handle the rest right now.

Payton slow-blinks at me again, her eyes seeming to have trouble focusing and her skin deathly pale. She's barely hanging on, and it pisses me off to no end that this all came down for something so fucking useless.

There's no way I would have authorized her to go after that fucking weasel, and she knows it.

"Why'd you have to do that?" I demand, guilt swamping me. She tries to answer me, her whisper is so faint I barely make it out. "I just..."

"What was that?" I lean closer, and she takes a breath that rattles like death.

"Just... wanted to make you... proud. Show you... show you I... can hold... my own."

I grit my teeth, that guilt all but choking me. She was one of the first to ever swear allegiance to me. She's been with the Reapers since the beginning. I was never gonna give her what she wanted from me, not on a personal level, but I damn sure appreciate and value her loyalty to what I've built.

"I am proud of you, Payton," I tell her. "Always have been."

Her smile looks more like a grimace, and she reaches for my face, her fingers sticky with blood and as cold as ice. They tremble, dragging over my cheek, and I grip her hand and hold it there.

She's weak as shit, but when she tugs against my grip, obviously wanting me to come closer, I let her pull me down to murmur in my ear, telling me what she and Luis found out from the guy they went after. Telling me like she thinks she has to, like I've gotta know before she goes.

I don't want selfless last words from her. I want her to hold the fuck on.

I shush her, pulling back and smoothing her blood-matted hair back from her face, pressing even harder on her chest wound. "It's okay. Don't worry about that now. Just stay with me, and we'll get you to Shane. It's all gonna be okay."

I keep repeating it, but when I meet Logan's eyes in the

rearview mirror, I see the truth we all know reflected in his bleak gaze. None of this shit is gonna be okay. And Payton—

"Oh god," Riley whispers, her voice thick with emotion and her hand, resting on my shoulder, the only warmth in the whole fucking world. She's staring down at Payton, and Payton's staring up at the roof of the Escalade, eyes open and lifeless.

She's gone.

20

RILEY

MY HEART CLENCHES as I look down at Payton. I've never seen a dead body up close and personal, but that's not really what I'm thinking about. I never liked her, but seeing her bloody and limp like this—knowing she's gone—isn't something I'd ever wish on anyone.

That's what I'm thinking about. That she *could* be anyone. This dead girl who was just trying to prove herself, trying to make a mark in the dangerous, deadly world we're all trying so hard to survive, isn't so different from my sister. It could have been Chloe. Or me.

Maddoc's jaw is clenched so tight it looks made of stone, and while I already know he's a master of staying calm in the face of chaos, a leader who's not ruled by emotions, he's obviously affected by this.

I'm not jealous. I know there was nothing personal between them, and that even if there had been, it would have had nothing to do with me. No, what I feel right now is a different kind of ache.

I wish I could take this pain away from him.

He finally lets go of her hand, laying it out over her chest, then passes his hand over her face to close her eyes. No one says a word until we get back to the house.

Maddoc looks up when Logan stops in the driveway with the engine still idling. An unfamiliar car is already parked there, and several more that followed us from where the shootout went down pull up and park at the curb.

"You gonna pull into the garage?" Maddoc asks, his brow creasing.

"No," Logan says as Dante twists around in the passenger seat, his face as serious as I've ever seen it.

"Nah, Maddoc," Dante adds. "You go in and deal with what you have to. We'll take care of the... of Payton."

Maddoc shakes his head. "Payton is my responsibility. I'll—"

Dante reaches back and squeezes his shoulder. "No, Madd. Let us handle it. This ain't on you."

Maddoc looks like he's about to argue again, and I know damn well he can't be used to taking orders from others, but after a moment, he relents. He knows just like I do that Logan and Dante aren't defying him. Maddoc's still in charge, but they're his family. They're allowed to share some of his burden.

I meet Dante's eyes for a moment, and he gives me a small, subdued smile. Then he pulls his shirt over his head and hands it to me before jerking his head toward the door, clearly wanting me to follow Maddoc.

I nod, a cold shiver wracking my body as I gratefully take his shirt and slip it over my head, knotting it at my waist. I'd all but forgotten that I used my own to try and stop Payton's bleeding. I don't want it back. Being surrounded by Dante's lingering scent, the oversized shirt still warm from the heat of his body, is comforting in a way that I really fucking need right now.

The Escalade pulls away, Logan and Dante driving off with Payton's body. By the time I head into the house after Maddoc, several other gang members have already piled out of the other cars too.

They follow us into the house.

"This was West Point?" I ask, my stomach tight as I instinctively move closer to Maddoc.

His jaw clenches again. "Yes," he says tightly.

I already figured that much from what I overheard as we drove across town, but having him confirm it stirs up a level of panic in my gut that almost makes me feel sick. I don't like the Reapers' plans for Chloe, but if West Point finds out what they know and gets their hands on her—

I can't stand to even think about it, but after seeing what just went down, I know for sure that I'll do whatever it takes to make sure that never happens.

Maddoc leads us all into the living room, and a tall, skinny guy covered in ink and wearing a pair of small, round glasses approaches him. Maddoc's eyes flick down to the large black bag the man's holding.

"We don't need it anymore, Shane."

The man nods, his face solemn. "I heard. I'm sorry." He holds up the bag. "Does anyone else...?"

"You can find out in a minute," Maddoc says tightly, then looks around and beckons to a dark-haired man. "Luis."

Luis comes over, his face wrecked. "I can't believe—"

"Report," Maddoc says, cutting him off harshly. "I need details. What the fuck happened? Why the hell were you and Payton over near Cliffton in the first place?"

Luis breaks out in a cold sweat, but to his credit, he doesn't cower. "Payton got in touch this morning. She said she had a lead, something to help after what happened with Troy."

"So you're saying this was all Payton's idea?" Maddoc demands.

Luis's naturally olive-toned skin goes pale. "I didn't mean, I'm not trying to, I mean, it was hers, but, uh..."

The man's clearly uncomfortable blaming a dead woman, but Maddoc just waits out his stuttering, his face devoid of all emotion now. Finally, once Luis stutters into silence, Maddoc speaks.

"You both chose to disobey my orders today. I'm going to ask you why, but first I need the details about what went down. What did Payton tell you that convinced you it was a good idea to ignore my explicit directive not to engage with West Point at this time?"

It takes Luis a second, but he finally manages to answer. "Payton said that we'd be able to retaliate for what they did to Troy. Find out why they went after him and what they got. She said if we could be the ones to bring you that information, it would, uh, it would be worth the—" He swallows hard, his Adam's apple bobbing, and finishes the final part in a strained whisper, "—the slap on the wrist."

A wave of pure fury crosses Maddoc's face, there and gone in the blink of an eye. "The slap on the wrist?" he repeats in a deadly calm voice. "Is that what you call today?"

Luis looks down. "Yeah. Fuck. I mean, no. I'm sorry. It wasn't supposed to go down this way."

Maddoc's face stays blank, his hands loose at his sides, but I'd bet money that there's not a person in the room who can't see his bottled rage just under the surface. He doesn't just value loyalty, he lives and breathes it, and with Payton literally dying in his arms, I can only imagine that the weight of responsibility he feels about her death must be crushing.

He sets it aside to get the facts he needs from Luis, and it's not my business at all, but I'm suddenly beyond grateful that Maddoc has Logan and Dante in his corner to bear some of that weight.

Any Reaper in his organization would gladly lay down their life for Maddoc the way Payton just did, but Maddoc needs more than that. He can't keep everything bottled inside forever, but I also get why he can't let the people who look to him as their leader see how he really feels. Not when they count on him the way they do.

Maddoc lets his brothers in though, in a way that I can't imagine he allows with anyone else. He lets them see all the shit that's stuffed out of sight, kept locked away under the mantle of leadership he wears so damn well.

And maybe, for just a moment out in the car, he let me see it too.

"How exactly did you two expect today to go?" he asks Luis in a tight voice.

Luis swallows. "Well, uh, Payton knew you wanted to know what Troy told West Point before they, before he, you know. While they had him. And when she found out there someone from higher up in McKenna's crew out and about without any protection this morning, she figured we could extract that info for you if we got him on his own."

"And how did you plan to get him to talk?"

"The same way those fuckers did to Troy."

"That's not what I tasked you with last night," Maddoc says evenly. "If I remember correctly, you were assigned to watch the warehouses near Broadway and Fifth, and Payton should have been taking care of some business for me over at Hillside."

Luis grimaces. "Yeah, boss. But she, uh, Payton thought this would be better."

"Better?" Maddoc repeats in a dangerously calm tone. "Is she part of my inner circle? Does she know all the irons I've got in the fire? Can—" He pauses, then goes on, correcting himself to the past tense. "Could she see the big picture? Was that Payton's call to make?"

Luis shakes his head, finally cowering. As he should, in my opinion. He fucked up by following her lead, and everyone in this room knows it.

"Tell me how it went down," Maddoc says, staring down at

Luis with an intensity of focus that makes me think he's committing every word to memory as Luis nods eagerly and starts rattling off details about who Payton was tipped off by, how she planned everything, and what happened once they captured the guy.

And, of course, how it all went to shit, because he hadn't been on his own after all.

Maddoc keeps all emotion out of it as he dresses Luis down, and while I get what he's doing and why every man present needs to hear it, it hits me as he's talking that I don't know what my place is here. I guess I don't technically have one, but I... care.

I don't want to walk away even though I've got nothing to contribute here. And even though I stayed out of danger during all the shooting—stayed in the Escalade because when Maddoc told me to, his walls came down, just for a second, just long enough for me to see that he *needed* me to—I still feel raw from everything that happened today.

It affected me, and my emotions are in turmoil.

Once Luis finishes talking, looking wrecked and guilty after laying out just how stupidly he acted even if it sounds like it really was all Payton's idea in the first place, Maddoc addresses the whole room, taking a moment to make eye contact with every Reaper as he speaks. "Every single one of you swore your allegiance to me. You did it for a reason, and I take those oaths seriously. But make no mistake, I *am* your leader. I run the Reapers. When you go behind my back, this is the kind of shit that happens. Is that clear?"

They all murmur their assent, and Maddoc turns back to Luis.

"You fucked up, and we lost one of our own. There will be consequences for today's shit show. Consequences to our entire organization for the escalation with West Point, and consequences for you, personally."

Luis swallows hard, but straightens his shoulder and nods. "Whatever I've gotta do."

Maddoc's jaw clenches again, but then he relaxes it. "Blood for blood. We'll take care of it at the Yauger building, and then you'll be doing perimeter runs until further notice, the midnight shift." He pauses. "Once Shane clears you."

Luis doesn't argue, and I can only guess that "blood for blood" means some kind of... physical punishment. Which of course has me thinking of the "consequences" Maddoc gave me when I was the one who fucked up. Not that whatever punishment he's just assigned Luis will be anything like that, obviously, but still, I've got no doubt that he belted me for the same reason he's being hard on the young Reaper.

Because Maddoc feels responsible.

Because he cares.

Because he really is a good leader. The kind who deserves all the loyalty he gets.

Before everyone files out, Maddoc tasks them all with spreading the word throughout the organization.

"Every one of you needs to grow eyes in the back of your fucking heads," Maddoc says grimly. "What went down today is all on West Point for grabbing Troy first, but McKenna will take any excuse to escalate, so be extra careful and vigilant out there from now on."

"How about we just wipe out the weasels once and for all, so we don't have to worry about that shit anymore?" one of the Reapers suggests.

Maddoc pins him with a hard stare. "How about you follow my fucking orders? And right now, those orders are not to go after West Point. Not yet. It's my job to know when, where, and how to take the fight to them, and that's not today."

There's a little bit of grumbling, but none of them argue.

That's clearly not good enough for Maddoc, though.

"No one pulls any more Lone Ranger shit, is that clear?" he demands. "No one else acts without my say so."

This time, they all agree more forcefully, and I stay out of the way as they finally leave. Maddoc stands like a statue, rigid and tense as he watches everyone file out, but the moment the door closes behind the last of them his shoulders slump.

One hand goes to the back of his neck, massaging the tension there. I know it's not something he'd ever let himself do in front of his people, and even though he hasn't said a word to me, isn't looking my way at all, I know that he knows I'm here.

Which means he's letting me see him like this.

He's letting his guard down, now that it's just the two of us.

I swallow down a lump in my throat, fighting with my emotions. We've got so much fucking baggage between us, but seeing Maddoc so wrecked, so obviously hurting, makes my heart ache.

I'm not supposed to care about him. He's supposed to be my enemy. But I just can't see him that way right now. I want to help.

He sighs, his hand falling away from the back of his neck, and it hits me hard when I realize that it still has Payton's blood on it. Not just his hands. It's all over him.

I go into the kitchen and wet a towel with warm water, not letting myself think too hard about why it feels so right to do this.

Maddoc hasn't moved. He seems dazed and a bit out of it, and I can't blame him.

"Riley?" he rasps out, when I reach for one of his hands and start wiping the blood off. "What are you doing?"

I turn the hand I'm holding over, carefully running the damp towel between each finger. "I'm cleaning you up."

I know damn well it's not what he's really asking, but it's all I've got.

"Why do you care?" he asks after a moment, making no move to stop me.

I've got no answer at all to that one, so I just push his sleeves back and keep removing the blood, then go on to his other hand.

"Fucking Payton," he whispers, his hand spasming in mine, like it wants to make a fist.

I smooth it back out, straightening his fingers and gently wiping the blood off his palm. "It wasn't your fault, Maddoc."

"Everything that happens with my people is my fault."

His tone is harsh, hurting, but he doesn't pull his hand away.

I look up at him. There's blood on his chin too. I wipe it away. "*This* wasn't your fault."

Those mesmerizing eyes of his blaze down at me, the gray at the edges of his irises so dark it almost looks black. Then he blinks and looks away, his hand—the one I'm still holding—tightening around mine.

"I'm the leader. The one in charge. They rely on me. Follow me."

"They do," I agree, smoothing his hand open again and running the warm towel over it.

Maddoc swallows. "She fucked up, they both did, but she thought she was doing it for me. Even at the end..."

"I saw the way she looked at you. That's not your fault, either."

His hands are clean, but I don't stop running the towel over them. I can't.

"I knew she had a crush on me," he says in a low voice, staring down like he's mesmerized by the slow, gentle circles I'm rubbing on his skin too. "I should have shut that shit down, but I figured it was harmless and I was fucking wrong. She was trying to impress me."

I don't know what to say. At least, not anything I haven't

already tried to tell him. He's right about all of it. But it's still not his fault.

"You were there for her," I remind him. "You were with her at the end. She wasn't alone. That means something."

Maddoc barks out a harsh laugh, his hands tightening on mine again. "Does it? Because I never wanted her like that. The only one I want is—"

He breaks off, and when our eyes meet, my heart lurches, all the raw emotion I've been fighting, denying, right there in his eyes too. He's laid bare to me, letting me see what I know down to my soul no one else does, and it means everything.

We've both made mistakes, but life is too short, and right now, for this small moment at least, there's nothing but truth between us. I drop the towel and go up on my toes.

And then I kiss him.

21

RILEY

I HALF EXPECT Maddoc to shove me away. After all, I shot him just a few days ago, and the only other time I've voluntarily been in his arms was tainted by lies and betrayal. But he doesn't. He does the opposite, banding his arms around me and locking me against him with a groan that sounds like it claws its way up from the center of his soul.

Like he *can't* let go.

Like I'm his anchor.

"Riley," he mutters against my lips, his hands roaming my body and leaving a trail of pure heat in their wake.

"Yes," I say, even though it wasn't really a question.

He tugs my hair, tipping my head back, and I press even closer, moaning into his mouth. Flattening my breasts against his hard chest so I can feel his heart beating against mine, proving we're both alive.

The intoxicating flavor of desperation in his kisses tells me he needs this too. We stumble backward, but I only realize we've careened into the living room when we bump into the couch Dante fucked me on once.

The reminder has my body flushing with even more desire,

and I throw my head back, giving Maddoc access to suck on my throat, lick the desperation off my skin, bite and mark and claim as much of me as he wants. I need every single thing he can give me right now, and I want to be everything he needs too.

He lifts me onto the end of the couch, perching my ass on its arm and yanking at my clothes, tearing through what he doesn't have the patience to remove and tossing the scraps aside until I'm completely naked.

I don't even try to help, not with all the possessive, dominating energy pouring off him. It's hot as fuck and exactly what I'm craving.

"Need this," he mutters, his eyes glued to my pussy.

"God. Me too," I pant, then yelp and almost tumble backward when he slings my legs over his shoulder.

He growls, low and dark, and catches my hips, locking me in place with a grip tight enough to bruise.

It's fucking perfect. Heat shoots to my core, and when he buries his face between my legs like he's trying to suffocate himself, an orgasm rips through me without any warning.

"Oh fuck, shit, god, *Maddoc*."

He groans, but doesn't even pretend to come up for air. It's like he wants to drown in me.

Or else fucking kill me.

"Fucking delicious," he mutters, sending shivers through me when he moves his head back and forth, rubbing the rough stubble on his jaw against my most sensitive flesh.

He breathes in the scent of my arousal, then laps it up, making my breath hitch and my body squirm.

I'm still shaking a little from the force of my orgasm, my clit swollen and hyper sensitive, when he attacks it again, demanding and rough this time.

"Fuck," I gasp, grabbing his head even though I'm not sure if I want to push him away or grind against his face to draw it out.

Maddoc doesn't give me a choice, eating me out like he's starving for it. Using his mouth like a weapon of mass destruction as he licks and sucks, bites and thrusts, forcing me to come again.

And then *again*.

It's too much, but as the aftershocks rip through me, he just growls something against my clit that I can't understand and then shoves two fingers into my pussy, fucking me with them rough and hard while he sucks on my aching nub until I scream.

"That's it, baby. Fuck yeah. Give me more."

"Oh god, I can't... Maddoc, please," I pant, pulling at his hair. Trying to get him to stop.

He doesn't. He just groans and pulls me even closer, drawing it out like melted taffy, twisting the pleasure into something dark and decadent that hovers right on the border of pain.

"More," he demands, like a man not just obsessed, but possessed.

But my body is already trembling from overstimulation, and I can't come again. I fucking *can't*.

I don't even realize I've said that out loud until Maddoc mutters, "Yes you can."

His voice is deep and low, vibrating against my pussy in a way that sends me over the edge all over again.

"Oh fuck, fuck, *fuck*," I gasp, riding it out because he gives me no other choice.

"That's right, butterfly," he purrs, turning his head to press a hot, open-mouthed kiss against my inner thigh. "You're primed for it now. Almost ready to take my cock."

I shake my head, but the way my pussy clenches tight, my inner muscles rippling enough to send a jolt of pleasure to my core that has me crying out all over again, tells me I'm lying to myself. There's no way in hell I should even *want* to be fucked now, but when Maddoc surges to his feet, pulling my legs wider apart and shoving his pants down, I can't deny the truth.

I don't just want it. I need it.

But not while he's still wearing clothes stained with Payton's blood.

"Off," I demand, pushing his shirt up to expose rock-solid abs and the twisting, dark lines that form the base of the tattoo spanning his chest.

I splay my hands over his heated skin and he bites off a curse, his muscles rippling under my palms.

"This what you want?" he asks, staring down at me with burning eyes as he tugs the shirt over his head and tosses it aside. "You want nothing but skin between us, baby?"

I meet his stare and hold it, then lean forward and drag my tongue down the line of his six pack. He already knows I do. But instead of pushing my head down and making me take the thick cock bumping my chin like I expect him to, he surprises me by yanking me to my feet and kissing me hard, his hard length throbbing against my stomach.

He tastes like my pleasure, and I grab his shoulders, my knees giving out.

"Fuck, I can't get enough," he groans into my mouth, locking his arm around me to hold me in place... then fucking devouring me.

I'm just as hungry for him, kissing him back with a raw craving that feels almost feral, but when one of my hands brushes over the rough line of stitches in his shoulder—the aftermath of the bullet wound I put there when I was aiming for his heart—I freeze, a surge of conflicting emotions threatening to swamp me.

I shudder, and Maddoc pulls back and grabs my chin, staring down into my eyes.

"Fuck," I whisper, not at all sure what I mean by that.

My eyes start to burn, but I can't look away.

"No," he finally says after a minute, and before I can ask what he's denying—what it was he saw on my face—his mouth crashes back into mine, and I'm fucking lost.

Or maybe found.

The way he dominates all my senses grounds me back in the moment, my mind emptying of all the shit that I don't know how to deal with yet. My body takes over, driven by pure instinct and a primal need that frees me to let out all my emotions, raw and uncensored.

Maddoc hauls my body, and it's all the permission I need to let go. I bite at him, drown in his taste and claw at his back, and he takes everything I have and gives it right back with a brutal passion born from the same desperate need for something that neither of us is ready to name yet.

"Please, fuck, do it," I gasp, my pussy is slick, wet, and swollen from what he's already put it through, but I still ache for what he promised me.

He groans and gives it to me, lifting me into position without lifting his mouth from mine, then shoving inside me in one ruthless thrust that has me screaming for him all over again.

"Yeah," he grunts, all his muscles standing out in stark relief as he starts fucking me on the edge of the couch, every thrust rough and relentless and exactly what I need. *"This."*

A moan rips from my throat, and I'm coming on his cock before I even have a chance to catch my breath. He fucks me all the way through it and then pulls out and turns me over, bending me over the arm of the couch and holding me there.

He hasn't come yet, and I fully expect to be impaled. I *want* it. But instead, I feel a callused hand smooth over my ass while he uses the other to pin my wrists behind my back.

"Thought my marks would last a little longer," he says, his shaft—still as hard as raw steel and wet from my pussy—throbbing with heat as it rubs against the back of my thighs.

Then he spanks me.

I gasp, the sharp sting a perfect counterpoint to the syrupy exhaustion from all the orgasms he's wrung out of me. He does it again.

"Fuck, Maddoc," I whisper, my body feeling like it doesn't even belong to me anymore. Like I'm both disconnected from it and drowning in the overload.

"You look damn good in red," he says, grabbing one of my ass cheeks in a rough, possessive grip. Squeezing. Kneading. "Seeing the stripes my belt left on you that night had my cock in pain." He spanks me again. "I got so fucking hard for you. And the way you sounded..."

His palm cracks into my ass again, and a seductive darkness swirls inside me as the fresh pain twists around the languid heat left over from coming so hard, so many times in a row, making me whine.

"Yeah," Maddoc grunts. "Like that. I could tell this kind of shit turns you on when I used my belt to you."

"No," I whisper, already arching back in a silent request for more.

Maddoc's low chuckle calls me out for lying, and then he gives me what we both know I really want, kicking my legs apart and lighting me up with a hard flurry of spanking that leaves me gasping, overheated and aching for him.

"Asshole," I say when he stops, my thighs trembling.

"Oh, is that where you want me to fuck you? In that sweet little asshole? Tempting, butterfly." He tightens his grip on my wrists and thrusts his hand between my legs, palming my pussy. Then he shoves two fingers deep inside me as he leans over my back to whisper in my ear. "*This* is what I want right now, but maybe next time."

"Fuck," I pant, too lust addled to get more words out. And then I stop trying, because he removes his fingers and fills me with his cock again, driving in hard and not stopping. Fucking into me like he really is possessed. Like he's reached his breaking point and is determined to find mine too.

It's here. Right fucking *here*, with my clit grinding against the couch and my ass on fire from his spanking. I know he's close, I can feel it in the harsh grip he's got on my hips and the pounding force he takes me with, and everything—*everything*—disappears. I want to be fucked like this forever.

And then he snarls out my name, and it pushes me over the edge.

"*Maddoc*."

He comes with a hoarse shout right after I do, his cock swelling inside me as he grinds against my ass and unloads everything he's got. It goes on forever, waves of pleasure that draw out into a long moment of silence in the aftermath that feels deceptively peaceful. I'm barely in my body, so fucked out —exhausted and sated—that it feels like I'm floating above myself.

But of course, like all good things, it comes to an end.

Maddoc pulls out, the loss of his cock followed by a warm flood of cum that drips down my leg, an undeniable reminder that the messy world is still right here, waiting for us both.

I push myself up from the couch and turn to face him, but he's already moving away, eyes shuttered and expression locked down completely as he uses his shirt to wipe off his cock, his eyes sliding down my body and then looking away.

"You should get up to your room. The guys will be home soon."

His cool dismissal snuffs out everything warm inside me, and I stiffen. But it's for the best. We obviously both needed what just happened, but nothing has actually changed just because we finally fucked without any deception between us.

Nothing except how raw and vulnerable I feel.

"Thanks," I say, snatching up my clothes and walking past him.

I'm not thanking him for the fuck, but for the reminder. There are walls between us for a lot of reasons, and I quickly put mine back up and keep them there as I shower and wash up, my body far easier to clean than the mess of thoughts and emotions inside me.

"Shit," I whisper, finally letting just a few of them out as the hot water pours down on me. I lean against the wet tile and squeeze my eyes closed, safe to come unraveled—at least a little bit—in the privacy of the steam and silence.

Fuck. I can't believe I let that happen.

I soap up my hand and move it between my legs again, even though I've already washed away all traces of his cum. I'm on birth control, so at least *that's* not an issue, but still. That level of raw connection and intimacy isn't something I ever meant to let happen with him again. It definitely isn't safe for my heart.

I can't seem to keep things straight anymore, not with my feelings about these men getting constantly tangled, twisted and knotted into something impossible to unravel.

It's almost like we're right back where we started. They're helping me against West Point again, all of us working to try and keep Chloe safe from the brutality of Austin McKenna, and it's seductively easy to fall back into old patterns. To imagine that the Reapers are actually on my side, the way it started to feel like they were before we got Chloe back the first time... and to imagine that I'm on their side too.

That they need me, and will be there for me when I need them.

That I *see* them, and it's my place to be a comfort and support to them.

That the connection between each of us is just as deep and true as it felt today.

But how can I be on their side when they've already betrayed me? And how can I ever let myself believe they're on mine, when I already know that they're planning on doing it again?

"Easy answer," I tell myself, straightening up and turning the handle with a decisive twist, replacing the false, comforting warmth of the water with an icy blast that brings me to my senses. "I can't."

22

RILEY

I'm shivering as I step out of the shower, but at least my head feels a little clearer. Clear enough that, when I hear voices downstairs and realize that Dante and Logan are back, I don't let messy emotions get in the way. The three of them are talking, and while I may not want to see Maddoc again right now, I do want to know what's going on.

I need to—more importantly, Chloe needs me to—so I quickly dress again and head downstairs.

As usual with these three, they're clustered around the kitchen island when I walk in. They all go quiet when I walk in the room, and my stomach drops.

"What happened?" I ask, the question making Maddoc's jaw clench in a familiar tell.

Whatever it is, it's not good.

I steel myself, making eye contact with each of them. "Just tell me. Is it about Chloe?"

Maddoc's the one who answers. He looks less wrecked than he did before, but his face is just as closed off and emotionless as when he dismissed me after we fucked.

"Payton managed to get some information out of the West Point guy she and Luis targeted," he says.

I flash back to the moment before she died, when she pulled him down to whisper her last words to him. Was that what she took the time to say? I'd figured it had been a last gasp declaration of her feelings, and the fact that it may not have been—that she may have been looking out for the good of the gang right up to the end—makes me think a little more highly of her. She obviously had her faults, but the Reapers clearly have a code of ethics that really does set them apart from other gangs in Halston.

"What did he tell them?" I ask, wiping my suddenly sweating hands on the sides of my pants. I know "tell" is a euphemism. Payton and Luis had to have extracted the information the same way West Point got whatever it was they wanted out of Troy.

But I don't care. If that makes me a bad person, then fuck morality. It may not be smart to let myself think I'm on the Reapers' side, but I'm sure as shit not on *West Point's*.

Still, I send up a silent prayer that Maddoc's not about to tell me Austin McKenna has my sister again.

He doesn't.

"West Point knows Chloe is alive, and just like we figured, that got them curious about why."

"Madd's mobilized our whole organization, trying to get her back," Dante adds grimly. "We tried to keep it on the down low, but that wasn't ever gonna last for long."

"So they know we're looking for her?"

The three of them exchange looks, but this time, it's Logan who answers. "Worse. They found out she's the heiress to William Sutherland's estate."

"Fuck," I whisper, my stomach cramping with tension. *This* is what I actually need to remember. That I can't trust them because, even though they're not lying to me about their intentions anymore, their intentions are to use my sister, and her money, like a pawn in their fucking gang war.

Except Logan's right. This really is worse. With both gangs competing for control of Chloe and both sides having already shown how ruthlessly they'll attack each other, her chances of staying safe out there on her own have just dropped hard.

"Hey," Dante says, walking over and tipping my chin. "It's not all bad news, princess. It's not like McKenna's got any more leads than we do."

I give him a wan smile. "An even playing field? That's what you're going with?"

"Who said anything about even?" he asks with a lazy smile, holding my gaze. "We've got you on our side."

He's just trying to reassure me... and it works.

A little.

I let out a breath I didn't realize I was holding, some of the tension leaking out of me. It *is* bad news, and I know I won't be able to trust the Reapers once we find my sister, but right now I guess we really are all on the same side.

I nod to let Dante know I'm okay, and he drops his hand but stays close to me, his shoulder bumping into mine as the talk turns back to what I assume they were discussing before I walked in: the implications of what went down today.

"West Point is becoming more of a threat every time we turn around," Maddoc says, his eyes catching mine as guilt stabs through me.

I shake it off, though. If they'd stuck to their word in the first place, Chloe never would have had to run, and recent events wouldn't have happened.

Troy and Payton would still be alive.

"It's not your fault," Maddoc says, both the words and the hint of softness in his tone catching me off guard. Then his face tightens up again and there's nothing soft about him at all as he continues. "This has escalated far beyond the shit they were pulling before, and we all know what will happen if they get a hold of Chloe."

213

I don't know... but I can imagine.

"It'll be bad," Dante says. "So let's not let it come to that, yeah?"

Maddoc nods. "Now that McKenna knows how valuable she is, he's going to make it personal. Especially after the shootout."

My stomach twists. "But they won't hurt her, right?"

"They're not gonna be the ones who find her, princess."

"Right." I huff out a breath, telling myself I believe it. "But I'm just saying, if they're after her money too, they'll need her, um..."

"Alive," Logan says flatly.

It's what I meant, but it's not reassuring. I already know Austin McKenna is a sadist, and given his history with Maddoc and the fact that Troy was technically still "alive" when West Point got done with him too, the idea that the West Point leader might try to find a way to have his cake and eat it too unnerves me.

"Is he going to retaliate for what happened today? Would he use my sister to send you another... message?"

Three sets of grim eyes meet mine, and my heart leaps up into my throat when, instead of an answer, a rapid, staccato knock sounds at the front door.

I jump, and all three men reach for the weapons they keep on themselves, swinging around to face the front of the house.

"Logan, Dante," Maddoc says, exchanging loaded looks with his seconds. They all nod as if they've actually just had an entire conversation, and Dante takes my arm as Logan flanks me on the other side, all of us moving toward the door.

All three men keep their bodies angled in front of mine, and while none of them have actually drawn their weapons, it's clear that they're just as on edge as I am... and that for some reason, they're acting protective of me.

Maddoc answers the door. A man I've never seen before

waits on the other side, but apparently I'm the only one who doesn't know who he is, because the tension in the room ratchets all the way up to the red zone.

The man doesn't smile. "Mr. Gray," he says, inclining his head slightly to Maddoc. "They sent me with a message for you."

"West Point?" I blurt, even though this man isn't wearing one of those gaudy gang rings and looks nothing like the goons Austin McKenna brought to my apartment when they took Chloe. This man looks more... polished.

He tilts his head to the side, looking me over with an assessing gaze. "And you are?"

"No one," Maddoc growls as all three of the Reapers close ranks around me, their big bodies crowding me back so quickly that I almost feel claustrophobic. "Come inside. If you've got a message from The Six, it doesn't need to be broadcast to the whole fucking neighborhood."

"No," the visitor says in a bland tone that still feels loaded with layers that I don't understand. "It doesn't. You know how little they care for public attention."

The Six. I've heard the name referenced before, but I've got no idea who they are. All three Reapers obviously do, and the energy between them gets so strained when the man drops that comment that I'm surprised no one snaps.

They usher him inside without another word, and as soon as the door closes behind him, he gets down to business.

"The Six know what happened today."

"The shootout," Maddoc says grimly.

It's not a question, but the man nods anyway. "It was very—"

"Messy," Dante throws in.

The man blinks, his expression not changing in the face of the apologetic grin Dante throws in.

"Public," he says after a moment. "It drew attention, and The Six aren't happy about that."

The way all three Reapers go unnaturally still at that makes me think it's a threat, and I bristle.

My go-to response to being pissed off or scared is to snap someone's fucking head off, but before I can, Logan and Dante both press their bodies against mine, sandwiching me between them, almost as if they could somehow tell I was about to let loose with a snarky reminder that obviously no one is *happy* about what happened today.

I take a breath and force myself to relax. Whatever's going on here, it isn't my fight. I'm not a Reaper, and obviously I've got no right—or any reason—to feel protective of the men who betrayed me.

No matter what my heart tries to tell me.

"There will be a meeting," the guy representing The Six says, giving a time and a place. Tomorrow, somewhere I've never heard of downtown.

"Just us?" Maddoc asks, no emotion in his voice at all.

"West Point is being summoned as well."

Maddoc nods. "We'll be there."

"Of course you will," the visitor says with a cold smile, then he turns and lets himself out, and the tension snaps—along with any pretense of Maddoc being unaffected—with the string of low, vicious curses that Maddoc lets loose with as soon as the door closes behind him.

23

MADDOC

Once The Six's representative leaves, I pinch the bridge of my nose and allow myself one breath—no, two—to get my shit back under control after letting my temper explode. Then I refocus, my emotions shoved to the background and my mind racing ahead as I mentally play out possible ramifications of getting on their radar like this.

I sigh. None of them are good, but since I've built an entire organization that counts on me to lead it, I'm gonna have to figure out how best to handle the newest shit sandwich we've been served up and still come out on top.

And luckily, I don't have to figure it out alone.

"We've got twenty-four hours until the meet," I point out, meeting the eyes of my seconds. My brothers. "Let's make sure we've got everything in order so we make a good showing. Your thoughts?"

"Those fucking weasels," Dante spits out, his eyes dark with an uncharacteristic anger that he doesn't usually let show. "It never would have come to an open shootout if Payton hadn't been retaliating for a move they made first. *They* started this shit by killing Troy."

"Over Chloe," Riley says quietly, her face pale.

Dante immediately tamps down on his rage.

"Nah, princess," he says, bumping her shoulder with a little smile. "None of this is on you or your sister. McKenna's a stupid jackass who didn't even know what he was hoping to get when he took Troy. The Six wouldn't be up in our business at all if it weren't for how fucking reckless he is."

I grit my teeth. He's not wrong. And yeah, it pisses me the fuck off too.

"But you guys said West Point interrogated Troy to find out what—who—you were searching the city for," Riley argues in a tight voice. "And that's Chloe."

"Let's stay focused," I say sharply. I don't like hearing the worry and guilt in Riley's voice. Besides, we're getting off track, me included. I've long since learned that getting pissed off over Austin fucking McKenna is a waste of time. It's why I plan on destroying him... eventually. But right now, our priority is getting through this meeting with The Six.

Riley gives me a short, tight nod. "Fine."

I should leave it at that, but I don't. Something in me drives me to give her back the words she offered me earlier today too. "Dante's right. It really isn't your fault."

She smiles—a small one, but still enough to make something inside me unwind a little.

Then she looks away, and it tightens up again.

Dante lets out an explosive breath, running a hand through his chocolate-brown hair in frustration. "Not even a little bit your fault. McKenna set this train wreck in motion."

"The Six aren't going to care who started it," Logan says flatly. "They don't use their power to play mediator, trying to make everyone here in Halston get along. They use it to keep order."

Riley's brow crinkles. "So The Six are like, what... an enforcement group? Gang war police?"

"No," Logan says.

"I mean, sorta," Dante throws in with a shrug. "They do keep the various criminal elements here in Halston in line."

"And if our current conflict with West Point has drawn their ire," Logan adds, "it's bad."

"What kind of bad?" Riley asks, looking between the three of us.

My brothers look to me, silently questioning how deeply I'm willing to share our world with her. But at this point, there's no reason to keep or hide anything from her... and one very important reason to make sure she's well-informed.

Her safety.

Whether any of us intended it or not, Riley *is* part of our world now—and once we secure Chloe's inheritance, she'll continue to have ties to it forever. It's best she knows more about how Halston really operates.

"Are they a rival gang?" Riley presses.

"No," I tell her. "The Six are a lot bigger than just a gang. They came into power a couple years ago, and you could say they're sort of the royalty of the underworld of Halston. They keep order among the various criminal elements in the city."

"And they enforce that order strictly," Logan adds. "They don't interfere with how we operate or try to control every little thing that any one organization does, but they've got eyes everywhere and the power to make sure everyone stays in line."

My jaw starts to tic again. "And that no organization draws the kind of unwanted attention that can disrupt business."

"Do they... work with the police?" Riley asks, her brow furrowed. Then, because she's not just gorgeous, she's smart as hell, she immediately shakes her head. "No, of course they don't. Is that what that guy meant? That they don't like that the cops know what happened today?"

"Right," I say. "The Six know more about the dark underbelly of Halston than the police ever will, and they've made it clear that that's how they want to keep it."

Dante nods. "They don't give a shit about our war with West Point, but if they're calling both us and McKenna in to discuss it, then they're seriously pissed that it escalated to the point that it's drawn that kind of attention."

"What will they do? What are they like?" Riley asks, her gaze bouncing between Logan and Dante.

But not me.

She's avoiding my gaze.

I'm the one who deliberately put some distance between us after we fucked, so I'm not surprised that she's acting a bit closed off.

What surprises me is how much it bothers me.

"The Six keep to themselves," Logan tells Riley.

His dry delivery makes her laugh, even though I know Logan was just being factual as always.

"So you're saying none of you have actually met them?"

"Not yet," I say, my grim tone reminding us all that the clock is ticking. I turn the discussion to practical matters, then break up our little huddle once everyone knows what needs to get taken care of.

Dante and Logan head off, but when Riley tries to follow I catch her arm, stopping her.

She raises an eyebrow, her guarded expression silently asking me why.

Fuck if I know, but I have to say something, and what comes out of my mouth, surprising us both, is—

"Just wanted to thank you."

She stares up at me, and for the life of me, I can't read her expression this time at all.

Fair enough. Since I don't even know what the hell it is I'm thanking her for, or if that's even the right word for what I'm feeling right now, there's no real reason to expect I'd have some great insight into her frame of mind, either.

She holds my gaze, clearly waiting for more, but I don't think I can give it to her.

Not won't.

Can't.

All I know for sure is that I was in a rough place today, and she brought me back from the edge of that. I needed her, needed what we did, in a way that went deeper than I'm comfortable with. And yeah, I'm grateful for it, but gratitude isn't all I feel. I just don't have the words for the rest.

"Okay," Riley says quietly before I can find them.

She pulls free of my hold and slips away to return to her room, and I let her go. I don't have time to go all soft anyway. Hell, there's never a good time for that. Sienna taught me that one, loud and clear, and even if Riley seems different—

Nope.

I shut that shit down fast and head down the hall to my office, putting my focus on where it needs to be tonight. On shoring up our defenses to get out ahead of the West Point threat and doing whatever else I can come up with to make sure that when we walk into that meeting with The Six tomorrow, we don't just walk back out, but we come out on top.

I stare at the map on my wall, my mind spinning. I don't want to challenge The Six. But getting on The Six's bad side would put everything I've been building since the day I decided to not follow in my father's footsteps at risk.

Which is why I won't let it happen.

I scrub a hand over my face, then get to work. But despite my best intentions, amid all my focus—the planning, the strategy, the hustle—I can't for the fucking life of me seem to stop thoughts of Riley from slipping in too.

"Fuck, Madd, you look like shit. Did you get any sleep at all?"

Dante grins at me and I flip him off, gratefully reaching for the coffee Logan hands me when I walk into the kitchen the next morning. We're all up early, but they're just as aware as I am of how much we need to do today to make sure our house is in order, so none of us linger once we've brought each other up to speed on the night's developments.

I'm not the only one who barely got any sleep.

Logan stays at the house, holing up in his room to continue coordinating the search for Chloe and Dante heads out to make the rounds of some of our allies, shoring up those relationships to ensure that whatever comes down tonight, we're in a position of strength to deal with it.

I spare a brief thought for Riley, but then dismiss it. She'll keep herself occupied for the day, I'm sure, and I can't afford distractions today. I need to fortify our territory against West Point. Go out and personally see to it that our perimeter is solid and my organization is secure.

It takes me all fucking day, and it's worth it.

When I get back to the house that evening, it's time to head out for the meeting with The Six. I'm going on a day and a half without sleep, but it's not my first rodeo and I'm more than capable of pushing through, especially with so much on the line.

"I'm driving," I tell Logan when his eyes stray toward the Audi. I know damn well that being in control helps him stay centered and focused, but tonight he'll just have to deal.

Luckily, he knows me just as well as I do him—and knows all the reasons I need to stay in control right now—so he just nods and heads to the passenger side of the Escalade without any argument, Dante and Riley taking the backseat.

I glance in the rearview mirror as I start up the engine, meeting Riley's defiant gaze as I prepare to pull out of the garage. The light catches, sparkling. She's switched out the blue jewel she had in her nose earlier for another one. I liked the way the other one picked up the vibrant color she's got in her hair, but this one—a bad-ass-looking little black diamond skull—definitely suits her.

Kind of like she suits *us*.

Dante clears his throat, and I jerk my eyes away from her whiskey-brown gaze and get us on the road. It's only once we're halfway to downtown that I realize she never actually asked if she could come tonight. And that it didn't even occur to me to stop her.

"Fuck," I mutter, scrubbing a hand over my face.

"Problem, Madd?" Dante asks from the back seat, leaning forward.

I shake my head, but the real answer is... maybe.

Despite everything, I'm getting too fucking used to having Riley around, and bringing her tonight probably isn't the right move since she's an unplanned variable. Not to mention that she'll be a hell of a lot safer if she stays off The Six's radar.

What's done is done though, because I'm not turning around.

And if I'm honest—even if it bites us in the ass later—I'm not sorry she's here.

Shit was different with Sienna. Dante and Logan and I each have different strengths and weaknesses, but we always work in sync and always have. Except when she was around. She always managed to throw our rhythm off even before she betrayed me with McKenna, but having Riley here is different. Riley may have shot me, but Dante's right. I respect her reasons for that, and instead of throwing the three of us off, it's more like she balances us out.

That's not an excuse to put her in danger though, so I'll just have to make sure we don't.

"Traffic's bad heading into downtown," Logan says, looking up from his phone. "You'll probably want to take the bridge on Le Grand."

I nod and make the adjustment.

"So what is this place we're headed to, The Six's headquarters or something?"

"Not sure where *that* would be," Dante answers Riley with a low chuckle. "They keep their details pretty private, and for good reason. But I have heard that they do a lot of business out of Saraven when they need to have meetings on neutral territory, so sure, I guess you could call it the public version of their headquarters."

"You've never been? Really? None of you?"

I shake my head, and Logan doesn't bother answering.

"Nah," Dante says. "The place is pretty upscale. A members-only club that's pretty exclusive about who they let in the door, and that's most definitely by invitation only."

"And those invitations aren't necessarily the kind you want to get," Logan says drily.

Riley laughs, but I hear the nerves behind it. Probably why she's asking so many questions.

"And it's downtown?" she presses on. "Is that, um, does that territory belong to The Six?"

This time, Dante's the one who laughs. "All of Halston belongs to The Six, princess. But for tonight, consider it neutral territory. Not ours. Not West Point's. And not anywhere even McKenna would be stupid enough to start anything, no matter how this all goes down. Not right under the nose of The Six."

"So, you're saying it's safe."

Logan goes still in the seat next to me, and I meet Dante's eyes in the rearview mirror again. I've got no doubt that they can hear the nerves in her voice just like I can... and that all three of us are having the same thought.

Dante's the one who voices it.

"Uh, *safe* ain't a word I would use for tonight," he says after a beat. "Or ever. Not when The Six are already pissed off like this. But—"

"But you'll be safe, butterfly," I cut in. "You're under our protection. We'll make sure of it."

"Thank you," she whispers, finally going silent. There's really not much to say, nothing else we can prepare for until we find out what they want with us.

Once we arrive at the club, we pass through a large, luxurious space that reminds me a bit of pictures I've seen of upscale speakeasies from the twenties. It's massive, with a dining area and bar, a lounge, and what looks like smaller private rooms spread around the space. Cocktail waitresses in form-hugging dresses serve a clientele that pretends not to see us as we're led down a corridor to a large room in the back, and once we enter, I've got no doubt at all who I'm looking at. We may not run in the same circles as The Six, but even with the way they work to stay behind the scenes when it comes to running Halston's criminal underground, each one of them has a reputation.

I nod in greeting, keeping Riley behind me as Dante and Logan spread out to either side. The Six are seated behind a long, ornate table on a raised dais, and it's not lost on me that there are no other chairs available. I don't give a shit about their power plays, though. I only care about their actual power.

And what the fuck it is that they plan on doing with it right now.

The well-dressed attendant who led us to the room backs out of it silently, but my attention is focused on the group ahead of me. No one knows enough about them to get an edge, but what I do know is that they own this city.

None of them say a word, all six of them giving us assessing looks, like they're taking our measure. Or else waiting for us to break.

I narrow my eyes. They're gonna be waiting a long damn time if that's what they're after. They called us here. They'll tell us why when they're ready. Until then, I settle in, giving them the same treatment right back.

The dark-haired woman with the laser-sharp blue eyes has got to be Ayla Fairchild. That would be clear even without the sleek prosthetic peeking out of her right sleeve. Marcus Constantine has the dual-tone eyes, one as brown and deep as Riley's, the other a mix between brown and light blue.

Ryland Bennett is dark and brooding and fucking jacked, covered in more ink than even Dante, but it's Theo Harrington who reminds me most of my laid-back brother from another mother. Theo has lighter hair and eyes, but they both share a certain charm that probably masks their deadlier side.

The fourth man is the most mysterious of The Six, the one I know the least about, and the other woman, with a stunning face, auburn hair, and a demeanor as cold as ice, has got to be Victoria Tatum.

Each of them is deadly in their own right from everything I've heard... but if any one of them threatens what's mine, I don't give a shit how much power they wield in this city, I'll do my best to take them down.

"Reapers," Marcus says in greeting, dipping his chin in a nod.

Another door opens before I can reply, spitting out McKenna, Sienna, and a half dozen low-rent goons flashing gold WPG rings across their knuckles. Without missing a beat, Marcus adds smoothly, "And the West Point Gang. Thank you both for coming."

"I always wanted to see the inside of this place," McKenna says, his eyes hooded and greedy as he looks around at the simple but obviously high-end furnishings.

Marcus's face drops the facade of warmth. "And now you have," he says crisply. He turns his attention back to me. "Anything from you before we begin, Gray?"

I hear him, but I can't respond. I can't tear my gaze away

from McKenna, not while something cold and furious is busy slithering down my spine, like the memory of Payton's last breath just grabbed a hold of it with icy fingers now that I'm in the same room with the fucker who caused her death.

When McKenna flicks his eyes toward me with an oily smirk, I clench my jaw, hit hard with a sudden, visceral need to return that particular favor.

"Maddoc Gray?" Marcus prompts, his voice muffled by the blood rushing through my ears.

My hands slowly curl into fists as I stare McKenna down, and for the first time in my life, I'm not sure if I can hold my shit together when I need to. And maybe I couldn't if I was alone... but I'm not.

As if they sense my rage—and how fucking close I am to doing something about it—Dante and Logan each move in toward my sides, closing ranks, and Riley rests a soft hand on my back, grounding me. It drains some of the fury away, reminding me why I'm here.

"Thank you for inviting us," I answer Marcus's question calmly, back in control again.

"I can't say it's a pleasure," he replies baldly, "but now that everyone's here, let me tell you why we asked you to come."

I nod. Bring it. They may be The Six, the power behind the city, and McKenna may have shown up with more muscle than sense in a useless show of power, but I don't need all that shit. Whatever it is that they're about to throw at me, all I'll ever need is my two brothers by my side to handle it.

My brothers... and Riley.

24

RILEY

ON THE DRIVE OVER, when Maddoc had referred to this group as Halston's underground "royalty," I figured he was just using the word for effect. Now I'm not so sure. There's definitely something regal and commanding about the four men and two women arrayed behind the deep mahogany table, and while they aren't actively doing anything threatening, the potential for danger is unmistakable. The air practically crackles with it.

It's all the more reason to keep my mouth closed and my eyes open until I can get a read on the situation.

"I'm Marcus Constantine," says the man who's done all the talking so far, his uniquely colored eyes resting heavily on first Maddoc, then on Austin McKenna, as he introduces himself. "And I'm sure you each know why you're here."

It's not a question, but Maddoc gives a single nod anyway.

Austin juts his chin out imperiously. "Yeah, we do. Your man said it was about the way the Reapers attacked us yesterday."

The asshole crosses his arms over his chest, his goons all smirking around him like they're actually stupid enough to think it's smart to bring that kind of attitude in front of people like this.

Maddoc doesn't react to Austin's attempt to shift the blame, but one of the women at the table—the one with dark hair and a prosthetic arm—sits up a little straighter, her blue eyes boring into the West Point leader.

"It sounds like you misheard," she tells him with a cold smile.

Austin makes a rude sound under his breath, and the body language of the men at the table is subtle but telling. They're protective of her, and three of the four react in a way that makes me wonder if she's playing them off each other.

"What Ayla means," Marcus says icily before Austin can get a word out, "is that we don't care which one of you attacked the other, or what it is you were fighting over. What we do care about is the attention you attracted."

"And your carelessness," one of the other men, the heavily inked one, adds. "You took your shit public and put the issue on the cops' radar."

"That's their fault," Austin snaps, flinging a hand and a death-like glare at us.

Maddoc keeps his cool and doesn't try to defend his actions, and I know instinctively that it's the right move. The other woman at the table, the stunning-looking one whose expression could have been carved from ice, confirms that instinct when she leans forward, staring at Austin McKenna like he's something she accidentally stepped in and needs to scrape off her shoe.

Austin's face turns red, but this time, he holds his tongue.

I don't care how intimidating the woman looks, I decide I like her.

"Did we ask whose fault it was?" she finally asks Austin.

No one waits for him to answer.

"Just because we don't usually get involved in street gang level shit," Marcus says, "it doesn't mean we're not keeping tabs on what happens. If you both want to keep operating your organizations here in our city, you'll need to start settling your disagreements more quietly."

"Understood," Maddoc says.

Austin scoffs, and six pairs of eyes zero in on him.

"I'm sure we can all agree that it would be bad for everyone if we have to get more involved than we have been, can't we?" Marcus asks with a smile that's a clear threat.

"You both need to keep better fucking control of your people," adds another of The Six.

Austin glares. "That Reaper bitch we took out came to Cliffton. To *our* territory. We had every right to go after her."

I didn't even like Payton, but I see red, my hands balling into fists so fast and hard that my nails carve bloody crescents into my palms. Before I can do something stupid, the first woman—Ayla—cuts Austin down with a single look. "We didn't bring you here to listen to your whining, and we don't care how you solve your differences."

She doesn't lean forward or raise her voice, but she utterly commands the room. She truly does look like a queen, and I can't even imagine what it must feel like to have your shit together the way she so obviously does.

"What we do care about is that you've now got Halston's finest crawling all over parts of the city that they don't need to be looking so closely at," she goes on, calmly eviscerating Austin's excuses and actually managing to shut the man up while I watch and learn. Or at least, I try to.

I'm no more inclined to take anyone's shit than Ayla is, but in contrast to her strong, regal bearing, my version of strength has always been more of the whatever-it-takes-to-get-by variety. I've always done what I had to do, but that generally means I'm operating minute by minute, always scrambling to carve out a place in the world for me and Chloe and constantly doing whatever I have to do to stay one step ahead of all the things that threaten to tear it down. Things like Austin McKenna.

I can't afford to let my rage at everything he's so intent on taking from me get the best of me—not right now, and not here on this neutral ground—so I block those thoughts out and focus on The Six, trying to get more of a feel for this group that the Reapers are being so carefully respectful of.

As soon as we find my sister, I'll find a way to get us both out of Halston and away from this fucked-up world The Six seem to rule, so it's not like figuring them out should matter to me... but I can't squash my curiosity. Especially when I realize that the vibe between Ayla and the three men I'd initially thought she might be playing off each other isn't that at all.

If I'm reading their body language right, it's more like she's actually *with* them. With all three of them.

I've never seen a relationship like that.

A heated frisson of excitement goes through me, and I try to tell myself it's because the men at that table are all hot as fuck in different ways so it's easy to see why Ayla would want to scratch an itch with any one of them. It's not really that, though. Reading body language is something I had to get good at when I was stripping, and what I see between the four of them makes it seem like there's more than just scratching an itch going on. A lot more.

I swallow hard, suddenly far too aware of the three Reapers and the protective stances they've all taken around me. The three men that there's no point denying I'm attracted to. That I have... feelings for.

Not that this is the time and place to dwell on that shit, obviously. Hell, there may never be a time or place. Admitting that my feelings are real—complicated and messy, but definitely real—doesn't change the fact that the three of them betrayed me. Or that they still want Chloe. Or that one of them plans on *marrying* her.

A sound escapes me, just a puff of pained breath since the thought hurts on a level I'm not at all prepared to deal with right now, but it really isn't the time or place, so when Dante flicks his gaze at me, a faint frown on his face, and Logan sways a little closer, I flinch away from the both of them and refocus on the reason we actually came.

"If you're not gonna interfere with how we carry out our business," Austin is saying to The Six in a belligerent tone, his goons bristling all around him like they really are more muscle than brain, "then why the fuck did you even want us to come here?"

"They already told us," Maddoc says without bothering to look over at him. "We attracted attention."

Ayla nods. "And if it happens again, we won't interfere." Her smile doesn't reach her eyes. "If your shit gets too out of control, we'll shut it down."

I can tell Austin wants to say something else stupid, but Maddoc speaks before he gets the chance. "Thank you for the warning."

Marcus gives him a hard look, like he's trying to figure out if Maddoc's being sarcastic or not, but whatever he sees on Maddoc's face must satisfy him, because after a moment he relaxes back in his seat.

"Take it to heart," he says in a clear dismissal.

The same elegantly clad hostess who escorted us through the club when we arrived shows up to lead us back out. Except this time, it's not *just* us. Austin, with Maddoc's ex hanging off his arm and all his goons trailing after him, leaves the building at the same time as we do, and if I thought the air back in that room with The Six felt dangerous, it's nothing compared to the tension and anger seething between our group and his. Everyone's blood is running high after all the violence that's burst out between the two gangs lately.

"Neutral ground," Logan murmurs almost inaudibly.

"It ain't neutral once we pass through the doors," Dante says just as we do that, pushing me behind him with a hard look on his normally easy-going face.

The three Reapers turn to face off with West Point on the sidewalk in front of Saraven and Austin McKenna signals to his men to spread out, blocking the way to our Escalade. Then he spits on the ground in front of Maddoc.

"You heard them," Maddoc says, his voice like sharpened steel. "We've got freedom to handle our shit however we need to. But not where it's gonna get attention."

Austin smiles like he mistakenly thinks bringing twice as many men as the Reapers gives him an edge. "Scared?"

"Biding my time," Maddoc corrects him with a dangerous smile of his own. Then the smile drops. "Now get the fuck out of our way."

Rage sweeps across Austin's face, and I'm sure the only reason they haven't already come to blows with the Reapers or started shooting at each other yet is that both gangs respect The Six's authority here. Even if we're not technically on neutral ground anymore, if they get in a fight right here on the sidewalk everyone will be in trouble... and from the sound of things back inside, it will be the kind of trouble that could seriously change the layout of that map on Maddoc's wall.

Austin's hand twitches toward the ill-concealed weapon under his jacket, his face darkening. "You don't fucking come into *my* territory and expect to walk back out, Gray. Oh, but you didn't, did you? You sent that girl in to try to handle shit for you."

He spits again.

It's disgusting.

Then he looks up with a sly smile. "You got a thing for relying on girls to handle your business? Isn't that why you're after this Chloe bitch?"

I stiffen at the mention of my sister's name, terror icing my veins.

"I don't know what you're talking about," Maddoc growls. "But if you want to find out how I handle my business, I'll be happy to take this conversation away from Saraven."

Austin glares. "I'm not fucking stupid. You've been on the hunt. Imagine my surprise when I found out that the one you were hunting for was actually mine?"

"Chloe's not yours," I snap, all that ice inside me transforming into a burning rage.

Austin's gaze drills into me. "I remember you. The sister. You were there when your old man paid off his debts, so you know she *is* mine."

"Fuck you," I shout, lunging forward.

Logan stops me, pulling me against him as Maddoc and Dante shift in front of me, blocking my view.

Austin cackles. "Imagine how happy I was to find out I hadn't lost out on my investment after that Capside deal I sent her to handle went south. Thought the chick died with the rest of them, but I get it now. I found out what she's really worth." He sneers at Maddoc. "Too bad you let her slip out of your fingers after going to all that trouble to get her, but that's kind of a thing with you, isn't it? Not being able to hold on to a woman?"

He yanks Sienna against his side, and the bitch gives Maddoc a cold smile.

Maddoc doesn't smile back. After a moment, his eyes flick away from her dismissively. "I hold on to what matters."

Sienna's eyes narrow. "You fucking *wish*."

"Shut up, Sienna," Austin snaps without looking at her. "But this other girl you want, Gray? Get used to wanting, because we'll get to her first. As far as I'm concerned, that inheritance of hers already belongs to West Point since her dad sold the little bitch to me in the first place, so if you think you're gonna get your hands on the money before I do—"

"We don't want her money," Maddoc cuts in with a snarl,

slashing his hand through the air. "We're not going after that, and we'll sure as shit make sure *you* don't get your hands on it either. Or on Chloe. Not fucking ever."

My eyes go wide, my heart suddenly trying to pound its way out of my chest in a way that has nothing to do with fear or rage this time. I can't think of a single reason Maddoc would say something like that.

Not unless he actually means it.

25

RILEY

"You don't want the money?" Austin scoffs in Maddoc's face. "You've put too many fucking resources into tracking the girl down for me to believe that shit. Unless... oh." He glances my way, then smirks back at Maddoc. "I see."

"You see shit."

"I see that you're fucking weak."

A vicious sound rips out of Maddoc's throat, his body jerking forward like he wants to hit the man.

Dante and Logan stop him, and Austin laughs.

"Weak," he repeats. "It's why West Point is gonna wipe you Reapers out. Maybe not today, maybe not tomorrow, but make no mistake. It's gonna happen."

"Not worth it, Madd," Dante says quietly, the killer that lives so quietly under his laid-back charm visible just under the surface for a moment when he meets Austin's eyes. "No point goading this shithead into doing something we have to respond to. Not here, where we'll regret it."

Austin's eyes narrow and the look on Maddoc's face says he wouldn't regret a single second of it. I feel the same. But Maddoc doesn't have the reputation as a leader that he does for no reason, so instead of showing Austin why West Point will *never* come out on top over the Reapers, he reins it in.

"Let's go," he bites out, giving his seconds a sharp nod to let them know he's got his shit under control again.

Of course Austin doesn't leave it alone, but we all ignore the final, taunting comments he throws out and split away, heading back to the Escalade.

Maddoc slips behind the wheel, and I flick a concerned gaze toward Logan and Dante. Maddoc's agitation is obvious, but Logan just stares back at me impassively while Dante's lips curl up at the corner as he gives me a small shake of his head.

Fine. They know him best.

I slip into the back seat with Dante while Logan takes the front.

"We need to ramp up the search for Chloe," Maddoc says as he pulls away from the curb, tires squealing. "Logan, you need to get in touch with Isaac."

Logan nods as Maddoc keeps rattling off orders that he needs his seconds to give the Reapers, and Dante leans forward as the three of them start up a rapid-fire conversation about protecting their territory. "We need to find a way to do it without sparking another fucking blowup between us and West Point."

"We can't afford that," Logan agrees, glancing up from the phone screen his fingers are flying over for a moment. "But the upside is that McKenna can't, either. That alone will help keep more violence from blowing up."

"That, and the smackdown we both just got from The Six. McKenna's gotta know they're not fucking around."

"He knows," Maddoc says grimly.

Logan's lips tighten with disdain. "But does it matter when the man doesn't always behave rationally?"

"That's why we're gonna stay a step ahead of him," Dante says, going on about the logistics of how they plan to do that.

I tune out the details, my mind still stuck on what Maddoc said to Austin McKenna back there.

I know how deep their rivalry goes. I've seen how much that sadistic bastard tests Maddoc's control. So Maddoc *could* have just been trying to throw Austin off the scent when he told him that the Reapers weren't going after Chloe's inheritance anymore. It could have just been some kind of strategic move totally divorced from their actual plans.

That makes the most sense, because over the time I've been with them, I've gotten a good idea of how badly they need the money if they really want to put an end to this gang war. Their plans for my sister still aren't okay, but the last few weeks have given me plenty of opportunities to see the kind of difference it would make to their organization and understand where they're coming from even if I can't forgive it.

Unless he really did have a change of heart. That would change everything.

I look out the window but don't register the sights. My hands are trembling in my lap and my stomach jumps with nerves as my mind ping pongs between hope and disbelief.

I half expect Dante to notice how agitated I am the way he usually does, to lean in and call me princess and remind me that I'm not alone here. But he doesn't, because the three of them are still talking about finding my sister. Which means that no matter what Maddoc told Austin McKenna, they haven't given up on doing that.

Was he lying?

Are they still planning on using her?

Will they still try to force her to marry one of them?

Or are they actually helping me for some other reason now?

I suck in a slow, stuttering breath. Then another. This truce with the Reapers was always tenuous, and the idea that maybe I won't have to fight them when we finally find Chloe, that I won't have to cut and run and leave whatever it is between the four of us behind, has me totally twisted up inside, both scared and dangerously tempted to believe it.

As soon as we get back to the house, I get in Maddoc's face, because I need to know.

"Did you mean it?" I demand, putting my hand in the center of his chest to stop him when it looks like he actually thinks he's going to head straight back to his office without talking to me after dropping a bombshell like that. "Did you mean what you said about my sister's inheritance?"

"Get out of my way," Maddoc growls, even though we both know if that's really what he wants, he can just push past me.

"Not until you answer me," I say when he doesn't, curling my fingers into the material of his shirt and then smoothing it out again.

Maddoc's face may not give anything away, but under my palm, his heart is racing as fast as mine is.

"You told Austin McKenna that you don't want my sister's money anymore. Is it true? Did something change?"

Maddoc looks away. "McKenna was trying to start shit with us, and no goddamn way was I going to let him get away with that. Not right there in front of Saraven. The Six would have destroyed us for that."

That's not an answer. It's also not the way it seemed to me.

Maddoc's control cracked. His emotions were clearly high. It felt like he cared.

And he *still* isn't pushing me away.

"Just fucking answer me already," I say, my voice shaking a little. "Yes or no, are you still planning on using Chloe once we find her? Is that why you're doing this?"

Maddoc scowls. "No one's going to do anything with Chloe or her money if we don't fucking find her. So if you still want that to happen, then get the hell out of my way. West Point's gonna double down to try and get to her first after today, and the only thing standing in their way is me, Logan, and Dante. We've got work to do."

With that, he finally plucks my hand off his chest and steps around me, then stomps off down the hall.

My heart is still pounding, and I look to Logan and Dante for... something. "You heard him."

I mean it as a question, but I can't bring myself to actually ask it again.

"We heard," Dante agrees, giving me fucking nothing.

Logan nods. "And he's right. We do all have work to do."

"What? *Logan*. You know that's not what I meant!" I yell at his back when he heads up the stairs toward his room, hands on my hips. Behind me, Dante snickers, and I round on him. "Was he doing that on purpose?"

"Doing what?"

"Not answering me."

"Who? Logan, or Maddoc?"

"Both! Dante!" I smack his shoulder. "Now you're doing it too."

He grins, catching my hand and holding on to it. Then his smile slowly fades into a more sober look. "We really do have to get to Chloe before West Point does, princess. Maddoc's right about that. McKenna ain't gonna fuck around. Not now that he knows the kind of money at stake with your sister's inheritance. And not now that..."

"Now that what?" I prompt him when he pauses, my stomach full of nerves.

Dante sighs, then turns my hand over and strokes his fingers over my wrist. "Now that McKenna knows it *is* personal for Maddoc."

And then the fucker drops my hand and heads up the stairs after Logan without bothering to explain that comment either, proving that there's more than one way the man makes me want to scream.

RILEY

MY FIRST IMPULSE is to follow, to track him down—hell, any one of the Reapers—and demand a straight answer about what Maddoc said. But the intensity of that meeting with The Six left an impression on me, and I take at least some of Maddoc's words to heart.

Now more than ever, we have to be the ones to find Chloe first, and the last thing I want to do is get in the way of whatever it is they're all putting into motion to make that happen.

It's late, so I head up to my room and try to convince myself to get some sleep. Instead, I'm stuck on the same emotional rollercoaster as before, and when it finally feels like I'm about to vibrate out of my own skin from pure frustration, I give up and go looking for answers.

Not from Maddoc. If he's coordinating efforts to find Chloe, I'm going to leave him to it. And not from Logan either, since I still never know what to expect from him no matter how my feelings about him may have shifted.

I go looking for Dante, and I finally find him in his studio, painting.

He looks up when I walk in, and any worries I had about

whether or not he'd mind me intruding here without an invitation go up in smoke when his eyes crinkle at the corners, a pleased smile spreading across his face. "I was just thinking of you, princess."

"Were you?" My eyes are fixated on the brush in his hand. It drips with familiar thick red paint, and my body instantly reacts with some kind of sense memory that heats my blood in a way that's far too distracting given that I came here for answers. I drag my eyes off it and meet his heated stare. "So this is the important work you had to rush off to do?"

Dante laughs. "Nah. I already did what I needed to, and we've got things in motion. Don't worry about that. This is... you know."

I do. He told me. It helps him get his head in the right space, and knowing that about him feels intimate in a way that goes way beyond the times we've been physical. It's just one more reason I have to know if Maddoc meant what he said.

"What's up?" Dante asks, turning back to the canvas he's working on and giving me the opening I need.

"I don't understand what Maddoc's problem is," I say, frustration coloring my voice. "Why can't he just give me a straight answer? Was he just fucking with me?"

"Cut him a little slack," Dante says as I cross the room. He adds a violent burst of paint to the center of the canvas. "Madd's got a lot on his mind right now."

"When does he ever not have a lot on his mind?" I mutter. "I've got no idea where I stand with him. No way to tell if he's telling me the truth or lying. How am I supposed to know—"

If I can trust him, is what I want to say. But admitting that, showing that I want it, makes me feel too vulnerable right now.

So instead I go with, "If he really wants to help, or if he's just using me again."

Dante turns to me, finally putting the brush down. "Maddoc has reasons for not opening up to people."

I cross my arms over my chest. "We all do."

"Fact," he agrees. "But not gonna lie, princess. His reasons probably make it a little harder for him to be straight with you than if it was someone else. Actually, scratch that. If it were anyone else, he wouldn't even try."

"What's so special about me?"

He gives me a hot look, then grins. "Where do you want me to start?"

It's tempting to go with the flirting. To stay in the moment and take what Dante's offering. But I need to know... and damn, I like Dante even better when he figures that out without me having to say so.

He doesn't make me work for it, obviously seeing something in my face that has him dropping the charm and giving me a look that's somehow even more appealing. That's more *real*. "You know about Sienna?"

I nod. "Maddoc's ex who's now with Austin McKenna."

I half expected her to make some kind of scene when she showed up with him at Saraven, but beyond hanging off Austin's arm and shooting a few contemptuous looks toward us, she was mostly silent.

"That's right," Dante says. "And that shit really fucked Maddoc up when it happened."

"He loved her?" I ask, something barbed and ugly twisting inside me.

"Huh. Love?" He cocks his head to the side, squinting a little, like he's replaying it all in his head. "I don't know about that," he finally says, "but she was definitely the only other woman he's ever been serious about."

My heart trips, my hands suddenly sweaty. "The only *other* woman?"

Dante gives me a long look, but doesn't actually answer. "It was bad enough that she cheated on him," he says instead.

"That shit was..." He shakes his head. "You know how he feels about loyalty."

"I do."

It's one of the things I'm attracted to the most... although I definitely don't hate how hot he is, either.

Dante nods, continuing. "He demands it. Fucking deserves it. And since he doesn't give his own trust lightly either, finding out about the cheating after he trusted that bitch, plus the way she defected to West Point afterward—not just choosing McKenna, but betraying our whole organization like that? Let's just say it's left Madd with some trust issues, especially when it comes to getting close to someone like that again."

Again.

It's that last word of his that sends my stomach into a little spasm of jitters. I wipe my sweaty palms on my thighs, then lace my fingers together to try to keep my hands from shaking.

Everything Dante is saying makes me hurt for what Maddoc went through, but it also feeds that tiny spark of hope inside me in a way that the shitty realities of life have always taught me was too dangerous to put any faith in.

People always let you down, and good things don't last. Those two lessons are ones I learned early, well, and often, and I'm not sure which idea is more frightening right now—that the Reapers are still playing me, or that, this once, things might actually be different.

Dante's watching me carefully, and I know without him having to spell it out that he'd never share details about his brothers like this lightly. And that if he thinks I'm not respecting the information in the spirit he's offering it, he'll shut it down hard and fast.

I lick my lips carefully. "So, you're saying Maddoc doesn't trust me. None of you do."

Dante trails the backs of his fingers down my cheek, then cups it. "That sharp mind you've got is hella sexy, not gonna lie.

But yeah, that's what I'm saying. And Maddoc's trust issues hit pretty close to home when it comes to you, which makes it interesting to see him trying."

I snort. "This is him trying?"

Dante laughs. "More than you probably realize. Hell, more than he'd probably admit. Even Logan..."

He cuts himself off, shaking his head.

"Logan doesn't trust me either? Of course he doesn't." I answer my own question before Dante has the chance. "But why? It's like he hated me from the start. What did I ever do to him?"

"Nothing, but believe me, he has his reasons. But you know how private he is. You wanna know those reasons, if you want the whole story, you'll have to ask him."

"Would he actually tell me?"

Dante shrugs. "If he wants you to know."

A few weeks ago, I would have said there was no chance in hell. I wouldn't even have *wanted* to know Logan's story, I'd just have wanted to get the fuck away from him. But now, I do. I want that and more. I want something I've never even honestly believed in before. Something I caught a tantalizing glimpse of at Saraven that can't exist unless Logan is a part of it too.

Unless they all are.

"I need to know if Maddoc meant it when he told Austin McKenna that you guys aren't going to go after Chloe's inheritance," I say, my heart pounding. "Have things changed?"

He gives me a long, assessing look. "Shit's been changing here since the moment you walked through these doors, princess."

That's still not an answer. "Did he mean it?" I press.

"Today was the first I'd heard about a change in plans," Dante says, making my heart sink. But then his lips tilt up, his eyes softening in a way that warms me all the way through as he

245

adds, "But when it comes to you, Maddoc always says what he means. It's been that way from the start."

I blink. Has it? Even after Maddoc betrayed me, after I fucking shot him, he's always insisted that he never lied to me. And... he hasn't. Not that I know of. He's pissed me off. Hurt me and betrayed me. But everything he's ever told me, he's followed through on.

Everything.

My throat tightens, a wave of emotion all but choking me. Oh god, Dante's right. Maddoc did mean it.

I instinctively try to protect myself, ducking my head and looking away as I blink fast to clear the hot prickle of tears that threatens to expose me.

Dante doesn't let me get away with that. He tips my chin back up and tucks my hair behind my ear, those vibrant green eyes of his—as compelling as anything he's ever put on a canvas —staring into mine like he can see right into my soul.

I'm completely exposed to him, and I've never felt so vulnerable... or so completely okay with that.

"Don't be so surprised, princess," Dante says with a smile that feels like a promise, a secret shared just between the two of us. "You're too damn sharp not to have caught on by now."

"Caught on to what?" I ask, swaying toward him. Resting my hands on his chest and then sliding them up to his shoulders.

He cups the back of my head, cradling it in one of his big, callused hands while his other one settles around my throat, tipping my face up toward his. "I've been telling you this whole time, you're different. You affect us. All of us. Did you think I was the only one here who's been catching feelings for you? 'Course Maddoc's gonna do right by you."

I suck in a sharp breath, his words landing on the rough tangle of emotions inside me like a spark on dry tinder. They're not the only ones with trust issues. But then Dante smiles down at me and the spark catches, and everything that's twisted me up

246

all day and held me back from believing I can actually have what I want with these men goes up in flames.

Dante smooths his fingers over my throat. "Princess?"

"Shut up," I say, all my doubts turning to ashes.

And then I kiss him.

27

RILEY

I MAY HAVE BEEN the one to start it, but Dante takes over the minute our lips touch. He *owns* my mouth, taking the kiss from spontaneous to scorching so fast that I'm left reeling. And then it gets even hotter. He breaks away just long enough to pull his shirt over his head and toss it aside, then he shoves mine up too, so we're skin to skin with one of his hands down my pants and the other back around my throat.

"More," I pant into his mouth, grinding against his body as he takes mine apart.

Dante chuckles, a low, sensual vibration I feel all the way through me, and delivers. Sucking and licking. Biting and soothing. Driving me crazy when he shoves a hard thigh between my legs to give my aching, wet pussy something to grind against.

I get lost in heat and hunger and passion, and when he tugs on my hair, tilting my head back and exposing my neck as he forces us both to come up for air for a moment, I have no idea how much time has passed.

I don't care, either.

"Damn, princess. You taste better every fucking time," he says with a dirty grin.

"You sure about that?" I ask, getting another low, rumbling laugh against sensitive skin in reply.

He grips my throat again, just tight enough to send a bolt of pure fire down to my core. "I'm sure." His eyes bore into mine as my pulse flutters madly against his palm. "But maybe I should keep checking just to be positive, yeah?"

"Fuck yes," I breathe out, then make a sinful sound when he leans down and licks a long stripe up my neck. I can't resist teasing him a little, though, so I add, "Unless you want to get back to your painting."

"Good idea," he says, rolling his hips against me so I can feel how hard his shaft is. "You remember how you painted in here with me before?"

He's got me mostly undressed now, but still has too much on himself. And by too much, I mean his jeans.

I want his cock out. And then I want it inside me.

And *he* wants to talk about painting.

"Do I remember... what?" I pant, rocking against him.

"Painting, princess." He grins down at me, hot and dirty, and smooths my hair back from my face. "You were fucking gorgeous. Wild and free. Paint with me again."

I thought we were going to fuck.

No, I *need* to fuck.

"You want to paint? Right now? Instead of sex?"

Heat flashes across his face, his eyes hooded and dark with lust as he steps away from me. "Hey now, no one said anything about one or the other."

My whole body is thrumming, blood hot and skin prickling with want. It clouds my ability to think, or to make sense of it when he grabs the canvas he was working on when I walked in —still half bare and dripping with thick, sensual globs of paint— and sets it against the wall. He places the palette of those same thick, rich paints right next to it, then beckons me over, pulling me against him and running a hand down my body. "No reason to have to choose. I want it all."

I grind against him. "Then take it."

His grin is positively filthy. "Give it to me. Sit on my face, right here. Give me that taste I need while you finish this painting for me. Wanna see what you do with it while I make you come on my tongue."

I laugh, heat flashing through me at the crazy suggestion. Then I realize he's actually serious when he hands me a brush, and all that heat turns into molten, liquid lust that pools hot and slick in the cleft between my legs, like my body is begging him to take that taste he just told me he wants.

"Is that a yes, princess?"

"Yes," I pant as he quickly finishes stripping off my clothes and lowers himself to the floor.

He pulls me up to straddle his face, hands hard and commanding on my hips as he drags his tongue through my center.

Fire licks in its wake, sending a demanding spike of pure need and urgent want through me.

"Fuck," I gasp, lurching forward and bracing my hands on the wall, one on either side of his dripping canvas.

He groans and does it again, licking me like candy. The rough, end-of-day stubble on his chin abrades my thighs, sending little zings of sensation through me in perfect counterpoint to the warm slide of his tongue through my slit.

"So fucking good, princess."

"God, yes," I pant, flexing my thighs in an effort to lift away from his face so he can breathe.

He yanks me back down with a throaty laugh. "No hovering. I need you to soak my face. Get it wetter than that canvas, babe. I want to drown in you."

I can't.

I want to.

He doesn't give me a choice, holding me against him tight enough to bruise and burying his face in my pussy like he has gills.

"Dante, shit, please... don't... don't stop," I beg, shamelessly grinding down against his wickedly perfect tongue and riding it hard.

The hungry sounds that spill out of him spur me on, and I lose myself in it. In *him*. In the hot, musky scent of sex as it mingles with the rich, earthy paint odors. Dante eats me out with a messy, single-minded determination that has me right on the brink of coming before I can even catch my breath.

Then he reaches up and pushes two fingers in my mouth, twisting his face to the side and pressing a hot, open-mouthed kiss against my inner thigh while I suck them.

"Get them sloppy for me, princess. And grab that paint brush."

I moan and nod, lathing his fingers with my tongue before sucking them deep. I'd do anything for him right now.

"So good for me," he mutters. Then he dives back into my pussy and slides his wet fingers out of my mouth with a pop, barely giving me a chance to whine about the loss before I'm gasping and cursing him out when he slips them into my ass instead.

"*Fuck.*"

It's a burning invasion that pushes me right to the edge, but then Dante pulls his mouth away from my clit and growls at me, "Paint. Do it. Show me. In color."

His words don't make any sense and all I care about right now is how fucking good he's making me feel, but somehow, I understand him anyway. He wants to see it. He wants to see all the hot, urgent, spiraling need inside me thrown onto the canvas.

And he's not going to let me come until I do it.

"You motherfucker," I gasp, scrabbling for the fallen paint brush and blindly stabbing it at the palette.

Blue. The paint that coats the soft bristles looks slick and wet and decadent.

I slather it on the canvas, leaving a thick purple smear behind as the new paint mixes with the red that was already there.

"Fucking beautiful," Dante mutters, humming against my clit in satisfaction. Then he sucks on it hard, two fingers still buried in my ass and stretching it to the point of pain, and an orgasm rips through me that's just as hot and sloppy as his mouth.

"Oh fuck, yes, *Dante.*"

He smiles against my pussy, I feel it, but he doesn't let up.

Of course he doesn't.

"Again," he demands, fingering my ass in a hard, fast rhythm that makes me crave his cock. Then he plunges his tongue inside me, fucking me with it in the same rhythm, and I'm right there. Ready to give him exactly what he wants. *Needing* to.

Then the fucker stops.

"Paint, princess."

I stare down at him, his face slick with my arousal and his green eyes almost seeming lit from within, thin, vibrant rings of color around pupils blown wide with lust as he stares back up at me.

"What?" I pant, rocking over his face as my inner muscles clench and yearn, my body already greedy for more. "*Dante.*"

His lips spread in a hot grin, his voice muffled and thick, and he plants slow kisses along my slick thighs, never taking his eyes off me. "I know exactly what you need. I'm also pretty sure I told you to paint."

It takes a minute for the meaning of his words to trickle through the cloud of need I'm floating on, but when it does, I shakily scoop up a dollop of bright green paint with the brush—

paint that's the same color as Dante's eyes—and splatter it onto the canvas.

Dante instantly rewards me, and the wave of fierce pleasure that rocks through me as I come again almost whites out my vision.

"Fuck. Oh fuck, please," I babble, my thighs shaking as the aftershocks shudder through me.

"More," Dante mutters. "Fill it."

I want him to fill *me*, but I know he means the canvas... and it doesn't matter that I've just come twice in a row. His tongue is addictive and the filthy onslaught of my senses as his thick fingers fuck my ass turn me into a greedy bitch who wants him to push me harder. Give it to me again. Make me scream for him.

I moan his name and slash the brush across the painting in front of me without any rhyme, rhythm, or reason other than to make sure he doesn't stop. Every color on the palette is a bright jewel, and they crowd together in random bursts and messy swaths that burst with the same vivid pleasure he pulls out of my body.

The canvas starts to look like I sound.

Shameless.

Desperate.

Carnal.

It's fucking beautiful, just like Dante said.

He hums against my swollen clit, lapping at it until I'm begging again, until I'm babbling and right on the cusp of another bone-melting orgasm. He's pulled back each time I've forgotten to paint for him, edging me to the brink of insanity, but this time he doesn't stop. He tips me right over that peak, and I scream his name.

"*Dante!*"

I fall forward, the paintbrush in my hand leaving a long, wet smear down the left side of the painting. Dante's sinful mouth never leaves my pussy, and I catch myself with both hands against the wall, my shoulder smacking into the canvas as the overload of pleasure leaves me trembling and boneless.

"Not done yet, princess," Dante mutters, hauling me back where he wants me.

"I can't," I whisper, already wanting it anyway even though I don't think I can take it.

Dante proves me wrong, and this time, he doesn't force me to paint for it again.

This time, I'm pretty sure he's just as gone as I am.

He straight-up growls, eating my pussy like a man possessed until he makes me come for him again. Then he slides out from under me and hauls me up to my knees, pressing up against me from behind, our bodies molded together from shoulders to groin.

"Look at it," he rasps, the rough denim of his jeans sending shocks of pleasure through me as he rubs up against my ass. He slides his hands up my sides and cups my breasts, rolling my nipples between his fingers before he pinches them hard enough to light me up again, his breath falling hot and moist against the side of my neck... and smelling like *me*. "Look at what we fucking made together."

I am. I can't look away. It's an explosion.

It's like I painted everything that happened to my emotions today.

"Same, princess," Dante growls. "I feel the same."

I've honestly got no idea whether I said that shit aloud or if he just already knows me that well. I don't care, either. Not when I feel him shove his jeans down and rub his cock against my back.

"I need to be inside you," he says, pulling away for a moment. "Spread your legs."

I do it, bracing my hands on the wall in front of me on either side of the canvas.

"So soft," Dante says almost reverently, nudging my wet pussy with the blunt head of his cock as he grips my hip and lines himself up. "Gonna take you hard."

"Do it," I pant, greedy for everything he wants to give me.

He groans, then buries himself balls deep with a single, brutal thrust that shoves me forward into the canvas.

I gasp, the wet paint thick and slippery and sensual against my breasts, cold and bracing on my overheated body. The unexpected sensation sends a tingling pleasure through me as he gathers my hair in his fist, wrapping it around and around to anchor himself, and starts fucking me hard. Making me slide against the canvas as he takes me apart like a man possessed.

"Jesus... fuck... princess." Dante's breath is choppy and harsh as he pounds into me. "You take me so fucking well. You like this? You like my cock splitting you open?"

"Yes," I gasp, my fingers scrabbling against the wet canvas and scraping long furrows through the swatches of color there. "I need it."

"Insatiable," he mutters, his hips slamming into me like he's trying to fuck me right through the wall. "You're perfect."

Hot, spiraling pleasure tightens in my core, and I squeeze my eyes closed as it starts to build, overcome with sensation. Then Dante's hand cracks into my ass, and the sharp, bright sting makes my eyes fly back open as I gasp, my whole body clenching around him.

He groans. "Yeah, that's it." He spanks me again, and I almost come. "Milk me, princess. You're so fucking tight. You feel incredible."

If he spanks me one more time, I know I'm going to come again, but instead he pulls out, so abruptly that I whine, my thighs trembling. Without thinking, I shove my hand between my legs, needing just a little more to tip over into another brain melting orgasm.

"Oh *fuck* no," Dante growls, capturing my wrist and

tumbling backward with me. "You need something to get you there, it's gonna be my cock. Ride me."

He rolls onto his back and manhandles me into position, and when I kneel above him and reach back to guide his shaft to my pussy, his eyes go dark with desire as they rake over my body.

"Gorgeous." His lips quirk up and he reaches up to trace the smeared paint on my chest. "You're almost as colorful as I am."

"Almost," I pant, arching into his touch as he drags his fingers through the jewel tones already drying on my skin. They're nothing like his ink, though. He's got it everywhere, and I still want to explore every tattoo someday. Find out what each intricate piece of art means to him.

But not right now. Right now, I need to be fucked.

"Make me come," I beg, taking him inside.

Dante grunts with pleasure, his big hands clutching at my waist when my pussy clenches around him. Then he gives me a dirty smile. "I'm just here to paint. You want to come, princess? Make it happen."

"Asshole," I lie, calling on muscles earned with years of pole dancing as I brace my hands on his chest and take him up on the challenge, rising up and then lowering myself again. And then again. Using his cock like my own personal sex toy as I start to lose myself in it. Riding him hard, chasing the building pleasure that he's made me such a glutton for and letting it carry me away.

But then Dante's hands are on me again, rubbing fresh, wet paint into my skin. Drawing sensual patterns over my stomach, breasts, clit. Reaching around to my ass and kneading it, spanking it again, forcing me to go faster and harder as he paints me like I'm a fucking canvas.

"Beautiful," he grunts, sexy-as-fuck tremors going through his muscles as his cock swells inside me. "Do it, princess. Let me see you fall apart again. Wanna feel you come on my cock."

I'm close. So close I can't stand it but so fucking greedy that I never want it to end.

It doesn't end. He grabs my hips and drives up into me, and pleasure explodes through me in an unstoppable wave that feels like it will *never* end.

"That's it. Fuck. It's always so... fucking... *good* with you."

Hearing it sends another wave crashing through me, and he rolls me onto my back and drives into me hard, fucking me right through. Smearing the bright colors he painted onto my skin over the both of us. Panting against my throat as his hips finally start to stutter, his rhythm cracking as he gets close.

"Come," I whisper, my body tightening around him. I scrape my nails down his back and grab his ass. "Give it to me. I want everything."

Because he's right. I'm insatiable. Greedy as shit when it comes to him and his cock and the cum I want inside me, filling me up. Greedy for the sizzling connection I feel as his eyes blaze into mine, burning deep, like he doesn't want it to end, either.

But then it does. I tighten my inner muscles and Dante's face contorts as he shouts, and he gives me exactly what I asked for. Everything.

And just like he said, it's so fucking good with him.

Every. Single. Time.

28

RILEY

"You good, princess?" Dante murmurs, sprawling out on the floor next to me.

He tugs me against his side and presses a kiss against my temple, then settles my head on his shoulder, idly tracing the patterns of drying paint on my body.

It's nice.... and I'm beyond good.

"Quit fishing," I say, biting back a smile.

He snorts quietly. We've both got our eyes trained on the canvas, but I still catch his grin in my peripheral vision.

"Want me to go grab us something to drink?"

I shake my head without bothering to raise it. I've got no interest in moving again, possibly ever, and from the total relaxation I can feel in Dante's body right now, he seems to feel the same.

I lazily wave a hand toward the canvas, both my brain and body buzzing with afterglow. "What are you going to do with that? It's a mess."

"Nah. It's beautiful. The best one yet. Maybe I'll hang it in my room. I've been thinking of putting something up there."

I laugh. He's over the top. But I can't deny that the idea of Dante sleeping under that particular painting sends some heat through me. "Is that what you were planning for it? Painting something for your room?"

He shrugs, his shoulder rippling under my head, but doesn't answer.

I roll onto my side and prop myself up on my elbows, resting them on his chest. "No, really. What was it going to be?"

When I walked in, the half-finished canvas was full of the bold colors I always associate with Dante now, but laid down in a way that seemed almost violent. It sucked me in, just like all his art does, and I want to know.

I want to know *him*.

"I was just painting out a dream I had," he finally says without taking his eyes away from the canvas.

"Must have been an intense one," I tease.

He grimaces, then shrugs again. "Yeah. It was pretty bad."

"Oh." I know there's a lot more to him than the easy-going charm that's usually on display, but I'm not used to him letting me see it. "A nightmare?"

"Not my first," he says, his lips quirking up as he finally tears his eyes away from the painting and looks at me. "Bad shit tends to surface in the still of the night, you know? Painting is a pretty good way of dealing with it, though."

I remember that he told me something similar the first time he showed me his studio, about how painting helps him unwind and process things, and I wonder if the "bad shit" he was putting onto the canvas is somehow my fault. Something to do with all the shit that's come down on the Reapers thanks to our ongoing search for Chloe.

Dante smooths a hand down my bare back and cups my ass. "What is it, princess? I can feel you thinking too hard."

I scoff, but I don't hate the idea that he sees me that well. "You can't feel something like that."

"Sure I can. Come on now, tell me."

I look back at the painting. At the red explosion he

decorated the middle with, and how my body softened it. Spread it around and changed it. "I was wondering what your dream was about. What kind of bad shit you wanted to work through."

"My dad."

The tension he must have picked up on eases out of my body with his answer. I'm glad it's not my fault. But now I'm also curious. Dante hasn't told me much about his past, but he did give me the impression that he had a good relationship with his father. Nothing like what Chloe and I have had to deal with in Frank. But if Dante's having nightmares about the man...

"Did something happen to him?" I ask hesitantly.

Dante sighs, his gorgeous face going bleak for a moment. Then he nods.

For a moment, I think he's going to leave it at that, and I decide not to push. Just because he's admitted to having feelings for me doesn't mean I'm entirely sure what to do with those feelings, or whether they can really go anywhere.

But then he opens up.

"A lot of shit happened to my old man. He was a hitman. Freelance. And since I trained up with him, some of what I saw, what we did, pops up in my dreams from time to time. But those are just memories, not really nightmares." He glances at me for a moment, then looks away again. "Killing doesn't bother me."

I wonder if he thinks I might judge him for that.

I wonder if I *do* judge him for that.

I sit with it for a moment, and realize I don't.

Death happens, and there are plenty of pieces of shit out there who deserve to die. Plenty who deserve a hell of a lot more than that too. I just can't find it in me to give a shit that Dante's the one who sometimes deals out the sentence. It's not even really a surprise, given his position with the Reapers.

And maybe, if I'm brutally honest with myself, that

darkness inside me finds that part of him just as appealing as all the rest.

"Then what does bother you?" I ask, thinking of the red paint he attacked the canvas with again.

Dante sends me another long look. "The way he died."

Not that he died, but the way it happened. Or maybe both.

I fold my arms on his chest and sink down, pressing our bodies together again as I rest my chin on my folded hands. "Tell me?"

Dante smiles, a small, soft one, and cups the back of my head, lifting his for a kiss. Then he folds the arm that's not gripping my ass under his head and looks back at the painting.

"Dad started training me before I could walk. Even before he let me touch any tools of the trade, it was the rest. How to read people. Situational awareness. Picking out targets, noticing a tail, all that shit. As soon as I was old enough not to fuck up the job for him, he started taking me with him."

An involuntary shiver goes through me. "He killed people in front of you?"

Dante's eyes crinkle at the corners. "My degree wasn't the book-learning type, princess. Some skills gotta be hands-on."

I nod, my eyes lingering on his bicep, flexed and bulging in this position. I can't help wondering if any of the intricate patterns and images inked onto his body—maybe the row of dark birds drawn in silhouette that wander across his arm there —represent that part of his past. If they represent his kills.

Maybe someday I'll ask.

"Anyway, it's not that shit that gets to me, is my point. And in some ways, it's not even watching him die." He pauses, then shakes his head. "No, it is that. He was taken out right in front of me, and it never should have happened. Not like that. He was too good. I mean, I'm better." His lips briefly lift in a familiar cocky smirk that's just as sexy as the first time I saw it, "But he was too good to be taken by surprise the way he was."

261

"Someone set him up," I guess, putting the pieces together. "Or... betrayed him?"

Dante's face darkens. "That's right. Not the first shithead who tried. Dad worked for a long time. Decades. He pissed a lot of people off and had a fuckload of enemies... or he would have, if all those pissed-off motherfuckers had known for sure it was Dad who pulled the trigger. But even though the right players knew who to call when they needed a hit, Dad was hella good at covering his tracks. Unless you were the one who hired him, you could never be sure he was the one who'd actually done the deed."

"But?"

"But then someone double-crossed him. Someone he'd done a lot of work for passed his name to another interested party. Let them know that Dad was responsible for taking out a key player in their organization. And since Dad trusted the guy, he wasn't watching his back the way he should when he agreed to a meet."

"And you were there."

Dante's lips compress into a thin line, and he nods, eyes fixated on the painting we made again. "I was there. Got recurring nightmares about it now, and what, a dozen? Two dozen canvases maybe? All with that moment—or with, you know, my feelings about that moment—splashed across them."

"The moment he died?"

"The moment I took out the son of a bitch who was responsible for it."

"Does it help?"

He drags his eyes away from the canvas and looks down at me, his expression softening. "Yeah, princess, it does."

"How old were you?"

"Fourteen."

My heart clenches. He was so young. And from what he's told me before, alone after that. Alone and looking for family, looking for a place to belong where loyalty was a real thing instead of the mockery of it that his father had found.

"Hey now, I don't want your pity."

I narrow my eyes, my heart tripping. "You've got to stop doing that."

"What, reading every thought and emotion on that gorgeous face of yours, like you're a wide open book?" he asks with a grin.

I laugh, because yeah. Exactly that.

He rolls us over, pinning me beneath him, and kisses me hard. "You'll have to get used to it." Then he sighs, resting his forehead against mine. "But I didn't tell you that shit to make you feel sorry for me."

"I don't."

It's the truth.

"Good," he says, "'cause as far as I'm concerned, pity's a wasted emotion. It's never gonna change anything. Doesn't get you ahead. So what's the point? Life is fucking chaos, all the time. Unpredictable. Messy. Full of pain. Shit happens, and you roll with it or you die. And I know you get that, because I've seen you do the same."

I nod, my throat tightening up with emotion. I do get that, and I love that he sees me so well. That he noticed. And if I also still feel a little sorry for him anyway, for all the shit he had to go through at such a young age, for the loss and the years before he found what he's got now, then *he'll* just have to get used to it.

Or at least get over it.

Or... fine. I just won't mention that part to him. Ever. But I'm suddenly fiercely, violently glad he found the family and loyalty he craves with the Reapers. That he has Maddoc and Logan now, two men who will *always* have his back. Who would sooner cut off their own arms than sell him out to suffer the fate his father did.

"I don't pity you," I tell him, "but I do feel..."

He cups the back of my head. "What?"

263

"Close to you." My throat almost closes over the whispered words. I'm not used to being so vulnerable with people. I'm also not used to feeling safe enough to want to. This time, I'm the one who cups his cheek. "Thank you for telling me about your father."

He turns his face and kisses my palm. "I want you to know me, princess. I want..."

"What?"

He shrugs. "A lot of shit." Then he grins. "But like I said, life is chaos. It's not like I'm actually expecting to get any of it."

God, can I ever relate to *that* sentiment.

Dante's right when he says I understand his philosophy about pity, about life. I've wanted a lot of shit over the years too. And, like Dante, I never expect to get much of it and have never been all that surprised when what really happened instead just made life all the harder.

But sometimes, like right now, things actually turn out... kind of fucking wonderful.

I bite my tongue. I don't want to jinx it, so I'm sure as shit not going to say so, but I'm also full of feelings. Feelings I don't have words for, or maybe just not the courage to say.

But this is Dante. He doesn't need words.

With Dante still pinning me down, I can't reach the paintbrush I dropped near the canvas, but I can reach the palette. I reach for it and drag a finger through the messy swirl of thick paint on it, coating my finger in the vivid red of blood Dante chooses for so much of his art and the deep blue of tears and sorrow and pain. They blend into the same shade of purple in my hair, and in all that mess, there's a bright, vivid green too. The color of Dante's eyes. The color of life, instead of all that death that haunts his nightmares.

Dante gives me a bemused look. "You want to paint some more?"

"You're the one who told me it's a good way to process things."

"Fact," he murmurs, letting me push him back just enough that I'm able to smooth my clean hand down his shoulder and rest it against his chest.

He already has color there. Gorgeous, intricate ink that I could get lost in. But unlike the full sleeves on his arms, his chest still has unmarked skin in some places too.

One of those places is right over his heart.

I touch the messy finger I dipped into paint to his skin. I don't know what the fuck I'm doing and I'm certainly no artist, but he's already shown me that neither of those things are necessary for this shit. For working through feelings. For painting *emotion*.

"Fuck," Dante whispers, his cock hardening against me as he swoops down and captures my mouth, trapping my painted finger between us. When he comes up for air, he looks down at his chest. "It kinda looks like my birds."

I tilt my head. I see it. He means the row of ravens I noticed on his arm earlier, but this one is bigger. Bolder. And not black, but bright. Not a crisp, well-defined silhouette, but messy and chaotic and colorful. It looks exactly how I feel.

He rubs his thumb over the top of my right breast. The paint I marked him with smudged onto my skin too, but unlike the bare spot over Dante's heart, my entire chest is already a colorful mess. The new mark is just one more slash of color, blending in with the rest.

Dante rolls off me and grabs the brush, dipping it into the blood-red paint and bringing it to my skin.

"More? You already painted all over me."

"I want to mark you up a little more," he says, intent on doing just that.

The wet paint is so smooth that it feels like liquid sex, and my nipples pebble with desire as he carefully drags the brush over the fresh paint we smudged onto me when we kissed.

"You were made for this color," he murmurs, his eyes trained on whatever it is he's painting on me. He finishes up and tosses the brush aside, then covers my breast with his hand, fingers splayed wide to frame the mark he made and palm rubbing against the hard nub of my nipple. "I like seeing this shit here."

I look down, trying to see it too.

It's... not a thing. Not a *picture*. But it's definitely an emotion. A curving, spiraling, twisting mark that's bold and dangerous-looking and hopeful. It's a burst of color—the crimson shade that Dante once told me is his favorite—that feels like all the sex we just had, and all the reasons we had it.

His cock swells where it's trapped between us and I spread my legs, arching up against him as I grab the back of his head and pull him down. "Kiss me."

"Yeah," he says, his voice a husky murmur. "We can start with that."

But we don't, thank fuck, *end* there... because apparently, every once in a while, good things actually do last.

29

RILEY

I'M up late enough with Dante that when I open my eyes the next morning to find my bedroom filled with pre-dawn light, the first thing I want to do is roll right over and go back to sleep. I grab one of the extra pillows on the bed and pull it over my face with a groan, sluggishly wondering why the hell I'm actually awake this early. I've never been a morning person, and the faint soreness between my legs reminds me of exactly why I deserve a little extra sleep.

I smile, an echo of pleasure rippling through me as my tired thoughts drift back over the time spent in Dante's studio, but then I remember exactly why I'm awake. I shove the pillow away and scramble out of bed, fueled by a surge of adrenaline-laced anticipation. Logan promised to take me around the city to check out some of the potential areas that Chloe might be hiding out this morning, based on the areas we marked when we went over the map the other day.

I'm showered and dressed and practically bouncing when I walk into the kitchen a few minutes later.

Logan is already there, and he hands me a travel mug filled with coffee already doctored exactly the way I like it. "You don't want breakfast."

267

I'm not sure if he's asking or if he's simply saying it to prove that he understands my state of mind. Either way, I nod in agreement, then moan with pleasure as I take the first sip of the coffee he made for me.

The sound makes Logan go utterly still, his pale eyes locked on me.

"What? It's good," I say, feeling self-conscious for no good reason.

He blinks, shaking his head slightly, and turns toward the garage. "I'm glad you like it. We'll take the Audi."

"Okay."

I follow him out to the sleek, sexy car and slip into the passenger seat, extra grateful for the coffee as he silently pulls away from the house and heads toward the part of Halston we agreed to start searching in. Sipping it gives me something to do since Logan doesn't say more than two words to me once we're on the road.

The silence is pretty much what I'm used to with him by now, and even though I feared him in the beginning, I can't help but wish things were different now. I can't get a read on him, and it might be greedy of me, but after Dante's confession last night and seeing what I thought I saw between four members of The Six—I want to.

Logan slows the car. "This is still Reaper territory," he says, scanning both sides of the road. "But barely."

He parks in front of a run down, empty storefront sandwiched between a sketchy corner store and a brick building pockmarked with what looks suspiciously like bullet holes. It's a part of the city we decided to check because I know Chloe is familiar with it, but I'm torn between hoping she hasn't been hiding out in such a sketchy part of town and hoping that we'll actually find some clue about where she is.

Or find *her*, of course.

"God, this fucking city," I whisper as we both get out of the car.

It's one thing to worry about Chloe from the safety and comfort of the Reaper house, but out here on the streets, the danger she's in feels even more real.

"So if this is your territory, that means West Point won't have people in the area looking for Chloe, right?" I ask.

"They shouldn't," Logan says, a dangerous glint in his eyes. "But let's go find out."

We split up, Logan heading into the corner store with a comment that makes me think he's familiar with the owner and might be able to get something useful out of him, while I start checking the other side of the street. I'm not sure what exactly I'm looking for—anything really, any sign that Chloe might have been there or any clue about where she would have gone—but after a while, I start to lose hope of finding it.

I tell myself it's a good thing. Hopefully, she's holed up somewhere safer.

I head down an alley a few blocks from where Logan parked. There's a check cashing place with a backdoor that lets out into it, and the guy who runs it, Wayne, isn't a total asshole. His cousin went to school with Chloe. There's a chance she could have stopped by, but she's too smart to have gone inside where the cameras they've got rigged in the front of the shop would have caught her. If she's been here, she would have come this way.

The narrow passage is blocked off by a chain link fence, and it's empty other than a dumpster and some garbage blowing around. I'm not sure what I hope to see exactly, but when I notice a distinctive orange wrapper for Chloe's favorite avocado bacon burger among the trash, there's a painful surge of hope in my chest.

Maybe she really was here.

Maybe she knocked on the back door of the check cashing place and hit Wayne up for a place to stay.

Maybe—

"Find something?" Logan comes up behind me, looking over my shoulder as I crouch down to poke at the wrapper.

It's... a wrapper. I sigh. "No. Maybe? Chloe might have eaten this."

I gingerly pick it up and Logan cocks his head to the side, as if he's actually considering it as a clue.

A little frisson of hope goes through me. It's ridiculous, but then again, this is Logan. His brain seems able to make connections that anyone else would swear don't even exist.

Then again, it *is* just a wrapper. Even Logan can't pull miracles out of his ass. A wave of despair goes through me, and I crumple it up and chuck it toward the dumpster with a curse.

"Forget it," I say, stomping past him, back toward the street.

A guy is standing at the end of the alley, blocking the way. He's also clearly tweaking. Not surprising for this neighborhood, but since there's a fair chance that he bought whatever he's on around here, it means he may have seen my sister.

"Hey," I call out. "Have you seen a girl hanging around here recently?"

His left shoulder twitches twice, then he lurches toward me aggressively. "I see, yeah. See a girl. See one right now."

I roll my eyes. He's as useless as the wrapper. "Whatever."

The guy moves to block my way when I try to brush past him, a sick leer on his face. "Where are you going, baby?"

"Away from you." I try to side step when he grabs for me, but he moves with me, his hand darting out to latch onto my arm in a claw-like grip.

He's not the first to try that shit with me.

I twist away from him, sending my knee toward his balls.

"*Bitch,*" he grunts without letting go, spittle flying in my

270

face as he shoves me back against the pock-marked brick behind me and presses his clammy body against mine. His ragged nails dig into my skin, and his pupils are dilated wide.

And then, just like that, he's gone.

"Don't touch her," Logan says in a flat, it's-not-a-threat-it's-a-promise voice, holding the man by the throat.

He gurgles, clawing at Logan's wrist in vain, but none of the sounds he's making are anything like words.

"Did he hurt you, wildcat?" Logan asks, his pale death-gaze locked onto the tweaker.

"No. Uh, no. I'm fine."

"You're shaking."

I am, although I have no idea how Logan noticed since he still hasn't looked away from the asshole who grabbed me.

I brush my hands over my arms, scored red now by the tweaker's nails.

"I'm okay."

Logan's gaze finally swings in my direction for a second, raking over me like he needs to see it for himself. Then he gives a decisive nod and drops his hand. "If he touches you again, I'll kill him."

"I doubt I'll run into him again," I say as the man scuttles away, broken curses trailing after him.

Logan's eyes narrow, flicking toward the fleeing tweaker. "Maybe I should just kill him now to be sure."

"Logan," I start, my heart suddenly pounding when his icy gaze returns to me. Except it's not icy at all this time, and I'm not sure what it is I meant to say anyway.

When he'd yanked the tweaker off me, he'd stepped between us, protecting me from him, and he still hasn't moved away. Now, we're standing close enough that our breath starts to sync... and I can't move.

I lick my lips, and Logan's gaze drops down to follow the movement.

"I, um..."

Logan waits like he doesn't have anywhere else to be, his body unnaturally still in that hyper-focused way only he can pull off. I can still hear the fading sound of the tweaker's feet pounding down the street, almost covered by the sounds of traffic from the main road, but Logan waits like nothing else exists except the two of us.

It's like he goes through the world always a little bit separate from it, and yet right now, I feel more connected to him than to anything else around us.

I rest my hand against his chest, and I'm a little shocked to feel his heart beating madly when he looks so calm and unflappable on the outside. "Thank you," I whisper, realizing that's what I'd meant to say all along.

He opens his mouth, but then closes it again and just nods, the movement looking awkward.

Then he turns away and scoops the wadded-up orange wrapper from the ground. "We should check..." he smooths it out and glances down. "Chester's." The name of the burger place. "They might remember her."

"Okay. Yeah. Of course. It's over on—"

"Fourth."

I smile. I'm not even sure why. Of course Logan knows, though.

He leads the way out of the alley. "I like their zucchini."

It startles a laugh out of me. "What?"

"Zucchini. They bread it. Then fry it." Logan's gaze flicks toward mine. "At Chester's."

I grin. "Yeah, they do. I didn't realize you ate fast food like that."

It seems so un-Logan-like.

He shrugs. "I used to... live around here. Sometimes I ate there."

"Around here?" I look around at the shitty little businesses and empty, boarded-up storefronts. "Are there apartments above some of these places?"

"I didn't have an apartment."

I frown. Then it clicks. "Were you living on the streets?"

Logan gives a sharp nod, striding purposefully down the cracked sidewalk toward Chester's. It's a little hole in the wall a couple blocks over.

"Why?" I press, hurrying to catch up to him.

Logan doesn't answer, doesn't even look at me, and his silence would have felt unnerving a few weeks ago. But now I'm not pushing just because I'm curious. I feel like I *need* to know. I want to understand him, and that means understanding where he came from.

I reach for his arm, pulling him around to face me. "Logan, why were you homeless? What happened? When was this? Before you joined the Reapers, right? Before you met Maddoc?"

He doesn't shake me off, which feels like a win even though I can tell he's not going to answer. But then he surprises me and gives me something.

"I used to pick up work from Maddoc's father. That's how we met."

"How old were you?"

"Twelve when I started working for Jonas Gray. Thirteen when I first met Maddoc." He pauses. "Ten when I... left."

"Ten when you left your home?"

He gives me another one of those sharp little nods, all precision and control and economy of movement, and starts walking toward Chester's again. "I had to. Everyone was dead. It wasn't safe to stay there."

"Who was dead?" I whisper, catching up with him. "What happened?" Then I remember. "You had a sister."

He mentioned her once.

A bleak look flashes across Logan's face, and something inside me cracks in two.

His steps speed up. "Her name was Emma," he says without looking at me. "But the mons—my mother killed her, right after she killed my father. I tried to... Emma was standing too far away from me. I couldn't get between them in time. I couldn't protect her, and then it was too late and I had to get out before she killed me too."

"Oh, Logan."

I stop walking, but he doesn't. So I run to catch up and get ahead of him, blocking his way.

When he stops, I put my hand on his chest to keep him there and just like back in the alley, the rapid patter of his heart is at odds with his emotionless demeanor.

"That's horrible," I whisper. "I'm so sorry."

It's not enough, but it's true. My own father is a certified piece of shit, but a parent who would do something like *that*...

I genuinely can't imagine. Or maybe I just don't want to. It definitely puts all Logan's odd behavior and obsessive tendencies in a different light, and I'm not sure what to do with all the feelings that are stirred up when I think of him trying to survive that kind of terror at such a young age.

And I sure as shit can't fault him for using whatever methods he needs to, to deal with it.

"There are a lot of horrible things in the world," Logan finally says, obviously uncomfortable with my sympathy even though he doesn't make any move to push me away. "It's full of them."

"Them?"

"Monsters." He pauses. "Us."

I shake my head, splaying my hand even wider across his chest. "You're not a monster."

There was a time I hadn't believed that, but now I know it's true. He may have survived one, but that didn't make him one.

Logan cocks his head to the side. "But I am. I've always known it, and you've seen it too. I have her DNA inside me. I can't get it out, but I've learned to control it. Use it. But I won't, don't, do the things she did to us. And never to *children*."

He spits out the last word with pure venom, and something deep and pure opens up inside me.

Chloe and I weren't abused as children. Our father used us, neglected us, but even though he never hurt us—not the way it sounds like Logan's mother must have—I can still relate to that venom.

I recognize that poison, because it lives inside me too.

Even before Chloe was taken, there's never been a single day that I haven't felt the crushing weight of needing to stand between my little sister and the horrors of the world, and never a moment I haven't fought against the knowledge that I'm not enough, not on my own, to truly keep her safe.

But like Logan, there was never anyone else, so I've had to try anyway.

And also like Logan, the one I had to protect her from first was the very parent who should have cared enough that I'd never have to.

"You're not a monster," I repeat softly, willing him to believe it.

I can see that he doesn't.

His ice-blue eyes burn into me like he really can see into my soul... but now I've had a glimpse of his too.

I cup his jaw with my free hand, and after a minute—under my other hand, the one still splayed open on his chest—his heart starts to slow from a frantic gallop to a strong, steady beat.

I did that.

He has to feel this connection between us too.

It makes me want to kiss him.

"I promise," I whisper instead, holding his gaze. "You're *not* a monster."

Logan finally breaks eye contact, looking over my head, down the street toward Chester's.

"We're going to find your sister."

I nod, letting him change the subject because he makes that sound like a promise too.

"I know we are."

I don't let my voice waver. The only future I can let myself believe in is one where Chloe is safe... but I'd be lying if I said that being out here, seeing that wrapper that she may or may not have left in the alley after eating a burger huddled in the cold while dodging asshats like that tweaker, made me feel anything but frantic about it.

Even if West Point hasn't found her yet, she's *not* safe. Not while she's living out on the streets, all on her own... like Logan once was.

The thought makes my throat close up, and even though I'm pretty sure I don't make a sound, Logan looks back down at me.

"We'll find her," he repeats sharply. "Chloe's smart, she's strong, and she's keeping herself alive."

"She is." My voice cracks, but I have to believe it. I *do* believe it. But then my fears force themselves out of my mouth anyway, my fingers curling around the fabric of his shirt and holding on tight. "Are you sure? How do you know?"

The ever-present ice in Logan's pale eyes thaws, just a bit, and his mouth softens in what I'm almost sure is his version of a smile. "I'm sure because she's your sister."

Then he gently pulls my hand off him and side steps around me, striding off toward Chester's again as if that's all he needs to say to prove his point. As if, when it comes to protecting Chloe, he actually thinks I *am* enough.

As if Logan believes in me too.

30

RILEY

The kid working the counter at Chester's remembers Chloe coming in. It's not a lot, but it's something that proves Logan was right about her being alive. It also proves that my instincts about where to look for her are spot on. Neither of those things point us in a new direction, but I'm still filled with a cautious feeling of hope as we arrive back at the Reaper house.

I dial back the hope, keeping only the caution, when I see that the driveway is full of unfamiliar cars.

"What's going on?" I ask Logan, relaxing a little when I see that he is. Whoever's here, they're not anyone he's concerned about.

"Reaper meeting," he answers me in his usual cryptic style as I follow him inside.

"Oh. Okay."

I half expect to find the house bursting at the seams, but there are only about a dozen unfamiliar people there when we walk in. Still, I'm sure they don't want me listening in on their business, so when Logan heads toward the living room where they're all assembled, I veer off toward the stairs, figuring I'll hole up in my room until they're done talking.

Dante steps out of the kitchen just as I walk past and stops me.

"Where are you headed, princess?" he whispers, his lips brushing against the side of my neck and his hand landing on the small of my back.

He doesn't give me a chance to answer as he steers me ahead of him into the living room, right into the thick of things, and then pulls me down on the couch to sit beside him. I stiffen, but no one tells me to leave even though, clearly, it's not my place to be here.

Dante sprawls out like he doesn't have a care in the world, manspreading with one arm thrown across the back of the couch while his other hand rests heavily on my thigh, like he's trying to keep me in place for some reason. When Logan takes a seat on my other side, I get the distinct impression that they want me to stay. I'm not sure *why* they'd want me here, but I relax a little, deciding not to fight it.

If I'm being honest, I might even kind of like it, even if I don't really understand why they're including me.

Maddoc's eyes land on me with no expression, but when he calls the meeting to order, he doesn't comment on my presence. It quickly becomes clear that everyone in the room—everyone but me, obviously—is a high-ranking member of the organization. Maddoc seems to have called them all in to discuss the shit that's been happening recently, although from the grim expressions on everyone's faces, I suspect he wants to reassure them that he's still got it under control as much as make sure they're up to speed.

"You heard about our meeting with The Six?" he asks, looking around the room.

"West Point's talking shit about it all over the warehouse district," a bearded man missing part of an ear says. "You want us to put a stop to that, boss?"

"If it's just talk, no one engages with West Point," Maddoc says firmly. "Is that understood?"

Everyone nods, even though not all of them look happy about it.

"We're not going to let McKenna goad us into fighting on his terms, especially not with The Six already taking notice. I want each of you to make sure everyone who reports to you stays alert right now. If shit goes beyond just talking, then no one responds alone. You need to make sure every single person in our organization knows they don't engage without backup."

"Troy isn't happening again," someone murmurs.

Maddoc's jaw starts to tic. "Damn right. And we *will* get vengeance for that, and for Payton, but right now, nothing happens unless West Point initiates. Is that clear?"

Another round of nods and sounds of assent, but the bearded guy with the chunk out of his ear crosses his arms and gives Maddoc a challenging look. "But if they do start something more than just talk, we get to take them out, yeah?"

Maddoc stares him down until he blinks. "The Six pointed out that what went down with Payton and Luis drew too much attention from the cops. They're right. That can't happen again. Not like that."

"But—"

Maddoc raises his voice as he talks over the guy's protest. "I'm tasking each of you with the job of making sure every Reaper knows they're to avoid violence and stand down if at all possible. But if West Point initiates, if our people need to defend themselves, then yeah, Vic. We go for blood. There's no fucking middle ground right now. We're not ready to take the fight to them, but if they bring it to us, we fucking end it."

Vic stands down, looking satisfied, but a couple of the other Reapers shuffle restlessly, brows furrowing.

"It's not all shit talking over in the warehouse district," one of them says, "they've also been fucking with our businesses there."

"Fucking no man's land," another one mumbles with a dark look.

"The warehouse district isn't a no man's land," Logan says, giving him a cool look, "it's a nexus."

The guy glares. "A what now? Because I've been saying for years we should just clean house and take it the fuck over."

I try to picture what I remember of that map on Maddoc's wall, pretty sure I can make a guess about which area they're talking about. It's a run-down, industrial part of Halston near where we snatched Chloe from the middle of that drug deal. It's also, if I remember correctly, the middle of a whole bunch of differently colored sections—gang territories—on Maddoc's map.

"Cool it, Amari," Dante says, a lazy smile on his face but a hard look in his eyes. "You know too much of the city's business runs through there. We disrupt that shit and everyone loses."

"Right now, we're the ones who are losing," Amari snaps back, scrubbing a hand through his hair. "West Point keeps fucking with our suppliers, and if we don't fix our cash flow, we're not gonna have any business *to* run through there."

Maddoc's jaw clenches. "I'm not going to let McKenna squeeze us out of business. Or out of Halston."

"Okay, but cash flow has been getting low, boss," one of the few women in the room says, her eyes flicking in my direction for a second. "Do we still have a plan for that? Because you know there's been some unrest in the organization."

The others chime in, discussing some of the logistical details of their various businesses and how the recent problems with West Point have been impacting Reapers' day-to-day lives, and I can feel the worry in the room like it's a living, breathing force. It's funny, because before today, I never thought much about the money side of Halston's gang activities. Listening in on this meeting gives me a new perspective, and I realize how badly they need the money Maddoc was planning to get by taking over Chloe's inheritance.

But I also notice that when he reassures his people that he's got it handled, he doesn't mention that as an option anymore.

"We're dealing with it, Tiff," he says to the woman who brought up cash flow. "My seconds have been working on establishing profitable relationships with some new players."

"Who?" she asks.

It's Dante who answers her. "People who have reasons of their own not to be dealing with McKenna behind our backs."

"Okay, but we've lost Mario Ricci's casino now, yeah?" the guy they called Amari asks gruffly, looking back and forth between Maddoc and the men on either side of me. "Who's gonna clean our money now that McKenna's gotten to him?"

Dante's hand tightens on my thigh. It's the only outward sign of his irritation. "We've made arrangements with a couple new businesses in the area," he says, his voice not giving any of his annoyance away at all. "Laundry ain't gonna be a problem."

Amari's shoulders relax. "Good. West Point's interference has always been a pain, but lately, not gonna lie boss, that pain has started to feel more like the kind of problem that's putting what we've got at risk, you know?"

I can still see that little muscle ticking away in Maddoc's jaw, but everything else about his demeanor radiates a cool confidence that his people respond to. The sign of a good leader.

"You don't need to worry about our business partners. My brothers have them handled, and nothing's at risk here. We're gonna hang on to every inch of Reaper territory we've ever claimed, and our businesses are just fine. None of that shit is going to fall into West Point's hands. Not ever." He pauses, taking a moment to make eye contact with each member of his crew. "And neither is Chloe Sutton."

I stiffen at the mention of my sister's name. I really don't want to be here to listen to their plans for her. I don't want to find out that what Maddoc said to Austin McKenna was a lie.

"Finding Chloe is our main priority right now," he tells his people, not looking my way. "This shit with The Six has lit a fire under McKenna, and now he's fucking rabid. We need to keep her from falling into West Point's hands. Understand? That's where your focus needs to be right now."

"Is she really worth as much as they're saying, boss?" Vic asks, making me curl my hands into fists.

Maddoc's eyes narrow. "She's worth it."

Vic grins. "We're talking in the six figures, right?"

"No," Maddoc bites out, giving Vic a look that wipes the grin off his face. "We're not talking about an amount. We're not talking about her money, period."

My heart trips over itself, but several of the Reapers make angry sounds and the rest just look confused.

"But, Boss—" one of the angry ones starts.

"Wait, I thought the plan was, uh..." Tiff says at the same time, shooting me a look that makes me think they all know exactly who I am. And who Chloe is to me.

"The plan has changed," Maddoc says, cutting them both off in a voice like steel. "We won't be using Chloe's inheritance, but we can't let West Point get their hands on it, either. Our top priority is keeping McKenna from getting his hands on her. We need to find her first and make sure she's secure. You got that? Because if I have to keep repeating myself, I'm going to start wondering whether I've put my trust in the right people in this organization."

All the Reapers make the right noises at that, falling into line, except for one of them, who frowns. "But if we're not gonna be using the girl's money, why are we putting so much into tracking her down like this?"

"Because Maddoc told you we are," Logan says in a tone

even colder than his eyes.

The other man swallows hard and nods once, then quiets the fuck down.

I don't blame him. I would too if Logan ever used that tone of voice on me. But... I don't think he would.

Not anymore.

Not with me.

I bite back a smile, because this isn't the time or place to get hit up by more feelings. Not that I have much choice about that. Not when Maddoc pins the guy who challenged him with a hard gaze, making those same feelings bubble up in my chest so fucking hard I almost can't stand it when he puts him in his place.

"We're tracking Chloe down because making sure West Point doesn't get their hands on her money will keep the playing field even between them and us," he says, spelling it out for them. "And once we've made sure of that, once we've got her secure and make sure they can't tap her funds either, it will be time to take the initiative ourselves. It will be time to move against McKenna."

He really means it. He's not planning on taking Chloe's money. He won't marry her. None of them will.

They're helping me for some other reason now.

"And what's that move gonna look like, boss?" Vic asks, rocking back on his heels and stroking his beard.

"It looks like us kneecapping the motherfucker," Dante answers before Maddoc can.

Maddoc nods, his lips curving up too, but not in anything I'd call a smile. It has too much predator in it. "Once we get Chloe back," he says, "our next move is taking West Point the fuck out."

The words hit his people like a bolt of electricity, taking the mood from tight and uncertain to energized and active.

Maddoc's so fucking good at this. Of course they follow

him. He makes them believe in him, and then he gives them every fucking reason to be sure it was the right choice. And as they wrap up their meeting, I can't help thinking he's given me a few reasons too.

I want to talk to him about it, *I* want to know, but I'm not sure I trust myself to have that conversation yet, so as his people start to file out I slip up the stairs to my room. With Chloe still out there, tension sky high between the Reapers and West Point, and The Six breathing down everyone's neck it may not be the time or place to get hit by feelings, but too fucking bad. That's exactly what's happening to me.

And it's too much. I'm not just overwhelmed, I'm... conflicted.

It's one thing to have caught feelings for these three hard, dangerous men who get me like no one ever has, but it's something entirely different to know what the hell to do with those feelings.

"Liar," I whisper, closing my bedroom door and leaning back against it with a sigh as I call myself out. It's not that I'm not sure *what* to do with those feelings. I've got a lot of ideas about what to do with them, some of which I can't quite bring myself to admit even here in the privacy of my own mind.

So the real question isn't what to do, it's whether I should do anything with them at all.

When we find Chloe, doing what's best for her will still need to be my priority, just like it always has... and I'm not sure if staying involved with the Reapers is going to be that.

And not just because dangling the temptation of her inheritance in front of them would always be an issue.

I can't quite wrap my head around that kind of money, not really.

I shove away from the door with a quiet curse, stripping off my clothes and pulling out something soft to wear to bed. It's a little early yet, but I don't have it in me to go back downstairs or deal with dinner. I need to just shut everything down for a bit and not get bogged down by thinking too hard about how Chloe's inheritance will change things.

Or how, for the Reapers, it would change everything.

I'd already started to suspect as much from some of the clues I've picked up while I've been living here with them, but being allowed to sit in on their meeting just now made that fact crystal clear. And as much as I hate to admit it—because the thought guts me on two entirely different levels—I can see why Maddoc thought marrying Chloe was the best thing he could do for his gang. Of course he did. He demands loyalty, but he doesn't just give it back, he lives and breathes it, so with Chloe's money in his grasp, he'd have to put the Reapers first.

Except now he's saying he won't.

I finish getting ready for bed, but when I consider screaming into my pillow just to release some tension, I settle for punching it into shape instead.

I hope Chloe has somewhere safe to sleep tonight. I hope she has something soft under her head too.

But I'm scared that she doesn't.

And I'm so fucking grateful that Maddoc is moving heaven and earth to make sure she will again.

"Goddammit," I mutter, rolling onto my back and staring up at the ceiling for far too long. Then I finally shut my eyes hard, as if I can shut out the hot mess of doubts and hopes clamoring for my attention along with them.

It doesn't work. Despite what Maddoc told his crew tonight about evening out the playing field by keeping my sister out of Austin McKenna's hands, it feels a hell of a lot like he's putting *me* first this time. Me and Chloe, both.

No one's ever done that before, and it's hard to believe it's real.

But more and more, it's even harder to believe it's *not* real.

I'm starting to believe in Maddoc too.

31

RILEY

"So we're going to check around the bus station again?" I ask Logan the next morning, biting back a smile when he hands me a travel mug with another perfect cup of coffee inside.

He doesn't smile or say anything about it, but he's so intentional and precise about everything he does. Taking the time to do that for me means something, even if I'm only just starting to trust what that "something" might be.

He nods in answer to my question, ushering me into the sleek car he seems to favor over the Escalade Maddoc always picks. It's way too fucking early again in my opinion, but I've got no complaints because we're going back out to look for Chloe.

Every day she's out on her own makes the knot of worry in my stomach twist a little tighter, but I'm feeling weirdly optimistic about things today. I'd blame it on a good night's sleep, but I know it's not really that. Something's shifted between me and the men here—something's shifted inside *me*— and it colors everything a little bit differently now.

I don't feel like I have to walk on eggshells with Logan today, so instead of sitting in the car in silence, I reach over and poke him lightly in the shoulder.

"That's all I get?" I ask when he glances over at me quizzically before quickly returning his eyes to the road.

His brow furrows, ever so slightly, and I can tell he has no clue what I'm talking about. He probably doesn't even realize I'm teasing him.

"The... coffee?" he asks after a moment. "Did you want breakfast as well? Yesterday, you didn't want to eat this early."

I grin, hiding it behind another sip from the travel mug. It's true. Not being a morning person, I've generally got no interest in food until I've been awake for a bit.

And Logan noticed because Logan notices everything.

"I don't need anything to eat yet," I reassure him. "I could definitely use more of an answer than just a nod, though. You know, conversation?"

He gets a tiny line of frustration between his eyebrows, and I think about the little I already know about him. Not just what he's told me, because that's not much at all, but also everything I've seen during the time I've lived with the Reapers.

Opening up obviously doesn't come easy to Logan, and he probably doesn't even know where to start. But he's not telling me no—or threatening me with bodily harm, the way he would have in the beginning—and that alone has me hiding another smile behind a sip of coffee.

"How did you and Maddoc meet?" I ask, holding my breath. Not because I'm scared he'll lash out at me this time, but because I know it can't be a pretty story. Logan already told me he was living on the streets by then, and he'd already survived the horrors with his mother too.

But I don't back down even when he takes a while to answer, because I genuinely want to know. I want to understand him. And I also figure a direct question is going to be easier for Logan to answer than something as open-ended and foreign to him as the idea of just making conversation while we drive for the heck of it.

"I used to pick up work for Maddoc's father," he finally says.

"Hm," I say, taking another sip of my coffee. Hopefully, the sound will encourage him to tell me more, but this hit of caffeine is also exactly what I need right now, so I don't push it. Not right away. I just close my eyes and enjoy the way it flows through me like liquid sunshine, feeling almost relaxed around Logan for the first time since I met him.

I take another sip. It's still early enough in the day that the warmth is as welcome as the caffeine. Still, even though we're not that far into summer yet, I know it's going to be hot as fuck later. It's why I threw on a short skirt and a thin top under my jacket this morning. Anything else will be torture if we're going to be walking the streets all day... and the way Logan's eyes dip, just for a second, to my bared thighs when he glances over at me is an added bonus.

I *do* affect this man.

I also want to know more about him. I still don't know exactly how far I can push since he's such a private person, but I give him an encouraging smile, and it seems to work.

"I was just running errands for him at first," he goes on telling me about working for Maddoc's father, the words coming out a little stilted, like he's genuinely not used to talking about himself. Or, from what I've seen, talking much at all. "After a while, he started giving me a little more responsibility. A few small jobs here and there."

Errands. Responsibilities. Jobs. Logan doesn't elaborate, but I get that it's all part of Halston's criminal underground. A world I'm familiar with since my own father has always skirted around the edges of it. One I know just enough to realize the dangers of. Some of which, over the last few weeks, I've seen firsthand.

And it would've been way too easy for Frank to have sucked Chloe into that shit as a kid—as young as Logan was when he got stuck in the middle of it—if I hadn't been there to keep her away from those dangers.

Something I failed to do in the end.

It makes my heart hurt, and I'm not sure if it's for my sister or for what Logan went through or both at that age. What had he said yesterday? He'd only been twelve when he started working for Maddoc's father.

I'm pretty sure Logan doesn't want my sympathy, so I tuck it away. I definitely want to know more though, so I also clear my throat and prompt him with, "So, you met Maddoc through his father?"

He nods, then tips his head toward the intersection we just drove through. "It was there."

"What, right here?" I say, twisting around to get a better look at the bleak corner. "Seriously? This spot is where you and Maddoc met."

Logan shrugs, but an almost-smile graces his lips as he gives me another teaspoon-full of information about his past. "Jonas sent him to collect a package from me. That was the drop spot."

"Small world," I mumble, since we're only a few blocks away from the bus station we'd checked the other day.

Logan nods and slides into an open parking spot on the street.

I follow him out of the car. "So, Maddoc was working for his father, too?"

Logan nods again, then darts a look to me, the faintest flush on his cheeks like he just remembered that I asked him to *talk*, and gives me some actual words. More of them than I expect. Speaking in fits and starts, he tells me a bit about his life on the streets as we start working our way through the rundown neighborhood, looking for any sign of my sister.

His childhood on the streets sounds bleak, dangerous, and just fucking *hard*, but when I say so, Logan shrugs again.

"No. It was... better."

"Better than...?" I start to ask, but I drop the question immediately when his eyes shutter.

And then I remember what he told me.

His mother. Right. She was a true monster, the kind I want to punch the world for letting her exist if I let myself think too hard about what *else* he must have gone through.

But I don't want to lose the unexpectedly relaxing vibe between us by dwelling on that, so I quickly change the subject.

"So you and Maddoc were kindred spirits right from the start?"

Logan gives me such a patronizing look that I can't help but laugh.

"Okay, okay, so how did he get you to warm up to him?" I press.

We've reached the bus station by now, and Logan opens the door, holding it for me. "He killed someone."

My eyebrows shoot up, but I clamp down on my curiosity as we walk inside. No way is Logan going to continue this conversation in front of other people.

He gives me the barest hint of a smile, his shoulders relaxing a fraction of an inch, when he sees that I understand that and won't push him. Not in here. I smile back and then move to question the ticket seller, showing her Chloe's picture while Logan prowls around the lobby quietly questioning people and staring intently in every nook and cranny, as if he sees the world differently than the rest of us and might actually suss out a clue from those scuffed, empty places.

But just like everywhere else we've checked so far, the bus station feels like just another dead end. It would be depressing as hell except, when we walk back outside, to my utter shock, Logan picks up where he left off without any prompting. Almost as if he *wants* to open up to me.

"There was a girl who Jonas used to use for deliveries sometimes," he says, staring straight ahead as we cross the street.

"She was—she would have been Emma's age. We called her Petal."

Emma... that was Logan's little sister.

I swallow hard, but he doesn't give me a chance to accidentally voice my sympathy. I'm not even sure I'd know how, not for something so horrific. Losing my own little sister is literally my worst nightmare. One I'm currently living.

But thankfully, not the way Logan had to.

He continues his story, speaking in short, jerky sentences. "Petal couldn't talk. Or just didn't. Not sure why she was out on her own, but there was a drug dealer..."

Logan trails off, darkness descending on his face for a moment. But then he shakes it off and goes on, his voice harder.

"Jonas should never have let Petal get near him."

"Jonas." I repeat the name. "That's Maddoc's dad?"

Logan nods, then corrects himself. "*Was*. Jonas was Maddoc's father. He was killed before Maddoc pulled us together and built the Reapers into what we are today."

It suddenly hits me that we've all lost parents. Maddoc, Logan, Dante, me. And Chloe's lost two, she just doesn't know it yet.

It's a pain that never stops hurting, but maybe it hurts a little less to know it's shared.

"What happened?" I whisper, absently rubbing at the sudden ache in my chest.

I'm not sure if I'm asking about how Maddoc's father died or asking Logan to continue his story about Petal, and when he answers me—scanning both sides of the street we're walking along and carefully checking each alley we pass instead of making eye contact—I can't tell which direction he's taking the story in, either.

"Jonas had his fingers in a lot of things," he says in that quiet, controlled way he has. "He wasn't the leader Maddoc is, but he managed to build up a loose organization of people he worked with, although none of them truly had each other's backs. And with all the things he tried to get into, he also managed to piss off quite a few big players in Halston, long before one of them finally took him out."

I blink. That's more words than I've heard Logan say at once in... ever. But then understanding clicks into place, and I can see it.

Logan doesn't let anyone in, and it sounds like Maddoc's father, Jonas, didn't trust anyone to get close. So of course Logan would have felt comfortable working for him, if "comfortable" is even a word I can use for a traumatized kid trying to survive on the streets.

But somehow, Maddoc changed all that for Logan. He broke through and got Logan to let him in. Logan said Maddoc did it by killing a monster, and I'm suddenly ravenous to know the rest. To know everything.

Before I can ask, Logan leads me into a narrow building with poor lighting. "Shoe Repair" is printed on the weather beaten sign above the door.

Logan shows the man working there Chloe's picture.

It's another bust.

When we walk out, I grab Logan's arm, stopping him before the self-preservation instincts that would have once kept me from grabbing him can kick in.

"What happened with Petal?"

Logan doesn't lash out, he simply shuts down. It makes my heart pound anyway.

He's so damn self-contained already that it's a subtle shift, but I'm paying close enough attention that I see it as clear as day. His body goes unnaturally still and his pale eyes lose all their brightness... but then I see the moment he pushes through that and decides to share some more of himself with me anyway.

I drop my hand, but I still feel connected to him, and it's a gift I really need right now. A spark of warmth to fight off the cold despair trying to creep over me as we run into dead end after dead end in the endless hunt for my sister.

We start down a different block.

"Jonas was... selfish," Logan says, hesitating over the last word as if it's not the one he's actually looking for. "I mean, he wasn't like Maddoc is." He shakes his head with a tiny sound of frustration. "In some ways, he was. Jonas taught Maddoc a lot. But Maddoc is who he is because of their differences just as much as because of what he picked up from Jonas about..." He flicks his hand in a way that makes me feel like he's taking in the whole city. "All of this."

I think I understand what he's trying to say. He means that Maddoc became the man he is because of his father's example, and that at least some part of that example was Jonas showing Maddoc who he *didn't* want to be.

Selfish. Maybe Logan means self-serving?

Maddoc isn't that.

He'll never be that.

"What happened with... the guy Maddoc killed?"

"Come on," Logan says, turning away abruptly and taking off in another direction. "We need to keep looking for your sister."

I follow, wondering if he's changed his mind and decided to shut me out again. But to my surprise, after a moment, he starts talking again.

"Petal shouldn't have been on the streets. Someone should have been protecting her. But Jonas didn't care about that. She was small and quiet and couldn't rat him out. All of that made her useful. She could get in and out of places where no one noticed her, but after the first time he sent her to the monster—"

"You mean the drug dealer you mentioned?"

He nods. "She didn't want to go back. She couldn't say why, obviously, but I could tell the fucker had scared her." He pauses, his voice dropping almost too low to hear. "I could tell he'd... hurt her."

My stomach clenches just to hear it, and my hands curl into fists.

I protected Chloe from our father when she was that age, but there had been other shitheads who tried to hurt her over the years. There always were.

And I agree with Logan. They're all fucking monsters.

"I told Jonas I'd take that job instead," Logan goes on, "but he told me to stay the fuck out of it. Said if the dealer thought I was getting interested in his business, it would hurt Jonas's arrangement with him, and I'd be the one to pay for that." He pauses, then says, "Maddoc overheard us talking."

"And he did something about it?" I guess aloud when he doesn't go on. Even though, shit, Maddoc must've just been a kid at the time too.

After a moment, Logan nods. "I didn't expect it. Everyone looks out for themselves out here. I figured that out fast, and Jonas lived and breathed it too. So it was stupid of me to follow Petal the next time he sent her."

"But you did."

He nods. "But I did."

Of course he did. She must have reminded him of the little sister he wasn't able to save. But he isn't telling me this story to remind me how fucking shitty the world can be. He brought it up when I asked how he met—

No, not how he *met* Maddoc. Why he let Maddoc in.

How they became as close as brothers, like they are now.

My steps slow as I connect the dots.

"Maddoc got to the dealer first," I breathe.

"He was already there when I showed up," Logan confirms. "Even before Petal arrived." And then, for the first time since I met him, he suddenly grins. Teeth bared and lips open wide. It's a vicious, dangerous, beautiful thing. "Maddoc made that fucker pay for his sins in blood."

Maddoc did more than that. He cracked through Logan's shell and showed Logan that he wasn't alone. He also earned one of the few, guarded places in Logan's heart with that act.

No wonder their bond is so strong. Logan isn't incapable of love, but after everything he's lived through, I can understand why he opens his heart so rarely. Rarely... but completely. He's totally committed to the bond he has with the two men he's found worthy of calling his brothers, and I have no doubt at all that he'd both kill and die for them without any hesitation.

Fuck, I'm so screwed.

I already feel something for him, something more than just darkness recognizing darkness, but seeing him in this new light leaves me with a deep yearning for more of him that I'm not sure what to do with.

That I'm not sure what he'll *let* me do with.

For now, I set it aside to focus on canvassing the city with him and enjoying the fact that he's decided to share anything at all with me. Especially because it feels like he's the only one.

Someone has to have seen Chloe. She must have left a clue somewhere. But by the end of the day, we still haven't found anything, or anyone who's willing to admit it.

I rub the center of my chest as we arrive back at the house, an ache there that I can't seem to shake. It's getting really fucking hard to stay optimistic when we keep coming up empty, but I refuse to believe anything bad has happened to my sister. I would know. I have to believe that, or else it will drive me crazy.

I don't know how Logan survived losing his own sister.

And selfishly, I hope I never do.

He hesitates when we reach the front door, blocking my way for a moment. "We'll find her."

"I know," I say, swallowing hard. Hearing it though, having him take the time to say it, just like he took the time to make my coffee this morning, eases the ache in my chest a little. "Thank you."

For a moment, Logan looks like he's going to say something else, but then he just nods and turns away, leading the way into the house. Dante and Maddoc are both there, going over some paperwork at the kitchen counter when we walk in.

They look up.

"Anything?" Maddoc asks.

I shake my head, my throat getting tight. Logan starts giving him a more detailed report of the area we checked, and who we talked to, and other random observations I didn't pick up on while we were out today, but it all still boils down to a whole lot of nothing.

"You okay there, princess?" Dante asks softly, coming up next to me.

"Sure," I lie.

He looks me over, his eyes warm in a way that has my throat tightening again. Then grins, bumping his hip into mine. "Come on. Let's get out of here."

I laugh despite myself. "I just got back here! And aren't you and Maddoc in the middle of something right now?"

I wave a hand toward the papers they were looking at.

"Nah, we were just wrapping up." Dante holds out his hand. "Come with me."

I hesitate, glancing over at Maddoc and Logan. They both look up as if they feel my eyes on them, and Maddoc gives me a small smile. Logan doesn't, but I still feel the way things have shifted between us. Between *all* of us.

I think I was right last night. It's time to believe in them.

"Okay," I tell Dante, my stomach getting a little jittery when he grins again and tugs me out of the kitchen. But this time, it's with anticipation instead of the sick dread I've felt all day.

With Dante, we could be going anywhere. Up to his studio, out to breakfast-for-dinner, or hell, all the way across town to run naked through the fountain in the plaza Chloe and I used to get lunch in for all I know. Trusting him is always an adventure... but it suddenly hits me that I do.

I'm not sure when that happened, and it's definitely not without some reservations, but somehow, it did. I trust him enough to follow him, even now that I don't have to.

That doesn't mean I'm not curious, though.

"You're really not going to tell me where we're going?" I huff after he drags me out to the Escalade, acting far more annoyed by that fact than I actually am.

He raises one eyebrow. "Why tell you when I can show you?"

I shake my head and roll my eyes, but I'm smiling. He keeps me distracted from my worries on the whole drive, and when he finally stops the Escalade I realize we're at...

"A tattoo studio? You're getting more ink?" I ask, unexpected excitement surging through me as I follow him inside.

He laughs. "I'll be getting more until the day I die."

I bite my lip. That sounds hot.

Dante nods a greeting to the heavily pierced girl at the front, and she points us toward the back of the building like she's expecting us. Well, him.

He puts his hand on the small of my back and leads me to a small room that would have looked sterile and cold if it wasn't for the fact that the walls are all painted black and covered from ceiling to floor in framed art prints.

Wait, no. Not art. Tattoos. Fucking gorgeous ones.

Dante pulls his shirt off and tosses it onto a small rolling cart, then drags me toward the back wall, jerking his chin toward one of the prints. "Look familiar?"

"Oh," I say, my fingers reaching toward it before I catch myself. It's a jaguar. Gorgeous work. Bold and bright and fucking beautiful, but I've already seen the original. It prowls across Dante's left shoulder, its tail wrapped around his bicep and its eyes—the same vibrant green as Dante's are—promising danger. They practically glow, staring out from the solid curve of Dante's bulky shoulder.

"I found Nico a few years ago. He's done a lot of these," Dante says, turning his upper body this way and that to point out the rest of the art that's laid out around the big cat like a riotous jungle of color.

The whole effect is sexy as hell, and when I look up and catch his eye, I can tell he knows it.

He cups my face, and a warm flush moves through me.

"Tease," I whisper.

The corners of his eyes crinkle as he smiles at me. "Nah. Never that. I'll always follow through for you, princess."

Fuck, that's a tempting thought.

The door opens behind me, a man's deep voice calling out a greeting.

"Dante."

I whirl around, my heart beating fast in my chest and my whole body filled with the need to have him follow through on that promise.

Dante catches my eye and smirks like he knows it, then steps around me and settles onto the padded, adjustable, clinical-looking chair in the middle of the room.

"Hey, Nico," he greets the man who walked in. "Thanks for fitting me in tonight."

"Anytime," Nico says, his eyes flicking my way with a questioning look as he drops onto a rolling stool and adjusts some lights.

"This is Riley. Riley, Nico," Dante says, filling in the introductions. Then he nods toward another stool. "You wanna have a seat there, princess?"

Nico mumbles a greeting as I take a seat, then he does something to lower the back of the tattoo chair so that Dante is lying flat and starts asking him about the new ink he wants.

I'm only half listening, too absorbed in drinking in the sight of the art that's already on Dante's body as it moves and flexes with the subtle shifts he makes in the chair. I still want to lick it. *All* of it. But then I noticed Dante tapping his chest as he discusses the new piece with Nico, his fingers skimming the empty skin right over his heart, and I'm suddenly all ears.

All ears plus a stupid surge of possessiveness.

That's *my* spot.

Dante chuckles, a low, throaty rumble, and when my eyes jerk up to meet his, I see that he's noticed.

"You wanna chime in here, princess?"

"What?" I ask, feeling like I've missed something.

He shrugs, the casual movement belied by the intensity of his gaze. "Since you're the original artist and all, we gotta make sure Nico's work meets your standards. It's why I brought you."

Nico snorts without looking up as he cleans and then carefully shaves Dante's skin. "Should I be nervous?"

I doubt the lanky, heavily inked man has ever been nervous in his life.

I also have no idea what they're talking about.

"What are you having done?" I ask, careful to stay out of Nico's light as I roll my stool closer to see.

Nico carefully presses a translucent piece of paper over Dante's heart, patting it into place. I can easily make out the lines traced on the other side that will transfer to his skin, and the shape of it reminds me of... flying.

It looks like a messy, chaotic bird, soaring free.

Then Nico peels the paper away and I recognize it.

A lump forms in my throat. "I made that."

"And I'm gonna fucking keep it," Dante says in a husky voice. "Do you remember the colors you used?"

I nod. I do. Vivid red and deep blue, lush purple and

brilliant green. I'd marked him with all of them. I'd *left* my mark on him, dipping my fingers in the paint in his studio the last time we fucked. Claiming a piece of him with it.

And now Dante is making that mark permanent.

"Are you sure?" I ask as Nico gets to work.

Nico chuckles. "He better be."

He touches the first needle to Dante's skin, and Dante's eyes flare with pain.

Pain… and something hotter. Something I feel too.

I can't look away, and Dante's eyes stay locked on mine too as the image I first smeared across his skin takes a more permanent shape under Nico's hands.

I don't have any tattoos of my own, and I had no idea that the process would be such a fucking turn on to watch. Or maybe it's just Dante. He holds perfectly still, his breath smooth and even, giving nothing away. His body tells a different story, though. One that has a deep, urgent heat pulsing between my legs as I watch.

I squirm, then shrug out of my jacket and lay it on an empty shelf.

As Nico drags the needle over Dante's skin, small beads of blood well up and along the smooth, curving lines. A thin sheen of sweat appears on Dante's sculpted body as Nico works, and Dante's eyes burn into me like they're a direct conduit to every single sensation.

The bite of pain accompanying the whir of the needle.

The ache in his flesh as the new image is forced inside it.

All that color and chaos, contained and captured.

I'm flushed and hot and don't even realize I'm panting until Nico finally throws me an amused look over his shoulder as he lays down the final line.

"Virgin?" he asks, raising his eyebrows as he quickly scans my exposed skin for any sign of ink. "Everyone cleared out of this place when we closed about half an hour ago, but I don't mind staying a little longer if you want me to—"

"Nico," Dante interrupts him, slowly sitting upright with his eyes still locked onto mine. "Get the fuck out."

Nico laughs, but gets to his feet and gathers up the tools he used. "Maybe another time then," he says, tapping a packet near the door. "Don't forget your aftercare."

"Out," Dante repeats, his cock a thick, throbbing line of temptation pressing against the denim of his jeans as he continues to stare at me.

I lick my lips and Dante smirks, and I don't give a shit whether Nico is out of the room yet.

When he reaches for me, I almost come just from the brush of his hands over my skin.

"Did I mention how fucking hot you look in this little skirt?" he whispers as he pulls me onto his lap in the tattoo chair, his big hands sliding up my thighs and pushing it up to bunch around my waist as he cups my ass and encourages me to straddle him. "Fuck, you're practically bare," he breathes out, running his fingers under the thin g-string of the thong I'm wearing. "Have you been walking around like this all day?"

"Does it matter?" I settle on top of his erection and rock against him. "You weren't with me then."

"I am now," he mutters, his hands tightening on my ass and encouraging the motion. And then he's kissing me. Fucking inhaling me. Biting at my lips, then whispering sweet lies and filthy promises against my skin as he yanks the thin straps of my top down and lifts me up to give my breasts the same treatment.

His jaw is rough with a five o'clock shadow, scraping against my sensitive skin as he nuzzles between them. Then he palms my left breast hard, turning his head to suck my right nipple into his mouth like he's trying to swallow it, and pleasure arcs through my body like lightning.

"Fuck. *Dante*."

I arch against him with a gasp, remembering his fresh tattoo just in time to avoid touching it. I tunnel my hands through the back of his rich brown hair, holding him in place instead as pure, primal need takes over. Dante groans, his jaw rasping against me again as he switches to the other side, and I grind down on his hard length, riding his trapped cock like a woman possessed.

My thong is soaked through and my pussy is fucking *aching*. I need relief like I need air. I need his cock.

"Shit, you feel good, princess."

"Yeah, I do," I pant, tugging on his hair until he lifts his face back toward mine. "But I'll feel better once you make me come."

He smirks, sliding one hand down my body to grab my ass in a punishing grip. "Is that a request?"

"You said you weren't a tease." I slip my hand between us, popping his fly open. "Prove it."

His eyes go molten, and he yanks my g-string to the side as I flex my thighs, lifting just high enough to pull his cock out and impale myself on every last inch of it.

"*Fuck*," he groans, the tendons in his throat standing out as he throws his head back and sucks air in through his nose. Then he tangles one hand in my hair, wrapping the soft length hanging down my back around his fist, and squeezes my ass with his other one, staring into my soul. "Do it. Ride me, princess. Take what's yours."

His cock flexes inside me and I'm fucking lost. He feels so damn good that I can't stand it, can't stand to be still and have no patience for waiting. I do exactly what he said and ride him hard, slamming down on his cock over and over as he attacks my mouth with his and swallows down all the filthy sounds that spill out of me until, with no warning at all, I shatter. Coming so hard on his cock that all the chaos and color of the bird he just branded himself with takes off inside me and *flies*.

Dante grips me tight and takes over, fucking up into me so hard the tools laid out on the table next to the tattoo chair start to rattle and bounce. "Fucking gorgeous. *Jesus*, princess. Nothing's as good as fucking you. Fucking *nothing*," he groans, pushing me even higher until, with a gritty curse, he shudders and slams up into me one last time, filling me with everything he has.

And even then—with long, open-mouthed kisses and slow lazy thrusts that push his cum out of my pussy until my thighs are coated with it—he doesn't stop.

I don't want him to.

"It's always so damn good with you," he finally murmurs, both hands in my hair as he rests our foreheads together, his thick length just barely starting to soften inside me. "You're every color."

I have no idea what that means. Except, looking in his eyes, knowing he chose the tattoo that he did, maybe I do.

I run my finger around the edges of it, careful not to touch. "I can't believe you did this."

His lips tilt up. "I like being marked by you." He drags his hands down, resting them lightly around my throat. "Always thought it was fucking sexy to see our marks on you. I wanted some of yours too."

A slow wave of arousal washes through me, and I shiver, then lean in and kiss him.

There are no words I trust myself to say in response, but he's right. I feel the same. It's sexy as hell, and for all the pain I've endured at the hands of these three men, I can't deny how hot it is to see them leave something behind. Stripes from Maddoc's belt on my ass. Bruises and scars from Logan. The paint Dante fucked all over me and taught me to use to deal with all the feelings I've never had a good way to let out before.

He licks into my mouth, the kiss slow and sensual. I'm exactly where I want to be. Where I want to *stay*.

But life doesn't work that way.

Dante pulls back, tracing my lips with the rough pad of his

303

finger and then helping me slide the straps of the thin cami I'm wearing back up over my shoulders. "Such a shame to cover you up."

"It's not forever."

As soon as the words leave my mouth, my eyes drop to his new ink. *That's* forever.

Dante put a piece of me on him.

Forever.

He helps me off him and we finish cleaning ourselves up, he pulls me toward him for another long, drugging kiss.

"I like knowing your pussy is still sloppy with my cum," he whispers as we break away, nudging his nose under my ear and breathing me in. "I wouldn't mind sliding back in there when we get back to the house."

Another delicious shiver goes through me. My body feels well-fucked and as relaxed as I've been all day, but now that he says so, I wouldn't mind that either. I grab his hand. "Let's go."

He chuckles, but stoops to grab my jacket off the shelf I left it on before letting me drag him toward the door. "You want this?"

I shake my head. "You've got me plenty warm without it."

"Fair enough," he says with a cocky smirk, folding it over his arm.

My phone tumbles out of the pocket, and when I pick it up, there's a message notification waiting. A text I missed a little while ago.

My pleasure fizzles, the sight of my father's name on the screen leaving me cold.

Dante's eyebrows draw together. "What is it?"

I hold it up so he can see. "Frank."

Dante frowns as I open the message. But as soon as I read it, my heart leaps, tears springing to my eyes.

"Riley?"

I look up. "Oh my god. He heard from Chloe!"

Dante's eyebrows shoot up, and my hands shake, making me fumble the phone as I try to hit the call button.

"Does he know where she is?"

"I don't know yet. All he said was that he heard from her. I don't... why couldn't he just tell me more than that in the fucking message?"

I stab the red button to end the call when he doesn't pick up after six rings, then hit the green call button again.

Dante moves behind me, pulling me back against his chest as it starts to ring again and pressing a kiss to the top of my head.

"This is a good thing," he reminds me, his solid warmth grounding me.

"I know, I know."

But that doesn't stop my heart from trying to pound out of my chest as I wait for Frank to pick the fuck up already.

Dante's got one hand on my stomach, holding me against him, and I cover it with mine, tangling our fingers together to keep mine from shaking as I wait through another six rings. Then it goes to voicemail *again*.

I end it and hit the call button again with a curse.

"I'll drive you over there," Dante says as it starts to ring again. "Let me tell Madd and Logan where we're headed, then we'll—"

Dante's mouth snaps closed when Frank finally answers, his voice so faint I can barely hear him.

"Ri...ley?"

"Frank? Frank! What's happening? What did Chloe say to you? Is she okay? Did she tell you where she is? Is she with you?"

All I get back is the sound of his rattling breath.

It sounds unnatural.

Broken.

I squeeze Dante's hand so hard I lose feeling in my fingers, and he dips his head lower, pressing his cheek against mine, like he's listening in too.

"*Dad?*" I blurt into the phone. "What's happening? Goddammit, you piece of shit, answer me!"

Frank doesn't, and after a moment, Dante pulls me around to face him, his face grave.

"He's such a fucking asshole," I whisper, still clutching the phone. "Why won't he fucking say something?"

"He can't, princess," Dante says, his voice grim. "He's dying."

32

RILEY

I SHAKE my head in denial. "Frank? Frank! Dad? Just... just answer me!"

I hear another slow, wheezing breath—an exhalation that almost sounds like my name—and then nothing but the wet, rattling sound of a man choking on every inhalation.

Dante steps away, pulling out his own phone and getting Maddoc on the line. Once he's given him an update, he reaches for my hand. "Put it away," he says, nodding toward my phone. "Let's go."

I nod, feeling numb, but hit the "end call" button and do it.

As soon as we get in the Escalade, Dante peels out. "They're meeting us there."

"Where?" I whisper, that numbness making it hard to think.

He cuts a glance my way, then puts his foot down on the gas, blowing through a stop sign. "Frank's place. Maddoc and Logan are on their way." He reaches over and grabs one of my hands, squeezing it. "Hold on, princess."

I squeeze his hand back, and suddenly all the foggy numbness is swept away by a tidal wave of other feelings. Anxiety curls in my gut, my mind racing over all the questions

Frank couldn't answer for me on the phone. "Do you think he was lying?"

Dante glances at me again. "About Chloe getting in touch with him?"

I nod, my shoulder hitting the passenger door as he roars around a corner faster than the Escalade is designed for.

Dante yanks me upright again. "Let's go find out," he says, screeching to a halt in front of Frank's place. There aren't any other cars around, not even Frank's.

I fumble with the seatbelt, pissed off by the way my hands are trembling and so jittery I feel like I might be sick. Before I can get it open, Dante comes around to my side and opens my door.

"Come on," he says grimly, taking my hand again.

My steps falter as I notice that Frank's front door is already open, the wood around the knob splintered and cracked, as if it's been kicked in.

"Shit," I whisper, my heart lurching.

"Pretty much," Dante agrees, pushing me behind him and then dropping my hand to pull out his weapon. "Stay back for a sec, princess."

He cautiously pushes the door the rest of the way open, peering inside. I rub my arms, a sudden chill running through me, and go up on my toes to see over his shoulder.

Nothing moves. At least, nothing I can see. The blinds are all closed, and just a few slivers of dim light from the streetlights make it through the broken slats, barely penetrating the dingy front room of Frank's apartment.

"Wait here," Dante says in a low voice before silently slipping into the dark room.

I don't wait.

I can't.

"Dad?" I call out as I follow him inside, earning a quick, angry scowl from Dante. But then I hear my da—Frank wheezing, and I push past him and rush across the room. "Goddammit, Frank."

He's on the floor, and each slow, rattling breath he manages sounds like a painful struggle.

I drop down next to him. My knees land in a clammy, wet puddle that smells metallic and dank. I know it's blood even before my eyes adjust, and I don't realize I'm crying until my voice comes out thick and tight.

"He's been shot," I say, pressing my hands over the wound in his gut.

Frank grunts softly, the pale gleam of his eyes fixing on my face.

"Don't you fucking die."

He doesn't answer. Doesn't even flinch. Just keeps dragging in those painful, wheezing breaths, the space between each one getting longer and longer.

I lean in. "Frank! Where's my sister? Who shot you? Was she here?"

Dante's hand lands on my shoulder. "Princ—"

Something crunches out on the porch, and Dante whirls around, cutting the word off with a curse as he raises his weapon and moves between me and the door. Then he lowers it.

"Madd. Logan," he greets them, stepping to the side. "Someone got to Sutton."

Logan moves around the perimeter of the room as silently as a ghost as Maddoc comes closer.

"Dead?" he asks, his gun drawn as he approaches to stand behind me.

"Not yet." I clear my throat, lifting a shoulder to scrub my face against it when my vision blurs. I press down on Frank's wound even harder, his hot blood still oozing out between my fingers.

"We're alone," Logan says from behind me.

The men all tuck their weapons away, and Logan flicks on the lights.

My stomach heaves. The place has been ransacked, and there are smears of blood and broken pieces of furniture near the walls that make me think taking a shot in the stomach was the end of a much longer conversation Frank had with his attackers.

One that involved them trying to get something from him.

Something that must have to do with my sister.

"Don't you dare fucking die," I hiss, leaning in. "You *owe* me. Who did this? Was it West Point? Do they have Chloe? Where is she?"

Frank blinks so slowly I'm not sure he's going to open his eyes again. His skin is almost colorless, his shirt soaked in red from chest to groin. He's staring at me, but his eyes look unfocused, and even *I* know that no one can survive losing as much blood as I'm currently kneeling in.

"See what you can find," Maddoc tells Dante and Logan, directing them to pull whatever clues they can from the wreckage around us before crouching down next to me. He puts his hands on top of mine, pressing down hard enough that Frank groans. "Like this, butterfly. Press hard."

When he moves his hands away, I double down. "Keep him alive."

"I'm trying," he answers grimly, doing something in the bloody mess that has Frank's body jerking. "Shit, he's been bleeding out for at least an hour."

"That text came in around then," Dante says, referring to the one I showed him on my phone.

Frank must have sent it before they got to him. This happened while Dante and I were fucking.

"Did you tell them?" I demand, my voice feeling raw. "Whoever... whoever did this. Did you tell them about Chloe?"

310

His hand twitches next to my thigh, the barest flicker of movement, and blood bubbles out of his mouth.

"No! Don't you dare. Talk to me first! Dammit, you need to tell me what happened! You owe me that, you motherfucker! Did they know Chloe was in touch with you? Was she here? Was it West Point?"

"It had to have been West Point," I hear Dante say grimly from behind me. "This shit has them written all over it."

Logan approaches on silent feet, then crouches down on Frank's other side and picks up his hand, wiping the blood off Frank's finger and pressing it against a phone. Frank's phone.

Logan quickly flips through it as soon as it's unlocked, then looks up at Maddoc and Dante with a frown. "There's no recent communication with McKenna on here, but West Point must have found out that he'd been in touch with her. He doesn't have his fingers in anything else that would give them a reason to come here."

"So you think the timing is just a coincidence with this attack of conscience he had, reaching out to Riley like that?" Dante asks.

Maddoc looks up, his face like thunder. "I think McKenna has turned up the heat, just like we expected. Of course he'd have eyes on Sutton. The real question is, what did he find out?"

"You think he told him where to find Chloe," Logan says flatly.

"No," I whisper, panic rising up to choke me. "No, no, no, fucking no!" I dig my fingers into Frank's clammy skin, then shake him. I don't care if he was trying to fuck me over. I expect nothing less. But I can't stand the thought that he'd do this to Chloe not once, but *twice*.

He coughs up another bubble of blood, muttering something in a low whisper.

"What?" I lean down, adrenaline surging through me as a fresh wave of hot blood seeps up under my hands.

311

Frank's lips move again. "I'm... sorry... hon... honey girl."

My heart clenches, pain spiking through my chest. I'm not his fucking honey girl, and I don't want a goddamn apology. I just want to know what he knows about my sister.

I need to know what he gave up about her when West Point attacked him.

My father is the epitome of a weak man. No way would he have held back when they were hurting him.

"Are you sorry about Chloe? About selling her out? Telling Austin McKenna where she is? Dammit, Frank, *do you know where she is*? Does West Point know now? Don't waste your fucking breath on apologies, tell me something useful!"

His eyes roll back, a horrible rattle sounding on his next exhale.

"No! Tell me anything," I beg in a broken whisper that's nothing more than a desperate puff of air. My throat is raw and panic crushes my chest, closing around me like a vise until I can't breathe. "Just... god... please. Frank, say something. *Please.*"

Another bubble of blood starts to form at his mouth with the next rattling breath, but then it just... stops.

Everything stops.

He's gone.

33

LOGAN

I'm intimately familiar with death, and the last slow, rattling breaths Frank Sutton struggles to take reek of it. When they finally stop, Riley's shoulders slump as if a string has been cut, her body crumpling in on itself.

Silence descends around all four of us like a shroud, and Riley's face as she stares down at Frank's body looks... wrong. It's utterly blank, her eyes almost as flat and lifeless as her father's are now.

It bothers me.

Then she suddenly explodes, surging to her feet so quickly she slips in the congealing pool of blood that surrounds her, barely catching herself before she falls on her ass.

"You fucker," she yells as she glares down at her father's body, her beautiful face twisted with things I can't name, but that I recognize just as easily as I do death. Ugly, wrenching emotions.

She clenches her fists, her whole body vibrating with them, then suddenly turns away from the remains of the man who failed her, clutching her stomach and retching.

"Princess..." Dante starts, his eyes brimming over with concern.

"Don't," Riley croaks, flinging a hand out to stop him when he reaches for her.

He hesitates—not something I'm used to seeing my brother do—then lurches toward her when she suddenly goes from zero to sixty, from trembling in place, racked by hoarse, panting breaths, to completely losing her shit like a wild banshee.

She jerks away from Dante and punches the wall behind her, screaming as she knocks a crooked, framed picture to the floor. She stomps on the glass when it falls, grinding it into the worn carpet, then grabs a ceramic lamp and hurls it across the room, screaming out her pain like it's shrapnel when it shatters against the far wall.

Dante makes another move toward her, but I get to her first. I don't know why. I don't even know how. I honestly didn't realize I'd even gotten to my feet, and yet here I am.

"Don't fucking start! Don't you fucking start, Logan!" Riley wails, her fists beating against me as I pull her tightly against my chest. "I need, he can't, it's not, *ahhhhhhhhhhhhhhhhh!*"

She switches from fists to nails, clawing at me, but I ignore both the words and the long, red scratches she inflicts on me. It's all just more shrapnel, and I've faced far worse.

I lock my arms around her as she struggles. She smells like blood. Like death and fury and sorrow. The emotions pour off her in palpable waves, and I take a deep breath and hold her closer.

I know death.

I know fury and sorrow.

Each is as familiar to me as breathing, and none of them can be fought against, or hurt, or hit... but *I* can be. The monster inside me is good for something after all, because it deserves all those things and more, and it pleases something deep in my soul to keep Riley safe within the haven I'm giving her, the restraint of my arms. Safe from all the emotions bursting out of her as she screams out her fury and pain.

She writhes against me wildly, her nails digging bloody gouges in my forearms.

"I won't let you go," I promise, dipping my head down to whisper in her ear as I tighten my hold.

She slams her head back, a good defensive move, but I duck in time to dodge it. She immediately pivots and drives her knee into my thigh, twisting and screaming like a hellcat. Crying like her heart has just been ripped in two.

"Shhhh," I murmur, hugging her against me. It's instinct, a long-forgotten sound I used to make for someone else.

I rub my cheek against the top of her head and shush her again softly as the emotions drain out of her, a soul-deep exhaustion taking its place. One I'm also familiar with.

"Please," she finally whispers, her body slumping back against mine. "He can't be... he never said... *Chloe*."

I raise my eyes to meet those of my brothers. We all understand what Riley's trying to say. Frank didn't confess what it was he told West Point. We still don't have a lead on finding Chloe. His death was the final betrayal.

"There's gotta be something here that will point us in the right direction," Dante says, his face set in a grim expression that doesn't look natural on him. "Some clue. Fucking *anything*."

"Then let's find it," Maddoc says sharply. Riley's pain affects him too.

He gives me a hard look, his eyes flicking toward her in a clear command. Hold on to her while they search the place.

I do, but they find nothing.

"*Fuck*," Dante spits out once they've gone over the entire apartment.

"Leave it," Maddoc says when Dante makes a move to start another sweep. "Wipe it all down. We need to get out of here, and I don't want anything left that will get us any attention once the cops finally show up."

"They won't know we were ever here," Dante promises.

Riley finally stirs in my arms, looking over at her father's body. She swallows hard. "What about Frank?" she asks, her voice a painful-sounding, raspy whisper. "Shouldn't I, um..."

She starts to tremble, and I slide my hand up between her breasts to rest over the place I've marked her, pulling her back more securely against me. "No. You don't have to do anything for him. The cops can handle the body."

She sighs—a long, slow breath, like a balloon deflating—and lets her weight fall back on me. It's complete trust, and it feels odd to have that from her, but also unexpectedly right. As Dante and Maddoc get to work wiping the place down, she barely stirs. Her breath is slow and choppy and occasionally broken by a twitching shudder, but she stays in my arms and, once Sutton's place is handled, doesn't object when I lead her out to the Audi.

I buckle her in and make sure she's secure, exchanging a look with Maddoc before he gets into the Escalade with Dante. My phone lights up with his incoming call before I've even pulled away from the curb.

I throw it on speaker. Riley is quiet and seems completely numb to her surroundings now, but she's still a part of this. I want her to be included, I want her to feel confident that we've got it handled, even if the conversation does nothing more than sink into her subconscious as she stares blankly out the window.

"We have to assume West Point got something," Maddoc starts with, his voice filling the Audi as both vehicles head back toward the house. "I want people on all McKenna's key players. If they have a lead we don't know about, then they're already one too many steps ahead of us right now."

"We'll get our people to follow every fucking one of them, Madd," Dante says. "Do we think Sutton really did hear from Chloe, though? That wasn't just bullshit?"

I glance over at Riley.

She doesn't move, still staring blankly out the window, barely blinking.

It... concerns me.

I tighten my grip on the steering wheel, but refocus on the conversation at hand.

"Yes," I say in answer to Dante's question. "There was a call from an unknown number on Sutton's phone. It wasn't from Riley's number, which means Chloe must've gotten smarter and borrowed a phone or found some other way to call him—and that means tracking her down by pinging cell towers will be impossible this time. The call lasted four minutes and thirty-eight seconds, and came in three hours before he contacted Riley." I cut my eyes toward her, then force them back toward the road and continue. "That was, presumably, about four hours before... what we found."

Before McKenna's people showed up to interrogate Frank Sutton, which allows for plenty of time for them to have gotten wind of the contact from Chloe, if they were tapping the right sources out on the streets.

Sources *I* should have found.

My fury over that is useless right now. Best to store it until I need it. Specifically, when I find out why my own surveillance network failed and can use it to correct that failure... or to correct those who failed me.

"So, West Point breaks in to find out what Frank knows," Maddoc summarizes, "then they either kill him so he doesn't share the information with anyone else, or else they kill him by mistake, during the interrogation."

Dante makes a sound of pure disgust. "We know those fucking weasels just trashed that place as a bonus. Sutton probably caved as soon as they threatened him. No way would he have stood up to much in the way of torture, especially not to protect his daughters."

"Like he should have," I add tightly, rage flashing through

me again. That reason alone should have given him, should give any parent, the strength to withstand whatever West Point did to him.

"Like he should have," both my brothers agree grimly before wrapping up what we know and ending the call.

We're almost back at the house now, and Riley hasn't reacted to anything she heard on the call. It's almost like she's gone catatonic, which just proves what I already determined back at her father's apartment: Frank Sutton deserved to die.

He *should* have died protecting his daughters. Instead, it was the opposite. He betrayed both Riley and Chloe, too many times to count and always for selfish reasons, and that kind of weakness makes him an entirely different type of monster than the one I grew up with. One that the world is better off without.

When we reach the house, Riley finally stirs, unbuckling her seatbelt as soon as I stop the Audi and opening the door to leave the car before the engine stops ticking. I quickly follow. She's walking on her own, but doesn't acknowledge Maddoc or Dante as she passes them. It's like her body is on autopilot, and she doesn't seem to see or hear anything happening around her.

I catch up with her and take her arm, leading her toward the stairs once we're inside the house.

She lets me guide her, hold her, without any outward reaction. Maddoc has one, though. He stops me, a questioning look on his face as his concerned gaze bounces between me and Riley.

After a moment, he clears his throat. "Maybe Dante or I should help her get cleaned up. Stay with her for a bit. She's gonna need—"

"Me," I interrupt, tightening my grip on her arm to the point that I may leave a bruise. "I'll take care of it."

Again, Riley doesn't react, but Maddoc's eyebrows shoot up in surprise and behind him, Dante looks shocked too.

I don't blame them. It's out of character for me. But I'm still right.

Riley does need to get cleaned up, but she needs more than that, and I'm the best one to give it to her. The emotions overloading her right now aren't just familiar to me, I've lived, breathed, and battled them. They've seeped into my soul and become part of the fabric of my being. I have no experience offering comfort, but comfort isn't required. Riley simply needs to know she's not alone in the dark, empty place she's currently buried in. A place I know all too well.

I'm not sure how to put all of that into words, but these are my brothers, so I don't have to.

Maddoc exchanges a look with Dante, and an entire non-verbal conversation passes between them. Then Dante claps me on the shoulder, and Maddoc gives a sharp nod. "Okay, do it."

He scowls, then shakes his head without saying anything further. He doesn't like seeing her this way. None of us do. But they both trust me with her, and he turns away, following Dante out of the room.

I take Riley up the stairs and into the bathroom. She's covered in blood, and even though it's the middle of summer, I know she's cold. Not on the outside maybe, but death leaves a chill that creeps into the blood and bones and marrow if it's not rooted out.

I push the plug into place in the tub and turn on the water, adjusting the temperature until it's warm enough to do that.

Riley stands by the door where I left her, staring blankly at her reflection in the mirror behind me. I move in front of her, blocking her view, and strip off her ruined clothes, putting each blood-soaked item into the trash. The bruises I once put around her neck are long since healed, but the scar I left on her chest is still there. It will always be there.

And it's not the only permanent mark I've left on her.

I frown when I notice the stitches at her waist. The bullet

that grazed her didn't go deep, and she hasn't complained once. I remember touching her body, though. Piercing her soft skin as I lay down the line of stitches. Leaving my mark on her body in a way that will always connect us.

I haven't forgotten about the stitches. On the contrary, knowing she has something in her flesh that I put there is something I've thought of often over the last few weeks. But seeing them now, I realize they need to come out. Indulging my own desire to leave proof of my effect on her is hurting her.

I don't want to do that. Once, I did. But now...

"These need to come out," I say, running my finger over the rough line of precisely placed stitches.

Riley doesn't react.

I leave her for a moment to fetch the correct tools—razor-sharp medical scissors for precision work and a pair of sterile tweezers—and then kneel down next to her hip and do it.

I did leave them in too long. Small beads of blood form as I remove the sutures, her pale flesh pulling toward me as I gently tug each stitch out. The smooth curve of her waist is marred by the irritated line I leave behind, but a part of me is pleased. The scarring here will be subtle, but present.

I want her whole body covered in my marks.

I want to claim all of it.

I go still for a moment, the unfamiliar emotion almost overwhelming me. Then I carefully fold it tightly, then fold it again, tucking it away for later.

I dispose of the medical waste, check the temperature of the water in the now full bathtub, and put Riley into it.

"Sit," I tell her when she doesn't.

Riley doesn't respond, but a single tear tracks down her cheek.

I wipe it away and stare into her eyes. They're not empty. They're too full.

I can't take away the pain or the anger—those have marked

her just as surely as the knife and needle I wielded on her body, and will be scars she bears forever—but I can help her drain them. Reassure her that the fears they're wrapped in, fears for her sister, aren't going to come to pass.

We won't let them.

I lower her down into the water, crouching next to her as I start to wash away the blood. "Maddoc has had our people tracking West Point's activities ever since your sister left. Up until now, we've kept that to our own territory and the borderlands, but tonight changes that."

Riley doesn't respond, and when the water turns murky and dark, I drain some and add in fresh water, then start on her hair.

"Not one of McKenna's key players will be able to move without a shadow. If they get near your sister, if they even get wind of contact again, we'll know it. We'll get there first."

The water darkens the deep blues and purples she's colored her hair with, turning the natural brunette roots almost black. I work my hands through it carefully, massaging the shampoo through the heavy waves and carefully separating the tangles until the whole, lush mass of it is clean again.

Slowly, her body goes from stiff and unresponsive to something softer, but she still doesn't speak. Water trickles down her tight curves, beads on the smooth, satin expanse of her skin, blends with the tears which intermittently trickle down her cheeks as I go on, outlining all the measures we've taken to ensure that we find Chloe.

Once I've removed all traces of her father's death, I help her out and dry off every drop of it, then check the small divots left behind from the row of stitches. They're closing nicely and shouldn't need any further care, but I swab them with antiseptic anyway. This time, Riley tracks my movements, but she still makes no effort to take over. She's like a living doll, and I manipulate her body with precision and care as I finish.

Her trust, her total submission, does something to me. I've

had many people under my control under other circumstances, but all of that was taken. This is different. This is *given*.

I open the bathroom door, releasing a cloud of steam into the hallway, but I don't hear my brothers. They trust me to take care of Riley, and I will. When Riley makes no move to leave the bathroom under her own power, I lift her into my arms and carry her to her room.

It's late, but even if it wasn't, I know firsthand how drained she must feel. For a moment, I consider finding her something to wear, but then I dismiss the thought. I'll make sure she's warm enough under the blankets on her bed, and even though I'll leave her to sleep, I prefer knowing she's naked, with the marks I've left on her exposed.

I help her into the bed, and another tear spills down her cheek as I straighten the pillows and then arrange the bedding around her. I'm tempted to capture it and save it, maybe taste it, but when she lets her eyes drift closed I leave it alone. Sleep won't heal her, but it will restore her, and I want that.

I smooth the damp waves of her hair back from her face, then adjust the blanket again, tucking it around her shoulders before letting my fingers drift beneath it to trace my mark between her breasts. Another tear leaks out, and without opening her eyes, she wraps her hand around my wrist, holding it there.

I wait, and eventually her heart rate slows. Her breath evens out. Her grip goes slack.

I start to pull away, and her eyes snap back open, full of a silent plea. Still full of pain, and loss, and all the blood I tried to wash away too.

I hesitate, but she doesn't let go of my wrist, so I slip into the bed next to her, both of us on our sides facing each other as I continue to lightly rub the mark I left on her. This time, she doesn't close her eyes, and the silence wraps around us like another blanket, cocooning us together with the pain.

322

I've never laid in bed with another person. Never been close enough to a woman that I could feel each exhale flutter against my throat. Never touched someone's bare skin, touched their most vulnerable places, without the intent to cause harm. So it makes no sense that being here with Riley feels like coming home.

Or maybe it does. Pain has always been my home.

I blink. For the longest time, *home* was the place where terror lived. Then it became the horror I escaped from. Here, in this house, it's become a fortress of safety and order, but the feeling seeping into me as we lie in silence, breathing together, is something entirely new.

"I hated him." Riley's lips barely move, the whisper hoarse and raw. Under my fingers, her heart beats faster, pulsing, pounding against the tips of my fingers.

I press them into the scar. "He deserved it."

Her breath stutters, then she nods, finding my other hand and bringing it to her cheek. She tucks it under her head like a pillow, squeezing her eyes closed and letting tears flow onto my palm.

"After my father was killed... after she killed him..." *And Emma.* "I ran."

Riley nods without opening her eyes, the hollow emptiness inside her like a vacuum, sucking the story I've never told anyone—not fully, not even my brothers—out of the darkest depths of my heart.

"I didn't know she'd been caught until years later. I didn't realize..."

She hadn't even tried to cover it up, or hide. When the police showed up, I found out later, my mother was sitting next to the bodies eating the lunch she'd prepared for all of us. A true monster.

Riley's eyes open, and the words come again.

"I didn't realize she'd been captured until Jonas, Maddoc's

father, mentioned it in passing. He had his finger in a lucrative contraband ring up at Whitehorn, the women's prison upstate, and he didn't realize she was my... that we were related. He mentioned her crimes though, and I knew. I looked it up. I found out she was..."

Riley blinks, and I take a breath. Then let it out. Then another.

"She was on death row, but that takes years. I went to see her."

It was a mistake. I thought seeing her behind bars would fix something, heal something, but all it did was awaken the monster within *me*, like calling to like. I didn't want to see her behind bars. I wanted to gut her the same way she'd—

I slam the door down on the memory of Emma. I can't.

"She wrote to me afterward. Every week. She told me how bad it was there. How much she suffered."

A familiar flare of satisfaction blazes in my chest, and without thinking, I flex my hand, caressing Riley's cheek. Her eyes are latched onto mine like she's untethered and I'm the lifeline she can't let go of, can't even blink, without drowning. But I'm a monster too. She needs to see that. She needs to *know* that. I want her to know me in a way no one else ever has.

"I looked forward to each letter. To the proof that she was miserable. It still wasn't enough, but then she got cancer. She begged for my help. The medical care in prison is almost non-existent, and the type she had was brutal, and slow, and excruciatingly painful without treatment."

I close my eyes for a moment, savoring my memory of all the pain-drenched words she wrote like a fine wine.

If I didn't know firsthand that death deletes the living, erases them and replaces what once was with nothing but a yawning void, I could almost convince myself that Emma and our father still exist in some way. That they were able to reach through the veil that separates them from the living and fill

Mother's body with each and every nodule of that pain in retribution for what she'd done to us... or as a final gift to me.

But they're gone, so the cancer was some other form of cosmic justice.

When I open my eyes, I see the reflection of my mother's betrayal in Riley's eyes as she remembers Frank.

I hope she finds as much pleasure and satisfaction in his suffering as I did when I refused to help the monster who raised me, when I had a small part in drawing out the misery and torment of the devil who shaped me into what I became, simply by denying her.

It's not enough. It will never be enough. But it's something.

"My mother had to live with her cancer for five years. It ate away at her. It rotted her bones and strangled her organs. It gave her the death she deserved instead of the easy one the state wanted to give her for her crimes. She begged for help, for relief, just like they had. She *suffered*."

Riley's expression doesn't change, but her hand tightens around my wrist and her heart beats in a slow, steady beat—perfectly in sync with mine—as she stares unblinking into my eyes.

I've never felt as connected to another person, never let anyone see me as clearly. It's dangerous. It stirs the monster inside me. Makes me want to mark her again. *Own* her. Drag her out of the darkness she's drowning in and trap her in mine, where I can keep her and have this, always.

I don't mean to tell her any more, but Riley's not the only one drowning. I can no more look away than I can keep these horrors inside anymore.

"The prison mailed me a box of my mother's effects after she died," I tell her. "She didn't have much. I never answered her letters, and there was no other correspondence. Not with anyone. There was no one else in the world, no one living, for her to keep in touch with. But the one thing she had... that she'd kept with her... that she never should have been allowed to fucking *touch*..."

Riley turns her face toward my hand, still cupping her cheek, and breathes against my palm. In. Out. In again. It's not a kiss—in twenty-six years, no one has ever kissed me—but it's a connection that makes my throat tighten up with an emotion I've never felt before. Tighten up so much it *aches*.

The words force themselves out anyway, my voice raw and painful.

"She had my sister's bracelet. I'd given it to Emma for her fifth birthday. I found it in a field behind our house, blue beads, like Em's eyes were, with some white ones all around it. She was wearing it that day, when the monster, when our mother..." Rage sweeps through me, tangling my tongue before I manage to bite out the rest. "Our mother *kept* it. She took it off Em's body. It's in the box they sent. One of the beads cracked that day, and it's still stained with Emma's blood."

Maddoc and Dante don't know any of this. They don't know what the prison sent me. They don't know how I relished every letter that arrived before that for the deep, pulsing satisfaction I felt as I denied Mother any help, over and over... and how finding Emma's bracelet in her effects felt like it robbed me of that. Like Mother was able to reach out from the grave to claw me open again, show me that she'd kept a memento, a souvenir, of what she'd done that day.

Maddoc and Dante don't know because while they're both intimately familiar with the darkness that pulses through the veins of the world like a plague, neither of them have been touched by the kind of betrayal I have. The unforgivable kind of a parent who doesn't just fail their child, but takes pleasure in hurting them.

The kind of betrayal that Riley knows.

In lieu of pleasure, Frank Sutton let his weakness guide him down that dark path. He looked out for himself and only

326

himself, at the expense of his daughters' pain. It's just as unforgivable, and I don't blame Riley for wanting to retreat and escape it.

But I know she won't forgive herself, either, if she doesn't snap out of it.

Her little sister is still out there.

Chloe still needs her.

I spread my hand out, not just tracing Riley's scar anymore but covering it completely, her heart beating against my palm.

"I know what happened today. I know what it feels like to have your soul splinter inside you, cut right through your skin and shred you to pieces as it tears itself apart. You can't move. You can't blink. Not without jostling those shards and letting them tear you up all over again. I understand why it shut you down."

I won't give her empty words or false promises. Some things, once they're broken, can't ever be repaired. But I can show her how to go on living anyway. I can show her she's not alone. I can let her feel it.

I take her hand and put it on my chest, spreading it wide. "I *know*, wildcat."

She stares back at me, and I really do drown in her eyes. Drown in them until they spill over and she makes a small, broken sound, sliding her hand up from my chest to cup my face. And then, tasting of salt and pain and sorrow, she finally closes them and presses her lips against mine, pulling herself out of the darkness.

And igniting mine.

34

RILEY

I DON'T THINK about it before I kiss Logan. I'm not thinking at all—or feeling anything anymore, thank god.

At least, not until our lips touch.

Logan's lips are firm and warm and totally unresponsive at first, but I don't care. I need this. I need *him*.

I tangle my hand in the back of his hair and breathe him in, kissing him harder. Using the taste of him to beat back the pain inside me, little by little. And finally, his body uncoils like a striking snake, and he moves too.

He kisses me back with careful intensity, holding me in place as if he's deliberately mapping my lips with the same precision and focus he brings to everything. But I need more, I need to be overwhelmed, and when I part my lips and his tongue touches mine, everything goes from zero to sixty between one breath and the next.

For a split second, Logan freezes. Then he makes a tortured sound and rolls halfway on top of me with the speed of a striking snake, taking my mouth with a ferocity that has our teeth clashing, our lips moving together so hard I expect my skin to split.

It's everything I need right now. His mouth fucking owns

me and his hands are everywhere, rough and possessive, driving back the darkness and fog I've been caught in.

I kiss him even harder, wrapping my arms around him and impatiently tugging at his shirt, trying to find skin. Pulling him even closer. Making an obscenely needy sound of my own when I feel the unmistakable outline of his hard length, grinding against my hip.

Then he pushes me away.

I blink, gasping for air and staring at him in shock. What just happened?

"Logan?"

He put two feet of empty mattress between us, and his jaw is so tight it looks like it might crack. He's still here though, and his usual cold blankness is backlit by a raging fire.

He's holding himself back, but I have no idea why.

I touch my kiss-swollen lips. "You want this too."

"I can't," he bites out, looking away. "You know that."

"What? No, I don't. Why not?"

His gaze lurches back to me and drills a furious hole right through me. "You were making me lose control. I can't do that. I told you about my mother. You know what I am. What's inside me."

A monster. That's what she was, and it's what he thinks he is too.

I shake my head. "You're not like her." I won't pretend I don't see shades of something monstrous inside him too, because I do. I'm just not afraid of it.

"Riley," he practically growls, his pale eyes flaring like the heart of a flame. "You've seen—"

I press my fingers over his lips to shut him up, and his eyes widen with shock.

"Yeah, I have seen it. I've also listened to what you said about her, and I doubt she ever worried about being what she was. Did she ever try to fight it?"

I can see the answer in his eyes. She didn't fight it. She fed it. Right up until the end.

I take my fingers away from his mouth and scoot closer, keeping my eyes wide open and locked onto his as I lean in and press a chaste kiss against his mouth again.

He jerks his head back, and my heart races as I open it right up for him, laying myself bare.

"I'm not afraid of the darkness inside you," I whisper. "There's something in me that craves it. That needs a little pain sometimes."

He doesn't blink. Doesn't reach for me. But I feel something shift in the air between us, and I'm not above begging right now.

"Today fucked me up." The confession is ragged, my throat tightening as all the shit that exploded out of me back at Frank's place tries to rise up and choke me all over again. "I need this. I need you to make me feel something. Anything. *Please.*"

I can see the battle in his eyes, and a needy little whimper escapes me when it ends.

I move toward him again but he stops me, reaching up to wrap his hand around my throat to hold me in place. He doesn't tighten his grip, but it still sends a delicious thrill of danger through me.

There's no way Logan misses it. He's staring right into my eyes, and I'm wide open and vulnerable to him right now. He can read everything I'm feeling and destroy me with it if he's really the monster he claims to be.

But I know he won't.

His grip suddenly tightens, just enough to remind me of what he can do, and the tension flows out of me like water as I give in to him. Like I just told him, I don't just need this right now, I crave it.

"Pick a word."

"What?"

"A safe word," he clarifies, his gaze boring into me.

330

"Red," I blurt, relief flooding through me.

He stares hard for another minute, then gives a sharp nod of satisfaction. "Use it if you need to. And don't move."

I start to nod but then think better of it when his eyes flare with the darkness I just asked for.

With Logan, words matter. Don't move means *don't move.*

He gets off the bed and strips the blankets off completely, and I shiver with the sudden chill, goosebumps rising on my skin and my nipples pebbling under the intensity of his gaze.

He repositions me the way he wants me, then pulls out a knife—the same one he scarred me with—and makes quick work of slicing up the bed sheet into long, thin strips.

His actions are nothing like the controlled rage I saw when he shredded all my clothes and cut the ones I was wearing off me after I'd first come to the Reaper house, and yet somehow the quick, efficient actions feel even more dangerous in their deliberation.

I fight the need to squirm, my breath quickening and slick heat gathering between my legs.

Logan's nostrils flare like he can smell it, then he tucks the knife away and crawls onto the bed, using the shredded sheet to tie me up well enough that it's no longer a question of obeying him or not. I *can't* move.

He rakes his gaze down my body, then follows with his fingers, lightly skimming them over my waist where he removed the stitches before pressing them against the scar on my chest. Then he pinches my nipples, hard enough to make me jerk against my bonds as I cry out with the sudden, sharp twin bursts of pain.

Logan smiles, and my pussy throbs with a deep, yearning ache.

He drags all four fingers through the wet folds, then slaps my clit.

"Fuck," I gasp, my back arching off the bed as pleasure and

pain ripple through me in a twisted spiral that only leaves me wanting more.

He gives it to me, working me up with a clinical precision and a focused intensity that leaves me almost sobbing. Pushing my body to its limits in a way I've never experienced before. Every piece of me is fully exposed to him, completely at his mercy, and it's like he's figured out exactly how to turn each and every inch of my body into an erogenous zone.

And for every stroke, rub, tease, and slap he gives me, he adds in a twist of darkness, a sliver of pain, hurting me the perfect amount to keep me teetering right on the razor's edge between bliss and danger, between pleasure and pain.

But he doesn't kiss me again. He stays fully clothed and keeps his distance.

He's doing this *for* me, to me, but not with me.

At least, that's what I think until I notice the rigid line of his cock, trapped in his jeans.

"*Logan*," I whimper, my whole body aching with need. I want him inside me. I want him to fuck me. I need it. I'm almost delirious with it.

But he doesn't give it to me.

Instead, he forces me to come.

"Oh shit, fuck, god, *yes*," I pant, shuddering in the aftermath.

His fingers drip with my arousal as he finally rips open his jeans, his eyes still burning into me like pale fire, and frees his cock. He drops down on top of me, bracing himself with one arm so a few inches remain between us, and shoves the thick head against my swollen clit.

Once. Twice. And then I'm coming again, my body straining against the tight restraints as it rips through me.

Logan never breaks eye contact as he starts jerking himself off with short, violent strokes and then spatters his release across my stomach, marking me up all over again.

His cum pools in my navel and runs down my sides, and I want to taste him again so badly I could scream. I'm sure he feels the same. His lips hover just inches above mine, his knuckles brushing against my damp skin as his cock softens between us. But then he blinks and jerks away, rising up to his knees between my spread legs.

For a moment, I think he's going to bolt, but then his eyes flare with that pale fire again and he carefully catches the cum that's started to drip down onto the mattress, rubbing it into my skin. Spreading it out until I'm completely covered and working it in like he's trying to merge it with my flesh.

Finally, once he's satisfied, he unties me and rubs feeling back into my wrists and ankles where they were bound before repositioning me on the bed.

"Don't move," he says softly, echoing his command from earlier as he steps away from the bed.

"I can't," I whisper, letting my eyes drift closed. And it's the truth. I'm limp and worn out and completely sated, my body aching and well-used and utterly *done*. I may not be numb or empty anymore, but I'm still exhausted... and it's a far better feeling than the blankness and despair I felt before.

But still not as good as the kernel of warmth that spreads out from my center when Logan returns after a minute with a fresh sheet to fix the bedding around me as I sink down into darkness again. But a different kind of darkness this time, one that feels like coming home.

It's my last thought before sleep takes me hard, holding me under for the rest of the night.

35

DANTE

I'M STILL THINKING about the shit that went down at Frank Sutton's place as I finish getting ready in my room the next morning. I can't think of a single thing we missed at the scene, but my gut still says there was something to find, and that West Point found it before they took Sutton out.

I pause as I strap on the holster I always wear inside my pants. No one's gonna miss that piece of shit, but it still gutted me to see what his death did to Riley. And not gonna lie, it also surprised the shit out of me that Logan stepped up when she broke down.

But maybe it shouldn't have.

Not knowing what I do—which isn't all the details, but it's enough—about his past.

I shake off those thoughts and finish tucking my weapon into the holster, but now that Logan's on my mind, I think about the other thing that surprised me.

Coming up the stairs after Madd and I finished handling our business, there was no mistaking the sounds I heard coming from Riley's room, and my cock reacts now just like it did last night.

I've never known Logan to develop feelings for a woman

before. It's not just that he doesn't have much use for them, it's that he's got a soul-deep distrust for the entire gender, and it bleeds over into everything. Everything except Riley. She's gotten under all of our skins, and I'd be lying if I said that knowing my brothers have been just as affected as I am doesn't feel all kinds of right.

Hearing her moan for Logan last night was hot as fuck.

I palm myself through my jeans. If I had a do-over, I might have snuck in there to watch. But I know now ain't the time—not with West Point on the move, potentially with a lead we don't have—so I ignore how interested my dick is in picturing Riley falling apart for my brother, and head downstairs.

Logan's already there, sitting at the counter with the kitchen pristine and his standard boring-ass breakfast of an egg-white-and-spinach omelet with whole grain toast, as cool and controlled as ever.

"Morning," he greets me, not a single blond hair out of place or any other sign that he fucked our girl hard last night.

Or did he?

Shit, now I'm back to imagining all sorts of options I wouldn't have minded having a front-row seat for last night.

I grin at him, heading for the coffee. "Good morning after a good night, yeah?"

Logan pauses with his fork halfway to his mouth, giving me a flat look devoid of all emotion.

I laugh, not buying it, but don't push it. He's got a complicated relationship with his emotions, and even though it turns me on to think about the two of them together, I can be patient and wait to see how that shit unfolds and what it might mean for me and my brothers in a longer term scenario.

I turn back to the coffee machine and change the subject, filling him in on some of the steps Madd and I took last night to make sure we get ahead of McKenna's people. It doesn't surprise me that Logan's already brought himself up to speed on most of this, but we toss a few ideas back and forth as he finishes eating.

After a bit, I hear footsteps on the stairs. Too light to be Maddoc's, so I grab a second mug from the cupboard and start doctoring a coffee the way I know our girl likes it.

"You think we should lean on the Scorpions?" I ask Logan, stirring in the sugar as Riley finally stumbles into the kitchen.

He doesn't acknowledge her, just looks off into the distance for a moment before giving me a sharp nod.

"Miguel has no love for West Point."

The small-time gang in the east end of the city isn't an ally, but Logan's right about the rocky history between their leader and McKenna. Even better, the Scorpions make most of their money by running a stable of cheap whores. Even if none of Miguel's girls have seen Chloe, they might have heard talk from some of their johns.

"How are you doing this morning, princess?" I ask softly, handing her coffee to her as Logan starts tapping away on his phone, no doubt following through on my suggestion to put some pressure on the Scorpions.

Riley gives me a wan smile as she takes the mug, sipping it instead of answering me.

She looks fucking wrecked. Gorgeous, as per always of course, but tired and as if her spirit's been shredded by everything that went down yesterday.

I glance at Logan, but he shows no outward sign that he connected with her last night. He's also not being cold to her though, so that's something.

"Breakfast?" he asks as he stands and brings his dishes to the sink, not making eye contact with either of us.

It's not clear whether he's asking me or Riley, but when she gives a subtle shake to her head, he drops it, so I guess that answers that.

She stands at the counter silently drinking her coffee as

Logan and I go over a few more logistics, but not gonna lie, my mind isn't a hundred percent on it now. Watching the two of them dance around each other takes a chunk out of my attention, and if Riley wasn't feeling so obviously ragged still, I'd be enjoying the silent drama as each pointedly fails to acknowledge the other.

Something's there, simmering in the air between them, and I wonder how long it will take before they both admit it.

As for me, I'm done pretending I'm not all-in with Riley. She's the most amazing woman I know, and it kills me a little to see the toll all this shit is taking on her.

"More coffee?" I ask as she stares down into her empty mug.

"No," she says, not moving. She still seems a bit numb, but thankfully not as fucking catatonic as she was yesterday.

I take the mug out of her hands and set it onto the counter, pulling her into my arms. She doesn't resist, and when I bury my face in her hair and breathe in that spice-and-smoke scent I'm already fucking addicted to, she wraps her arms around me.

"This isn't over yet," I promise, liking the way she clings to me more than I'll ever admit.

Logan meets my eyes over the top of her head, the look a silent vow that he's backing that statement up. He turns away to take her mug to the sink as Maddoc comes in.

"We need to go over plans for the day," Madd says in lieu of a greeting, his eyes skating over Riley with a depth of worry I'd be shocked if he let himself voice aloud.

Something unexpected warms inside me at the solidarity I feel with my brothers upon seeing that. Logan, Maddoc, and I have a bond that goes deeper than any I'd imagined ever finding anywhere else in this life, but with Riley as a touchstone for all of us, what was already solid becomes something even more.

Riley stays pressed against me as Logan brings both of us up to speed on a few things, including a reply he got from the Scorpions.

"Miguel doesn't have anything on Chloe," he says. The mention of her sister's name makes Riley tense in my arms as he adds, "But he's making some noise about the warehouse fire that went down on Grandview the other day."

Maddoc makes a note of it. Finding Chloe is our priority, but that doesn't mean we can let the rest of our business slide. I frankly don't know what the fuck we're gonna do now that Madd's taken the girl's inheritance off the table. I don't disagree, but that doesn't change the fact that we're going to have to find another way to put McKenna and his people down for good.

But first things first. I can tell Riley's following the conversation even though she doesn't participate, and we strategize some options we haven't exercised yet on putting pressure on some key players for more information. With Sutton taken out and all that implies, we need to go flat out to get ahead of McKenna's crew on this.

Halfway through our planning situation, Maddoc gets a call. I see Shae's name on his screen before he swipes to accept the call. Shae is one of the gang members we assigned to keep an eye on West Point last night, and after sharing a pointed glance with me and Logan, Maddoc throws it on speaker.

"Got something, boss," Shae says, the sound of traffic behind him. "Those weasels you put me on last night are on the move."

"Are you still near Falls Court?" Maddoc asks, naming a section of the city where territory is contested.

"Yeah," Shae says, confirming it. "They've got no legit reason to have so many of their crew here, and there's too much sudden activity to be business. Something's going down."

"Does it have to do with my sister?" Riley blurts, finally stirring to attention.

The phone goes silent. I know Shae doesn't recognize Riley's voice or trust that he can disclose Reaper business in front of her, but Maddoc sets him straight.

"Report, Shae. Are they going after Chloe?"

"I've heard some noise, yeah," Shae answers slowly. "Sounds like West Point has a new lead on where she's been holed up. They're on the move now, headed over to the Rand District." Maddoc's phone beeps. "Just sent you the cross streets they mentioned, boss. I don't know that area well—"

"A lot of abandoned buildings there," Logan murmurs, tapping away at his own phone and no doubt making it give up secrets the rest of us would never manage to pull out of the ethers.

"Have you got eyes on them now?" Maddoc asks as the background sounds change, becoming muffled.

Shae must have gotten in his car.

"Yeah," he confirms.

"Good. Stay on them." Maddoc points toward the garage, giving me the signal to gear up and prepare to move as he pulls a few more details out of Shae.

I nod, then snag the keys to the Escalade, pulling Riley along with me.

"Come on, princess," I murmur, knowing there's no way she'll want to be left behind even though she's not at a hundred percent.

Logan and Maddoc follow, and the three of us grab some additional firepower from one of the locked cabinets we keep in the garage before piling into the Escalade. I drive with Madd in the passenger seat keeping Shae on the line to report on the weasels he's following. Riley gets in the back with Logan without a word.

I think about arming her for a hot second, but I don't know her capability and she doesn't ask. In the future, we may have to change that, but for now, speed is the most important factor.

"My bet is on 1041 Terrace Way," Logan says from the back seat as we approach the Rand District, a rundown mix of abandoned commercial buildings and state run housing. "The locals—" a minor gang with a chop shop, if I remember correctly,

"—keep running squatters out of it, but if Chloe was looking for a place to hole up and stay out of sight, it's a contender."

"I'm following those shitheads down Alameda Avenue right now," Shae's voice comes through from Maddoc's phone. "Does that track?"

"Yes." Logan's voice is clipped. "It intersects with Terrace Way and gives them access to the back of the building."

"Get there first," Madd says to me grimly.

I nod and push the Escalade a little faster, pulling up to the building in question as two silver Lincoln Navigators with blacked out windows screech to a halt from the other direction, coming from Alameda.

West Point. And Shae's low-slung muscle car thunders up right after them.

"Go, Logan," Maddoc says tightly.

Logan slides out the back passenger door, the body of the Escalade shielding him from West Point's view. I don't watch how he gets into the building, but if that's where Chloe's been squatting, I trust him to get in and get her out—or find any clues she left behind—while we take care of business out here.

"Stay in the car," I tell Riley as Maddoc and I pile out and face off with McKenna's people.

She doesn't listen, but at least she has enough self-preservation instincts to stay behind Madd and I as Austin McKenna steps out of one of the Navigators. That bitch Sienna follows him, draping herself over his back as she sneers at Maddoc.

"This isn't Reaper territory," Austin says, spitting on the ground as his people spread out behind him.

Shae had a couple of our crew in the car with him, and they fan out behind the weasels as Maddoc stares McKenna down, ignoring Sienna.

"It's not West Point's territory either," Madd says, his voice deceptively calm over a core of steel. "And neither is Whitton."

Frank Sutton's neighborhood.

McKenna's eyes narrow, but then he smiles, the expression sadistic and cruel. "No clue what you're talking about. We don't do business in Whitton." His eyes flick toward Riley. "That area is... dead."

Riley makes a low, furious sound behind me, and McKenna's eyes snap her way.

"Clear the fuck out," Maddoc says coldly, moving to block McKenna's view of Riley and giving the fucker a chance he doesn't deserve to avoid this turning ugly. "The Six won't be happy with how this goes down if you don't."

"We have business here," McKenna says, crossing his arms over his chest. "If you want to get in the way of that business the way you did before, that's on you. You cost me something in the warehouse district a couple of weeks ago. I'm here to get back what's mine."

"My sister doesn't belong to you!"

I grab Riley's arm before she does something stupid, just as Logan materializes next to us, moving like a shadow in the sun.

He's alone.

When Maddoc shoots him a hard look, he gives his head a subtle shake.

"The tip was good. She's been here. But she's cleared out," he murmurs under his breath. "Signs point to an extended stay."

McKenna overhears. "Search the fucking building," he shouts at his men, his face mottling with rage as he makes no pretense at all that they aren't here for Chloe too.

"I wouldn't follow that order," Shae says, cocking a gun behind them.

That sound is all it takes for every fucker standing to draw their weapons, including me and my brothers.

"Get the fuck behind me," I bite out, jerking my chin at Riley.

She still looks like she wants to lay into McKenna, but she

341

obeys, which lets me focus. With Shae and his backup surrounding McKenna's men, we're evenly matched in manpower, but since one Reaper is worth a half dozen weasels any day, we've still got the advantage as far as I'm concerned.

But Madd is right that we'll get exactly the kind of attention The Six warned us off from if this shit escalates.

There's no fucking way we'll be the ones to back down first, though.

"You want to see your crew's blood on *every* street in Halston?" McKenna asks with a manic gleam in his eye, making a pointed reference to Payton's death. "Because I'm happy to oblige. This shit hole would look a hell of a lot better painted in Reaper red."

Madd takes the safety off the Glock he's holding, raising it to aim between McKenna's eyes. "If you want to see blood, that can be arranged. Not that the view will be great with nine millimeters of metal buried in your skull."

McKenna licks his lips. "You've been doing a lot of burying lately, isn't that right?"

"What the fuck did you say?" Madd asks in a low, furious voice.

McKenna smiles, his own weapon never wavering. "You're welcome. But the way you've made my men work so hard, putting the job of thinning your herd on our shoulders? They deserve a reward for that. I think I'll give it to them in the form of some quality time with that hot little number we're here to collect. The young ones are always so... sweet."

Riley makes an inarticulate sound of rage.

"*Riley*," Maddoc snaps as half a dozen weapons swing around to point at her.

My brothers realize the same thing I do. Hearing that fuckhead threatening her sister like that could set her off.

Maddoc and I both move, but Logan moves faster. His arm lashes out, wrapping around Riley's waist and hauling her back against him as he swings them both around, his body providing her cover as the tension that was already at the snapping point comes to a head between one breath and the next.

McKenna cackles, a sound of unholy glee, and the sound of even more weapons being drawn and cocked echoes loud in the empty waste of a street. It's a sound that triggers the craving for blood to be spilled. It boils hot in my veins as Shae and his crew spit curses and scramble from their defensive stances, becoming an active threat.

West Point's players mirror it, and all my senses sharpen, my focus narrowing as I instinctively prepare to fight.

If anyone so much as twitches, it's gonna turn into a goddamn blood bath, and part of me wants that with a ferocity that I'd give anything to unleash. But we've got no fucking cover and I can't risk my brothers getting killed.

I can't risk a bullet finding *Riley*... or what they'd do to her if we went down.

36

RILEY

I SEE RED. Blood rushes in my ears as rage floods my body like a molten force, and if Logan doesn't get the fuck off me and let me give Austin McKenna what he deserves for the disgusting things he said about my sister—for what he's already done to her and the plans he has for her future—I'm going to castrate him.

Dante steps forward, a dozen weapons swinging toward him as he deliberately re-holsters his own and spreads his hands. "Not the time or place," he says, every muscle in his body still vibrating with readiness even as he lays on the charm and starts to de-escalate the tension.

Maddoc steps back, coordinating his movements with Logan's as they both block me from being able to see any of those West Point fuckers.

"Logan," Maddoc says with a pointed look that carries the weight of a full conversation.

Logan nods and loosens his grip on me, and Maddoc takes over. Pulling me back as he murmurs in my ear. "He's never going to touch her. You know I won't let it happen. Come on now, you need to stay calm so we can get to her."

I'm breathing so hard my chest is heaving, but Maddoc keeps up a low, steady murmur that lowers my heart rate and pulls the world back into focus for me. I don't want to stand down, but he's right. I've got the shakes, worry and anger and rage all warring for space inside me, but none of that shit is going to help my sister.

Logan said she was here. I'm not sure what he saw, but I trust him to get that right.

Chloe was here. Now she's gone. Now isn't the time for retribution on West Point, it's time to wrap this up so we can follow whatever clues Logan found in there. Because he *had* to have found some. If I don't believe that, I'll go fucking crazy.

"None of us can afford to spill blood in the Breakers' territory," Dante is saying, his voice reasonable and calm in the midst of a sea of potential violence. It's working, though. No one but Dante has put their weapon away, but most of them are lowered now.

Then Austin McKenna catches my eye, and smirks.

"Speaking of things no one can afford," he drawls, tugging his girlfriend around in front of him and groping her obscenely. "Looks like you went low rent on your replacement, Maddoc. Sutton offered me a twofer, but a washed up stripper?"

He spits on the ground again, and Maddoc makes a brutal sound, thrusting me behind him as he cocks his gun again. Dante and Logan draw theirs too, and although no one moves, it feels like shooting might break out at any moment.

And there's nothing between my Reapers and West Point's guns.

The hot rage that blinded me to good sense when Austin insulted my sister drains out of me, replaced by a flood of cold fear. I don't know what it is exactly that's happening between me and these men, but I can't lose them.

My hand is shaking as I raise it slowly, resting my fingers lightly on Maddoc's back. His tense muscles shudder under the light touch, and then, with a strained breath, he straightens and lowers his gun.

"Stand down," he grits out.

The tension remains so high it feels like the air is quivering, but the other Reapers instantly obey him—both Maddoc's seconds and the men who trailed West Point here.

Austin smirks again, then directs his men toward the abandoned building. "Search it."

Maddoc and Dante both stiffen, but Logan leans in to murmur quietly to Maddoc. "I stripped it."

They let the West Point men pass.

"They won't find anything?" I ask, worried about those assholes getting any closer to my sister than they already have.

Logan looks at me with his pale eyes. "I took care of it."

I relax, at least as much as I can. But I trust him. If Chloe left any clues, Logan found them and made sure West Point wouldn't.

After a while, they storm back out, glaring at us and muttering threats as they stomp back toward the two SUVs they arrived in. All except for Austin and Sienna.

Austin isn't smirking anymore. "You might wanna watch your back from here on out."

He pins Maddoc with a dangerous look, then turns his back on the Reapers and stalks toward one of the vehicles.

Sienna lags behind for a moment. "Or not."

The cold smile she directs at Maddoc turns into a hot glare as her eyes slide toward me. Then she sneers.

I don't give a shit. She has no right to be jealous after cheating on Maddoc.

She betrayed him, and I fucking hate her for that alone. The fact that she chose to be on the side of the sadistic asshole who's targeting my sister just puts the nails in the coffin. But finally, they leave.

Maddoc instantly turns to Logan. "Report."

"I found signs that Chloe had been there, and West Point must have got that from Sutton. She wasn't here last night, though, so she probably cleared out after that call she placed."

"Why?"

"It looks like she wasn't the only squatter. My guess is she felt unsafe, and did the smart thing and got the fuck out."

My stomach sinks. "How far could she have gone?"

None of them have an answer.

"Let's search the area to see if we can figure out where she headed."

Maddoc tells the Reapers who came to back them up to keep an eye out in case West Point comes back with the same idea, or whoever the other gang whose territory we're actually in shows up, and I spread out with the three of them to search around the building.

We don't find anything, and that numb despair that I was drowning in after Frank wraps icy fingers around my heart again as Maddoc gives his troops more commands, telling them to spread out and cast a wider net.

"Play nice with the Breakers if you run into them," he says.

"And if they don't let us, boss?" the bulky man they'd called Shae asks, cracking his knuckles.

"Do what you have to," Maddoc says grimly, "but remember, we need allies."

The men nod and disperse, and Dante wraps a hand around the back of my neck, offering support.

"Come on, princess," he says, urging me toward the Escalade. "Let's get back to the house and regroup."

I nod, but what do we have to go on, really? Chloe's been on her own too damn long. I'm scared for her.

"Riley."

I look up, startled out of my despair by the intensity of Maddoc's voice.

"We'll keep looking."

I nod listlessly, ready to get home already.

He grabs my arm before I can turn away, forcing me to turn back around as those Siberian Husky eyes of his burn into mine with a promise I can't ignore. "We'll keep looking *until we find her*. This doesn't end until we get her back. Until Chloe is safe. Don't give up."

I never will... but I needed to hear that. I'll *never* give up on my sister, but keeping up hope is hard.

It's a little less hard when I don't have to do it alone, though.

"Okay," I say, offering him a small smile.

He doesn't smile back, but his eyes soften. Then he finally nods and lets me go, the three of them forming a protective barrier between me and the world as they escort me back to the Escalade and take me back to the house.

Take me... *home*.

LOGAN COLLECTED a few things my sister left behind at the abandoned building, confirming it was really her, but when a few days go by without any further sign of her, I feel like I'm going to snap.

"How about Jameson Mathers?" Dante asks me as I pace back and forth in the Reapers' front room.

"Who?" I snap, even though he doesn't deserve it.

I'm antsy, nervous, and on edge, my heart feeling brittle as the days Chloe's missing add up.

Dante calmly repeats himself. The Reapers have been looking into everyone Chloe's ever had contact with on the off chance she reached out to someone besides Frank, and I don't even want to know what they hacked into—her cloud storage account? Her social media?—to come up with the list of contacts he's going over with me.

I remember Jameson now, though. Some boy from her school who used to sniff around, hoping to get a piece of her.

I shake my head.

"Okay," Dante says, tapping out a quick message to someone after quickly conferring with Logan. They're probably telling whoever they've got watching Jameson Mathers that he's not worth keeping eyes on, especially when there's so much other ground to cover.

I can't even imagine what this effort is costing them, especially since they're not doing it for the money anymore. Or at least, not to gain access to her inheritance for themselves.

Maddoc's made it clear that letting West Point get their hands on it isn't an option, but I know that's not the only reason they're devoting so many resources to finding my sister. They're doing it because of what's brewing between us.

I've never had anyone on my side like this before, and I appreciate it more than I can ever put into words. I'm doing everything I can to help track down every glimmer of a lead, but every minute she's out there on her own is another minute closer to Austin McKenna finding her first and it's getting to me.

I can't let myself think about what that sadistic bastard will do if he finds her. I *can't*.

"Let me run facial recognition," Logan mutters under his breath as he and Dante put their heads together.

Dante smirks. "Got live facial recognition right here," he says, nodding toward me as he flips his phone around to show me the screen. "How about these girls, princess?" Three girls. Chloe, laughing in the middle. Her hair dyed the way it was last summer and a worn brick wall behind them that looks like the high school we both went to. "No names or caption," Dante adds. "Do you recognize them?"

I blink. Maybe? I can't think. "This is fucking *useless*."

Logan doesn't flinch as he methodically works through whatever the fuck he has on his screen, but Dante gives me a patient look that makes me want to scream.

Then Maddoc's gritty voice sounds from behind me. "Take her down to CMA."

I whirl around, and he's leaning against the doorjamb, giving Dante one of those looks that speaks volumes I'm not privy to.

Dante tucks his phone away and gets to his feet. "Good idea, Madd."

"CMA?" I jump in. "What's that? Did you get another lead on Chloe?"

Maddoc's lips tilt up at the corners, but the pale eyes he's got me pinned with stay serious. "Not yet. CMA is a shooting range. You need to learn to handle a weapon."

I shake my head, turning my back to him and stalking over to the front window. I push the curtains aside and stare out into the empty street. "I don't like guns."

Behind me, Dante snorts and the rapid-fire sound of Logan's fingers on his keyboard go still.

"It doesn't matter if you like them as long as you can shoot them," Maddoc says calmly.

I whirl back around to face him, lashing out with all the frustration and fear that has nowhere else to go. "I *can* shoot. You know that. I just don't want to."

Maddoc just stares me down. "It's not about want. Sometimes we need to do shit we don't like. And there's a difference between pulling the trigger and knowing how to handle a weapon." He reaches up and touches his shoulder, the one that carries the scar from the bullet I put into him. "If you could actually shoot, you wouldn't have missed."

I grimace at the reminder of the night I shot him. And I see his point. We were standing so close together in the kitchen that it should've been easy for me to put a bullet in his heart.

But honestly, I'm not so sure that the reason I missed is because of my lack of weapons training. The truth is that even

350

then, despite how angry and hurt I was, some part of me didn't want to kill Maddoc.

His eyes soften as if he can read my thoughts, and he adds quietly, "Go to the range with Dante, butterfly. It's a dangerous fucking world, and you're right in the middle of it now."

It's a dangerous world that all three of these men have protected me from in their own ways. Put themselves between me and the line of fire, again and again. But he's right, they might not always be there to do that... and the fact that he's concerned about it, about *me*, means something.

"Okay," I say, all the fight going out of me. Besides, I'm not doing any good here right now, and releasing some of this pressure on a shooting range instead of by biting off the heads of the only three people besides my sister who seem to give a damn about me is probably a win.

Dante slings an arm around me, a grin stretching across his gorgeous face. "You, me, and some hot metal? Trust me, we're gonna have fun, princess."

"I'll go too," Logan says, methodically closing up the laptop he was working on and getting to his feet.

"You will?" I ask, a part of me startled that he wants to voluntarily spend time with me, even after the way things have shifted between us. But it also warms something inside my chest.

Dante, on the other hand, looks a little put out, his arm reflexively tightening around me. "You don't have to do that."

Logan returns Dante's gaze without any expression. "I want to."

I almost grin despite all the worry and frustration coursing through me. I've never once seen any one of these three have a problem with the way I'm growing close to each of them, but I'd put money on the fact that Dante was hoping for a little one-on-one time with me just now... and I don't hate the idea.

But I also don't hate the idea of being looked out for by *both* of them.

Dante holds Logan's eyes for another second before relaxing with one of his easy grins. "Yeah, all right. Then let's get out of here."

Maddoc's phone buzzes. "Take the Escalade," he says before he turns away to take it, leaving the room.

"Guess that means I'm driving," Dante says. "Go put on some different shoes, princess. Nothing with open toes. And no exposed skin here." He runs fingers over my exposed collarbones, then down my cleavage, exposed in the tank top I threw on this morning. "That's not gonna feel good if hot brass hits it. Put on something with long sleeves."

"You want your hair pulled back too," Logan adds, assessing me with his cool gaze. "Do you have a hat?"

I almost point out that I didn't have any of that shit when I shot Maddoc. I was naked, sweaty, and covered with his cum. My hair being down didn't get in the way of pulling the trigger *that* time. But instead, I just head upstairs to do as I've been told, leaving Logan quietly grumbling something about his Audi that makes Dante laugh.

When I come back down dressed in more protective clothing, we head out.

Once we get to the range, they run me through some basic safety instructions and make me put on protective gear for my eyes and ears, then finally hand me a gun.

"Keep it pointed toward the target, princess," Dante says before he releases it to my grip. "You gotta always assume any weapon you touch is loaded, and treat it accordingly."

"Okay," I say, my senses abnormally sharp as the cool metal gives me a focus for all the adrenaline in my system. "This one is smaller than Maddoc's, though."

I want to bite my tongue as soon as the words leave my mouth, not sure if I'll ruin things by bringing that up, even though Maddoc alluded to it himself earlier. But Dante just laughs, resting one hand on the small of my back, and Logan—flanking me on the other side—gives me a small smile too.

"It's a Ruger LC9s," Logan says. "Better suited to your stature, and it's a reliable, accurate weapon."

"Not gonna knock you on your ass with the recoil, either," Dante adds. He hesitates for a second, then adds, "It was Payton's."

The slim, compact gun is already warming in my hands. I'm not sure how I feel about knowing where it came from, so I don't dwell on it, just taking the knowledge the way I suspect it's meant. As acceptance.

"So what do I do with it?" I ask, spreading my legs and squinting one eye as I point it toward the paper target set up for me.

"This is an original model," Dante says, indicating the gun as he moves behind me. He wraps one arm around, pressing up against my back, and covers my right hand with his, his thumb nudging mine over a small lever. "It's got a safety you're gonna have to take off before you do anything."

The little lever under my thumb clicks.

"Now I shoot?" I ask, a surge of something that feels almost sexual moving through me as I grip the stock. My finger curls around the trigger, and I do it without waiting for him to say so.

The gun jerks in my hand, the metal hot and the recoil Dante promised wouldn't knock me on my ass still enough to get my attention.

I fucking love it... but the target looks pristine.

"Did I hit it?"

Dante laughs. "After taking off the safety, you might wanna aim first."

"I did," I lie, that hot rush of pleasure still simmering in my blood. I needed this, and I didn't even know it.

And I want to do it again.

I squint my left eye, steadying the gun with both hands as Dante releases me and steps off to the side, giving me room.

"Keep both eyes open," Logan says before I shoot again.

"What?" I ask, turning toward him. "Why?"

His hand darts out and blocks my wrist, guiding the barrel of the gun back toward the target.

"Sorry," I say, although even the embarrassment of forgetting that bit of gun safety can't dim the pleasure still coursing through me. This release is exactly what I needed, and Maddoc is probably right. It's a skill I should master.

Logan's expression lightens in a way that's not quite a smile, but still warms me. "Squinting your non-dominant eye can help you direct your focus, but it narrows your field of vision. Train yourself to keep them both open so you can have maximum awareness of your surroundings."

Logan moves behind me, taking the spot Dante was in before, pressing his strong, lean body against my back and sending a shiver of an entirely different kind of pleasure through me.

"Okay, so I just..." I raise the gun again and try to line up the little bump at the end, the sight, with the target.

"Yes," Logan says, reaching around me to subtly adjust my aim. "Keep the barrel level with the horizon."

"Trust your instincts, princess," Dante adds, a smile in his voice. "Don't worry too much about making it an exact science. You're not gonna have time to line everything up if you've got to defend yourself out on the streets. You just need to start developing some muscle memory."

When Logan shifts behind me, I react to a different kind of muscle memory, my pulse picking up speed.

His hands slide down my sides and settle on my hips. "Balance your weight."

"When it feels right, fire," Dante says.

I pull the trigger, better prepared for the recoil this time. A dark hole appears next to one of the outer rings of the target.

"I hit it!"

Logan's grip shifts, turning my body a little. "Your aim was high, the trajectory off by thirty-seven degrees."

Dante laughs. "Good enough to wing the fucker."

The targets are shaped like concentric circles instead of the outline of a body, but I think he's right.

"You've got seven in the clip, princess. Lay 'em down. The only way to learn the gun is to use it."

Logan clicks his tongue against his teeth, shaking his head as he moves away from me. "The muscle memory you need will develop by repeating precise techniques, with careful deliberation. Once you pull the hammer back to ninety percent—"

I lower the gun. "To what?"

Logan takes it from me and shows me what he means. "Once it's here, pause. Breathe out. Sight down the barrel..."

He fires, hitting the center of the target, then hands it back to me.

Dante grins. "Nah, just trust yourself, princess. We've got plenty of rounds. Go for it."

"Practice precision and control," Logan counters from my other side, crossing his arms over his chest. "Lay a good foundation."

They start to bicker, and I tune it out, lining up the gun and imagining Austin McKenna's smirking face in the center of the target. I pull the trigger again.

"Not bad," Dante says, his breath ghosting over the back of my neck. "Logan's right about balancing your stance if you can, though." He presses up against me, nestling my ass against his groin as he holds me steady. "Now let's try it again, like this."

He stays there while I shoot through the entire clip, the rush of release each time I fire something I think I could get addicted to. But when Logan takes Dante's place behind me for the next few rounds, it's another kind of release I start to crave.

My nipples ache, pebbled against the lacy bra that contains them, and when Logan moves my body into a subtly different position, taking charge of it in a way that echoes the way he took me apart in the bedroom, my pussy floods with heat.

"Slow your breath. Slow your pulse," Logan murmurs, the heat of him seeping into me from behind as I imagine what it would be like if I lowered the gun so Dante could come around to my front. Take my mouth. Pin me between the two of them while we all chased a different kind of release.

I'm a heartbeat away from suggesting it when Logan's front pocket lets out a shrill ring, the vibration shuddering through me as his phone goes off with a ringtone I already know means it's Maddoc calling.

Logan immediately drops his hands and steps away, pulling out his phone to take it. He doesn't bother with a greeting, and I can just make out the faint rumble of Maddoc's voice as Logan's eyes lock onto mine.

"Give me the gun, princess," Dante says grimly, taking it from me and quickly emptying it of bullets.

"We're on our way," Logan says into the phone after a moment, ending the call and pocketing his phone. "Chloe's been spotted."

"What?" I gasp, my heart jackrabbiting as my hands start to shake.

Dante quickly finishes dealing with the gun as I rip off my safety gear and toss it at a man Logan signaled to come take care of it for us.

"One of our street informants saw someone who matches her description," Logan tells us as Dante takes my hand and we all hurry out to the Escalade. "Maddoc is headed to the spot she was seen now. I'll drive. Keys?"

He holds out a hand and Dante snorts, his grip tightening on my hand. "I got it, brother."

Logan shakes his head, and something passes between them that I don't have it in me to wonder about.

After only a brief hesitation, Dante tosses him the keys after all. He ushers me into the front seat and gets busy tapping away on his phone in the back as Logan peels out of the parking lot, the big vehicle taking the turn onto the main road faster than I would have thought possible for something that size.

I still want to go faster, and I have to sit on my hands to stop the shakes. I'm terrified that this will just turn out to be another false lead, or that we'll be too late... but I'm something else too.

With these men by my side and the Reapers pouring everything they have into helping me find my sister, with my frustration burned off on the gun range and the solid wall of their support thrumming in the air between us, for the first time in longer than I can remember, I'm *hopeful*. Chloe's out there, and we're going to find her.

I'm going to get my sister back.

37

RILEY

It's all I can do to keep my mouth closed as Logan navigates through the streets of Halston. I want to tell him to hurry, but he already is. Even though he's driving with as much precision and care as he does everything else, he's breaking just about every speed limit the city has in place... and he's good enough to get away with it too.

It still doesn't feel like enough, though. Not when there's no way of knowing whether Chloe will still be where she was spotted by the time we get there, or if it was even really her in the first place.

"We'll find her, princess," Dante murmurs from the backseat.

I nod on autopilot.

"Breathe," he adds with a low chuckle.

I let out an explosive breath, one I didn't even realize I was holding until he pointed it out. It doesn't do a damn thing to make me feel any less antsy, though. I don't even realize my leg is jittering until Logan reaches over without taking his eyes off the road and rests a hand on my thigh, steadying me.

The unexpected gesture of comfort surprises me enough that I manage to tear my eyes off the road ahead of us for a second to look over at him. His eyes are still straight ahead, a look of total concentration on his face.

It almost makes me smile. Maybe it wasn't so much comfort as that the frantic motion of my leg was driving him crazy. Either way, I'll take it. Both of these men are reminding me in their own ways that I'm not alone in this. That they care too.

Logan rounds a corner at a speed that the Escalade shouldn't be able to handle, and I see a couple of vehicles parked in the street that I think I recognize as belonging to the Reapers. I'm not all that familiar with this part of the city and have no idea which gang claims it. In other circumstances, that might have put my guard up, but with Maddoc standing on the sidewalk in front of a storefront with bars on the windows talking to a small cluster of people I'm pretty sure are part of his organization, I don't worry about it. I'm not sure when I started associating one of Halston's most ruthless gangs with a feeling of safety and protection, but that's what the Reapers have become for me.

Now, I only hope they can be that for Chloe too.

"Is this it?" I ask as Logan pulls to a smooth stop next to the small group, my voice tight from the sudden constriction in my throat. "Is this where they saw her?"

"Yes," he answers succinctly as Maddoc looks up and meets my eyes.

I fumble with my seatbelt, hands shaking again, then hurry to his side as if drawn by a magnet.

"Where?" I ask, interrupting whatever he was saying to his crew mid-sentence. "Where is she?"

He takes the interruption in stride, holding a hand out to me and pulling me against him without a word of censure. "We heard someone who fits her description was seen ducking down that alley."

He nods toward it, and it's all I can do not to break away

from him and race down there to check myself. I know better, though. He got here first. He would have already done that.

"Where do we look?"

"We've already checked with the businesses on this street. She didn't enter any of them, but the owner of the pawn shop says he thinks he saw her walking past his windows."

"Is he your..." *What did Logan call it?* "Your street informant?"

"No," Maddoc says, which makes Dante break into a grim smile.

"So that's two confirmed sightings then," he says, getting an answering nod from Maddoc. "Sounds legit. Which direction was she going?"

"North," Maddoc says, jerking his chin up the street in that direction. "Levi's working his way up Grande, and I sent Kieran down Forty-Eighth. Take Greg and Amari and work the side streets to the west."

Dante nods and peels off with two of the Reapers.

"Logan, I want you, Kyle, and Jack to work your way east. It starts turning residential three blocks down." Maddoc looks at me. "Does she know anyone who lives around here?"

"I don't, um, I don't know. I don't think so."

But it's hard to think at all. I just want to *move*. I want to find her already.

But I also trust that Maddoc knows what he's doing, so I wait and let him call the shots.

"Go," he says to Logan and the other two, gripping my elbow. "Riley, come with me."

He sets off in the direction he indicated earlier—north—without letting go of me. I manage a small, grateful smile and get a long, steadying look in return. My heart is thundering in my ears and I feel so hyped up on adrenaline that his grip is the only thing grounding me, and I think he knows it.

"We looked up here earlier, but we're gonna go again now

that you're here," he tells me as we make our way down the street.

I nod, scared to get my hopes up but doing it anyway, because Maddoc's right. Even though there's no way Chloe could know about her inheritance yet, she knows enough to have stayed off the radar this long and to realize she's in danger out here. She also thinks a big part of that danger is the Reapers themselves, based on the shit that went down when she ran.

So she'll be hiding—hiding or running—especially if she sees the Reapers coming after her before she realizes that I'm here too.

We peer into alleys and check behind, under, and inside dozens of potential hiding spots that I hate picturing my little sister huddled in. I push those worries aside and focus, because that's exactly why we're here. So she *doesn't* have to hide anymore.

"Chloe?" I call out softly as we veer into yet another narrow, dank alley. "It's me. It's safe to come out."

There's no response and no sign of her, but I refuse to think that we got here too late.

I shake Maddoc's hand off and stomp to the end of the chain link fence blocking off the end of the alley, lacing my fingers through the rusty metal as I stare through it.

"Would she have gone over?" Maddoc murmurs, coming up behind me.

I blink, then shake my head. "No. Not unless she had to."

"No one was chasing her," Maddoc says. "It was just a sighting. Come on."

He tries to pull me back the other way, but doubt creeps in and turns my feet to lead. "What if I'm wrong?"

Maddoc gives me a small smile. "Then Kieran will catch sight of her. I had him circle around that way before you got here."

I nod jerkily and let him lead me out of the alley.

"Keep your eyes peeled," he says as we reach the end of the block. "We've got a lot of bodies out here, but you're the only one she's really gonna trust."

I nod again, then freeze.

"Chloe?" I whisper, pointing at a figure in the distance. One too far away to really make out much detail about, and wearing clothes I don't recognize—dark wash jeans and a baggy sweatshirt, head down and a baseball hat pulled low—but one that I *recognize*.

It's my sister. I know it is. I don't need to see her face to recognize the way she moves. It's her.

"*Chloe.*" I yell it this time, breaking into a sprint, but she's too far away and doesn't seem to hear me. Or maybe she just can't, not over the sound of an engine suddenly revving, loud enough that I can hear it from here as a sleek black van with tinted windows suddenly barrels out of a side street right next to her.

For a split second, Chloe freezes. Then she pivots and bolts in the opposite direction from the van, moving even farther away from me and Maddoc.

The van follows, and Maddoc is suddenly right next to me, grabbing my arm again. "Fuck," he spits out, racing next to me as we try to close the distance. "That's West Point."

Two muscle-bound goons tumble out of the still-moving van and grab Chloe, bringing my worst nightmares to life.

"No," I scream, my heart lurching as she struggles against them. "*Chloe.*"

I don't remember shaking Maddoc off, but I'm running flat out and with single-minded determination as they drag her into the van.

It's not enough. The door slams closed, and I don't even know if she heard me; if she knew I was here for her.

One of the blacked-out windows rolls down as the van peels

away, proving that those fucking West Point goons heard, though.

"No, god, fuck, no, *you can't have her.*"

My feet pound against the pavement as I race after them, every step jolting through my entire body. My vision narrows until nothing else exists but the black metal beast taking her away from me and the West Point monsters inside it.

Then the barrel of a gun appears in the window that came down, and the muzzle flares with bright fire as the staccato thunder of gunshots echoes down the narrow street.

Maddoc tackles me, shoving me into an alley and out of the way of the bullets, and I beat at his chest with blind fury as the van skids around a corner and disappears, taking my sister with it.

Taking Chloe.

"Let me *go*," I scream. "They can't—"

"Riley."

"We need to—"

"*Riley.*"

"I have to... have to..."

"I know," he says as I struggle against the iron cage of his arms.

But he doesn't know, or he wouldn't have fucking stopped me.

"*Maddoc.*" I wrench my face away when he reaches up to wipe my tears, his other arm locked firmly around my waist. "I have to save her. Let me fucking go!"

Instead, he cups my face and holds me even tighter, so tight that I feel the thundering beat of his heart against mine. Tight enough that the pain ripping through me only shreds me on the inside instead of ripping me all the way apart when I finally face the truth and break down sobbing against his chest.

We were too late. We lost her.

My sister is in the hands of a monster now.

363

38

MADDOC

I BITE off a curse and bottle up my impotent rage over McKenna getting the drop on us so I can absorb Riley's tears as she collapses against me. She's a fighter through and through, and has been since day one. This collapse is something else.

It's a sign that I fucking failed her.

Now I need to fix that... and the clock is ticking.

"She's gone," Riley whispers in a broken whisper that rips something open inside me.

"It's not over," I tell her, stitching that shit right back up because I have to, no matter how much I'm still reeling from how close she came to taking a bullet just now.

If they'd gunned her down in the street like they did Payton, it would have gutted me, but this—the raw pain she's radiating—is almost worse. My jaw clenches tight as she stares up at me with her eyes still overflowing, like she's begging me to make her believe what I said is true. Like she's still teetering on the edge of a fucking breakdown that I know damn well she understands we don't have time for.

Riley's breath hitches. "But what will they do to h—"

"Nothing," I cut in before she can start spinning horror stories that aren't gonna do us a damn bit of good to contemplate right now. "West Point is gonna keep her alive. They have to if McKenna's gonna get his hands on that money."

It's not sugar coated, but it's the truth. Most of it, anyway. West Point sure as shit won't have any reason to keep Chloe alive *after* they get access to her inheritance, and "alive" doesn't include any particular need to treat her well—especially not with a fucking sadist like McKenna calling the shots—but Riley doesn't need to hear that shit right now.

And not least of which because there's no way in hell that my brothers or I are ever gonna let it come to that.

"Do you understand?" I press when she keeps staring up at me blankly. "We've still got time to get her back. I need you to stay focused so we can get it done. The only way through is forward. Everything else can wait."

Everything else *has* to wait.

It's a lesson I've learned hard and often, and it's the same shit I say to myself each and every time I feel like I'm spinning out, or about to collapse under the weight of everything. Again, not sugar coated, but true. No matter how much shit life piles on—and the worse it gets, the heavier she dumps it—the only ones who get bogged down and buried in it are those who are too weak to keep going. You can always carry more, power through, if you're strong enough.

And I *know* Riley's strong enough.

After a moment, she nods, proving me right. I can tell it takes an effort and that she's barely keeping it together, but barely is good enough. I can practically see her spine stiffening, and then I feel it when she pulls away from me, throwing her shoulders back and angrily dashing the last of the tears off her cheeks.

"You're right," she says, her voice strained but determined. "Let's go. Do you know where they'll take her?"

"No."

For a split second, her chin wobbles, but then she grits her teeth and steadies it. "Okay. Let's figure it out. Let's find her."

I nod and call my people back, directing them to regroup at our vehicles. Riley turns to head back that way too once I get through to the whole crew, but before she can move I give in to the impulse to drag her back against me and kiss her hard and fast, just once.

It's a promise.

Once we all make it back, I gather them close. The street is quiet, but it's got eyes and ears. That's how we got our sighting in the first place. I'm not gonna waste time bringing everyone back to the house before we move on this though, so I herd them into a tight knot and keep my voice low.

"McKenna got Chloe."

"Mother*fuck*," Dante spits out, a curse echoed by half the group.

"You're sure it was them?" Logan asks, his eyes shards of ice as he skips the outburst and cuts to the action step.

"I recognized the players, but if you want to verify, it was a black Benz Sprinter. Plate number 8FCV723."

He nods, his phone already out as he moves to verify.

Kieran looks at me, eyes hard. "You want me to take Greg and Amari and head over to Cliffton, boss?"

West Point territory.

I shake my head, grinding my teeth. It's not the answer I want to give, but it's the right one. "We can't just bust into their territory."

"Someone will end up dead if we try to get her back that way," Dante adds.

"Sounds good to me, as long as the dead are all fucking weasels," Kyle spits out.

I give him a grim smile. "If I could guarantee that would be the case, we'd already be moving out. We need to be smart about this, though. A full frontal assault is McKenna's fucking wet dream."

And we all know he's too well fortified to risk it.

"So what then?" Kieran pipes up. "Where do you want us, boss?"

Riley leans into my side, her body so tense I can practically feel her thrumming, and I wrap an arm around her as I trade looks with my brothers. I trust their judgment and rely on their strengths, and it only takes me a minute to organize my thoughts.

I hand out assignments, making sure we'll have people in place once we figure out where the fuck we need to go, then get behind the wheel of the Escalade to head back to the house while Logan and Dante reach out to put pressure on everyone we know who has information about McKenna's business.

Riley stays focused but silent, even when we get back to the house and bust out a map of the city. It's the one I've got specifically marked up with all West Point's holdings, known safe houses, and the establishments under their "protection." The map is knowledge, which is leverage, which is the key to staying one step ahead of them at all fucking times.

"We can rule the cannery out," Dante says as we start to pore over the map, drawing a fat "X" over the spot as he explains his reasoning. Logan nods and makes a suggestion of his own, and Riley bites her lip, a furrow appearing between her eyebrows as we start working through it block by block, narrowing in on where to plan the extraction.

This isn't the same as when Riley was working with Logan to hunt for her sister, and I can see that she's battling a feeling of hopelessness as we go over what we know about McKenna's activities to work out where he would have stashed her.

"This is the club he had her dancing at, right?" Riley asks, stabbing at the map as her frustration bleeds through. "How about I go check *there*?"

Logan launches into one of his too-fucking-detailed explanations about why there's no way in hell McKenna would be dumb enough to hold Chloe at Club Prestige, and when he draws another "X" over it, Riley makes an inarticulate sound of rage, her frustration bleeding through.

Dante wraps his arms around her from behind. "Settle, princess," he murmurs in her ear. "This ain't a setback. It's progress. The more locations we can eliminate, the tighter our extraction plan will be."

Her eyes jump to mine, and when I nod in agreement, she takes a deep breath and squares her shoulders again, staring down at the map with a look of determination. "What about this bodega?" she asks. "West Point has some connection to it, right?"

Wrong, but it doesn't matter that she doesn't know how McKenna's fucked-up head works the way we do, or much about his gang activities. I still want her here. I want her to see progress being made. I want her to know we're not gonna stand by with our thumbs up our asses while she's hurting.

We work late into the night, Logan verifying shit online as we continue narrowing it down and hacking into city-wide cameras where he can, and Dante coordinating with our crew for on-site surveillance wherever we can manage it.

"We got enough to make a move yet, Madd?" Dante asks as Riley stifles a yawn, his face uncharacteristically grim. "I've got Shae over near The Barrows, but if we keep him there all night he's gonna get spotted."

I want to say yes, but I'd be a fucking liar.

I shake my head. "Send him home to get some rest, but tell him that come hell or high water, we're gonna get her tomorrow."

Dante nods, and when he hangs up with Shae, I manage to convince him that he should get some shut eye too. All three of us can and have gone on little to no sleep when we've had to, but this fucking day has taken a toll on each of us and it's better to stay sharp where we can.

Not that *I'm* planning on calling it a night yet. And not that Riley looks like she has any plans to close her eyes, either.

"Where else does that fucker do business?" she asks, glaring down at the map.

"Here," Logan says, tapping a few blocks in the heart of West Point's territory. "We can't get our people in there to check, but I'm going to go upstairs and hack into the ATM machine cameras in the area to look for that van."

I nod, and he heads up.

"Riley," I start, resting a hand on her back as she tries to drill a pair of holes through the map with those gorgeous coffee-colored eyes of hers.

"I'm not quitting."

"Of course not."

She's just strung out and fucking exhausted, and not doing a damn bit of good here. I hold back from saying so though, and keep working through the city with her as she sags against my side, closer and closer to passing out. Long after midnight, her body finally betrays her, and I lower her onto the couch, smoothing out all those vibrant purple and blue waves that frame her face the way I wish I could smooth out the pain that tightens her features, even now that she's given in to sleep.

I want to take that pain away.

I can't stand to see her fucking hurting like this.

And I stand there way too fucking long, staring down at her as I battle the rush of unexpected emotions before a thought occurs to me that I instinctively shove away before realizing what a dumb-ass move that is.

It might be a long shot and it's somewhere I've got nothing but shitty memories about, but there *is* one place we haven't checked out yet that I know damn well McKenna has used in the past when he wanted to stay under the radar. Under *my* radar, specifically.

He's got no idea that I followed Sienna to his little fucking love nest back when I first caught on to her cheating ways. Neither of them do. I confronted her about it after I saw them there, but I wasn't stupid enough to let my emotions cloud one of the most basic rules of survival. I told them what I knew, but I didn't give away how I knew it.

Neither of them have any reason to believe I know about the safe house they used to fuck in, but *I* know it's still leased in the name of one of the shell companies McKenna runs his legit-on-the-surface businesses through. I also know it's right on the edge of West Point's territory, and that if I don't go check it out right the fuck now, I'll lose my best chance to stop that asshole from moving on Chloe's inheritance at the start of banking hours tomorrow.

I stare down at Riley for another two seconds, then toss a blanket over her, grit my teeth, blow out a fast breath, and *move*.

The house is in a run-down residential neighborhood with trash in half the front yards and more street lamps dark than lit, and I cut the lights on the Escalade and coast to a stop three blocks down and one block over before cutting the engine. A dog barks from behind a rusted chain link fence when I slip out to cut across a few lawns, and I go still, waiting to see if the sound will bring unwanted attention from the direction of the West Point house.

It doesn't, and after a minute, the owner yanks a door open and screams at it, finally getting it to shut the fuck up. I curse under my breath when he lingers and do my best to blend into the shadows, waiting again to see if McKenna's men will react now that there's a human voice in the mix. But when the dog owner slams his door closed again, returning inside, and no one heads in my direction from the safe house, I finally figure it's safe to move.

And the minute I peer around someone's shed to look down the right street, I know I've hit pay dirt.

The house isn't empty. It's two in the damn morning, and while the shitty little bungalow isn't the only house on the block that's not dark, it's the only one with every single window lit up. The guards McKenna left around the perimeter are basically like a neon sign all on their own, but when I use the cover of another neighbor's rotting pergola to move a little closer, getting a visual of Chloe right through the back window cinches it.

She's here, and I'm getting her the fuck out.

I watch for a few more minutes to confirm my first impression. That fucker drugged her, and he's dumb enough to let it make his security slack, even with the guards he posted. It might be smarter to get some backup, or at least let my brothers know what's about to go down. Hell, there's no "might," it hands down would be. But remembering that pain on Riley's face, even in her sleep, I just don't have it in me to wait now that I'm so close to being able to make things right for her.

The weapons I always keep on me aren't enough if I'm going it alone though, so I turn and stealthily make my way back to the Escalade to better arm myself, justifying the risk I'm taking with the knowledge that there's no way in hell McKenna will be expecting me here tonight. The bullshit his men are pulling inside the house proved that, and even the guards he's got on duty are fucking off their responsibilities from what I've just seen. They continue to fail to make an appearance when that fucking dog—a Rottweiler, I see this time—starts up at me again.

I ignore it just like McKenna's guards and the dog's owners do, but if my Reapers ever act as incompetent as those West Point assholes? They won't *be* Reapers anymore.

When I finally make my way back to the West Point safe house, approaching from the back the same way I did all those years ago when I came here and found Sienna riding

McKenna's cock like the faithless whore she turned out to be, I know I've made the right decision to get Chloe out on my own. The two weasels that had been in the room with Chloe when I first arrived are now playing a card game in the kitchen, and the lights in what I know to be a couple of front bedrooms have gone dark.

I smile with grim satisfaction. McKenna's stable of lazy shitheads are all making my job easier. It's an ideal time to strike, and going in alone is gonna allow me to slip in and right back out with Chloe before McKenna has a fucking clue I've taken back what he never had a right to.

I move quietly, double checking positions of all the players I saw on hand to make sure I'm not in for any nasty surprises, then make quick work of the half-ass lock on the back slider and slip into the house.

Chloe is right where I first saw her, hands loosely bound and propped against an entertainment center with a first-person shooter game frozen on the flat screen at its center. The rest of the room is empty.

That dog starts up again, his late-night rage muffled this time, and I cut the bindings off her hands and haul her to her feet.

"Wha—" Chloe starts, shaking her blonde hair out of her face as she frowns blearily up at me. Her eyes widen just a fraction, and I can see panic trying to work its way through whatever they've drugged her with.

"Quiet," I whisper, stabilizing her when she sways. "Riley sent me. I'm taking you to her. You're safe, Chloe."

Chloe's eyes are a lighter brown than her sisters, but they gut me just as hard when they spill over with tears at those last three words. But the minute she nods in understanding, I ignore both the tears and the distraction of how hard her similarities to her sister hit me and tuck her hand through my arm, putting one of mine around her waist to hold her up and moving us toward the door I slipped in through.

The two shitheads playing cards laugh at something, and she mumbles something inaudible, shuddering against my side.

"Stay close. Stay quiet," I murmur.

She seems too out of it to follow directions, but when I keep moving, she stumbles after me obediently. We make it out the back without incident, and are ten feet from the Escalade before that fucking Rottweiler starts up again.

I make the mistake of assuming McKenna's assholes will continue to ignore it.

I'm wrong.

"The fuck?" I hear along with the sound of pounding footsteps behind me, a split second before gunfire lights up the night.

I shove Chloe to the ground and swing around to return it, picking off three of the guards racing toward my position when their muzzles blaze and give theirs away.

"Fuck," I bite out after the third one drops, reaching down to yank Chloe up as lights come on in every goddamn house in the neighborhood. More West Point men are on their way, and no matter how well armed I am, the only way out of this is to escape quickly now that my stealth plan has gone to shit.

I manage to shove Chloe into the car before any more of McKenna's people make it to our position, but when I dive for the driver's side, a familiar line of white fire blazes across my neck, the bullet slamming into the Escalade's framework.

I growl out another curse and slam the door shut as adrenaline does its fucking job and keeps the pain at bay long enough for me to peel out of the neighborhood and call for backup. Some of it shows up as I fly through Halston's streets, Reaper-driven vehicles blocking off the ones I can already see giving chase, and the rest is waiting for me back at the house.

I'm bringing Chloe home, and unlike that incompetent

motherfucker who doesn't deserve the territory he's laid claim to —or anything else in this city—I'll have a full protective detail in place. One who knows how to do their fucking job.

"Shit, boss," Vic, one of my lieutenants, growls when I finally make it back to the house and pull Chloe out, his black scowl promising pain to West Point.

Chloe is still drugged up, and it's not until I realize how out of it she is and sling her over my shoulder to carry her inside that I understand the grim nod Vic directed at my chest.

My shirt is soaked in my own blood and my neck stings like an angry bitch, but that shit doesn't matter. It's just a fucking scratch, and one that Logan will bitch less about stitching up than he will about the bodywork the Escalade is gonna need when we dig the bullet out of it. Right now, what matters is that I've kept my promise and brought Riley's sister home. What matters is that she was fucking hurting, but now I've brought Chloe back to her, she doesn't have to anymore.

And whatever it fucking takes, I'm gonna make sure she never has to again.

39

RILEY

I'M NOT sure what the noisy commotion that wakes me is all about, but it drags me kicking and screaming out of a sleep so deep it feels like being underwater. My body feels like lead and my heart is even heavier, and I swing my legs over the side of the... couch?

I blink groggily, but yeah. I'm not in my room, and breaking through the fog of sleep slowing down my thoughts feels like a bigger job than I can bear. At least, it does until I turn toward the deep voices of the three men who are starting to mean safety to me, who are starting to mean *home*.

They're not alone, and my focus sharpens fast. "*Chloe?*"

I must be dreaming. But as I scramble off the couch I don't remember lying down on, Maddoc carries her in and sets her on her feet in front of me, and dream or not, I don't want to question it. I just want to wrap her in my arms and never let her go.

"Chloe," I breathe out as I hug her tight, not even a little bit ashamed of the sob that escapes me once I finally feel her familiar shape in my arms.

It's really her.

I'm wide awake.

Somehow, the Reapers brought her back to me.

I squeeze her tighter, and she leans heavily against me as she mumbles part of my name. "Ri..."

I frown and push her back, keeping a firm hold on her shoulders. Her voice is slurred and she looks pale, tired, and ragged as all fuck.

"What's wrong?"

Her eyes well up, and she shakes her head, sagging into my arms again.

I rub her arms briskly. She's here, and that should be all that matters, but she's also cold and trembling and can barely stand.

I look at Maddoc sharply. "What did that piece of shit do to her?"

"She'll be okay."

That's not an answer, and Maddoc's eyes soften like he knows it.

"McKenna's men drugged her," he says. "Let's get her upstairs. It'll work its way out of her system once she gets some rest."

"Are you sure?" I ask, already moving to do it.

Chloe stumbles, and Maddoc steps in to help.

"Not sure what exactly he gave her, but yeah, I'm pretty sure," he says as we work together to get her up to my room. "I've seen shit like this before. They didn't hurt her. She'll be okay after a little sleep."

Except she was on the streets, on her own, for way too fucking long.

"I can get Shane here tomorrow to check her out, princess," Dante offers, as if he read my mind. He and Logan followed us into my room. He glances at Maddoc. "You okay with that, Madd?"

"'Course."

"Okay," Dante says, drawing the word out as I get Chloe settled in my bed. "So, you gonna tell us what went down now?"

376

I bristle for a second at his pissed-off tone, but then realize it's not getting my sister back that he's mad about. It's that, since Dante is asking, Maddoc must have gone to get her on his own. The last thing I remember is going over the map with him after Logan and Dante had both gone upstairs for the night, and if I didn't already know that the world they live in is way too dangerous for Maddoc to go up against West Point on his own, the fact that his shirt is soaked in blood now would be a dead giveaway.

But he did it anyway.

He did it for me.

"I thought of a place McKenna might have stashed her," Maddoc says.

"Great," Dante says, throwing his arms up. "And you didn't wake us to go with you... why now?"

Maddoc doesn't flinch. "I needed to check it out."

"Where?" Logan asks, just as intense as Dante even though his anger is more contained than Dante's.

Maddoc's jaw clenches. "A West Point safe house."

The three of them share a long look.

"It's barely even in his territory," Logan finally says, his voice flat. "McKenna's a fucking idiot."

"*You're* a fucking idiot," Dante says to Maddoc before he can respond to that. "Don't do that shit again, yeah?" He jerks his chin toward the dried blood coating Maddoc's throat. "Not without us."

"I got her back."

"Not the point."

"I mean, it's kind of the point," I say, squeezing Maddoc's arm with gratitude to break their stare off. "Thank you." Then I smack him. "But I agree with Logan and Dante. You could have died!"

Maddoc captures my hand and holds onto it. "It's just a scratch."

"Logan?" I ask, my heart beating too fast as Maddoc's beautiful Siberian Husky eyes hold me captive. "Is it?"

Logan came in with some first aid supplies, and he makes quick work of checking the bullet wound before giving a small shrug. "It just grazed him."

"Does it need stitches?" I press.

"No," Logan says with one of those almost-smiles of his as Maddoc—still holding on to my hand—slowly runs his thumb over the back of it. "No stitches required. He just needs to clean it up a little."

"Okay," I say, letting out a long breath. "Okay, then."

Maddoc keeps ahold of my hand, continuing with those slow caresses to the back of it, as he gives his brothers the rundown on how he got my sister away from West Point.

"Are they going to try to come after her again?" I ask. "Will they come *here*?"

"No," all three men say at the same time, their certainty settling my anxiety before it can bubble to the surface.

Most of it, at least.

"But they shot at you. They saw you. They'll know it was us —*you*, that took her back."

"Yeah," Maddoc says, "but I've got Reapers all around the house now. Even if McKenna was stupid enough to try, we're too heavily fortified for him to hit us here."

"And McKenna *is* stupid," Logan adds as he tidies up the first aid kit he used to check out Maddoc's... scratch. "But he'll also remember what The Six told him."

Dante snorts in what sounds like agreement, crossing his arms over his chest. "Trying to take the head of the Reapers' house by force? That fucker would bring down their wrath faster than he could blink."

Chloe makes a small sound of distress, stealing my attention. She's still asleep, just restless, and I smooth her hair back and adjust the covers as the men continue to go over the details of her rescue and all the measures they've put into place to keep her—to keep the both of us—safe.

After a while, they wish me good night and split up, each heading to his own room while I stay with Chloe. I definitely haven't had enough sleep, but I'm not even remotely tempted to lay down with her. Instead, I sit next to her on the bed, watching her sleep for a while and letting all the relief, all the gratitude I feel knowing she's finally here and *safe*, wash through me in gentle waves.

"We're okay now," I whisper, leaning in to kiss her forehead. I know there's still shit we have to figure out with this inheritance of hers and that Austin McKenna isn't going to just give up on this war he's got going with the Reapers, but I still believe it's true. I'll *make* it true, but this time, I won't have to do it on my own.

Chloe lets out a small sigh, her eyelids fluttering as she shifts position.

She doesn't wake up, and I smile. Knowing she's safe is *everything*... and it's all thanks to Maddoc.

I get off the bed and don't let myself stop to think as I head to his room.

I already thanked him. We both need our sleep. I've got no plan at all and when he opens to my soft knock—shirtless and with a damp, bloody cloth in his hand from finally cleaning the "scratch" on his neck—all I can do is stare at him.

He stares back, looking right into my soul, and when he slowly smiles, I realize I don't need a plan.

Right now, I just need *him*.

I slide my hand up his chest and wrap it around the back of his neck, taking care around the angry red line West Point's bullet left there as I go up on my toes. And then I take what I need... what I want.

I press my lips to his.

40

RILEY

Maddoc doesn't just kiss me back. He wraps his arms around me with a low groan, gathers me close, and takes charge in a way I don't even realize I crave until he does it. The heat of his bare skin burns right through my shirt, and when he slides his hands down to my ass and lifts me up, I wrap my legs around his waist without a second thought, trusting him to hold me.

"I want you naked," he murmurs, turning into his room and kicking the door shut behind us. His hands tighten on my ass, and the deep tone of his voice goes straight between my legs, flooding my pussy with wet heat.

"You'll have to put me down."

Maddoc's lips quirk up on one corner. "Will I?"

I shiver as he transfers my weight to just one hand, showcasing his strength as he slides his other hand up under my shirt, pushing it higher.

I loosen my grip on his neck and help him pull it off over my head, the smooth heat of his chest against my pebbled nipples making me gasp.

"Better," he says, slowly letting my legs slide back down to the floor.

"Better," I echo as he touches my chin, tipping my head

back so he can kiss me again. I press myself against him and moan into it when he runs his hands down my arms and wraps them around my wrists, pulling them behind my back so I'm forced to arch into him.

I already know Maddoc has a thing for being in control. What I didn't know until right now was how good it feels to give it to him freely. How safe it makes me feel... and how fucking hot it is.

"Riley," he murmurs, trailing hot kisses from my mouth down my throat. "I said naked, and you're not there yet."

"That's a problem. Why don't you fix it for me? You seem to enjoy doing that. Fixing things for me, I mean."

I smirk, an instinctive reaction to hide the vulnerability I feel right now, but I can see by the deep look he gives me that he sees right through it and hears what I'm really saying: *thank you.*

"I do enjoy it," he agrees, walking me backward until the edge of his bed hits the backs of my thighs. His eyes burn into me, through me, and I'm not just aroused. I feel things for this man that I don't even have words for. "Your problems are my problems now."

My breath hitches. No one has ever said something like that to me, but I don't call bullshit. Maddoc doesn't just mean it. He backs it up by doing things to prove it.

"Then finish undressing me," I say, the words coming out embarrassingly breathless.

Maddoc smiles—a slow, sensual promise that makes me want to lick my way right past it. Suck on his tongue and swallow his breath and beg him to get on with it already.

I don't have to, though. His cock, a thick ridge behind his pants, digs into the soft skin of my stomach as he presses closer. "I can do that."

He releases my wrists to stroke my sides, his fingers lingering on the fading line of divots where Logan removed the stitches he'd put in. Then Maddoc dips under my waistband, the rough drag of his calloused fingers sending a fresh wave of heat rolling through me.

But it's not that that makes me shiver. It's the care he's taking. It turns every little movement into something entirely new between us.

"You're such a fucking tease," I whisper, since he still hasn't gotten me naked yet.

"I never tease," he corrects me, finally opening my pants and sliding them down my hips. "Not when it comes to you."

He leaves my pants just low enough to expose the blue thong I'm wearing, then cups the back of my head with one hand while pushing the other between my legs to palm my pussy over the silken material.

I grind against his fingers, spreading my legs as wide as I can while he's still got them trapped this way.

He kisses me again as he works his hand over the wet silk of my thong. And then, finally, under it.

I gasp into his mouth, and he groans, those thick fingers of his thrusting into me until I'm panting, shamelessly clinging to him until it's too much and not enough.

I drop my head back, ripping my mouth away from his.

Maddoc doesn't stop, just sucks his way down my throat.

"You need to be naked too," I tell him, already close.

"You first," he mutters against my throat. "Get on the bed."

He doesn't wait for me to do it on my own, lowering me down onto the mattress and then settling on top of me to keep me there.

"We're not naked yet," I murmur as his hands roam over me, his thick cock grinding against my thigh.

I thread my fingers through his dark brown hair and pull him down for another kiss, arching up to rub my breasts against his chest while he takes me apart breath by breath. By the time he finally moves his mouth lower, my whole body is tingling with an electric energy that makes it impossible to stay still.

But I have to, because Maddoc holds me in place. He sucks and bites his way down to my nipples and then stays there, abusing them to the point that I'm practically in flames, gasping out his name as he brings me right to that perfect edge between pleasure and pain and holds me there.

I dig my fingers into his scalp. "More."

He chuckles, a dark, hungry sound that vibrates all the way through me, but instead of giving me what I want, he abruptly moves away.

Then I realize he *is* giving me what I want.

He gets to his feet, standing between mine at the foot of the bed, and lifts each of my legs, one at a time, to remove my shoes. Then he slides my pants the rest of the way off, holding my eyes and rubbing his fingers over the thin triangle of blue silk he's left me wearing.

"You look good like this," he says, his eyes hooded and filled with heat.

I arch and spread my legs a little for him. "In blue?"

"In my bed."

He drags his gaze down my body, pushing my thighs apart so I'm even more fully exposed to him and then lifting one of my hands.

He sucks my fingers into his mouth, his gray eyes locked onto mine, and fierce ripples of pleasure shoot through me. When he slides my fingers free, he pushes my hand under the little triangle of silk covering my pussy.

"I want you wet."

"I am."

"Do better."

I shudder as his gaze burns into me. He doesn't look away as he steps back and starts to strip his own clothes off, and the intensity of his attention is doing it for me as much as anything else.

I rub my clit for him anyway. Lightly at first, then harder when his eyes flare with hot pleasure. Faster.

I'm used to men watching me, but this feels different. This *is* different. It fills me up with feelings I can't put into words—or maybe just don't have the courage to yet—but my body is a different story. It shows Maddoc everything... and it gets me another one of those slow, filthy smiles of his.

I shudder even harder, a wave of pleasured heat ripping through me, and press my fingers against my clit as my breath starts to come a little faster.

"Good?" I pant.

"Fucking gorgeous," Maddoc says, his eyes flaring with desire. "But you can do better than that."

"*You* can do better than this."

That gets me a dark laugh that does delicious things inside me, along with another promise. "I will."

He shucks off the last of his clothes, all hard muscle and burning intensity and a cock that juts toward me and makes my mouth water. And then he's suddenly *right there*. Closing the space between us and flipping me onto my stomach without any warning.

I gasp, my fingers dragging across the bedspread as he hauls me backward by the hips. "*Fuck.*"

He chuckles again, the sound filled with heat. "That too."

"You'd better."

He gets my knees right on the edge of the bed with my ass in the air, and then those big hands of his are spreading me open, pulling my legs wider apart, answering me with the only kind of promise I need.

He plants a hand in the middle of my back and pushes my chest back down to the mattress, then peels off my thong.

"Oh fuck," I gasp, heat rocketing through me as he buries his fingers inside me, thrusting deep.

"You did good," he says, his voice rasping, "Got yourself nice and wet for me."

"Do something about it."

I mean for it to come out demanding, but instead I sound like I'm begging.

I *am* begging.

Maddoc rests his free hand on my lower back—a claim and a command— and leans over me, his fingers still driving me crazy as they fill me, over and over, the way I need his cock to.

"I'll do whatever you need, baby." His voice is a husky whisper, and the burning heat of his shaft nudges the back of my thighs. "I want you. Want to take you bare. Fill you up. Feel your heat sucking my cock in."

I moan, remembering the feel of his cum dripping out of me.

That was an accident, but this—

"Tell me you want it like that," he demands, fingering me faster. "Tell me to do it."

"*Yes*."

Maddoc groans, long and low, his cock throbbing against my backside. Then he pulls his fingers out of me so fast I'm left gasping.

"Your cock," I beg, expecting him to impale me. *Needing* him to.

Instead he turns me back over, pulling my legs up over his shoulders, slow and deliberate. He turns his head and kisses my calf. Then the other. Then he pins me in place with a gaze that's one part dominance and the rest masculine heat, and takes himself in hand.

"Look at me," he says, guiding his cock toward my pussy. He rubs it through my wet folds, circling my clit with his thick cockhead until I'm shaking.

"*Maddoc.*"

"Touch your breasts."

I do it, cupping them, brushing my fingers over nipples still overly sensitive from the attention he paid them.

Then I pinch them, and he thrusts inside me, bottoming out so fast that I'm overwhelmed by the dual sensations, and break the fuck apart.

"Oh fuck, Maddoc, *Jesus*," I pant, the orgasm slamming through me as he stays where he is and grinds against me, his cock buried so deep that my body, clenching around it with the waves of pleasure, feels utterly owned.

"You're fucking beautiful, butterfly," he says with a low intensity that drags my orgasm out with another fierce wave of pleasure.

Maddoc rests one hand on top of my pussy like he's staking a claim, his muscles standing out in stark relief as he holds himself still above me. Then, as soon as my orgasm starts to mellow down into a languid warmth, he... *moves*.

"Watch me, baby," he says, pulling back and then sliding home again. "Watch me fuck you. Watch me take you apart."

My breath hitches, my skin flushed with heat as he does just what he promised.

He fucks me with a slow, deep intensity that starts a deeper kind of heat coiling inside me, a delicious tension that pulls me tighter and tighter, a pleasure that's drawn out until it feels like it's going to utterly consume me.

"That's it, let me hear it," he demands, his eyes boring into me, pinning me down as his cock impales me, over and over, and I can't do anything but exactly what he wants me to.

I'm panting, moaning for him, arching off the bed as he moves my body where he wants it and fucks me a little faster. Harder. Each thrust a homing missile for the spot inside me that makes me want to beg; each one more powerful than the last, until every single one of them sends the headboard banging against the wall behind me and white hot pleasure shooting through my core.

"Good girl. Come on now," Maddoc demands as he slams into me again. "Break for me. Let me feel it. Come on my cock. *Break.*"

My body obeys, breaking apart all over again just because he asked me to. Because he *told* me to. Because I fucking trust him enough to let go and let my instincts take me over, despite everything that's gone down between us... but also because of it.

Because he's *earned* my trust.

My nails dig into Maddoc's shoulders and my spine arches, and pleasure rips through me like a tsunami.

"*Maddoc.*"

He fucks me all the way through it and then puts one knee on the bed, and then the other, without ever pulling out of me. My body feels like it's floating in the afterglow, but the thick, rigid length he's still got buried inside me has a greedy hunger sparking back to life even as my bones try to liquify.

Maddoc stretches out on top of me, hitching one of my legs over his hip and smoothing my hair back from my forehead with his other hand. His weight pins me down and lights me up, both at the same time.

"One more," he demands as his hips rock into me with a slow, rhythmic roll, his eyes burning into mine.

I don't tell him I can't—even though my body feels like soft, warm taffy—and he doesn't tell me to do it again; he just makes me. Shifts his hips and finds my g-spot and drives that steel shaft of a cock against it while he stares into my eyes, over and over and over, until I can't do anything *but* give him one more.

"Oh god, Maddoc," I gasp, a deep tremble starting in my core and threatening to shake me apart from the inside out.

"Fuck, that's it, butterfly," he grits out as it sweeps through me. "You feel so fucking good on my cock like this."

"*You* make me feel so fucking good," I admit as my sated body goes lax underneath him.

I cup his jaw as feelings that go way beyond the sex well up inside me and when Maddoc locks eyes with me, something passes between us that has my pussy clenching around him again.

He shudders, his face contorting as a raw, guttural groan escapes, and then he follows me. Fucking into me hard and fast until he finally buries his face against my shoulder and comes inside me with a hoarse shout that sounds a lot like my name.

I can feel his hot cum pumping inside me, his hips jerking against me in short, aborted thrusts as he pants against my sweat-slicked skin and then finally settles. His weight pins me to the mattress, locking me down with a sense of deep, primal safety that makes me feel more secure—more satisfied and cared for—than I can ever remember being before.

I float in it. For once, everyone I care for is under one roof, protected and safe, and it's... fuck. It's everything.

Eventually, Maddoc gets up, pressing a soft kiss to my forehead, and pads off to the bathroom. I don't move and he doesn't ask me to, and when he comes back, he brings a warm, damp washcloth to clean me up.

He makes quick work of it, then crawls under the blankets and pulls me into his arms. It's not until his heart is beating, slowly and steadily, under my cheeks, his hand settled on my hip as he holds me against him, that I realize it didn't even occur to me to go back to my own room. I'm exactly where I want to be.

It's my last thought as sleep takes me.

41

RILEY

It's been a long time since I woke up feeling at peace, and for a moment, before my eyes open, it's such an unfamiliar feeling I'm not even sure I actually am awake. But then someone stirs beside me, all muscle and warmth and strength, and I snap my eyes open, trying to remember where I am.

Maddoc's room.

I smile, that peace settling back around me like a warm blanket after my initial moment of disorientation. I can't remember the last time I woke up next to a man the morning after, and it's... nice.

Maddoc's arm is draped over my hip, heavy and secure, and the way my body is tucked up against his is something I could probably get used to. I try to tell myself it's a dangerous way to feel. He's still the leader of the Reapers, and his world will never be a safe place to live.

And then there's my sister.

Chloe will always be my first priority. She's off the streets, which means she's safe for now, but she's not safe forever. Not with that inheritance hanging over her head.

I sigh softly, rolling over to face Maddoc and letting my eyes roam over his strong features. They haven't quite softened in his sleep, but slumber seems to give them a hint of that same languid peace that filled me when I woke up. It makes me feel close to him.

No. I reach out, lightly skimming my fingers over the healing gunshot wound in his shoulder, a hairsbreadth above the skin. *It's not seeing him sleep that makes me feel close to him.*

It's not even this peaceful feeling of safety I've found in his bed. It's because the connection I've felt with him almost from the beginning, the one that made his betrayal cut so much deeper and his change of heart mean so much more... is real.

I bite my lip, nibbling on it as I try to wrap my feelings around that, and my fingers come down, feather-light, on the wound I gave him.

Maddoc's eyes spring open. Then they turn warm.

"Riley," he says, his voice rough with sleep as he reaches up to cover my hand with his, holding it against him as he holds my gaze.

"Good morning."

He smiles, a small but sincere-looking one, and leans forward to kiss me. It's soft and intimate in a way I'm not at all used to.

"How did you know where to find Chloe?" I ask when he pulls away, partly because I truly want to know, and partly to recover from how open and vulnerable I feel in the wake of all this.

"I remembered a place McKenna has used before, one he set up specifically to keep things on the down-low." He brushes some of my hair back from my face, letting his fingers trail over my cheek. "It's just outside West Point territory, so not where we had any eyes."

"Did one of your allies tip you off?"

"No. It's a safe house he's got in a residential neighborhood, away from typical gang activity." He hesitates, then adds, "It's where he used to meet up with Sienna."

I almost ask if he means "meet up with" when the bitch was cheating on him, but of course he does. The flat look in his eyes tells me so.

For a split second, I wonder if he still cares for her... and I hate her a little bit for that. Loyalty is *everything* to Maddoc. But then I decide she's not worth it, and since Maddoc seems to shake off the memory just as fast, his eyes warming for me again as he goes on with his explanation, I figure he feels the same.

"I figured it would be stupid of him to still use the place." His lips quirk up a little. "Which just made it all the more likely he might have her stashed there. So I thought I'd go check."

"On your own? In the middle of the night?" I ask, turning my face a little to press my cheek into his palm. "You should have woken one of us. Hell, all of us, Maddoc. You got shot."

He runs his thumb over my lips, his eyes following the motion before lifting back up to mine. "Not the first time."

"But why would you take a risk like that?" I whisper.

Maddoc goes still, looking at me in silence. Something passes between us that makes my stomach flutter.

"I didn't like seeing you hurt," he finally tells me, making my heart squeeze.

It's too simple, and yet it's true.

He means it.

I lean forward and kiss him, losing myself in it in a way that has nothing to do with wanting his cock again. I do, but not now. That's not what this is about. And the way he holds me so carefully, making me feel treasured, tells me more than any words that things have changed between us. And the way he came through for me with Chloe—

"I need to check in with my sister," I say, pulling away from him before the way his touch is heating me up leads to something more.

He nods, and I place a final kiss, butterfly-soft, against his jaw, his early morning stubble deliciously rough against my lips.

"Thank you for getting her back."

He gets out of bed when I do, his eyes raking over me appreciatively, and it's harder than it should be to leave his room. Until I refocus on Chloe.

I go to her room—*my* room—and get a lump in my throat, the hot prick of tears stinging the back of my eyes, when I see her lying there safely.

"Oh god," I say, covering my mouth to hold in a sob. Or maybe a laugh? Then I realize I don't have to hold in anything at all, and I rush to her side and gently wake her.

"Riley?" she asks, blinking at me blearily for a moment before she shakes off the grogginess of sleep and the aftereffects of whatever those fuckers drugged her with, bolting upright and coming alert all at once.

Street instincts.

She looks around, tucking a lock of dyed-blonde hair behind her ears.

"You're safe," I reassure her, hugging her hard. "Are you okay?"

I brush her hair back and kiss her forehead, and she nods. "I think so, yeah." She melts against me. "*Riley.*"

This time, it's not a question. It's pure relief.

I murmur nonsense to her just like I did when she was small, content for a moment to just *exist* in the moment. In this perfect one, where we're together again and, for now at least, totally safe.

But then Chloe stiffens, pulling out of my embrace and looking around the room until a spark of recognition appears in her eyes. "Is this the... the Reapers' house? Oh god, I thought I remembered them from last night. *Shit*, Ri. When you didn't come after me, I didn't know what to think. They... they caught you?"

"No, it's fine. We're safe here."

"How? You said they were going to betray you! You told me to run!"

"Yeah." I bite my lip. "Things have changed."

"How? *Why?*" she asks, looking up at me with big eyes that remind me that, for all that she kept herself alive out there and has had to grow up way the fuck faster than I wish she had, she's still my baby sister. She still looks to me, trusts me, to reassure her that everything will be okay.

Which I can, I'm just not sure how to explain it.

I know what I feel for the guys. For all three of them. I know what's happened between us, and what they've given up to help me this time. I just don't have the words to talk about that kind of thing.

And maybe I don't have the courage to trust it—to trust myself—quite yet, either.

But mostly, I don't want to confuse Chloe. Not after all she's been through.

"The Reapers are on our side now," I tell her, brushing her hair back again and leaving it at that. "They helped me find you, and they're going to help us... help us stay safe."

Chloe searches my eyes for a minute, then nods, her shoulders relaxing. "Okay."

"I'm sorry I wasn't there, Chloe," I say, a lump growing in my throat. "I'm sorry I couldn't find you sooner."

She shakes her head. "No, Riley. I'm just glad you're okay. I was—" Her voice hitches, her eyes welling up. She swallows it down, blinking before she allows any tears to fall, and lifts her chin defiantly. "I was scared. For you. I wasn't sure what they did to you. I thought..." She swallows again, and this time her voice is a cracked whisper. "I thought I heard a gunshot from the house when I was running away."

"You did, babe," I say, grabbing onto her hand and holding it tight. "I shot Maddoc."

Her eyes go wide. "Maddoc *Gray*? The leader of the Reapers?"

"Yeah, but he understands why I did it. He even respects it." I squeeze her hand again. "I was scared for *you*. I hated the idea of you out there on your own. And fuck, I'm so glad you were able to keep yourself hidden for so long."

"Not long enough," she says, looking away. Looking a little lost.

I turn her face back toward mine. "You did good," I say firmly. "Those West Point fuckers had people everywhere. It's amazing you managed to stay off their radar for as long as you did. We figured out you'd been staying at that abandoned place over off Alameda Avenue. Was that where you were the whole time?"

She shakes her head. "No, only for a day or so. I moved around a lot."

"Good girl," I murmur, running my hand over her hair.

"I tried to move mostly at night and found places like that one to stay out of sight during the day. I used that cash to pay for things... mostly."

She ducks her head.

"Hey now, it's okay. Whatever you had to do."

"I know," she says, raising her head and pinning me with a gaze older and a little harder than it should be. "You taught me that."

"Yeah." And part of me hates that for her, but the bigger part of me is damn happy that I taught her enough about how fucked up the world can be for her to realize that taking care of herself out there had to be her *only* priority.

She tells me a little more about her time on the streets, ending with—

"I had to steal a few things, break into one place when I thought I was being followed the second day, but I was doing okay." A tremor in her voice tells me that "okay" is a bit of a stretch—probably why she reached out to Frank when I took too damn long to find her—but then her chin firms again. "I figured you'd, um, you'd find me eventually."

"Always. You did good," I repeat, hugging her tightly. "Now come on. Let's go downstairs and get you something to eat."

All three of the guys are in the kitchen when we go down.

"Hey, princess," Dante says with a lazy smile. He raises his coffee cup in greeting to my sister. "Chloe. Good to see you again."

"Hi," she says cautiously, inching a little closer to me.

"Are you feeling better?" Maddoc asks her, leaning back against the kitchen island with a cup of coffee in his hands too.

My sister raises her chin, showing all the spine that kept her alive out there as she decides not to let her nerves get the best of her. "I'd feel better with some of that coffee."

Dante laughs.

"You really are her sister," Maddoc says with a hot spark in his eyes as they flick toward me that warms me from the inside out.

Logan, in typical fashion, just acts. Preparing her a cup efficiently and with the kind of precision only he can pull off. "Did you overhear any of West Point's plans for you?" he asks as he hands it to her, foregoing pleasantries.

Also typical Logan, but that's okay. Actions speak louder than words.

Chloe nods, the way her hands tremble a little as she lifts the cup to her mouth the only sign of her nerves. "They wanted money from me? But that's stupid." Her eyes dart my way for a second, flashing with guilt. "I had to spend almost everything in that envelope you gave me, Ri."

"That's fine." I accept a cup of coffee of my own from Logan, taking a stool and pulling Chloe down onto the one next to me. "It wasn't what they were after."

Her eyes widen. "Then... then how were they going to get more money out of me?"

"Not that," I say sharply, seeing exactly where her mind went. She doesn't know about the inheritance, but she obviously knows Austin McKenna is a brutal, sadistic shithead who wouldn't be above using her, pimping her out, or worse to fund his gang. I take a deep breath, knowing she'll have *feelings* about the truth, then give it to her. "Our mom... um, Heather Sutton, she wasn't actually your birth mother, Chloe. Frank had an affair."

"He... what?" she asks, sounding like a lost little girl.

I press my lips together to keep from blurting out what a fucking piece of shit he was on every level. It's better that he's gone. He *deserved* what he got. But Chloe always hoped he'd be better than he was, and this is one more piece of evidence that he never had been.

"He had an affair," I repeat. "Mom knew and she *wanted* you. But you—"

"I wasn't hers."

"You *were*," I insist, gripping her hand tightly. "Not by blood, but by everything that matters."

Chloe stares at me blankly for a moment, then inhales sharply and nods. "Okay."

I smile, squeezing her hand. She's trusting me to make this okay, looking to me to make sense of a shitty world even when *nothing* feels like it makes sense.

This time, though, I don't have to explain it all on my own.

"The woman your father had an affair with was a Sutherland," Logan steps in crisply, his pale eyes warming almost imperceptibly when I throw him a look of appreciation for taking some of the burden of telling her such life-changing news off my shoulders. "Your real grandfather, her father, was a man named William Sutherland."

Chloe stares at him for a second. Then—

"Was?" she asks in a small voice.

I understand. We never knew either set of grandparents and are all alone in the world. It might have been nice to have had someone else out there who cared.

"It's why McKenna wanted to get his hands on you," Dante says, conveniently leaving out the part where the Reapers had started out with the same idea. "Sutherland was a wealthy man, and you're the heir to his estate."

"The money West Point wanted was your inheritance," Maddoc adds.

Chloe is shaking her head. "I don't have an inheritance. I didn't even know him!" She whirls on me. "Did you know? Did you know we're not..." Her voice breaks. "Not really sisters?"

"We *are* really sisters," I say fiercely. "We share blood. We share DNA. We share everything. You're my *sister*, Chloe. You always were and you always will be."

The "half" I leave off is meaningless, at least to me.

"Okay," she says after a minute, her voice still a little shaky.

I run my hand down her hair, cupping the back of her head and looking into her eyes. "We will *always* have each other."

"Okay," she says more confidently this time, squaring her shoulders. She looks around at the guys. "So what happens now?"

"Now, we help you claim your inheritance," Maddoc says. Something raw passes over his face for a split second, but it's gone when he adds calmly, "And then we help get the two of you out of town."

Of course.

Of course we have to leave.

I stuff all the feelings I have about that down deep enough that they won't hurt right now, because this is about Chloe. Always.

"How do I claim it?" she asks.

Logan taps a small white box in front of him, one whose

corners are precisely aligned with the edges of the counter. "DNA. I'll swab you for it and send it in as proof."

"Proof?" She looks back and forth between us all in confusion. "But... but I thought he was dead?"

"The estate had a DNA sample taken from the grandmother. They're holding it to match against the heir, as proof."

He opens the little box efficiently, laying out each piece and instructing Chloe in what he needs to do to obtain a proper swab. As he takes it, Dante murmurs quietly into his phone, arranging to have a Reaper come pick it up and, presumably, deliver it to whoever it is who can confirm that Chloe is William Sutherland's granddaughter and heir.

Chloe snatches her coffee back up as soon as Logan's done with the swab, holding it with both hands and staring down into it. "So, once we get the money..."

She looks up over the rim, her eyes seeking out mine.

"We'll have to leave Halston," I say, a lump in my throat. "The way we talked about."

She nods.

"West Point still wants you," Dante says to her, sounding a hell of a lot more subdued than he usually does, which just makes my throat feel even tighter. "They're dangerous."

Chloe snort-laughs, then shakes her head. "I know."

"I killed some of McKenna's people," Maddoc says flatly. "We were already at war—"

"But shit's about to get even worse," Dante finishes for him.

Chloe nods again, then takes another drink of her coffee. She's not going to argue because she's smart enough to know this is what has to happen. She doesn't ask to stay, or complain about needing to leave behind everything she's known.

She also doesn't ask about Frank.

"Chloe?"

She looks up from her coffee.

My sister has the biggest heart of anyone I know, and I hate to be the one to bruise it. But even though Frank doesn't deserve how much she cared for him, how much she always *hoped*, she did care. And she deserves the truth.

Not that it makes being the one who has to tell her he's gone any easier.

I clear my throat. "I know you tried to get in touch with Frank. Um, we went there afterward, and he'd been—"

"I know," she interrupts me softly, sadness washing over her face. "I heard it happen."

42

RILEY

THE SPLIT-SECOND HINT of relief I feel over Chloe already knowing, over not having to be the one to break the news to her, is completely obliterated by the horrible scenarios my imagination supplies about *how* she might have heard that.

My heart thumps painfully in my chest. "What?"

Did she go to see him? Was she hiding somewhere in the room while West Point tortured him?

Maddoc must see the horror on my face, because he speaks up when Chloe hesitates. "We checked Frank Sutton's place thoroughly. The only signs of anyone else being there were McKenna's men. Not your sister."

I relax, believing him. Trusting him. But I still look to Chloe to confirm it.

She nods, then shakes her head. "No, I didn't go there. But I was getting desperate," she whispers. "The money was running low and I'd had a couple of close calls trying to dodge people who were asking around about me. It was getting harder to stay hidden, so I... I didn't know what else to do. I didn't know what was happening with you, Riley. So I called Dad."

I squeeze her hand in encouragement when she sniffles. "What happened?"

"He said he would help me?"

Chloe turns it into a question, looking up at me just like she used to when she wanted me to tell her everything would be okay, back when she was young. When she wanted to hear that the monsters weren't real.

Some of them are though, and our father was one of them. I honestly can't picture the piece of shit following through on the offer to help. If anything, he would have just found another way to use her. But he's gone and he can't hurt Chloe anymore, so I don't say it. I just lean in and kiss her forehead, giving her hand another squeeze too, and tell her to go on.

"Dad, um, *Frank* told me he needed a few days, but when I called back, I..." She swallows. "I heard them." It comes out as a strained whisper. "I heard West Point come in. I heard them when he dropped the phone. They were hurting him." She sucks in a breath, covering her mouth. "They were *killing* him."

But they didn't kill him. They left him alive. He died in my arms. Whatever Chloe heard over the phone must have been frightening and terrible, but she didn't *actually* hear him die.

It's not much, but it's something, and I cling to it.

"They knew he was on the phone with me," Chloe says, her hand trembling in mine. "It's why I ran from that place over near Alameda."

If she thought she had to run, then she heard him give her up. Either that, or she realized he would.

I hate Frank just a little bit more for that. I hug Chloe tightly. "I'm proud of you. Running was the right move."

She sags against me for a moment, but I understand completely when she almost immediately stiffens and pulls away. The Reapers are strangers to her. She won't let herself look too weak in front of them, and any comfort I can truly offer her will have to be later, in private.

I share a look with Logan as I let her go. If anyone gets what it is to have shitty parents, it's him, and it warms something in me to see the understanding in his pale eyes.

It warms me even more when he turns away and starts pulling ingredients out of the fridge.

He may eat the most boring stuff on the planet for his own meals, but I'm starting to understand him a little too, and I know it means that, in his own way, he's trying to take care of my sister. He's showing that he cares.

He's going to feed her.

Dante's phone rings and he steps away quietly. The low murmur of his voice as he deals with gang business creates a kind of background noise that has become reassuringly familiar to me over the last few weeks. While Logan starts preparing food, he and Maddoc discuss the steps they've taken to protect the house, and how to coordinate that with the rest of their gang.

Chloe still seems groggy and exhausted, but she's obviously recovering from whatever they drugged her with, just like the men promised she would. But it's equally obvious she still feels uncertain here, around them.

I want to reassure her again. I also want to find out every detail of the time she was out there on her own. But all of that can come later. For now, we talk about easy things, eat the food Logan made us, and slowly, I start to see her grow more comfortable and relax.

"Spend the day with her, princess," Dante whispers, pausing his phone conversation to press a kiss against my temple as he leaves the kitchen. "You fucking deserve it."

Chloe gives me a curious look when he walks away. "They really are on our side?"

"They really are," I say, a lump in my throat at the thought of leaving them behind. But I force it away. I've spent my whole life doing whatever I have to do to keep Chloe safe, and I'll never regret it. Instead, I take Dante's advice and spend the day catching up with her.

A *wonderful* day.

A relaxing day.

A day—and a reunion—that neither one of us ever could have had, if not for the Reapers making it possible.

43

RILEY

When everything Chloe has been through finally catches up with her, it's early evening. We did talk about some of what she went through on the streets throughout the day, and I filled her in a little more about my time with the Reapers too, but for the last couple of hours we've simply been hanging out— giggling a little, enjoying some snacks Logan quietly delivered to us, and snuggling together in the big bed in my room like we've done dozens of times before. Having a pajama party, we used to call it. Neither one of us have actual pajamas right now, but we do have unlimited streaming and found *Whip It*, a movie we used to watch with our Mom, on one of the services.

Chloe falls asleep halfway through the movie with her head on my shoulder. She passes out hard, dead to the world, and I sit with her as the movie wraps up, stroking her hair back from her forehead like I used to when she was little and feeling so fucking grateful to have this moment with her that my throat closes up, my eyes pricking with the hot sting of tears I won't shed.

I've done enough of that. I'm not going to do it now, when I'm *happy*.

I never would have gotten her back without the Reapers'

help. Not the first time, and definitely not the second. And I never would have had a day like today either, where I didn't have to worry about anything other than how happy I was to be reunited with her, if it hadn't been for them.

It's an amazing feeling to actually have people looking out for me and keeping the wolves at bay so I could have that, and I'm suddenly overcome with the need to... I don't even know. Be with them? Let them know how I feel? Thank them?

All of the above.

I pull the covers up to Chloe's chin and smooth them down around her shoulders, then head downstairs. The guys are all in the living room, and I'm hit with so many feelings when I see them that I freeze for a moment, not really sure what I'm doing here.

Yes, I'm grateful to them. Beyond grateful. They've done so much for me, all together and each of them individually. But I still never expected to develop feelings like this. For *all* of them.

"Hey there, princess," Dante greets me with a lazy, sexy-as-fuck smile that reminds me of the first time I saw him. The first time I slept with him. Maddoc's gaze is just as intense as the first time I met *him*, too... but there's so much more behind it now. And Logan?

I shiver as his pale eyes meet mine, but it's not with the fear that filled me when they first brought me here. Just like with his brothers, my feelings about Logan are... well, it's just hard to believe how much everything has changed in such a short time. How far we've all come.

And how much it hurts to know that my time with them will be over soon.

I take a breath and smile, because now is not the time for that kind of pain. Not while I'm still here. Not while I still have them. And suddenly, I'm thinking of that meeting we had with The Six. Of how one of the women there—the beautiful, dark-haired one who was missing part of her arm—seemed to have feelings for three different men in the panel who faced us.

No, more than just *feelings*. It looked a lot like all four of them were in an actual relationship, a kind of relationship that I never would have imagined working, much less wanting, before seeing how the four of them interacted... and before meeting Maddoc, Dante, and Logan myself.

These men, *my* men, are as close as brothers. They must know how I feel, and the way they're looking at me, I can't doubt how *they* feel. So maybe I'm not the weird one. Maybe none of us are. Maybe it's totally okay to have had sexual experiences, to have developed feelings, for all three of these Reapers.

And maybe I should use the limited time I *do* still have with them to do something about that

I go to Dante first, wrapping my hand around the back of his neck and pulling him toward me. Kissing him like he's the air I need as he wraps those big, inked-up arms around me and turns it into something just as sweet and dirty as every other time we've come together.

When we come up for air, he lets me go with an easy grin, and I turn to Maddoc.

He likes to dominate. Likes to be in charge. But right now, he lets me take the lead as I cross the room to him and tug his face down to meet mine.

Our lips meet, and his taste is fucking intoxicating. Even though he waited for me to come to him, now that I'm here, he *does* take charge. He takes my breath away, kissing me like everything we've done together, everything we've shared, has meant just as much to him as it's meant to me.

Of the three of them, it took me the longest to find my way with Logan, but now that I have, I want him just as much as the other two... but still have just the slightest hint of uncertainty when it comes to the unpredictable way he's reacted to me in the past.

And yet, when I go to him and then hesitate for a split second, he doesn't. He palms the back of my head, his lips tipping up in the faintest hint of a smile—the kind no one who wasn't looking for it would even notice—and kisses me. I mean, *kisses* me. As if everything that he keeps in check, the controlled way he moves through the world, is all containing an inferno of passion. An inferno that he unleashes on me the moment our lips touch.

When we break apart, my head is spinning.

And then it spins just a little bit more when that secretive hint of a smile from before spreads to a real one.

"Riley," he says softly, turning my name into a caress.

"Our princess," Dante says, holding a hand out.

Logan gives me a little push, and I move back toward Dante, taking his outstretched hand and letting him tug me onto his lap.

A hot thrill goes through me. This time, he handles me like he owns me, and his thick thighs—all hard muscle and seductive strength—bunch and flex under my ass as he positions me how he wants me, tangles one hand in the back of my hair and grips my jaw with the other one, and kisses me again. Taking control of this one until I'm panting into his mouth, clinging to his shoulders, and growing wet and ready for anything, everything, he wants to give me.

The kiss threatens to scorch me from the inside out, but when it ends, the hot challenge in his eyes is even more arousing.

"What?" I whisper, wanting to lick away the smirk on his lips and drown in the warmth of his vibrant green gaze.

He traces my mouth with his finger, then drags it down my throat. "Kissing my brothers in front of me was sexy as fuck, princess. Pretty sure they each felt the same. But as much as I liked it, you know what I liked even better?"

Heat rushes through me, a tingling, electric sense of urgency that just goes to prove whatever he's teasing me with now, I already want it.

Dante sees it on my face, because of course he does. This man has been able to read my emotions from the beginning. As ruthless and dangerous as he may be to the outside world, as hard as he can be around the edges, there's a part of him that's always connected with me on a level beyond that.

"Tell me," I say breathlessly.

He grins, his expression so heated that my heart starts racing, my blood singing with anticipation for whatever comes next.

I'm not the only one. I can feel it. I'm the sole focus of all three of these powerful men, and as Dante's finger dips lower, tugging the loose collar of my shirt down and running across my collarbone, then down between my breasts, Logan and Maddoc come closer, surrounding me.

"What I liked even better," Dante says, his voice taking on a rasping, husky note that has me pressing my thighs together as heat floods between them, "was hearing you with Logan the other night."

Behind me, Logan—always in control—makes a rough sound, almost a groan, but bitten off. It's hot as hell to think of Dante's words hitting him like that, and I squirm, gasping a little, as Dante's eyes flare with dark heat.

"I heard you and Madd too," he says in a rough whisper, his length swelling, hardening underneath me. "It was hot as fuck."

I want to look. I want to turn and look at the other two. To see if they're as turned on by Dante knowing what we did as I am. But I can't look away.

Dante leans closer. He forces my head back and turns it to the side, brushing the long waves of my hair back and giving me my wish. Maddoc and Logan's gazes both burn into me with scorching intensity as Dante's lips brush the sensitive skin just under my ear.

"I know they heard you with me too, princess. I know my brothers liked it, like *you*, just as much as I do. But maybe they want to do more than just listen, yeah? Maybe they want to see more than how fucking sexy you look kissing their brothers. I know I sure as fuck do. Maybe they want to watch something hotter."

"Yes," I whisper, my whole body on fire as he paints a deliciously dirty picture in my mind.

Dante nips my earlobe, and a shiver moves through me. "I want to fuck you again."

"*Yes.*"

"I want to fuck you right here."

"Fuck, yes," I gasp.

"I want to fuck you in front of my brothers, let them see how gorgeous you are when you scream for me, and then I want to see how good you look taking their cocks too."

A flush of arousal moves through me like a tidal wave, and the burning looks Logan and Maddoc have locked onto me send flutters cascading through my stomach.

I want this. I'll have to leave soon, and when Chloe and I get the fuck out of Halston, I know it won't be safe to ever look back. I *want* this, but not just because of how turned on I am at the idea of being watched, of having all of them, of sharing such a hot sexual experience with the three men I crave like a drug, but because... because it's *them.*

Because of what I feel for them.

Because I want what I saw with The Six, even if it's just for tonight.

I want all three of them.

"Will you do that, princess?" Dante asks, pressing a hot,

open-mouthed kiss to the side of my throat. "Will you let us have you like that?"

I moan softly, more turned on than I can remember being in... ever.

And then I nod.

44

RILEY

As soon as he gets my yes, Dante uses his grip on my jaw to turn my face back toward his. Then he takes my mouth like he owns it, doing his damnedest to make me forget everything that isn't the heat and taste and feel of him.

I moan, surrendering to the kiss completely as his hard length grows beneath me.

I can't forget everything else, though. I'm hyper aware that we're not alone... and that none of us want to be. The men want to share me, and the deep, throbbing need in my core is all the evidence I need that I most definitely want to be shared.

"Fucking beautiful," Maddoc murmurs from behind me, the subtle sounds as he and Logan shift position—as they *watch*—turning me on even more.

Dante's hands span my waist, then slide up under my shirt, sending heated shudders through me from the rough calluses on his fingers as they trail up my sides, pushing my shirt higher. He breaks our kiss long enough to pull it over my head, then pulls his own off and takes my mouth again, his hands cupping my ass and rocking me against him.

"That's it, princess," he murmurs against my lips when filthy sounds tumble out of me. "Let me hear you."

I'm wearing a bra today, and suddenly other hands are on me. I don't know whose and I don't care. They open the clasp on the back and ease it off me, and then I'm skin to skin with the hard planes of Dante's incredible chest.

My nipples pebble hard, and I gasp, pressing myself against him as he tunnels his hand into my hair, pulling my head back.

Someone groans, and then I'm suddenly lifted off Dante's lap, the rest of my clothes stripped off me.

"Fucking gorgeous," Dante murmurs as I stand before him, his brothers' hands supporting me.

Dante splays his hands wide, framing my shaved pussy with them, then leans forward and presses his flattened tongue against my clit before sucking it into his mouth... *hard*.

Pleasure spikes through me, and I scream, lurching forward and bracing my hands on his shoulders. He looks up at me with a devilish grin, then kisses my clit again, eyes locked with mine. His hands are moving below, but I can't see what he's doing. Can barely think of anything but how much I want him as he nips at the sensitive skin of my navel, then slides his hands up the back of my thighs, urging me forward.

It's only when he lowers me back down to his lap—guiding me to straddle him this time—that I realize what he was doing before. He was unzipping himself, pulling his cock out and getting it ready for me.

And as he lowers me down, he fucking *impales* me on it.

"Oh god," I gasp as his thick cock forces me open in the best possible way.

The sound of rough breathing comes from behind me, Maddoc and Logan murmuring in low voices laced with desire, but I can't focus on them. Can't focus on *anything*. Not while Dante has me speared so deeply like this.

"You take me so fucking well," he says, the green of his eyes darkened with the same desire bleeding off his brothers, making the air around us so thick with sex that I almost feel drunk on it.

"Nothing feels as good as being inside you, princess. Come on now, ride me. Fuck yourself on my cock."

His hands stay firmly on my ass and I dig my fingers into his shoulders, lifting myself up. Dirty sounds escape me at the exquisite feel of his length stroking me from the inside out, and when I hear Maddoc—or maybe Logan?—inhale sharply behind me, letting the breath out on a low, quiet moan, my body clenches around Dante's cock, fierce pleasure spiking through me.

Then I drop down, grinding onto his lap.

And do it again.

And *again*.

"Oh fuck, that's it," he grits out, his inked muscles going taut as his rough palms grip my ass even tighter. "Take what you need. Get it, beautiful."

"Dante," I breathe out, a fierce, hot, addictive pleasure coiling tightly within me as I fuck myself on his glorious cock. "*God.*"

He's got a firm hold on me, but he's doing exactly what he said. Letting me take what I need, letting me take control of this fuck and drive us both crazy. Keeping his eyes locked with mine... until he doesn't.

He looks over my shoulder, his cock flexing inside me.

"You're making my brothers so fucking hard, princess," he says. "They're watching you. Remembering how good it feels to fuck you. Watching your sweet little body do what it does best. What we've all dreamed of doing with you since the minute you walked in and captivated us. *Fuck*, Riley. Do you know how incredible you are?"

What I know is that I'm going to come hard, and I'm going to come fast. Between the intensity of my feelings for these men and the heartbreak of knowing I'll need to leave them soon—and the hot rush that comes from knowing they're watching me *now* —I can't do anything *but* come hard and fast.

Dante grins at me, a fierce, possessive affection in his eyes that almost undoes me.

"You," he says, gripping the back of my neck and kissing me hard enough to put me *right there*. Then he lets go and I use muscles I haven't flexed since I last had my legs wrapped around a stripper pole, letting my head fall back and the purple and blue waves of my hair cascade down my back. The passion rising up in me like an unstoppable tide drives me even harder, and I ride Dante's cock all the way to the teetering edge of screaming pleasure he's taken me to so many times before. And then—

"Nothing better than this," he mutters as I slam myself down on his cock and moan. "*Nothing.*"

—I fall right over that edge, waves of hot bliss shuddering through me as my orgasm turns me inside out, my body clenching in rippling undulations around Dante's swollen, steel-hard shaft.

His big hands slide up, supporting my upper body, and he tilts me backward. "Let my brothers see you, princess. Let them watch me fill you with my cum."

I shudder hard, an aftershock of pleasure ripping through me at the thought. "*Yes.*"

I want that.

I want his cum inside me.

And once he gives it to me, I want Maddoc and Logan to each fuck me, wet and dirty too.

Dante drags me up his cock with a groan, his big hands on my ass again, spreading me wide. Giving Maddoc and Logan a view. Then he pulls me back down, his hips thrusting up to impale me hard, and the insatiable need these men awaken in me rekindles, deep in my core.

"Do it," I beg him, my thighs shaking as he uses me like a cock sleeve, bouncing me on his lap even faster. "Come inside me."

"You want that?" Dante asks, his breath getting choppy and his grip tightening on my ass almost to the point of pain. "You want me to make you into a mess? Get your pussy sloppy with my cum?"

"I want everything you can give me," I say, which is nothing but the truth.

"*Fuck*," Dante groans, yanking me down on his cock and giving me exactly that. *Everything.*

"You two look hot as fuck together," Maddoc says in a low growl as Dante pants through his orgasm, filling me up just like he promised.

A greedy, hungry shudder ripples through me at the visceral reminder that all the men are sharing this moment. That they're all going to share *me*. These three have spoiled me. They've each given me some of the best orgasms of my life, and as sated as Dante's cock always makes me, my body already craves more.

I lightly trace his still-healing new tattoo—*my* mark, permanently imprinted near his heart—and Dante tunnels his fingers through the back of my hair, palming the back of my head and tipping it forward toward his.

"Nothing better than this," he repeats softly as his cock slowly stops pulsing inside me.

He rests his forehead on mine, looking into my eyes with a hot, tender smile, and reaches between us to take my hand, flattening it over his tattoo.

He hisses a little, and I smile. It must still be tender, but just like me, I know that does it for him. Just like every single thing about him does it for me. Him *and* his brothers.

Dante's tender smile turns downright filthy, and he tips my head like he did before we fucked, turning it so I can see Maddoc and Logan watching us.

"You came so well for me, princess," he whispers in my ear. But then like he's reading my mind again, he adds, "but this doesn't have to stop here."

Maddoc's gray eyes are locked onto me and burning with fire. Logan's pale gaze is so hot that I can't remember how I ever thought they looked like ice.

"You spent last night with Madd," Dante says, his softening cock flexing inside me again. My breath hitches, and Dante chuckles, low and dirty. "Do you want him again?"

"Yes," I breathe out, heat tightening my core again as that fire in Maddoc's eyes flares bright.

"Did he fuck you good last night?"

"Yes."

I gasp as the memory sends an aftershock of pleasure ripping through me, forcing my body to milk Dante's cock as it starts to harden again inside me.

We both groan, and I'm pinned in place, frozen with fire by the intensity of Maddoc's gaze and the pulsing weight of Logan's too. Their focused attention ripples through the air between us like the kind of heat that pulses off the seemingly quiet desert.

"It was so good," I admit, still holding Maddoc's eyes and letting my tongue loosen, opening up like I never do. "Maddoc fucks like a god."

He smirks, his lips lifting just a tad at the corners, and Dante chuckles, a vibration I can feel where we're joined.

"You want to be fucked like that again?"

I want to be fucked like that always.

"Answer him," Maddoc says in that demanding leader-of-the-Reapers tone that reminds me of just how controlling he can be... and just how much I fucking get off on it.

"I want to be fucked like that again," I say obediently, my voice coming out just as breathless and needy as my body is feeling.

Dante's big hand rubs up and down my bare spine, sliding under my hair and pressing me closer to his chest. My nipples rub against his pecs in a maddening tease, and he leans in to bite at my ear again, his cock almost fully hard inside me now.

"What do you want?" he whispers. "Tell us *exactly* how you want to be fucked tonight. What are you craving, princess?"

I shake my head. I'm not afraid of dirty talk, but opening up like this is so much easier with my body than my heart.

Dante chuckles. "Not good enough. Do you want more cock?"

I close my eyes, my pulse quickening. "Yes."

"Look at me," Maddoc demands.

My eyes snap back open, and he smiles, hot and predatory.

"Whose cock do you want, princess? My brothers'?"

"Yes." I swallow, my body tightening with desire again. Something that another low chuckle from Dante tells me he definitely noticed. "I want... I want all of you." The way Maddoc's eyes flare and the low, quietly indrawn breath I get from Logan spurs me on. "I want you to share me," I whisper. "I want to be taken and used and owned. I want to belong to *all* of you."

I wanted to be marked, in whatever way they're willing, so that when Chloe and I have to leave, I'll have something—even if it's just a memory—to take with me.

"Good girl," Dante whispers, kissing my temple as he continues to hold my head firmly pointed in Maddoc's direction. "I knew you were fucking perfect for us."

"Then show me," I challenge, my eyes boring into Maddoc's. This is a man I can push as hard as I want, knowing he'll push back when I need it and stand strong—strong enough to let me break against him—when I need that too.

And right now what I need, what I crave, is exactly what I get.

Maddoc takes me up on my challenge, striding toward us and plucking me bodily off Dante's lap before lifting me into his arms. "You want to be fucked again, butterfly? You want to know how well you fit here?"

Dante groans, wrapping his hand around his swollen cock as his cum runs down my thighs, making me into exactly the mess he promised.

Maddoc doesn't seem to notice or mind... or maybe he does.

Maybe he notices, and it turns him on just as much as it does me.

He holds me against him, kissing me hard and possessively, and everything I felt in his arms last night roars to life inside me all over again. The kiss is everything I just found the courage to ask for. It's a deep, dirty claim, making me feel taken and used and owned. Making me feel like I belong to him.

And belonging to Maddoc *is* belonging to all of them. I've seen how they are. As selfless with each other as they are ready to defend what's theirs against all others.

He sucks on my tongue and takes command of my mouth, his arms rock solid as he supports my weight against him and fans the flames inside me until they're back to an all-consuming blaze. Knowing Dante and Logan are there makes that blazing fire burn out of control, but the way Maddoc kisses me—like *yes,* he'll fuck me, but only when he gets around to it and he's got no intention at all of hurrying things along—takes over all my awareness until I'm lost in it.

He barely lets me breathe, kissing me like he's inhaling me—kissing me on and on and *on,* until I'm burning up and melting into pieces. Until I *need* his cock.

"Maddoc, please," I gasp when he finally lets me come up for air. "I need—"

"I know," he growls, setting me down on my feet without letting me go. He rests one hand against my throat while the other one holds me firmly against him, and kisses me again. Kisses me like *he* craves it. Like he can't stop.

But this time, the thick length of his cock digs into my

418

stomach, his clothing scraping roughly against my overly sensitized skin.

He's still fully clothed. They all are, other than Dante having taken off his shirt and freed his cock. And I shiver, suddenly feeling vulnerable and exposed in a way I never did while stripping.

Maybe because the three men watching me have a different kind of attention trained on me. One that, like Dante said once, feels like it sees me all the way down to my soul.

Not that I want to be anywhere else. I don't. I don't want to be *with* anyone else—and I don't want any of these three men to be anywhere but right here with me—either. But I've opened up more to them more than I ever have to anyone. In some ways, in the most private of ways, even more than I've ever opened up to Chloe. And... it's a lot.

My heart starts to race.

My body starts to shake.

I'm so wet, so freshly, deeply aroused, that I almost can't stand it.

"Riley," Maddoc says, looking down at me with an intensity that tells me he sees it. Senses it. Sees *me*. "I've got you."

"I've never done this before," I admit breathlessly, staring up into his eyes but acutely aware of both Logan's and Dante's, trained on me too. "I've never... been watched." He knows I stripped, but he also knows what I mean. "I've never been with more than one man."

Or with *any* man that I cared about like this; like I care about each of *them*.

"Good," Maddoc says with a possessive kind of satisfaction that settles my nerves and leaves nothing but the fire burning in my blood for this man. For all three of them. "You're gorgeous, and I like knowing that's all for us."

"As it should be," Dante murmurs, his hand moving lazily over his erect cock.

Logan makes a low sound of agreement—a sound that's somehow both completely controlled and also so hungry and raw and *real* that my stomach flutters with a whole new batch of nerves. The best kind. The kind that heighten my arousal and flutter in my stomach.

Maddoc sees that too.

"Do you want a drink to take the edge off, baby?" he asks, stroking my throat like he's already imagining the smooth slide of good whiskey going down it.

"Oh fuck, *yes*," I admit, falling for him just a little bit more, just because he offered.

He smiles, reaching down to lift a half full lowball off the side table next to us. He keeps his eyes on me as he lifts it to his lips, the smooth golden liquid making my mouth water. He lowers the glass and then lowers his head, taking my mouth again... and spits the whiskey he just sipped onto my tongue.

I moan. It burns so good... and even better, it tastes a little bit like him now too.

It goes down just as smoothly as I imagined, spreading a different kind of fire through me. One that turns me on just as much as swallowing something Maddoc had inside him first.

He sets the glass down and cups my jaw, tilting my head back. "You told Dante you want me again."

"I do."

"You told him you liked the way I fucked you last night," he says, his eyes glittering with a dark light that tells me he finds this little game just as hot as I do. And even better, that it's more than a game. It's Maddoc knowing what will get to me, and giving me all of it.

Heat floods between my legs, and I suck in a breath, pressing my thighs together.

"I do," I repeat in a husky whisper. "And I want it again."

He smiles, slow and sexy and utterly feral. Then he spins me around and pulls my back against his chest, holding me there while one hand roughly squeezes my breasts and the other plunges between my legs.

"Oh god," I gasp as his fingers thrust into my cum-drenched pussy with a deliciously obscene sound that makes me feel deliciously dirty.

Dante's eyes burn into me, his hand still wrapped around his cock—hard and wet from being inside me and enough to make my mouth water as he slowly works it over, watching me with his brother. Logan is watching too, his entire body so still that on anyone else it would be unnatural. On Logan, it's hot as hell. It tells me just how focused he is on this.

And the thick bulge in his pants tells me just how much he's enjoying it too.

"I'm going to give you exactly what you want, baby," Maddoc whispers in my ear as he fingers me deep. "Bend over and grab your ankles."

I hesitate. No matter how turned on I am, the idea of letting him dominate me like that—

"Do it," Maddoc says, pulling his fingers out abruptly and taking a step back. "Let me back in that pussy."

I fold myself in half, spreading my legs and wrapping my hands around each ankle, just like he said. My hair sweeps the carpet and Dante's cum runs down my thighs, and the idea of letting Maddoc dominate me like this turns me the fuck on, is what it does. Everything else is secondary right now. I *need* this. I need him to take me in front of his brothers.

His fingers plunge back inside me, and he spanks my ass hard enough to make me clench around them with a gasp.

"Perfect," Maddoc says. "I want to feel that around my cock again." My body tightens, desperately wanting that too, and Maddoc's voice drops low. "*Just* like that."

His fingers leave me and I hear his zipper come down. He grabs my hips hard enough that his fingers dig in, giving me a bite of pain that makes it that much better and the hope for a few bruises to remember this by when he's done.

Then he notches his cock at my entrance and buries himself inside me in one, brutally perfect thrust.

He groans, grinding against me for a moment, balls deep and hitting it exactly where I need it. Then he smacks my ass and starts to fuck me, holding me in place as he pushes me higher and higher.

"Those sounds you make are sexy as hell, princess," Dante murmurs, his voice reminding me that I'm not just getting fucked, I'm getting fucked in front of all of them. "You look fucking amazing taking Madd's cock like that."

"She *feels* amazing," Maddoc grunts. "She feels fucking perfect."

His words, his cock, the weight of the Reapers' eyes on me and the blood rushing to my head, it all comes together to ramp my arousal up in a way I've never felt before. I'm dizzy and close —*so* fucking close—and when Maddoc grits out more filthy words of praise, telling me how much he loves fucking me, I break.

"Jesus, baby, fuck," Maddoc grits out, fucking me through it as I sob out my release, this second orgasm cracking through me like a whip, all sharp, intense lines of pleasure followed by a deep, throbbing afterglow that feels like it's marked me for real. Marked me as *his*.

Then Maddoc finishes inside me with a string of low curses, the rough rasp of his pants against my bare thighs and ass driving home all over again just how hot it is to be dominated like this, used like this, by someone who's already proven just how far he'll go to take care of me too.

He pulls out of me and helps me straighten up, then holds me against him, and kisses me possessively.

It's hot, but what's even hotter is when he breaks the kiss, rubs his thumb over my lips like he wants to make sure it takes, then turns me toward his brother. Toward Logan.

I should be sated. Physically, I've been more than satisfied and my body feels deliciously wrung out from the way Dante and Maddoc have already had me. But I'm greedy. Hungry to know I'm Logan's too. Eager to feel that deep, dangerous connection between us consume me the same way his pale gaze is right now.

I want more.

I want *him*.

But I'd be lying if I said I wasn't a little nervous as I walk toward him. I've never felt anything like what's grown between me and Logan. We share things that I've never had with anyone else, but he's also got what he calls that monster inside him.

I know he's not that, but even if he's not dangerous to *me*, he is a dangerous man. A deadly one.

And one who I want to fuck me almost desperately.

He doesn't move, but his eyes track me with a feral-looking hunger that meets and matches my own, driving it higher. His stillness is that of a predator, ready to pounce, and when I stop in front of him, his eyes drop to my pussy.

I suck in a sharp breath, desire spiking through me. But then almost immediately I wince, realizing what a filthy mess I am.

Logan likes things clean and neat. Organized and under his control. Coming to him messy like this, used hard by his brothers with both Maddoc and Dante's cum leaking down my thighs, is almost guaranteed to turn him off.

I move my hand in front of my wet, swollen pussy, and Logan's hand lashes out just as fast, stopping me.

"No," he says, the raw hunger in his voice flipping everything I know about him on its head.

He wants me. Wants *this*. Needs things to be orderly and predictable in the rest of his life, but can share me, wants to share me, with his brothers just as badly as I want to be shared.

"I'm a mess," I whisper, shaking with renewed need.

His eyes burn back into mine, then they drop to my pussy again. He releases my wrist. "Clean yourself up."

"What?"

"Stuff it back inside. My brothers are leaking out of you."

"Fuck," someone mutters behind me with a low chuckle. Maddoc? Dante? I don't know, but Logan's filthy demand has my body reacting. Clenching tight again as desire throbs hot and urgent in my core.

It forces more hot cum down my thighs, and—equal parts shocked and turned on—I do what Logan told me to. I catch it. I scoop it off my thighs. I push it back up inside me and then can't help the quiet, needy sounds that spill out of me as my fingers fill me the way these men have.

The way I'm desperately hoping Logan will too.

The appreciative groans from behind me tell me his brothers are hoping the same thing, but when I try to move closer to Logan again, he stops me.

"I can't," he clips out, the thick bulge in his pants calling him a liar.

"You... what?"

Logan presses his lips together, an uncharacteristic flush coloring his cheeks, and stares at me with a fierce hunger that directly defies his words. He's got himself locked down though, and when he doesn't answer, I push him.

"You can't fuck me?"

"She's ours, Logan," Maddoc says when Logan still doesn't answer.

We can all hear what he means. *Ours*. I belong to them. All three of them. Maddoc wants Logan to have me too.

But instead of following Maddoc's lead, Logan takes a step backward, away from me, his eyes shuttering.

Pain slices through me. "You don't want me?" But then my breath catches, that connection between the two of us burning bright enough to illuminate the truth. I reach for him, resting my hand over his heart before he can move away again. "You don't trust yourself with me."

It's not a question. I'm sure of it.

Logan answers anyway. "You know what I am."

He means a monster. He *doesn't* trust himself... but I do. I want him, and I'm not afraid of him. I just need to show him that. To prove to him what I already know. That he *can* be trusted, at least with me.

"Logan," Dante starts from behind me. "You—"

I shake my head, grateful when Dante backs off. Then I hold out my hand to Logan. "Give me your knife."

My nipples pebble with the memory of the way he ran it over my skin when we were intimate before.

He looks confused for a moment, and I lightly stroke the scar he left between my breasts.

"Give me your knife, Logan," I repeat in a gentler voice, hoping he can see everything I'm feeling on my face.

He should. He's observant like that. Now I just need him to believe it.

He hesitates for another moment, then finally holds it out to me.

"Sit," I say without taking the knife from him.

His eyes narrow a little, no doubt balking at any hint of not being the one in control, but he's already trusted me this far, and a visceral thrill goes through me he trusts me with this part too.

He sits, and I lean closer, taking his hand and guiding it up so the knife rests against my throat.

I hold it there, the blade biting at my skin like it's made of the same darkness that he and I share, and crawl onto his lap.

Logan instantly stiffens, flinching backward... but taking care, just like I knew he would, not to let the knife break my skin.

"I know you have the control not to hurt me if you don't

425

want to," I tell him, my pulse tripping. Not with fear, but with arousal. "You're the most precise person I know. You don't ever do anything by accident. Do you want to hurt me?"

He hesitates. "No."

"Then you won't," I promise in a throaty whisper, knowing that we both understand what's been left unspoken.

He *has* hurt me.

And I've liked the pain.

But the kind I need, the kind he enjoys dominating me with, isn't what we're talking about here.

Logan silently holds my gaze, something throbbing in the air between us, but he still doesn't move. He still hesitates, even as his body reacts to me.

I can see how torn he is, at war with himself and his demons, but they're not going to win. This isn't a war he gets to fight alone. Not when I know that none of his self-doubt is justified. Not with me.

"You won't hurt me," I repeat, starting to grind against him as his brothers' cum drips out of me, soaking into the rough denim of his jeans. "Not in any way I don't want you to."

Logan's eyes flare and his cock hardens even more beneath me, the tendons in his wrist going taut beneath my fingers.

My breath hitches in my throat, and I moan as I roll my hips against him a little faster, feeling it in my thighs after riding Dante so hard but not letting that stop me. Not when Logan feels so good.

"Logan," I whisper, touching him because I need to. I release his wrist and trail my fingers up his arm, skimming them over his firm chest and then dragging them down his sternum, stopping to hover just above his waistband.

I half expect him to stop me.

I desperately want him to kiss me.

I wait for the knife to waver, for his barely leashed control to snap, for all that coiled intensity brewing inside him to break.

Instead, he finally *moves*, lifting his other hand to the back of my head and gripping it tight.

I'm not sure if it's an invitation or a dare, but either way, I take him up on it. I lean forward to kiss him, slowly pushing against the knife blade as he retreats it just enough to keep it from cutting me, until I'm finally close enough to taste his breath.

For a second, I think he won't let me go any further... but then he *makes* me. Uses his grip on the back of my head to urge me forward until our lips finally touch, then flips the knife over to put the flat of it against my throat instead of the edge of the blade. He takes control of my mouth with a precision and focus that have me panting, and I reach between us to unzip his pants.

Logan's breath catches, a tremor going through him as he kisses me even harder.

"Have you... done this before?" I ask when he finally releases my mouth, dozens of tiny clues clicking into place in my head.

He holds my gaze with a burning intensity for a moment, his cock thick and hot as it throbs in my hand. Then, "No."

"You've never had sex?"

The question makes his cock jump in my hand.

"I've never needed to."

Needed to.

His choice of words doesn't escape me, and my heart flutters at the implication.

I lick my lips. "Do you need to with me?"

Those pale blue eyes of his blaze with something that has me squirming on his lap.

"You're ours," he finally says after a moment, sending a delicious shudder rolling through me.

"Then take me, Logan."

That almost-there smile hovers around his lips for a

427

moment, then the hand he's got on the back of my head fists in my hair and he uses it to guide me where he wants me.

The knife against my throat never wavers as I flex my thighs, lifting myself above his leaking shaft and then slowly sinking down onto him. A sound that could easily be mistaken for pain punches out of him as he enters me, and for just a moment, that knife wavers.

"Logan," I whisper. "Please..."

He fists my hair hard enough to make my eyes water, and it feels so fucking good. So *real*, grounding me firmly in the present moment.

"Ours," he repeats, using his grip on my hair to urge me into motion.

He stares into my eyes as we start to fuck, neither of his hands ever wavering, and it's so intense I almost feel like I'm having an out of body experience. My body is equal parts soft and loose from being used so well by Maddoc and Dante, and buzzing with an electric tension that tells me this next orgasm is going to wreck me. Logan makes me do all the work, but there's no doubt at all that he's in total control.

Until I finally see that control of his start to crack.

"Riley," he grits out, his skin flushed red and a tremor going through his rock-hard thighs. He immediately presses his lips together with a little groan, as if he didn't mean for my name to slip out like that, and for the first time since he entered me, his gaze wavers. Drops. Skims my mouth before drifting lower with a hungry look of possession that almost has me coming then and there.

I know what he's looking at, and I don't want him to hold back.

"Take what you want, Logan," I gasp, my core starting to clench tight as I ride him faster. I tip my chin back, arching my chest toward him with one hand braced on his shoulder. I trace the scar he gave me between my breasts. "I'm *yours*. Mark me again. Show me."

Logan's eyes snap back up to mine and behind me, I hear his brothers groan with appreciation. Then Logan does it, carefully dragging the knife from my throat down to my chest, and once it's precisely lined up with my scar, tilting it just enough to break the skin.

"Oh fuck," I gasp, the pain blooming into a raw, sinful kind of pleasure as he carefully places a second line exactly parallel to the first. Bright red blood beads up from it, then runs down my center, and I come so hard and so suddenly that it steals my voice.

"*Riley.*"

My name sounds like it was ripped from Logan's throat, and the knife clatters to the floor as he grabs onto my hips and slams his cock up into me, fucking me through my silent scream.

"Fuck, wildcat," he groans hoarsely, sounding completely wrecked. "I can't... I can't..."

His shaft pulses inside me, the hot gush of his cum flooding into my overfull pussy and running back out to make a mess on his thighs.

He crushes me to him as he fills me, then lets me cling to him in the aftermath until I can breathe again. Until I realize that he's clinging to me just as hard.

Not just clinging, but kissing me, pressing his lips against my forehead, my temple, my jaw... a slow, deliberate progression until he finally takes my mouth again in a kiss that's more intimate than anything we've shared before.

It leaves me boneless and replete, changed down to my essence... by all three of them.

I don't want to move and none of the men make me. Not for a long time. When I finally muster the energy to open my eyes, looking over at Dante through my drooping eyelashes, I get a heated, tender smile in return.

"Fucking sexy as all hell, princess. That's our good girl."

Our good girl.

I smile. Like Logan said, I'm theirs now.

And even though I can't stay, a part of me will always belong to the Reapers.

LOGAN

My morning workouts always start at precisely 4:10 a.m., and while I work different muscle groups each day, each routine has a precise sequence that allows me to finish at exactly 5:59 a.m. Having control over my body is important to me, and the order this schedule launches my day with is even more so.

Which makes the fact that I should have been done ten minutes ago and just lost count of my reps again infuriating.

I bite out several quiet curses when I notice the clock. I can't stop thinking about what happened with Riley last night, and I've gone through my entire workout with the distraction of an erection. It's unacceptable.

My stomach grumbles, reminding me I'm now behind schedule for breakfast, but I ignore it and pick up a heavier kettlebell. My routine is already broken, but the most important thing now is to push myself hard enough to refocus my mind and stop replaying the feel of being buried inside a woman for the first time.

No, not just "a woman."

Riley.

Now that I've had her, I want her again. What I told her is

the truth. Sex has never felt necessary to me before. But Riley doesn't just feel necessary, she feels disturbingly addictive now that I've had her and been invited to share her with my brothers.

But addiction is a weakness, and Riley is leaving.

The kettlebell slips out of my hand on the upswing, and I retrieve it with a string of quiet, vicious curses that shame me with my own lack of control.

From the moment Riley walked into our lives, I wanted her gone, but now that it's set to happen, I'm on edge in a way that I can't ever remember feeling before, my gut twisting in a distinctly unpleasant way that stirs the monster inside me, making me feel a little bit murderous.

I ruthlessly quell those feelings and work myself to exhaustion, then put the gym back to rights and head upstairs to complete my usual morning routine, determined to keep everything else predictable, even though I'm late with it.

Thoughts of Riley resurface once I'm in the shower, the soft warmth of her body and the breathy sighs as she clung to me making my cock swell with a speed and intensity that almost alarms me. I don't... *do* this. I don't feel out of control like this. Not ever.

I ignore the insistent throbbing of my shaft and the heat pooling in my spine and pretend I don't still taste the phantom echo of Riley's sweetness in my mouth, and by the time I head to the kitchen for breakfast, I'm myself again. Once I finish my omelet and toast, I set about making breakfast for the rest of them, and after a bit, the others all make their way into the kitchen.

Maddoc claps me on the shoulder, making a beeline for the coffee and Dante stifles a yawn as he pulls Riley close enough to nuzzle for a moment, jumping into the kind of easy banter he excels at.

Chloe holds herself a bit apart, but mumbles a quiet thank you when I hand her a plate. I look away when she starts to eat.

The genuine appreciation on her face as she bites into the omelet I prepared is irritating me for some reason.

They're leaving. Last night was... not something I have words for, but even though I can't quite bring myself to regret it, I do know that the way it's obviously changed things between my brothers and Riley—softened some edges and deepened the ties—is foolish. They'd be smart to keep themselves removed now that we've all had her. She's *leaving*. Whatever existed last night, whatever it is that's been growing ever since she came, is basically already over.

The handle of the empty mug I'm holding snaps off, the ceramic biting into my flesh. The four of them all look over.

"Okay there, Logan?" Dante asks with a little furrow in his brow.

"Fine."

I turn away from them and clean up the pieces, assessing and then ignoring the scratch it gave me once I've rinsed off the minor beads of blood... the ones that bring to mind the way Riley's blood beaded up so beautifully when she asked me to mark her again.

When she agreed to belong to us, even though she's leav—

My phone pings, and I unclench my hands and snatch it up, grateful for the interruption to my spiraling thoughts.

It's the results of Chloe's DNA test, and for a split second, I almost delete it. Forwarding this confirmation to the executor of Sutherland's estate will put the ball into motion, but there's never been any point in avoiding the inevitable, so I conquer the weak impulse to manufacture a delay and swipe it open, letting my eyes quickly skim over the results while I start to plan out the next steps in helping Chloe claim her inheritance and seeing the Sutton sisters on their way.

Then I blink, my brain stuttering to a halt, and read through it again more deliberately.

"Logan?"

I look up. The question came from Maddoc, but they're all four staring at me.

I hold up my phone. "Chloe isn't the one."

"The one what?" Chloe asks, her brow crinkling in a way that reminds me so much of her sister I have to look away.

"Your DNA isn't a match for the Sutherland heir," I tell her, my brain rapidly clicking through odds and impossibilities.

"What... what does that mean?" Chloe asks as Riley moves next to her and wraps an arm around her waist, hugging her close.

My brothers both look stunned, and I don't blame them. I do *not* make mistakes.

"Could McKenna have sabotaged the results somehow?" Dante asks after a moment.

Maddoc makes a rude sound, and I have to agree.

"He's not that sophisticated."

"Are the results of these things always accurate?" Riley asks. "Maybe we just need to... to have her do it again?"

They're all fumbling for answers, but I retreat from the conversation for a moment to mentally reexamine the facts. I don't make mistakes... but sometimes, I do make assumptions.

"Riley," I interrupt, drawing everyone's attention. "It could be you."

"What?"

"You need to take the test," I tell her, already moving toward the supplies I'll need to swab her according to the protocol. "I may have... misinterpreted things."

"Walk us through it," Maddoc demands grimly, an assessing gleam in his eye as he looks toward Riley.

I quickly sort through the medical supplies I have on hand and collect a fresh DNA kit from the multiples I ordered out of my usual habit of redundancy.

"William Sutherland's daughter left her family and changed

her last name, obscuring her identity," I start. "The family took care to bury whatever scandal caused her to break with them, but I was able to document enough to realize that she had... a relationship."

"With Frank," Riley says in a faint voice.

I nod. "I knew that Frank Sutton had an affair. And when the Sutherland heir's trail led to him, I thought..." I swallow, unexpectedly embarrassed to have to admit my failing. "I *assumed* that she was his mistress."

"Wait, now you're saying she wasn't?" Dante asks, his brow furrowing.

"That's what we're going to find out," I say grimly. "Because if Chloe isn't the heir, then her biological mother wasn't a Sutherland."

"You think... *mine* was?" Riley asks incredulously, the shock on her face stirring something inside me that I quickly put a stop to. "You think Mom would have stayed with *Frank* if she came from something... better?"

"Not necessarily better," I correct her, the thing I thought I put a stop to putting its claws into me. "Wealthier, yes. But I wasn't able to find out why she cut ties with them. And—"

My throat spasms, as if trying to deny the sentimental words, the words of comfort, that want to come out.

"And?" Riley presses, looking at me with a desperate need for answers that wrench them out of me.

"And she did stay for something better. She stayed for you two."

Riley's eyes fill with tears, and Chloe stifles a sob. It's incredibly uncomfortable... and yet it's all I can do not to pull Riley against me the way she was after I came inside her body last night. To hold her and let whatever it is clawing me apart inside open my chest completely and make room for her there.

Instead, I remind myself again that she's leaving, and

quickly finish the DNA swab before calling in one of our crew to run it over to a guy I know who can run the test quickly.

Chloe and Riley speak in low voices, murmuring softly and comforting each other through the upheaval they must be feeling, but I turn away. One way or another they'll need to leave, and feeding my addiction to the distracting emotions I'm swamped with will only cause more of the kind of pain I swore to myself I'd walked away from forever when I left my own monster of a mother's home so many years ago.

I turn away, heading back toward the gym. If I work myself hard enough, my body's exhaustion will make me numb to those kinds of distractions.

But Dante stops me with a smirk.

"Sometimes you just gotta fucking feel it," he says quietly, knowing me too fucking well... including all my coping mechanisms.

I grit my teeth, wanting to be pissed at him for calling me out, but he's right. I don't need to bury this, I just need to get over it.

Instead of heading to the gym, I go up to my room and try to get some work done, resisting the urge to pester my contact about the test. He's already being paid to rush it. Interrupting him isn't going to speed that along.

Eventually, I give in to the urge to check on Riley, scrolling through the security cam footage until I find her and her sister in their bedroom. It's easy to see how close they are. How tender Riley is with Chloe, and how much Chloe relies on her.

That kind of love, that kind of *family*, is more precious than anything. It's why we have to let her go.

My chest aches, and eventually, I realize my eyes have gone dry and gritty as I watch them together. But wanting something out of reach has never changed a single damn thing, so I force myself to stop. I may have been wrong about Chloe's parentage,

436

but I'm not wrong that one of the sisters is the Sutherland heir, and as soon as we get that confirmation, Riley will leave.

Clenching my jaw, I drag my gaze away from the video feed of Riley's room, and I don't let myself look again... not until later in the day, when my phone finally pings with the result of her DNA test.

46

RILEY

"WELL?" Maddoc says once we're all together in the living room.

Logan doesn't beat around the bush. "Riley's the heir."

Chloe squeezes my hand, and the guys all start to talk at once, but even though Logan basically said the same thing this morning, hearing it confirmed has me stunned.

I'm the heir to the Sutherland estate. It's hard to believe.

"Weird, huh?" Chloe whispers, leaning in.

"Yeah." I clear my throat when there's a break in the guys' conversation. "So, what happens now?"

Maddoc gives me a long look, but I'm not really surprised when he finally answers. "We stick to the plan."

Dante slings an arm around my shoulders. "We'll help you collect your inheritance, princess, then get you and Chloe out of town."

I'm even less sure that I want to go now that it's not Chloe who's in danger, but nothing has actually changed. We *should* still leave Halston. It really is the only way to make sure we're both safe.

"You on board?" Maddoc asks, holding my gaze.

I swallow hard. I want to say no, but that's not really an

option. And the minute I say yes, everything jumps into fast motion.

The next couple of days go by in a whirlwind as Maddoc and the guys make preparations for me to claim the estate. I'm not much help with the logistics, so I spend most of my time with Chloe, trying not to count down the hours left until they move us both to the safe house they want us to stay in while all the legal stuff goes through.

"We can't just stay here?" Chloe asks me quietly after Logan finishes updating us on the stepped up security they've put into place around the house.

I stare after him after he leaves the room, then shake myself out of pointless longings and answer her. "No. West Point is still out there, and they still want the money."

She shudders. "Do you really think they'll try something?"

"If they do, the Reapers will stop them," I tell her confidently.

Maddoc, Dante, and Logan have already proven that they'll protect us, and I know they've also arranged to have a whole contingent of their gang members escort us to the meeting with the estate manager. We'll be safe... I hope.

Chloe's shoulders relax as she takes me at my word, but I can tell something is still on her mind.

"What?"

She bites her lip for a second, then blurts, "I know it's what we talked about before but things have changed, right? Are you really still okay just leaving all this behind?"

"Leaving what behind," I joke, "our shitty apartment? Stripping? Because you know I can do that anywhere, and now I won't even have to anymore unless I want to do it for fun."

"No, that part will be nice," Chloe says, shaking her head. "But I meant... these guys. The Reapers. Can you really leave them now? I can see that something's going on with all of you."

My heart lurches. I've told Chloe that things changed

between me and the guys after she ran away, that I trust them, but I definitely didn't get explicit about my feelings. She was dead passed out the other night when I fucked all three of them, but the way she's watching me with knowing eyes right now tells me that I haven't been as good about keeping my emotions in check as I'd hoped.

For her sake though, I need to.

I shake my head, denying how huge and intense the connection between us is.

"There's nothing here for me," I lie, trying to put her at ease. The last thing I want to do is have Chloe feel like I'm not going to be a hundred percent there for her as we build our new life together.

"Riley," she starts, her eyes going soft.

"Shh," I say, hugging her tight... partly to avoid her seeing too much truth in my face. "It's fine. We're leaving. It's for the best."

She hugs me back without pushing it, and I'm glad. It's not that I want to hide the truth from her, because I am falling for the guys. For all three of them. And yes, a part of me wishes I could pretend things were simple enough that that means something. That circumstances were different, and we could stay here in Halston and I could see where it goes with them.

But being the Sutherland heir doesn't change anything between Chloe and I. I'm still her big sister. I'm still determined to give her the good life she deserves. And even before we got tangled up in Halston's dirty underbelly and caught the attention of the gangs we'd spent so many years avoiding, I knew that that better life for her wasn't going to be here.

I can't leave her. I won't. And that means I need to leave Halston.

No matter how much I might wish things could be different.

47

RILEY

I spend longer than I should staring into the darkness after Chloe falls asleep for the night. I've never been an indecisive person, so the fact that I'm lying in bed thinking about the three men I'm about to leave instead of actually heading downstairs to spend some final time with them is just another sign that things have gotten all jumbled up and weird.

I don't want to leave them that way though, so I finally get fed up with myself and roll out of bed.

"Everything okay?" Maddoc asks when I silently pad into his office.

Dante and Logan are with him, all three of them clustered around his desk, and my heart starts to thump with a longing I don't have time for. "Yeah. Fine. I was just..."

Already missing them.

"Everything's in place for the morning, princess," Dante says with a warm smile that just makes the idea of leaving even worse. And suddenly, I can't stand the thought that they've done so much for me and don't know—not *really*, at least—how I feel about them.

"I want to give you guys some of the money," I blurt out, which makes all three men freeze and stare at me like deer caught in the headlights. I swallow, the idea sinking in and feeling right when nothing else about leaving them does. "Tomorrow, after I claim my inheritance," I go on, "I want to give the Reapers a cut for all your help."

I owe them, but it's more than that. They changed their minds about trying to force Chloe—or me now—to marry one of them so they could take it all, and that means everything.

But to my shock, Dante stays quiet, Logan's face goes blank, and Maddoc's gaze turns hard and flinty.

"No," he bites out. "We're not taking your fucking money."

It feels like a slap.

"You deserve it," I say, which just seems to piss him off even more.

This time, Dante speaks up before Maddoc can. "That's not what any of this is about, princess."

"I know you guys need it."

"Is that what you think we did this for?" Maddoc spits out, advancing on me. "For a cut of your inheritance?"

"I think you've used up a lot of resources helping me and Chloe out."

And all for no gain.

Maddoc's eyes narrow. "And, what, you decided it was some kind of fucking *business transaction*?"

The accusation cracks into me like a whip, and he storms out before I have a chance to stop reeling. Logan follows him out, as tense and stiff as he's been ever since the night we fucked, making me seriously wonder if I was mistaken about everything.

It... hurts.

"Hey," Dante says softly as I stare after his brothers.

I quickly wipe the tears off my cheeks and glare at him. "Hey, what?" I snap. "Are you going to throw the money back in my face now, too? Money I *know* you guys need?"

He pulls me into his arms and kisses my temple. "It's not

that they're not grateful for the offer, princess. They just care too much, and neither Madd nor Logan is used to that shit. They've got no fucking clue how to handle letting you go."

I swallow hard, all the hurt draining out of me and leaving a different kind of pain in its place. "What about you?"

"I care too much too," he murmurs, his green eyes dropping to my lips, "but unlike my brothers, I know exactly how I'm gonna handle it."

I tremble, but he doesn't leave me hanging. He swoops down and kisses me until I'm breathless... and he doesn't stop.

"Dante," I gasp when he scoops me up into his arms, still trailing hot, open-mouthed kisses down my throat as I cling to him.

"I've got you."

He takes me up to his room and doesn't let me go until I'm naked and panting against him, all my confused feelings and the hurt about the way things are going to have to end buried for the moment under the deep, consuming lust that fires my skin.

"Please tell me you're going to fuck me."

Dante's lips slowly curve in a smile so deliciously dirty that I shiver. "Oh, princess. I'm going to do so much more than that."

He proves it with that wicked mouth of his, laying me out on the bed and making me come twice before he even bothers taking off his clothes. And once he does...

"Fuck, Dante. You're gorgeous," I breathe out, trying to lock those vibrant green eyes and miles of inked muscle into my memory.

He looks me over with hooded eyes and one hand wrapped around that thick cock of his. "Back at ya." I reach for him, but he shakes his head. "I want to try something."

He lowers the lights, and my heart skips a beat when he lights up a series of candles arranged near his bed instead. They're tall and blood-red and their flickering light turns the night into something new.

Dante climbs onto the bed behind me. "Virgin skin," he murmurs, tracing designs between my breasts with his rough, callused fingers before trailing them down my stomach.

He stops just above my shaved pussy and I spread my legs for him, eager for him to use me in whatever way he wants. Anything to keep this night going. To fill the time we've still got together with memories my body can hold on to.

But instead of plunging them inside me or, better yet, finally fucking me, he reaches for one of the candles. "Trust me?"

I nod, and he smiles with a hot, possessive gaze that shoots straight to my core, reaching past me to fish something out of his nightstand.

"Is that... baby oil?" I ask as he squirts some between his hands and rubs them together.

"That's right."

He palms both my breasts, rolling and pinching my nipples between his fingers, and the slippery slide of the oil in contrast to the roughness of his hands has me moaning in no time. At first, I think he's decided to old-school romance me with flickering candlelight and a baby oil massage, but as soon as he has my skin coated with the oil, he lifts one of the red candles out of its holder and tips it above me, sending a thin stream of hot wax splattering down onto my body.

"Oh fuck," I gasp, my back arching off the bed as the searing droplets of wax hit my skin.

"Now *that's* fucking gorgeous," Dante murmurs, his eyes heating up as they rake over the blood-red pattern he created. He leans down and scrapes his teeth over my collarbone, and my nerves flare to life like the wax somehow took my normal sensitivity and ratcheted it up to eleven.

When I gasp, he chuckles with satisfaction, then rocks back onto his heels and tips the candle over my body again, snaking it down my center.

"*Dante.*"

It's the most perfect kind of pain. The initial shock of hot, burning intensity fades to a dull warmth that leaves everything feeling heightened. Dante does it over and over, until my body resembles one of his paintings.

Then he reaches for the baby oil again, pours some directly over my clit, and follows with a hot stream of wax.

"Oh shit, shit, *shit*," I gasp, almost levitating off the bed.

Dante holds me down, setting the candle back on its base and then scraping his blunt nails over the wax on my breasts.

It's too much. I scream for him.

He captures my mouth and swallows it down, then flips me onto my stomach and plunges his dick into me.

"Oh god."

The friction of his soft bedspread on the heightened sensitivity of my skin is overwhelming, and the furious pace he starts fucking me at doesn't give me even a single second to catch my breath.

I don't want one.

It's perfect.

Dante has always known how to play my body like an instrument; how to fuck me until everything else ceases to exist. But this time, it feels like something more. It feels like he's determined to find each and every way he can pleasure me while we still have the chance.

"Oh fuck, princess," he groans, holding me down as he pounds into me. "Can't ever get enough of you."

I'm close to coming again, my core tightening in a delicious coil as he works my body over, and then suddenly, he slows down. Lays himself over the top of me, one hand on my hip and the other pushing the long waves of my hair aside.

"Can't ever get enough of you," he repeats, murmuring the words against the back of my neck.

He kisses me softly there as he fucks into me so deep I can practically taste him. His cock fills me up, over and over until

I'm whimpering. And when I come again, he comes too, pulsing inside me like he's trying to leave a mark that will never fade.

Breathing heavily, he finally draws out of me, but even then, he's not done. His fingers dip into my well-used pussy, gathering the cum that's leaking out of me before he rolls me over to face him and lifts his fingers to my lips.

"Open," he breathes, his voice hoarse. "Taste how fucking good we are together. You and me."

I wrap my lips around his fingers, swirling my tongue to gather it all. And he's right. We taste too fucking good together. I bite his fingertips gently, trapping them between my teeth for a moment before I release them.

"It's good," I admit quietly, and I hope he knows I'm not just talking about the taste of our combined arousal.

"Best I'll ever have," he murmurs.

Then he gently rubs the wax off my body, his large hands soothing the sensitive skin. When it's all gone, he pulls me close, wrapping me in his arms like it's exactly where we both know I belong.

I settle against his big frame, feeling turned inside out. Both raw and soothed.

Feeling like I'm home.

And not letting myself think about how, in the morning, it will be time to say goodbye to all of it.

48

RILEY

I WAKE up with a pleasant ache between my legs and a hard cock pressed against my ass.

"Morning, princess," Dante whispers in my ear, his big body spooning me from behind and his hand splayed wide across my stomach, holding me against him.

I close my eyes against the sun streaming in through his windows. Today is going to change everything, and I'm suddenly greedy for anything that will put it off a little longer. I'm greedy for *him*.

And Dante, just like he always does, reads me perfectly.

"One more," he says, hooking my leg over his from behind and sliding into me.

"God, *yes.*"

He smiles against the back of my neck, pressing a hot kiss there and then pushing me forward. Rolling me onto my stomach as he slowly pumps into my body, building a slow heat that starts to consume me.

"You feel so fucking good," he murmurs, his body blanketing mine completely as his hands settle on my hips, holding me in place. "Love those sounds you make for me."

I dig my fingers into his mattress, rocking back to meet his thrusts, and give him what he wants. Let him hear *exactly* how good he makes me feel, my orgasm creeping up on me without any warning and rolling through me like a wave.

"Oh fuck, *fuck*. Yeah, like that," Dante groans, shoving me down into the mattress and finishing himself inside me before resting his forehead on my back for a moment. "Gonna miss this," he says quietly.

I sigh. "Yeah."

But we both know it doesn't matter, so after he presses one more kiss to the back of my neck, he rolls off me and we both get out of bed.

"I should go make sure Chloe's up," I say, standing in front of him, naked. "Do you know when we're supposed to head to the meeting?"

"A couple hours, I think," Dante says, cupping the back of my neck and running his finger down between my breasts. My skin is pale again, other than the twin scars from Logan, and I almost wish the hot wax had left more of a mark. "Logan's got everything set up with the estate manager."

A lump tightens my throat. Of course he does. I'll be claiming my inheritance today, and that means that once we head out, I won't be coming back to the Reaper house.

Not ever.

"I should shower," I whisper.

Dante's lips quirk up, then he nods and kisses my forehead. "Go."

I swing by my room to collect some clothes and find Chloe already awake and in the middle of packing.

"Is it okay to take all this stuff?" she asks, rooting through my drawers and holding up a few of the things Dante bought for me after Logan shredded my clothes.

I nod, forcing a smile. "Yeah, it's all ours. Get yourself ready, okay?"

Chloe has nothing, not since we rescued her. But that's okay. We can share.

I escape to the shower before I do something stupid, like get emotional, and when I finally finish getting dressed and step out of the bathroom, Maddoc is there.

"Were you looking for me?"

"We need to get going," he says, his voice cool and his eyes shuttered.

I lift my chin. "I'm ready. Let me just go get Chloe."

He nods sharply, turning toward the stairs. But then he whirls back around and grabs me, his fingers digging into me hard enough to bruise.

I gasp, my body flaring to life. "Maddoc. What—?"

His only answer is to press me back against the wall, pinning me there with his body as he grips my throat and tilts my chin back. His eyes are blazing now, that alluring light gray ringed with darkness like the center of a flame. Then he takes my mouth, hungry and consuming, kissing me like a starving man.

I cling to him, kissing him back just as desperately. It tastes like everything that he's shut off between us since the night I fucked all three of them, and when he wedges a thick thigh between my legs and starts to take me apart with his dominance, I let myself forget—just for a moment—that this is it.

But then it's over. We break apart and he stares down at me in silence for a moment, then sighs, his hand gentling around my throat.

"Butterfly..."

He breathes the nickname he gave me what feels like forever ago, gazing down at me like he's trying to discern something in my expression. Or maybe he's just trying to memorize my face, since there's a good chance he'll never see it again after today.

I bite my lip, holding in words that there's no point in saying now. Not unless he's about to ask me to stay.

But of course he doesn't. It's like he just needed to say my nickname to say goodbye.

"Riley?"

It's Chloe this time, calling to me from our bedroom, and Maddoc drops his hand, his face shutting down again.

"I'll see you downstairs," he says, turning and leaving without another word.

I touch my lips, then turn and go to Chloe. "Got everything ready?"

She nods, but she's tugging on her hair like she's nervous. "I think so."

I force a smile. "Don't worry. If we've forgotten anything, I guess we can just buy it now, you know?"

She laughs, shaking her head. "That's crazy. But yeah, I guess? Do you really think they're going to just... just give you the money like that?"

I shrug. "I guess so."

Chloe's laughter dies, and she gives me a serious look. "Nothing is ever that easy."

I go to her and kiss her forehead. "I know, but it will be fine. I trust these guys."

Chloe looks deep into my eyes, then gives me a tentative smile. "Okay. Let's go, then."

We grab our bags and head downstairs, handing them over to Dante as he and Maddoc coordinate logistics with some of the Reapers they've called in to escort us. Dante takes everything to the Escalade and Maddoc gives Chloe and I a brief acknowledgment before stepping outside with a couple gang members I recognize but don't remember the names of. Logan is busy preparing coffee in a couple of to-go mugs that, knowing him, are probably for me and Chloe.

He hasn't looked at us since we've come down, and the way

he's shutting me out reminds me so much of my first few days in this house that it makes my chest hurt. I've seen behind the blank mask he so often wears, and even though I get that it's a way to protect himself, after what we've shared, seeing it back in place like this just drives home the fact that whatever I found here with the three of them is over now.

Chloe looks back and forth between the two of us, and whatever she sees on my face puts a look of sympathy on hers.

Logan finishes doctoring the mugs and turns to hand them to us. "You can drink these on the drive over to the attorney's office," he says flatly. "There isn't time for a full breakfast."

"That's fine," I say, knowing my stomach is too twisted up to worry about food anyway. I take the mug he's holding out to me, but instead of taking hers, Chloe backs away.

"I, um, I think I might have left something upstairs," she blurts, scampering out of the room. "I'll meet you in the car!"

Logan stares after her, unblinking.

I move in front of him, forcing him to look at me. "Logan?"

He finally blinks. "We should go."

I put my hand on his chest, stopping him. "Thank you."

He nods stiffly, his eyes skipping over mine and settling on the travel mug he gave me.

I laugh softly, shaking my head. "Not for the coffee." I bite my lip for a moment, not sure what I want to say but definitely wanting to get through to him that... that he *matters* to me. "You're not the monster you think you are," I finally whisper. "Or if you are, you're one I'm lucky to have known."

His blank mask finally slips, just for a moment, and his heart rate ticks up under my palm. But before he can say anything Maddoc comes back inside, his face grim. "Time to go."

Logan nods sharply, and pulls my hand off his chest... but before he drops it, his thumb rubs over the back of my hand in something a lot like a caress. Or a goodbye.

Chloe comes back downstairs, and the guys hustle the two

of us into the Escalade, coordinating with the caravan of other vehicles that fill the driveway as we all head toward a part of town that makes me feel incredibly out of place.

"Here," Chloe says, slipping something into my hand in the backseat of the Escalade.

I look down. It's one of my favorite nose rings, the black faux-diamond skull that she always says makes me look badass.

I smile at her, and switch out the blue teardrop-shaped one for the skull. I slipped the blue one in yesterday, feeling sentimental, but she's right. Now isn't the time for that.

Logan pulls into a parking garage under a high-rise office building, a half dozen Reaper vehicles following us in and arraying themselves around the spot he parks in.

"Ready, princess?" Dante asks, turning to face me from the front passenger seat.

I squeeze Chloe's hand and nod, but it's only true because they're going inside with me.

Maddoc speaks quietly into his phone, coordinating with his crew, and then finally gives us the go to head inside. A handful of his men accompany the five of us, and for a moment, a frisson of nerves twists my stomach into a knot. I'm not sure whether Maddoc actually expects there to be a problem here, or if these are just the kind of precautions he's learned to take as leader of the Reapers, but I half expect to get turned away before we even get started.

Instead, the uptight-looking older woman seated behind a massive reception desk looks a bit taken aback when we walk in, but quickly rallies and shows us into the attorney's office.

The estate administrator, a slim woman in an expensive suit, zeroes in on my skull mood ring the minute we walk in. "Ms... Sutherland?" she asks, a pinched look around her lips as she looks me up and down.

"Sutton," I correct her, straightening my shoulders. "Riley Sutton."

452

"I see. And you have documented evidence of your relationship to the Sutherland family?"

I've been so focused on what I'm losing here—leaving the Reapers behind and losing the connection I've found with these three men—that I honestly haven't given much thought to all that I'm gaining. The well-masked distaste in her voice gets my hackles up, though. This is my birthright. *My* inheritance. If she doesn't like the fact that I've shown up to collect it looking the way I do, or in the company I choose to keep, then fuck her.

"Yes," I say, staring her down. "We've got everything in order."

And thanks to Logan, we do.

He lays it all out for her, answering question after question as she rifles through the paperwork he's put together. Chloe keeps a hold of my hand, Maddoc and Dante flanking us on either side, and even though I keep waiting for the other shoe to drop, the woman finally admits that everything checks out.

"I'll need you to sign a few things," she finally says to me, pushing a stack of papers across the desk toward me. I follow her directions, putting my signature in a dozen places while my heart tries to beat out of my chest... *still* waiting for the other shoe to drop.

But it doesn't, and once all the paperwork is handled, she gives us instructions for accessing the money, and the meeting ends.

"That's really it?" I whisper to Dante as we walk out.

He nods, one hand resting protectively on my back until we all shuffle back into the Escalade. He gets behind the wheel, and Logan takes the front this time while Maddoc slides into the back with Chloe and I, conferring with the other Reapers before giving Dante the signal to head out.

"That's really it, princess," Dante says as we exit the parking garage in the middle of a caravan of SUVs bristling with gang members. "The money is yours now. Once we get you to the safe house, you can—mother*fucker*."

Whatever he was about to tell me I could do is cut off when a sleek silver car skids into the lane in front of us, cutting us off from the caravan of Reaper vehicles. Dante cuts the wheel hard to the left, taking the Escalade up onto the sidewalk to avoid a collision. It puts us parallel to the silver car, and I see its windows start to lower as Maddoc shoves me and Chloe down.

Then the other car opens fire.

49

DANTE

"*FUCK*," I grit out, slamming on the brakes and throwing the Escalade into reverse.

Chloe screams from the back seat as muzzle fire breaks out from the silver Charger, and Logan lets out a string of vicious curses when my wheels jump over the curb, causing his phone to slip out of his hands.

I slam the Escalade back into drive and twist the wheel hard, skidding out as bullets thud into the side of the SUV. Two more cars roar up from behind us, and there's no fucking time to figure out where the rest of our escort went because reinforced or not, the Escalade's side panels aren't going to hold up to the level of firepower bearing down on us for long.

"Go, go, go," Maddoc yells, covering the girls in the backseat as I tear down a side street. "They're fucking trying to isolate us."

I nod grimly, my vision narrowing as I trust in my brothers to return fire while I do my fucking damnedest to keep us ahead of the West Point shitheads who were clearly lying in wait for us.

"How the fuck did they know she was claiming her

inheritance today?" Maddoc spits out as I take a corner fast enough to put us up on two wheels.

"We'll find out," Logan answers coldly, cracking his window to return fire.

There are three West Point cars on my ass now, but two of ours finally appear in my peripheral vision, doing the fucking job we brought them for. One of them rams into McKenna's henchmen—Luis, I'm pretty sure—cutting them off, and the other Reaper vehicle goes neck and neck with the other two, working hard to give us the space to make a break for it.

Another West Point car suddenly pulls onto the street in front of me, playing fucking chicken, and I stick my gun out the window and make those fuckers duck, then spin the wheel hard, veering off onto another street as the other Reaper cars we brought along for protection finally find us again.

They try to cut off our pursuers, but McKenna's men are starting to box us in. My brothers are both firing out their respective windows and Chloe's whimpering in the back seat, staying low like Maddoc told her to, but Riley's unarmed.

I can fix that.

"Princess," I bite out, my eyes meeting hers in the rear view mirror for a moment. That steel I fucking adore in her blazes in her eyes, and I toss my gun back to her. "Take a few out."

She nods, then lowers her window and opens fire. She looks serious and focused, and the time we spent at the shooting range pays off when she takes out the tires of the car behind us.

"*Fuck* yeah," Maddoc says as I fishtail around another corner. He leans out as the West Point car Riley hit starts to spin out behind us, the driver hanging out the window and taking aim at us.

His mistake. Maddoc puts him down with one shot, and I finally break away from the West Point pursuit, trusting the rest of our crew to draw their fire and keep them off our tail.

"We clear?" Maddoc asks.

I scan around us. "Maybe."

"I'm tapping traffic cams," Logan adds. "I don't think they —*fuck*. Four o'clock, Dante."

I bare my teeth as I catch the vehicle Logan warns me about, coming up fast from a side street as we rip past it. I steer hard into a turn, looking for a route that won't take us back into the fray as Logan rattles off route options and Maddoc and Riley both open fire out the back windows again.

"Fucking hell," I growl, adrenaline sharpening my vision as the car—it's that fucking silver Charger again—barrels up on our ass. I take a few sharp turns and then lay down a string of curses when the last one brings me eye to eye with a series of orange construction cones. "*Motherfucker*."

The Charger is coming hard and the street in front of us is empty of construction workers but with the asphalt torn the fuck up, I know it will eat the hell out of our tires if I try it. There's nothing on the left but I see the shadow of an alley up ahead on the right, so I gun it and skid into the narrow opening, banking on our luck holding.

It doesn't. A chain link fence blocks off the back of it, and a steel dumpster blocks the other side, making the option of ramming through not a viable one. Before I can throw the Escalade into reverse, the Charger is on us, boxing us into a space so narrow I doubt we can even get our doors open.

Next to me, Logan goes utterly still, and I meet Maddoc's grim gaze in the mirror.

Fuck. We're stuck... and the only way out is to carve a way out in West Point blood.

50

RILEY

"Oh god," Chloe whimpers as everyone springs into action at once.

Logan reaches under his seat and efficiently reloads as Dante jerks the wheel, angling the Escalade across the alley to give us the maximum protection it can provide. My heart races, my stomach sour with fear and the gun Dante gave me shaking as I try to focus on what I need to do.

Protect Chloe.

Hold them off.

Maddoc doesn't give me a chance. He hustles me and Chloe out the door that's angled away from the West Point car, opening fire over our heads. Dante grabs a spare weapon from beneath his seat, then he and Logan slide out and use the Escalade for cover, their guns blazing the minute their feet hit the pavement.

"Clear an opening," Maddoc directs them grimly, keeping his big body between the West Point shooters and me and Chloe. "We'll go over the fence."

All three Reapers have their weapons raised, the continuous sound of their gunfire as they try to create a path out of this shit creating a deafening roar. Bullets ricochet between the brick walls that make up either side of the alley, and I don't even realize I'm screaming until my throat starts to feel raw, the gun in my hand growing so warm it feels like a living beast.

Maddoc shouts something, but I can't hear what he's saying, and just when he starts to wave us toward the back of the alley, another car tears around the corner and joins the one that has us blocked in.

Austin McKenna gets out, a handful of his goons tumbling out after him and spreading out in a formation that allows them to spray the back of the alley with their firepower.

Austin stares at us from behind his row of goons, a smirk on his face that makes me want to see it smeared across the pavement.

"You're not going anywhere, Maddoc," he yells, a gun he's not firing held loosely in his hands as he lets his men do all the work for him.

"Wrong," Maddoc says, his jaw clenching so tight that the muscle starts to tick.

Austin laughs mockingly, but Maddoc ignores him, his eyes scanning the alley again as he assesses the situation. I hold in a sob. Even I can see that West Point has cut off any chance we might have had of making it up and over the fence behind us now, and there's nowhere else for us to go.

The steel I see in Maddoc's spine tells me he's not conceding defeat, though. West Point has us outgunned and boxed in. I don't know what he thinks he can do, but I understand. He'll never surrender to Austin McKenna. It's not in his nature.

Chloe clings to me, her head down and her body trembling. "Riley?"

"We'll be okay," I lie, my eyes darting toward the three Reapers as they talk in low tones that the gunfire almost masks completely, still trying to figure a way for us to get out as Austin yells at his men to get us out from behind the Escalade.

The West Point goons start to advance, and the Reapers go silent, their focus on returning fire.

"You don't have to die here," Austin yells. "Just give up the Sutherland girl."

Chloe whimpers, her nails digging through my jeans where she clings to me, and I take aim and do my best to take Austin's fucking head off.

My shot misses, and his eyes narrow as his gaze lands on me. "You're the one the meeting was with, yeah?" He spits on the ground, his eyes flaring with a sadistic light. "Only Maddoc Gray could have had a gold mine like you right under his nose for so long and not even fucking known it."

"We know what she's worth," Maddoc calls back grimly, a tone in his voice that makes my chest hurt.

Austin won't understand, but *I* hear it, and Maddoc's not talking about my inheritance. It makes me want to cry. These three men gave up so much to help me. Even now, a quick glance at their grim faces tells me the truth.

They'll give up *everything*... except me. But no matter how determined they are, they'll die if they stand their ground right now. *Chloe* might die. Even if the other Reapers who were escorting us today somehow make it here, it will be too little, too late. Austin is all but toying with them now, taunting Maddoc for his own sadistic pleasure but making sure his goons keep us pinned down while we use up the last of our ammo.

And I can't let that happen.

I can't let my sister fall back into Austin McKenna's hands.

I can't let these three men lay down their lives for me.

I *can't*.

A shot from one of the West Point goons ricochets off the Escalade's door, making Logan duck and curse. Dante's gun jams, and Maddoc—who's been shooting two-fisted ever since we all tumbled out of the Escalade—tosses his spare to his brother as Austin's men open fire again.

"Don't hit the girl," he shouts, pistol whipping one of his own men when the new slew of gunfire makes me duck. "We need her alive to claim the cash."

"That will never fucking happen," Dante says, ejecting the clip he just used up and popping a new one—the last one, from what I can see—into the gun Maddoc gave him.

One of Austin's men shoots it out of his hand, and something in me snaps. I rise to my feet, holding my weapon loosely above my head in a gesture of surrender.

"Stop!" I call out, my heart thundering as loudly as the gunfire that suddenly ceases all around me.

Austin grins with a manic light in his eyes. "You want something, baby?"

I want him to die... but I want the men I care for, the Reapers, and my *sister,* to live even more.

I lift my chin. "I'll go with you if you let them go." Logan rears back and Dante spins to face me, but I keep my eyes trained on Austin, hating myself a little when my voice cracks. "I'll... I'll marry you, if that's what you want. So you can have access to the money."

"The fuck you will," Maddoc spits angrily, grabbing for me.

A shot rings out from one of Austin's men, making him yank his hand back, and I hold Maddoc's gaze.

"I'm sorry," I whisper.

"You're not doing this," he growls, crowding me against the side of the Escalade as Chloe starts to cry.

I cup his face, staring into his eyes as my heart starts to crumble. "I have to."

"No," he rasps, covering my hand with his and pressing his jaw into my palm. His eyes burn into me, seeing right into my soul exactly the way Dante claimed they would, and I don't blink—I can't—as I lean in and press my lips against his. Breathe in his breath. Let the rough stubble against my hand ground me in this moment, just for a second.

And then that second is over.

I step back, walling off the pain in my heart. Maddoc reaches for me, something wild flashing in his eyes. I know he's going to try to stop me, and I can't let him do that. So I bring up my gun and take the safety off, the harsh click unmistakable as I cock it and aim it at his heart.

My hand shakes, but Maddoc freezes, getting the message. He grits his teeth, his jaw going tight and emotions that neither one of us ever had the courage to put into words cascade across his face.

Finally, he rasps, "You won't shoot me."

"But this way, neither will they." I steady the gun and take another step backward. And then another. "You have to let me go."

"You're making a mistake," he grits out, his gaze locked onto mine.

"Keep Chloe safe."

He closes his eyes for a split second, but not before I see the war of grief and rage there. When he opens them again, he's pulled the mask of the Reaper leader into place. His body is unnaturally still. Poised to pounce on me the minute I waver... so I don't.

My eyes flick toward Dante and Logan, and the expressions on their faces are so raw and tortured that I almost break. Chloe has tears streaming down her face, but the way she shakes her head frantically is just a reminder of how all this started. I'll do whatever I need to, to keep the ones I love safe. Everything else may have changed over the last few weeks, but *that* never will.

Especially not now that my sister is no longer the only one I'm trying to keep alive.

I keep the gun steady, a reminder that I won't change my mind, and touch my fingers to my heart, tracing a spiraling, twisting shape as I hold Dante's eyes. He permanently inked my mark onto his body, but I remember the way he marked me too.

He nods, the vibrant green of his eyes blazing with recognition, and I drag my fingers to the right, running them over the twin scars Logan gave me. Logan's mask slips, the emotional distance he's put between us since the night we all fucked ripped away in an instant.

I look to Maddoc. He hasn't blinked. He barely looks like he's breathing. And I fucking hate that he's about to see another woman walk away from him and into Austin's arms.

"I'm not her," I say, holding his gaze.

His jaw ticks. "I know."

"Tick tock, baby," Austin calls out, tapping the gaudy gold watch on his wrist. "If you want me to leave any of these Reapers standing, time is running out."

I want to say something else, to promise things I can't, but my throat is too tight with unshed tears, and all I can do is hope that they know.

Then rough hands are on me, snatching my gun away and shoving me roughly into the back of the silver car. Austin slides into the back seat next to me, his hand twisting my hair into a leash, and one of the goons slips into the driver's seat, gunning the engine before the doors even close.

The last thing I hear as we speed away from the alley is a hoarse roar of fury from Maddoc.

But he's alive.

They all are.

And if this is what it takes to keep them that way, then it's worth it.

BOOKS BY CALLIE ROSE

Boys of Oak Park Prep
Savage Royals
Defiant Princess
Broken Empire

Kings of Linwood Academy
The Help
The Lie
The Risk

Ruthless Games
Sweet Obsession
Sweet Retribution
Sweet Salvation

Ruthless Hearts
Pretty Dark Vows
Pretty Wicked Secrets
Pretty Vengeful Queen

Fallen University
Year One
Year Two
Year Three

Claimed by Wolves
Fated Magic
Broken Bond
Dark Wolf
Alpha Queen

Feral Shifters
Rejected Mate
Untamed Mate
Cursed Mate
Claimed Mate

Kingdom of Blood
Blood Debt
Dark Legacy
Vampire Wars

Printed in Great Britain
by Amazon

28532300R00270